D0093037

LOVED

A HOUSE OF NIGHT
OTHER WORLD
NOVEL

LOVED

#1 *NEW YORK TIMES* AND *USA TODAY* BESTSELLING AUTHORS

P. C. CAST + KRISTIN CAST

BLACKSTONE
PUBLISHING

Printed in the United States of America

First edition: 2017
ISBN: 978-1-5384-3112-2

1 3 5 7 9 10 8 6 4 2

CIP data for this book is available
from the Library of Congress

Blackstone Publishing
31 Mistletoe Rd.
Ashland, OR 97520

www.BlackstonePublishing.com

To our House of Night fans,

HAPPY 10th ANNIVERSARY!

You are the wittiest, most creative, most loyal readers any author could ask for, and when you spoke, we listened. This book is our love letter to you.

Dearest Readers,

For those of you who need a House of Night recap—or those of you who might be entering the House of Night world for the very first time—here is a brief summary to get you up to date for our newest adventure!

What is a House of Night?

It is a school that fledgling vampyres go to after they are Marked. Over the next four years there, they will either mature into adult vampyres and make the Change, or they will die horribly.

Tell me about the House of Night vampyres! I hear they're not like other vamps …

You're right! They aren't!

HoN vampyrism is based on biology with a little goddess magick sprinkled in. In some young people going through puberty, an amazing physiological chain reaction begins. This reaction gives them flu-like symptoms as their bodies begin to Change from human to vampyre.

Vampyre Trackers follow the pheromones these teens release. When the Tracker makes contact, the teenager is Marked magickally by the Goddess as a fledgling vampyre, and the outline of a sapphire-colored crescent moon appears in the middle of his or her forehead. The youth then must go to a House of Night, as the only way the reaction within him or her can be semicontrolled is by being around adult vampyres, and even then many of them die horribly as their bodies reject the Change.

All House of Night schools are autonomous and matriarchal. They have their own society that exists apart from the country in which it is located, and their own religion. Once a student is Marked and becomes a fledgling vampyre, he or she is legally emancipated from their human families and can choose a new name and future.

If a fledgling makes the Change, their crescent tattoo is magickally colored in and expanded into a unique facial tattoo, which is a gift from the vampyre goddess, Nyx.

The Goddess Nyx is the deity most vampyres worship, though she does not require that worship, and she has many faces and names as she is worshipped by vampyres all over the world.

Vampyres are not immortal, though they do live abnormally long lives (two hundred to a thousand years). They flourish in the arts. They can Imprint with humans through drinking their blood, and they often take human mates. They also often choose a vampyre consort. Vampyres cannot become pregnant and give birth, nor can they father children or create new vampyres in any way.

Two different species of HoN vampyres have developed. Blue vampyres are the original type of vampyre. They are nocturnal, but can go out in the sunlight, though it isn't pleasant for them. Some are gifted by Nyx with affinities for an element or an animal (cats are the usual vampyre familiar), or are given other special abilities. Red vampyres are considered a mutation—though in our HoN world, led by our heroine, Zoey Redbird, they are not considered less than blue vampyres. Red vamps can be destroyed by sunlight. They cannot enter a private home without an invitation. They can influence human thoughts, though that is a skill that is not encouraged.

Most teachers at the HoN are called Professor, though there are some discrepancies. Example: Kramisha, (Loren Blake before her) is the Vampyre Poet Laureate. She teaches, but her main job is being Poet Laureate. Kramisha is also, like Shaylin and Aphrodite, a Prophetess of Nyx. This role circumvents the title of Priestess or High Priestess. Prophetesses of Nyx have different abilities, but all of them are oracle-like in nature, as they can either read signs and portents, or they get actual glimpses of the future. Kramisha's prophetess gift comes in the form of prophetic poetry. Shaylin's gift is that she can read auras. Aphrodite gets visions of traumatic future events.

Priestesses and High Priestess form most of the governing bodies for all Houses of Night. A priestess is simply a young High Priestess in training. Some priestesses never attain the level of High Priestess, which is a sign of having a special connection with Nyx—High Priestesses are wise and mature, and respected by all vampyres and fledglings.

Gender roles are fluid in the HoN. Warriors do tend to be male, and High Priestesses are usually female, but everyone is encouraged to follow his or her own path.

Humans have varied reactions to vampyres. Traditionally, vampyres segregate themselves from human societies, though Zoey and her group are working hard to change that, but as is typical with human beings, fear and ignorance breed racism and hatred, and our vampyres struggle with that—especially in Oklahoma, our setting for the Tulsa House of Night.

MAIN CHARACTERS

ZOEY REDBIRD is our heroine. She was Marked just before she turned seventeen. From the beginning her Mark was unusual because the Goddess Nyx chose her as special. She is of Cherokee descent and is very close to her grandmother, **SYLVIA REDBIRD**, who is Cherokee. Nyx gifted Zoey with an affinity for all five elements: wind, fire, water, earth, and spirit. Zoey fights against Darkness and was the first person to realize that Neferet, the High Priestess at the HoN, was trafficking with Darkness and had turned from Nyx. Zoey has a tight group of friends who call themselves the Nerd Herd (they weren't exactly the most popular group in school!). Her friends have special abilities, too, though none have been as gifted as Zoey.

Zoey has a tumultuous history with boys, and although in the matriarchal world of the HoN she has the right to have multiple partners without being judged and slut-shamed, she's not very good at juggling guys. Her Warrior, **JAMES STARK**, is much more than her boyfriend—he is bound to her through blood and oath. He can feel her emotions and they are very much in love, though Z will always have feelings for her childhood sweetheart, **HEATH LUCK**, who was killed during the battle between Light and Darkness.

At the beginning of *Loved*, Zoey and the Nerd Herd have made the Change and are full vampyres. Almost a year before the new book opens, Zoey was named the High Priestess of the North American Vampyre High Council—which is a big responsibility for a girl who isn't quite eighteen.

STEVIE RAE JOHNSON is Z's bestie. She's a true Oklahoma girl who loves country music and everything Okie. She was Marked before Zoey and welcomed her to the HoN as her roommate. Tragically, Stevie Rae's body rejected the Change and she died—though she was reborn as one of the first red fledglings. Nyx gifts Stevie Rae with an affinity for earth. Her mate is Rephaim, a magickal being who is the son of Kalona (see below). Because of crimes against humanity he committed with his father, Nyx sentenced Rephaim to be a raven during the day and a boy after sunset. Though Rephaim's love for Stevie Rae caused him to turn from Darkness and Nyx forgave him for his past, the goddess believes he must take responsibility for those mistakes. At the beginning of *Loved*, Stevie Rae and Rephaim are living at the Chicago HoN where she is High Priestess. With the rest of the Nerd Herd, she returns to Tulsa to celebrate Z's eighteenth birthday.

APHRODITE LAFONT started the series as the mean girl in charge. She has visions of death and destruction given to her by Nyx, though she was not using them in a manner that helped humanity. Her father was Tulsa's mayor, killed in *Revealed*. Her mother is a nightmare. Throughout the series Aphrodite matures and grows and becomes one of Zoey's closest allies and friends. She is a fledgling who sacrifices herself so that Stevie Rae and the red vampyres can maintain their humanity, and in doing so she loses her Mark, but becomes Nyx's Prophetess. She is bonded with the vampyre Warrior, **DARIUS**, who is completely devoted to her.

DAMIEN MASLIN is one of the Nerd Herd. He is studious, wise, kind, and very cute. Nyx gifts him with an affinity for air. His true love is **JACK TWIST**, a fledgling who is tragically killed by Darkness. Damien is the first male to be appointed to the Vampyre High Council. He is in charge of the New York HoN, and with the rest of the Nerd Herd, he returns to Tulsa to celebrate Z's birthday, though none of them realize that he has been struggling with depression since he was a child.

SHAUNEE COLE is another member of the Nerd Herd. Her affinity is for fire. She is confident and smart—smart enough to understand that her friendship with another member of the Nerd

Herd, **ERIN BATES** (gifted with a water affinity), had become all-consuming and unhealthy. Sadly, Erin did not complete the Change and died during *Revealed*. Shaunee's boyfriend is **ERIK NIGHT**, a vampyre who once dated Zoey *and* Aphrodite. She is High Priestess at the New Orleans HoN and she, too, (along with Erik) returns to Tulsa for Z's birthday.

SHAYLIN RUEDE is not an original member of the Nerd Herd, but after she was Marked as a red fledgling and gifted with the ability to see auras, she also discovered she had an affinity for water, and she took Erin's place in Zoey's circle. Shaylin was blind before she was Marked, so she has a unique viewpoint and a special maturity. Her partner is **NICOLE**, who is a red vampyre. Currently Shaylin and Nicole live at the San Francisco HoN— both come to Tulsa for Z's birthday.

KRAMISHA is the Vampyre Poet Laureate and also a Prophetess of Nyx. She receives prophecies in the form of poetry.

NEFERET was the High Priestess at the Tulsa HoN when Zoey was Marked. She was an especially powerful vampyre with abilities to see into people's minds and to communicate with cats. She was born in the late eighteen hundreds in Chicago, where her father molested and abused her before she was Marked. Neferet chose revenge instead of healing, and that choice set her on a life path that led her into Darkness. Over the course of the HoN adventures, she revealed herself as a ruthless tyrant. She becomes an immortal Tsi Sgili witch and awakens Kalona, a fallen demigod who was once Nyx's consort. Neferet is Zoey's sworn enemy. Her greatest desire is to rule the world and make humans subservient to vampyres, which she would have accomplished if not for Zoey and her friends. Instead of being Goddess of the World, Neferet is entombed for eternity … or at least that's what Zoey and the Nerd Herd hope.

KALONA is a winged, fallen demigod. He and his brother, **EREBUS**, were created to be friend and consort to the Goddess, Nyx. Erebus was Nyx's friend—like a brother to her. Kalona was her true love and consort, but jealousy caused him to listen to the destructive whispers of Darkness and he betrayed his Goddess, choosing to Fall to Earth and be banished from Nyx's realm rather than open himself to truth and trust. When Kalona fell he was filled with anger and hatred—for himself and for humanity. He spent eons committing crimes against humanity until Native American Wise Women finally created A-ya, a magickal maiden brought to life from the earth. A-ya's only purpose was to love Kalona and to compel him to follow her within the earth where his powers were weak enough that the Cherokee Wise Women were able to trap him and free their people from his tyranny.

Led by Darkness, from his prison within the earth, Kalona began whispering to Neferet so that she would fulfill the prophecy to release him. At first he was Neferet's lover, pretending to be Erebus and intending to rule humanity at her side, but over the course of the HoN series Kalona found himself again and eventually gained the trust of Zoey and her friends. He was key in defeating Neferet, and was finally able to kneel before his true love, Nyx, and ask the Goddess for forgiveness, which she joyfully granted him. He now resides with Nyx and is her true love and consort.

The **WHITE BULL** and the **BLACK BULL** are living symbols of pure good and pure evil.

The White Bull = Darkness
The Black Bull = Light

The White Bull was Neferet's ally until she refused to be his consort, though it isn't clear whether he has totally turned from her or not …

(

As *Loved* opens it is almost one year since Neferet was defeated. Zoey and the Nerd Herd are fully Changed vampyres. They created the first North American Vampyre High Council, and then the group scattered to fulfill their assignments at other House of Night schools. It is almost Zoey's eighteenth birthday. As a surprise for Zoey, Stark gathers all of the Nerd Herd to celebrate at the Tulsa House of Night, where Zoey is High Priestess.

LOVED

1

Zoey

The dream started innocently enough. I mean, really, don't most of them? One second you're happily flying across the sky like Superman, and the next spiders are raining all around you while Yoda, Tim Gunn, and Beyoncé play strip poker in the middle of an episode of *America's Next Top Model* as you keep score for them—naked.

So when my dream-self realized I was back at Capri, standing in the rooftop garden of the ancient Vampyre High Council, looking out at a Mediterranean Sea illuminated so brilliantly by a full moon that it almost hurt my eyes, my subconscious didn't scream, *Nightmare!* If it screamed at all it was something like, *Ooooh, pretty,* as my dream-self strolled over to the grove of potted orange trees in full bloom and waited for my imagination to conjure something awesome like a tea party (and by tea, I mean brown pop) with Zac Effron and Michelle Obama. It wasn't until I heard *his* voice behind me that I began to wonder if something might be wonky.

"It's been a long time, Zoey Redbird."

1

I sighed and didn't turn around. "I thought you were done creeping in people's dreams."

"Creeping?" He chuckled softly. "Why must I be creeping? Can we not simply call this a visit? I thought we had become friends."

He joined me at the edge of the balcony and I glanced at him. "Friends wear shirts when they visit other friends—unless the dream visit is, well, a *different* kind of friendly." Kalona started to speak, and I held up my hand. "And that's a kind of *friendly* I thought you'd reserved only for Nyx."

"You misunderstand my intent. I simply thought you would enjoy the familiar scenery. We have been here before, Zoey. Remember?" He smiled at me with all the force of his ridiculous immortal gorgeousness and, even though I am absolutely *not* interested in anything even vaguely romantic with Kalona, there was no denying his beauty. But just because there was no denying it, that doesn't mean I had to give in to what Grandma would call his *shenanigans*.

I turned to face him, rolling my eyes so dramatically even Aphrodite would've approved. "Oh, yeah, I remember this place. This was where you snuck into my dreams and tried to get me to join you in one of your sneaky, sexy 'let's take over the world together' plots." I air quoted. "So *that's* what this setting reminds me of."

The eternally charming smile slid from his face. "Perhaps I did misjudge the setting for this little conversation. And my clothing choice."

"Ya think?"

He cleared his throat, looking uncomfortable, then with a snap of his fingers his muscular chest was covered in a simple black tee (that had slits for his amazing white wings). "Yes. And I apologize. Is that better?"

"Absolutely," I said. Noting how chagrined he looked, I added. "And I didn't mean to be overly sensitive."

"Thank you." He paused. "Would you be more comfortable if I changed this as well?" Kalona gestured at the incredible scene surrounding us.

"No, never mind. It's no biggie. Oh, and I do like your new white wings." I studied them as I spoke. "But they're really not white. They're more like the inside of an oyster shell—all sorts of pretty shades of light merged together to form white. They suit you better than the black ones."

He glanced behind him, as if he was shocked that the huge wings tucked against his broad back were no longer black. Then he met my eyes, his expression unreadable. "I appreciate the color change as well. White pleases me."

The silence stretched between us, becoming awkward until I finally broke it with a sigh and said, "Well? Why are you here?" When he just frowned and wouldn't meet my eyes, I started to get worried. "Is Rephaim okay? Did something happen to Stevie Rae? I just talked to her yesterday. She said the Chicago House of Night was having some growing pains, but—"

"They are fine. I apologize again. I don't seem to be making myself clear." He ran his hand through his thick hair. "In my mind this went much better."

"Look, whatever it is, just say it."

He drew a deep breath. "I believe danger is coming."

Ah, hell. "What kind of danger?"

"I do not know. I can feel something stirring, though, and I had to warn you—no matter what Nyx says."

I felt a jolt of shock. "Nyx doesn't know you're talking to me?"

"Not exactly."

"What the hell does 'not exactly' mean? And be exact," I said.

"The goddess has given me the freedom to visit the mortal realm whenever I wish," Kalona said.

"I need more exactness than that."

"I didn't need to tell her I was going to speak with you because she already made it clear I could visit whenever I so desired."

"But you did tell her you felt danger coming to the House of Night?"

"Yes. And when I could not be more specific, she didn't believe worrying you was worth it," Kalona said.

"And yet here you are."

"Yes, here I am. I wanted you to be forewarned and prepared," Kalona said. "After what you've been through—what we've all been through—I decided to err on the side of being a worrier."

He looked so uncomfortable, vulnerable even, that I realized this was probably difficult for him. He and I definitely had a past, and since he'd died and then been reconciled with Nyx almost a year ago, I could imagine that it would be super awkward for him to step outside his comfort zone and come to me with a warning his consort and goddess believed wasn't necessary. Of course, that probably meant that his warning *wasn't* necessary since Nyx knows her stuff—but still. I had to give him some credit for having his heart in the right place.

"Okay, well, that's nice of you. So, I'll keep my eyes open for trouble. And I'll tell Stark, too. Thanks for the heads up."

"There's something else you can do," he said. "You can read Neferet's childhood journal."

My body suddenly went cold. "Whoa, wait! Neferet has something to do with this feeling of yours?"

"Yes. No. I'm just not sure. And because I'm not sure, you need to be prepared for anything. That is why I want you to read her journal."

"I don't understand. What is this journal you're talking about?"

"When Neferet was a child—before she was Marked, she was a human named Emily Wheiler."

"Yeah, yeah, I know that. She lived in Chicago and when she was young, before she was Marked, her father raped her."

"Yes, and she kept a journal—a diary of sorts—wherein she

recounted all that happened to her. She buried that journal in Oklahoma more than one hundred years ago. I think it would be wise if you read it. *If* the danger that is coming is from Neferet, you're going to need every piece of information available to defeat her."

My mind was spinning and my stomach felt sick. "Don't you mean defeat her *again*? And why the hell didn't you mention this journal last year when she declared herself a goddess and tried to take over the world?"

He shuffled his feet and looked down. "I was embarrassed. It was through the energy that seeped from Neferet's journal that I first began to influence her. I used her to free myself from imprisonment with A-ya. I made a terrible mistake and I feel great remorse, and embarrassment, because of it. When I joined you against Neferet I simply did not want to give you a reason to mistrust me again."

I blew out a long, frustrated breath. "Okay, I get that. But you still should have told us about the journal."

"I'm telling you now, even though I know it brings up the Darkness in my past. I hope that shows you how serious I am about the impending sense of danger I feel."

I nodded. "Yeah, it definitely does that. So, where is this old journal?"

"She buried it at the base of the ancient Oklahoma rune stone in 1893."

I blinked in surprise. "You mean the Heavener Runestone? I went there on a field trip in eighth grade. Ugh. Ticks."

"Ticks?"

"Yeah, I remember picking like a zillion ticks off of my legs after we got back on the bus. Not important, just gross. At least it's winter, so ticks won't be an issue. There'll be mud, though. It's been raining like crazy, but I'll take mud over ticks any day. Uh, 1893 was a long time ago. What if it's all disintegrated and whatnot?"

"The journal is in delicate condition, but you won't have to search through mud to find it. Neferet dug it up decades ago when she first came to be High Priestess at the Tulsa House of Night. She hid it under the floorboards beneath the bed in her chamber."

"What? You mean it's still there? Under *my* bed in *my* chamber?" It made me feel vaguely nauseous to think that Stark and I were at that very moment happily snoozing away just above Neferet's crazy journal—almost like we were sleeping over her grave—if she wasn't immortal and was actually dead, that is.

"Ah, of course. You took the High Priestess' chamber."

"Yeah, 'cause I'm the High Priestess," I spoke confidently. Almost one year ago, I'd become the first High Priestess of the New North American High Council—a position and title I'd only recently begun to feel comfortable with. Well, I was fairly comfortable when I wasn't dealing with the grumpy *old* High Council that still liked to try to rule North America from Italy. Like it was still the dark ages. Or at the very least the out of date, pre-Internet ages.

Kalona was looking at me oddly. "What?" I asked.

"It is just difficult for me to imagine you in Neferet's bedchamber."

"I redecorated." My voice sounded bitchy, but only because I didn't want to remember that he had, of course, been in Neferet's bedroom—and bed—many times when he was still a bad guy and they'd been plotting to take over the world. "You wouldn't recognize it."

He shrugged. "The chamber is of no importance to me. The journal isn't even of any importance to me. I have never read it. Neferet told me about it, though. She named it a recounting of what made her strong. She used to liken herself to a sword forged in fire. One night she told me that she'd dug up the journal and put it to rest under the floorboards beneath her bed."

"I wonder why she dug it up," I heard myself asking.

"She said it was there lest she forget," he said.

"Hum, well, okay. I'll have Stark help me move the bed and find it. Good thing I decided against wall-to-wall carpet when I redecorated."

"You truly will read it?" He seemed genuinely relieved.

"Well, yeah. Like you said, if what you sense has anything to do with Neferet, I'll need all the help I can get." I paused and added, more to myself than to him, "I wonder if I should tell the rest of my circle. I mean, they're scattered all around the country right now, but maybe they should be prewarned, too."

"Do what you believe is best, Zoey. Your circle is strong, even though you are not still together. Perhaps I give them more credit than does Nyx because of the time I spent with all of you, but I believe you and your circle can handle the worry." He grinned a little sheepishly, lessening what I could have taken as his being critical of Nyx.

"Alright, I'll get the journal and put my circle on prealert."

"Excellent," he said.

"Good," I said. We just stood there and I finally blurted, "So, how's your brother doing?"

"Erebus is well," he said.

"And Nyx? The goddess is good, too?"

"Nyx is spectacular."

"Good to hear it. Tell her I said hi."

"I would rather not," Kalona said, looking super awkward. Again.

"Huh?"

"She asked that I not worry you," he said.

"Oh, right. I get it. Okay, so, have you talked to Rephaim lately?" I continued to try to make small talk with him, wishing Shaunee were with me. She was a lot better at talking normally to Kalona than me.

He opened his mouth to answer and then his words broke off as he tilted his head like he was listening to a voice on the wind only he could hear. "Forgive me, Zoey Redbird, but I must return to the Other World. The goddess calls. And I do apologize, again, if I went about this in the wrong way. I hope we part as friends."

"Friends? Sure. And no problem about all of this." I gestured out at the gorgeous Mediterranean Sea. "I do like it here. Thanks for the warning. I'll be sure I—" It was about then that I realized Kalona had gone. "Well, that's typical. He's not on the Dark Side anymore, but he can still be weird as hell." Shaking my head, I stared out at the moonlit sea, trying to process the decidedly bad news he'd just delivered.

(

Preoccupied by the moon and the message, Zoey didn't notice that as Kalona departed, his shadow wavered, shivered, and changed, morphing from the familiar winged immortal into swirling smoke—white smoke that formed the outline of an enormous bull before disappearing completely.

2

Zoey

"Me-uf-ow!"

I opened my eyes to find Nala so close to my face that she was just a fat orange and white blur.

"Good morning," I whispered, trying not to wake the warm body pressed against my side.

Nala promptly sneezed directly in my face and then climbed over my chest (how can such a fat cat have such little, tiny, *sharp* paws?) to circle three times and curl in donut form against my hip, where she turned her purr machine on high.

"Why does she sneeze so much? Do you think she's allergic to people?"

I turned my head to look into Stark's gentle brown eyes. "Sorry," I was still whispering. "I didn't mean to wake you up. And I'm pretty sure Nala sneezes so much because she likes to sneeze *on* people—not because she allergic *to* people. I mean, how often do you hear her sneezing randomly when she's *not* near someone's face?"

"Good point. Why are you whispering?"

"Because I didn't want to wake you up," I said in a normal voice.

"Too late. You started mumbling and twitching in your sleep a little while ago. I could feel something going on with you. Bad dream? But wait. Before we get into that—come here, my High Priestess. My Queen." With one hand Stark lifted the covers he'd cocooned around himself, showing me a lovely amount of his bare, muscly chest, while his other hand slipped under my shoulders, drawing me against him.

I snuggled close eagerly, putting off the bad news Kalona had delivered for at least a few more minutes. I kissed his neck and then let my hand trace the broken arrow–shaped scar that had been burned into the flesh over his heart. I kissed him again, this time lingering. His lips were warm and eager, and when his hands slid down my back, kneading the tension Kalona had brought on, I felt like Nala and wished I could purr.

Instead I explored his body, which never got old. His chest was the right amount of muscle. And I loved his scent. He was sexy man mixed with red cherry licorice, his current snack obsession. He was smooth in all the right places and hard in all the right places—and we fit together perfectly.

Soon the dream was temporarily forgotten as I lost myself in the heat and passion that was Stark.

"My beautiful Queen," he murmured as he kissed my ear as we eventually came back to the present.

"I love it when you call me your Queen."

"Because you like to pretend you're British?"

I grinned up at him. "Oh, kind sir, you know me so well," I said in my best bad British accent.

"Sssh," he pressed a finger against my lips. "Don't speak. Or at least don't speak in that awful accent."

"Hey! I've been working on that accent. Someday soon I'm going to be victorious in my quest to get tickets to the Harry Potter play in London. I'm preparing." I muttered against his finger, which he refused to move.

"Sssh again. I want to pretend like you're *not* going to try to use a British accent while we're over there."

"I thought it would be polite."

"If by polite you mean *disaster of monumental proportions*, then yes. Polite."

"Good sir, my accent is simply not that ba—" I tried to speak through his finger in said awesome accent, but he covered my entire mouth with his hand.

"Trust me. It could start an international event. It's that bad."

I scowled at him and bit his palm. Stark yelped and pulled his hand back.

"Aphrodite said my accent is good."

His brows shot up. "And you never considered that she might be setting you up?"

I opened my mouth and then closed it. Sighed. "She's setting me up."

"Absolutely. Now, how about good morning round two, my Queen?"

"Certainly, kind sir."

This time Stark used his lips to stop my unfortunate accent. And all I'll say is that his lips had a decidedly positive effect.

Several minutes of kissing later, it was Stark who—uncharacteristically—pulled back and, brushing a stray strand of dark hair from my cheek, reminded me of what he temporarily had me forgetting.

"So, bad dream? You haven't had a scary Neferet nightmare in months."

"It wasn't a Neferet nightmare. Or at least not exactly. It was Kalona."

"You had a Kalona nightmare? That's weird."

"Well, it wasn't a nightmare. It was a visit. Or at least I'm pretty sure it was." Stark's look darkened with the same memories that had made me snap at Kalona, and I hurried on to explain. "But not a creeper visit, like he used to do."

"That's good. Did Nyx send him to you?"

"No. Actually, he said Nyx doesn't know. He came to warn me. Apparently, Nyx thinks he's being, I don't know—overly cautious, I guess, which he admitted was a possibility."

Stark sat up and grabbed his T-shirt from the bedside table, pulling it on. He ran his hand through his adorable bed-headed hair and sat across from me looking very Warrior-like and alert. "Explain, please."

I sat and rearranged the pillows behind me, causing Nala to grumble. "Kalona said he felt that danger was coming. Here. To the House of Night. He wanted to warn me and recommend some reading material."

"I don't get why Nyx didn't want him to do that."

"I think it has something to do with the recommended reading material," I said.

"Which is what?"

"Neferet's old journal. And by old, I mean *really* old—as in written when she was still Emily Wheiler."

Stark's face paled. "Shit. Neferet again? That's bad. Really bad."

"Well, Kalona couldn't say for sure that he thought the danger had to do with Neferet. But he also couldn't say for sure that it *didn't* have to do with her. So, he thought he'd warn me and tell me about the journal."

"His reasoning?"

"That if something was going on with Neferet—again—we'd need to know everything we possibly can about her." I raised my hand to stop him as he started to mumble something about that being *too little too late*. "Yeah, I know. I asked him why he was just now telling me about the journal. He made a semilame excuse."

"Sounds like him. He's not a bad guy anymore, but that doesn't mean he's not still a pain in the ass," Stark said.

"Exactly. So, I'm supposed to read the journal and put our circle on a big trouble alert, even though they're scattered all over the US right now. Or, I think most of them are still in the US. Last time I talked to Damien he was going on and on about needing to open a new House of Night." I waggled my eyebrows at Stark. "In the Caribbean on Grand Cayman Island."

Stark grinned through his worry. "That couldn't have anything to do with the fact that it's December and New York City is having record cold temps, could it?"

"Um, yes. I think, as Damien would say, there is a direct correlation." I swung my legs over the side of the bed and put on my cushy slippers. "But he's still reachable. I'll text him and Stevie Rae, Shaunee and Shaylin—just to put them on alert. You know, it's weird. I usually hear from all of them at least once a day, but lately they've been pretty quiet." I froze and met Stark's eyes, feeling my first wave of foreboding. "Oh, Goddess! Could something have happened to them? Hell! I didn't even think about that when Kalona was warning me." I started to reach for my cell phone, which was turned off but charging on my night table. "I'm such an idiot. If they're in danger and I didn't—"

Stark intercepted my hand. "They're fine. Nothing's happened to them."

I realized my hand was shaking when he took it in both of his. "You can't know that," I said, feeling frantic. "I'm calling them. All of them. Now."

Stark blew out a long breath and then reluctantly said, "You can't. They're in the air."

"Huh? What do you mean? What's going on?"

"Z, what's today's date?"

I frowned at him. "I don't know. Um. The twenty-third. Of December. I think."

"Yeah. It's the twenty-third. What's tomorrow?"

"The twenty-fourth." And then I knew what was going on. "OMG, are they surprising me for my birthmas?"

"Well, they *were* surprising you. And I kept the damn thing secret for months." He shook his head. "Aphrodite's gonna kill me."

"Wait, for real? They're coming here for my birthday?" Even

13

Kalona's weird visit and ominous message couldn't dampen the flutter of happiness that lifted inside me. "All of them?"

"All of them."

I jumped up and down, giggling. "Seriously?"

"Seriously. You didn't think your circle was going to ignore your eighteenth birthday, did you?"

I lifted my shoulders. "I'm pretty used to my birthmas being a disaster of smooshed holidays, so yeah—I did."

"I hate that your birthday has always been so crappy," he said. "I really wanted to change that for your eighteenth."

"Hey, there were little bits of good with the crappy. Grandma always gave me something cool, and my little brother, Kevin, used to sneak me silly little things he made or got from the Dollar Store because my mom's awful husband, the step-loser, used to only give me Jesus-themed gifts because, you know, the baby Jesus' birthday is the only one that should be celebrated in December."

"Oh, right, of course," Stark said sarcastically.

"But it's awesomesauce that my friends are surprising me! And well-timed awesomesauce, at that. I can give Neferet's stupid journal to Damien. He'll love studying it, and I can already hear him lecturing us about making it required reading and such for all House of Night students—a cautionary tale or whatever."

"That's probably a good idea. So, where is it?"

"You're not gonna like this part."

"Just *this* part? When it comes to Neferet, I don't like *any* part," he said.

"Neferet hid the journal in the floorboards under our bed," I said.

Stark's jaw clenched and unclenched before he spoke. "You're right. I don't like that part. At all."

I sighed, giving our giant four-poster bed a long look. Stark and I had designed it ourselves. The tall posters were carved to look like four trees, their branches joining above us like a living canopy. "I wonder if it's as heavy as I remember it being."

14

"Well, as Stevie Rae would say, let's get 'er done."

(

"That thing was way heavier than I remembered it." I wiped sweat from my face and tried to peek over Stark's shoulder. He was on his knees using a pocketknife to dislodge the thick wooden panel in the floor that had made the ominously hollow sound as we'd knocked over every square inch beneath our bed.

"Uh, Z, you don't remember the bed being heavy because the Sons of Erebus Warriors and I hauled the thing up here and put it together to surprise you. *I* remember how heavy it was."

"Oh, well, that would be why then. OMG, there it is!" I gasped as Stark pulled a bundle that was wrapped in an old linen cloth from the hidden floor cubby. I held out my hands and he passed it gingerly to me, like it was an unexploded bomb. Carefully, I unwrapped it and found a worn, brown leather journal. The slender book was longer than it was wide. Its faded cover was unadorned, except for the very center. There, in surprisingly easy-to-read cursive, were the words "*Emily Wheeler's Journal,*" which were marked through with an ominous X. Beside them, in the same handwriting, only much bolder, much darker, was the new title: *Neferet's Curse.*

"Looks like we found the right book," Stark said. This time it was his turn to peek over my shoulder.

"Looks like it," I said.

Neither of us moved.

"Uh, you gonna open it?" he asked.

"I wish I didn't have to." I looked up from the journal to meet his concerned gaze. "How about we get breakfast first? Everything seems better after a big bowl of Count Chocula."

"And brown pop?"

"Breakfast of champions," I agreed, pulling on my sweat pants that were decorated with fat orange tabby cats.

"I'd usually say we shouldn't procrastinate about this, but you're right. It's gonna read like a horror story, and that'll be better on a full stomach. Plus, I need coffee. Now."

I brushed my teeth and stuck my hair up in a messy ponytail, glad that one of the first rules I'd proposed when I'd officially become High Priestess of our new Council was to relax the dress code of the professors' dining hall. Holding the journal carefully, I beat Stark to the door and opened it. Aphrodite fell forward, barely catching herself in time to not knock me over.

"Seriously? You're lurking outside my bedroom door?" I shook my head at her. "That's creepy AF."

"Please don't use text abbreviations when we're talking. Out loud. I realize it's your special little way to use cuss words without actually cussing, but it's not cool," she said, patting her flawless hair back into place.

"Aphrodite was just bein' polite. We heard that bed a thumpin' so we thought we'd wait until you was done. Like Aphrodite said—it didn't take long." Kramisha shoved past Aphrodite, eyes narrowed at the bed that was totally catawampus, off-centered and rumpled. The Vampyre Poet Laureate shook her head, making her gold, waist-length Beyoncé braids swirl as she sent Stark a *look*. "Boy, you got you some excess energy."

"I don't know whether I should be impressed or squeed out." Along with Kramisha, Aphrodite was staring at our displaced bed.

I felt my cheeks flush with heat. "No, no, no. First, you're wrong. Second, we're not having this conversation. Third, what *are* you two doing here?" Magnet-like, my gaze was pulled to the lavender notebook Kramisha clutched in her hands.

"Yeah. It's what you think. A poem woke me up. First time in almost a year," Kramisha said.

"And because misery loves company, she woke me up," Aphrodite said. "Have I mentioned how much I hate poetry?"

"Not for about a year," Stark said.

16

"Thank you, Bow Boy," she said. "And, as per usual, I couldn't figure out what the hell the stupid thing was saying—hence the fact we're both here."

"Poems ain't stupid," Kramisha said firmly.

"Why do we have to keep going over this? 'Ain't' isn't a word," Aphrodite countered.

"How 'bout we go over this—I'm gonna kick your tight white ass if you keep disparaging poetry. Is that a word?" Kramisha said with mock sweetness.

"That's a bunch of words." Aphrodite flipped her hair back. "And I don't think the vamp Poet Laureate is supposed to resort to violence."

"If you had to read the awful poems them kids be writin' in my class you'd know that we in a war. A literacy war."

"But I think that war's figurative—not literal." Aphrodite paused, shrugging her smooth shoulders. "What do I know, though? I'm shitty at figurative language so, war away. Just not on me. It's unattractive."

"Stop. I can't deal with bickering today," I said, and the two of them turned to face me. Instantly their expressions changed.

"Something's up," Aphrodite said. "Right?"

"Right," I said.

"Double right," Stark said.

"Yep. I knew it. That's why I wrote this." Kramisha thrust the purple pad at me, but before I could (reluctantly) take it, Aphrodite interrupted.

"What's that?" She pointed at what I was still holding.

I drew a deep breath and then spoke quickly, like ripping off a Band-Aid. "It's Neferet's journal from when she was young. Kalona showed up in my dream last night. He told me where to find it. He said I need to read it because he felt like trouble was on its way. Again."

"Neferet? Oh, Goddess, no . . ." Kramisha's voice was a strained whisper.

"Oh, for shit's sake. Not again!" Aphrodite said.

3

Zoey

The professors' dining hall was nowhere near the students' cafeteria—something I didn't fully appreciate until I wasn't a student any longer. Here's the thing about becoming a teacher—at any age. You find out real fast that students are equal parts awesome and awful, often at the same time. It is universally acknowledged by teachers that in order to save what's left of our sanity, we have to have a place at school to escape to that's off-limits to students. Hence the creation of that shabby yet magical place called *the teachers' lounge.* Here at the House of Night, everything is at least several steps up from a "normal" high school—including our escape from the students' area. Oh, we have a teachers' lounge, but instead of it being a dingy, windowless closet with an overripe refrigerator, our *Professors' Sanctuary* (yep, that's really its name— it's on a gold plaque and everything) is a smaller, more comfortable version of the New York Public Library's Rose Main Reading Room, complete with a ceiling mural of puffy clouds.

Our dining hall is equally as awesome. Ever been to the Palm Court at the Plaza in New York City? Well, no need. I could save you a trip if you were allowed in the professors' dining hall in T-Town. Sadly for you (and happily for us), no one except House of Night professors, Sons of Erebus Warriors, and High Priestesses are allowed.

Oh, and since I became the new Council's High Priestess, every Tuesday is officially Spaghetti Madness. Just sayin'—it's good to be Queen. Um, or High Priestess.

The four of us went directly to my booth—a huge, soft, leather thing that circled around a linen-draped booth already set for ten people. It was super early, meaning the sun had barely set, and we had the room all to ourselves.

"Your usual, High Priestess?" asked the slender young priestess-in-training whose turn it was to rotate through the dining hall this semester.

"Call me Zoey," I said automatically, like I did every day. And, like every day, she smiled shyly, nodded, and then never called me Zoey. "And, yep. Make my brown pop a double."

"So a glass of pop and a glass of ice?"

"Yep and yep," I said.

"Just bring me coffee and a breakfast bagel," Stark said.

"I want one of them chai lattes. Extra whip cream," Kramisha said, then added, "Please."

"And I'll take my usual," Aphrodite said.

"Mimosa—hold the orange juice," parroted the priestess.

"Actually, today bring me a small orange juice on the side. Emphasis on small," Aphrodite said. The priestess nodded, bowed respectfully, and walked away, leaving us staring at Aphrodite. "What? I told Darius I'd eat healthy, but you know I can't abide polluting my champagne with—" she paused and shuddered delicately, "juice. But—and you'll probably only hear me say this once in this lifetime—enough about me. Let's see the death journal."

I'd filled the two of them in on Kalona's dream visit on our

19

way to the dining hall, and I could feel a terrible prickly sensation in the air between us—a sensation I hadn't felt in almost one full year—a sensation I hadn't missed for one speck of an instant. It was fear and dread mixed with a healthy dose of WTF.

I handled the journal carefully. It was pretty well preserved, but the pages were fragile and the ink faded, though still pretty much legible. I took a deep breath as we stared at the title, *Neferet's Curse*.

"That's not creepy at all," Aphrodite said softly.

"And yet I have a feeling the title is totally going to fit," I said. "Okay, here goes." Gently, I opened the journal and read aloud:

> *January 15th, 1893, Emily Wheiler's Journal. Entry: the first. This is not a diary. I loathe the very thought of compiling my thoughts and actions in a locked book, secreted away as if they were precious jewels. I know my thoughts are not precious jewels. I have begun to suspect my thoughts are quite mad.*

"Ding! Ding! Ding! Correct answer," Aphrodite said.

"Damn, 1893. That shit's old," Kramisha said. "And she been crazy since then. That's a lotta crazy. Keep reading."

So, I did. And as Emily Wheiler's sad, scary, abusive life unfolded, I was surprised by the sense of pity I began to feel for Neferet.

"Oh for shit's sake," Aphrodite interrupted as she sipped her third glass of champagne (her orange juice remained untouched). "Did she just describe a statue of a giant *White Bull* in her garden?"

My stomach clenched. "Yeah, that's exactly what she just described."

"And it's the only place she felt safe or comfortable." Stark shook his head in disgust. "That damn bull was stalking her all the way back then."

"Makes me feel sorry for her," Kramisha said before I could.

"Don't." Stark's voice was sharp. "No matter what happened to her—Emily Wheiler, and then Neferet, had a choice in how she would react. No amount of awful, abusive father excuses what she became—what she did."

"And yet Kalona thinks it's important that we understand what happened to her. It makes me think there might be a point to pitying her," I said.

"Don't let her suck you in." Stark's eyes were as hard and sharp as his voice. "That girl—that sixteen-year-old Emily Wheiler—she stopped existing more than one hundred years ago. Remember that while you keep reading."

A chill skittered down my spine. "I will. We will."

"Here, I'll take a turn reading," Aphrodite said. "You're eating. I'm drinking my breakfast. It's easier to drink and read than eat and read. Plus, I like to do the voices."

"The voices? You mean like the ones in your head?" Stark asked, eyes widened in mock innocence.

"My cat will eat your cat," was all Aphrodite said before she turned to a new page of the journal and kept reading. "*April 27ᵗʰ, 1893 ...*"

I chewed my Count Chocula while I listened to Emily's tragedy unfold. My eyes looked from Aphrodite to Stark and Kramisha. The journal had definitely captured their attention. Except for an occasional, "Ah, shit, that's bad," or other sounds of shock, no one spoke.

The journal wasn't long. The ornate clock on the wall chimed seven bells as Aphrodite turned to the final entry, made on May 8, 1893, that described how a newly Marked Emily had been rescued from her father's brutalization and rape by the Tracker, and how she'd had a choice. She could have turned her back on the human world, making a new life at the Chicago House of Night—or she could have allowed what her father had done to her to poison her new life.

We all know what choice she made. After Emily had healed from the rape, she'd returned to her father's house as Neferet and killed him—strangling him with her dead mother's pearls. I understand exactly why. Emily had spelled it out for us.

I am not mad.

The horrible events that befell me happened because, as a young human girl, I had no control over my own life. Envious women condemned me. A weak man rejected me. A monster abused me. All because I lacked the power to affect my own fate ...

... No one will ever harm me without suffering equal or more in return ...

... No one will ever know my secrets for they will be entombed in the land, safely hidden, silent as death. I regret none of my actions and if that curses me, then my final prayer is to let that curse be entombed with this journal, to be imprisoned eternally in sacred ground.

So ends Emily Wheiler's sad story and so begins the magickal life of Neferet ... Queen of the Night!

After Aphrodite read Neferet's final words, the silence at our table was thick. I felt shell-shocked and unaccountably sad for *Emily*. Not for Neferet. Like Stark had pointed out—Neferet had a choice. She chose Darkness, violence, and selfish hatred. But Emily Wheiler hadn't had any choice. And I couldn't help but pity her.

"Damn. That was bad," Kramisha said.

"Well, at least now we understand why she hates men so much. Especially human men," Stark said.

"And why she was such a control freak," Aphrodite said.

"I understand her anger now," I said. They gawked at me, and I held up my hand, stopping Stark before he could add his two cents. "I didn't say I agreed with it. And I also don't think I would have made the same choices she did, or at least I hope I wouldn't have. But I understand her, and I have a feeling that was Kalona's point."

"In case she somehow gets out of the grotto, you mean," Aphrodite said.

"Yes." I turned to Kramisha. "Okay, your turn." She tore a page from her lavender notebook and handed it to me. Kramisha's handwriting was pretty—something that I hadn't taken time to realize a year ago when she'd started writing prophetic poetry, which we'd used to save the world. More than once. But in the year since, our Poet Laureate had been teaching at the Tulsa House of Night, and I'd sat in on several of her classes. She had a raw, honest, irreverent teaching style that totally worked with students. She also had one of the most unusual adult vampyre tattoos I'd ever seen. From a distance, Kramisha's elaborate sapphire tattoo stretched on either side of the crescent moon resting in the center of her forehead—the same crescent that Marked us all, whether in sapphire or scarlet—looking like an indecipherable script of indistinguishable letters. But when you got closer and really studied it, you could make out words hidden within the script. Words like *create, imagine, inspire.* And I swear the words change because I can never seem to find the same one again in the exact same place. It was weird and cool, a lot like Kramisha.

"Are you gonna take it, or am I readin' it to ya?"

"Oh, yeah, sorry." I mentally shook myself. I took the purple paper, holding it almost as carefully as I'd held the ancient journal, cleared my throat, and read aloud:

Snowflakes—each unique
yet while falling from
    one existence to another
they might touch
    come together

and in this Joining

find themselves again.

But only if each

agree

to sacrifice

who they were to be formed

anew.

Sometimes it

        just

            needs

                to

                    snow.

"So? Anything? Anything at all?" Aphrodite asked.

I sighed. "Doesn't mean anything to me—or at least nothing that hits me right away." I glanced at Stark. "You?"

"I got nothing." His eyes found Kramisha. "What about you?"

"No clue."

Aphrodite snorted. "No clue at all? Are you or are you not a prophetess?"

Kramisha narrowed her eyes at Aphrodite. "I got to gets to class, so I don't have time to take you out back and smack that smug champagne smile off your thin lips. So, I'll just say this—do you understand your visions? *All* your visions?" She made a disturbing hissing noise when Aphrodite tried to speak. "No. They's rhetorical. Don't speak 'cause you is suddenly reminding me why we used to call you a hag from hell." Kramisha stood and bowed formally to me. "Merry meet, merry part, and merry meet again, High Priestess. Text if you be needing me." Braids swaying in time with her slinky walk, Kramisha exited the room.

"Damn, she's touchy. She should drink more." Aphrodite glanced at her fingernails. "And I need a manicure. So, let's hurry up this next part."

"Next part?" I asked stupidly.

Aphrodite raised one perfectly plucked blond brow at me. "Seriously? Like you're not heading to Woodward Park to check on Neferet's grotto jail?"

"Oh, that next part. Yeah, I am."

"*We* are," Stark corrected.

"What he said."

"Okay, hang on just a sec." Aphrodite's fingers tapped over her phone. Then she sighed, smiled, and delicately fluttered her fingers at the waitress. "Another champagne," she said. Then, grimly, she picked up the untouched glass of orange juice, and—like it was a shot—gulped it down. Shuddering, she dabbed her mouth.

"Aphrodite, what in the hell are you doing? Like you said, we're going to Woodward Park," I said.

"Yeah, and like Stark said, you're not going alone. I texted Darius. I just have time to suck down another glass of my morning grapes before he shows up. And please make note that I drank that orange stuff." She shuddered delicately. "It was completely naked and not mixed with the salvation of alcohol."

"You are such a piece of work," Stark said.

Aphrodite's grin was Cheshire. "Thank you, Bow Boy."

4

Zoey

"OMG, who *is* that deliciously handsome Son of Erebus who just walked through that door?" Aphrodite cooed.

I didn't bother to look over my shoulder. Stark made a noise between a snort and a sigh.

"Wait, I know who it is. It's my man!"

Aphrodite tilted her head back, perfectly timed for Darius to bend down, murmur, "Hello, my beauty," and kiss her. He straightened and shook his head slightly. "Champagne for breakfast?"

"Always, handsome," Aphrodite said. She flicked her finger against the empty orange juice glass and added, "But I made it healthy with this."

Darius glanced at me. "She actually drank that?"

I nodded. "Yep. Gulped it down like a trooper."

"It was just orange juice. It tastes good," Stark said.

"Then next time *you* drink it," Aphrodite said.

Stark looked utterly baffled. I just shook my head and rolled my eyes. Sometimes—actually, most times—it's easier to just go with whatever craziness Aphrodite spouts versus trying to actually make sense of it. Stevie Rae told me once that she listened to Aphrodite like she read Shakespeare—not actually getting every word, but eventually understanding the basic message. As usual, I agreed with Stevie Rae.

"What is the urgency, my beauty?" Darius asked after bowing formally to me and nodding to Stark.

"Kalona showed up in Z's dream warning of danger. He told her to read Neferet's journal. We did. It's as bad as you might imagine. Now we're going with Z to Woodward Park. Hopefully shit is *not* going to go wrong. Which would be the first time. So, I sent out the Bat Signal, and here you are. The end."

I watched as several emotions flashed across the Warrior's face—surprise, fear, anger. He glanced at me. I nodded. He sighed.

"And I was naively hoping the emergency was that the dining hall had run out of champagne."

"That would be more on the lines of tragedy than emergency," Aphrodite said.

"Has Neferet truly begun to stir?"

"We don't know." I spoke with much more bravado than I felt. "But we're going to find out."

(

"Tell me why we decided to walk again?" Aphrodite said as she leaned on Darius, lifting up her foot to study the red sole of her Louboutin stiletto boot. "OMG, *gum*? I stepped in some Neanderthal's *gum*?"

Stark and I were walking ahead of them. I glanced over my shoulder. "We're walking because it's a beautiful December night— not too hot and not too cold—and midtown is all dressed up in holiday lights. Aphrodite, it's *pretty.* I wanted to enjoy it." I didn't add, *While we can, because if Neferet somehow gets loose we'll probably all die,* but my unspoken words hung over us.

"We told you to put on sensible shoes," Stark added.

"Last season's Louboutin's are as sensible as I get," she said as she scuffed down the sidewalk, trying to get rid of the last of the gum.

"Check out Utica Square. I love how it looks all lit up for the holidays. It reminds me of a giant snow globe," I said.

"I'm averting my eyes," Aphrodite said.

"Is she still boycotting Utica Square because of Miss Jackson's closing?" Stark whispered to me.

"Yes, I am," Aphrodite answered. "Fucking barbarians. Do they expect me to shop at Saks? Like the rest of the upper-middle-class people?" She shuddered. "No. I've resorted to online Nordstrom purchases."

"But, my beauty. You just returned from a shopping trip to Dallas. You said the Nordstrom there was a paradise," Darius said.

"Hyperbole," she muttered. "Sad, sad, hyperbole."

At the corner of Twenty-First and Utica, we turned left, crossing the street and walking past festively decorated office buildings and the yummy McGill's restaurant. There was a little rise in the road and then we were looking down at Woodward Park.

"Ah oh," I said.

"What the hell?" Stark asked.

Aphrodite and Darius caught up to us, and we all stared at what should be a dark, deserted park lit only by the vintage-looking streetlamps. Currently it was anything but deserted and dark. There was a large crowd of what appeared to be reporters, complete with a big Channel 2 News van and several cameras surrounding a woman who was standing in front of a podium (Podium? At Woodward Park? Huh?) facing the throng of people. Camera lights flashed, but we were too far away to hear what was being said.

"Oh, for shit's sake. That's my mother."

The three of us gawked at Aphrodite. Then our gazes swiveled back to the park scene and, sure enough, now that I was looking closer I could see that the woman was indeed Aphrodite's beautiful, hateful mother, Frances LaFont.

"I wonder what she's up to?" Stark said.

"Nothing good," I said. "That's for sure." I glanced at my friend, who was staring at her mom with a kinda shell-shocked expression, her face washed the white of a porcelain doll. "Have you talked to her since your dad died?"

"No. I called her after we beat Neferet. I thought she'd want to know that I was okay. I don't know why I thought that, but still. I called. Her PA passed along Mom's message to me, which was that she is 'permanently not available to talk to the person who used to be her daughter,'" she air quoted. "That was last year."

"She is consumed by anger and ambition," Darius said, sliding his arm around Aphrodite's shoulders and holding her close. "That is what you escaped, my beauty."

"Hey, Stark and I can go down there. Go back to McGill's and order a glass of wine. We'll do some recon and meet you in a few," I said.

Aphrodite shook her head. "No. She said it. I'm not her daughter anymore, so she doesn't get to fuck with my life anymore."

Darius touched her cheek gently. "Bullies seldom stand when confronted by those who *aren't* weak or alone. You are neither."

"Yeah. Especially not alone." I took her hand and squeezed.

"And definitely too hateful to be weak," Stark said, his smile making it the compliment he intended.

Aphrodite blinked several times and then drew a deep breath and stood a little taller. "Okay, let's go see what kind of shit she's stirring now."

Closing ranks around Aphrodite, we followed the sidewalk down, crossed the street, and moved slowly to the outskirts of the group of people just as a familiar voice from the crowd called out a question.

"Mrs. LaFont, the next mayoral election isn't for almost a year. Why announce your candidacy so early?"

Aphrodite sucked in a shocked breath.

Mrs. LaFont's cerulean eyes searched the crowd until she spotted the reporter. "Chera Kimiko, so lovely to see you. I was afraid we'd lost you to marital bliss. Glad to see you're back with the news, though I do prefer Fox's sensible politics to Channel 2."

Aphrodite made soft kiss-kiss sounds.

"Thank you, Mrs. LaFont," Chera said without losing a beat. "And I think reporters should report the news and not fabricate it. Would you like me to repeat my question?"

"No, dear. I remember the question perfectly well. I am announcing my candidacy for mayor of Tulsa early because I believe the good people of our fair city need to be given hope."

"Hope? Tulsa's unemployment rate has fallen 1.5 percent over the past year, and is currently at its lowest since the oil boom. Housing sales are up. We've finally raised teacher pay competitively, and the construction on Harvard Street has actually been completed." Chera paused as the crowd laughed softly before concluding. "What does Tulsa need to hope for?"

"Do you remember the Biblical story of Sodom and Gomorrah?" Mrs. LaFont said, an icy smile on her perfect face.

"Oh, shit. Here we go," Aphrodite murmured.

"Those twin cities thrived, too, even as they were rotting from within. I'm sure their unemployment rate was down, as well. Just before God, in all His wisdom, smote them for harboring vile sinners. If you recall, angels of the Lord couldn't even find ten righteous men to save the cities."

"I'm sorry, Mrs. LaFont. I don't understand. Are you saying Tulsa is harboring sinners and you need to save us from them?" Chera asked.

"Well, *I* didn't say that. You did. And since you did, let me explain. I don't think it does any of us good if we gain wealth, but lose our souls in the process."

"Ma'am?" Chera asked, clearly as baffled as the rest of the crowd.

"Vampyres." LaFont spoke the word as if she'd bitten into a lemon. "Vampyres are the vileness we're harboring."

"Ah oh," I said softly. "Maybe now would be a good time for us to leave."

"Not a chance," Aphrodite said.

"But Mrs. LaFont, Tulsa has spent the past year working *with* the House of Night. There is even a new program in the works that will allow area students to take classes at the House of Night—tuition-free. There's a farmers' market on the school grounds every Thursday night, which is open to the public, and their new High Priestess, Zoey Redbird, has instituted a cat rescue program in conjuncture with Tulsa Street Cats. Human–vampyre relations have never been so good," Chera said.

"And don't forget, the House of Night saved us from Neferet!" called another reporter I didn't recognize.

"Don't *you* forget Neferet came from the House of Night. They are the reason she loosed her evil on our city. If it hadn't been for the House of Night, those twelve hundred people, my husband included, would be alive today. How many of them were your brothers and sisters? Husbands and wives? Sons and daughters?" LaFont paused to let the crowd murmur restlessly.

Into the pause, Chera asked, "What is it you're proposing, Mrs. LaFont? What will be your mayoral platform?"

"That's simple. My platform is: *Make Tulsa Strong Again.* I believe that says it all."

There was a pregnant pause, and then Chera said, "What exactly does that mean?"

"Well, it means that we need to depend upon the good Christian people of this community to come together to preserve our culture and identity. We're strong when we're Tulsa—not when we harbor a ticking time bomb in the heart of our beautiful city. If I am elected your mayor, I pledge to rescind the House of Night's lease on the old Cascia Hall Preparatory School and to escort every last vampyre out of our city. We need to take Tulsa back!"

"Ooooh! Question! I have a question over here!" Aphrodite had stepped forward and was doing an excellent imitation of Damien, flailing her hand with way more enthusiasm than she had ever shown in class.

Her mother's cold blue eyes lit on her daughter. I saw them widen for an instant as an emotion flicked over them—shock, maybe? Or sadness?

Then those eyes that were exactly the shape and color of her daughter's narrowed, and I realized what the emotion had been—anger.

"Would my security detail please escort this young lady from the park." Mrs. LaFont said in a dead voice.

"Um, no, *Mother.*" Aphrodite sounded like she was lecturing a petulant child. "This is a public park. I have every right to be here. Well, right now I do. If you're elected I'm sure that'll change. Hey, maybe you can bring back marking undesirables with a yellow star, you know, to encourage the *good people of Tulsa,*" she pitched her voice to sound exactly like her mother's, "to jump on the bully bandwagon. Because, like we all know, a bully only has to beat up a few kids in the schoolyard and then the rest of the sheep will start to follow you or avoid you out of fear."

"This press conference is over," LaFont said. "And this person—"

"Who happens to be your daughter!" Aphrodite interrupted.

Which didn't phase LaFont at all. "This person has proven my point. She and her vampyre family have disrupted a free human gathering. Again. I will see you all on the campaign trail. Good night and may God bless Tulsa!"

Smooth as a snake, Mrs. LaFont glided from the podium. Her security team closed around her, hurrying her to a waiting limo.

"And they called *me* a hag from hell," Aphrodite said, shaking her head in disgust.

"Oh, some people still do," Stark said, obviously trying to lighten the tension between us.

I was watching Aphrodite closely. Her eyes were suspiciously bright. Darius was practically velcroed to her side.

I understood what she was going through. My mom betrayed me, too. But I still loved her. I couldn't help it. And I didn't think Aphrodite could, either.

"Come on. Let's circle around through the rose gardens. By the time we get back here the reporters should be gone," I said.

"Aphrodite LaFont?" Suddenly the lights of a camera were shining in our direction and Chera Kimiko was pointing a puffy microphone at Aphrodite.

"Yes, I'm Aphrodite. I dropped my last name, though. Kinda like my mother dropped me." She tossed back her hair and smiled directly into the camera.

I thought she deserved an Oscar. She definitely has the hair for it. I mean, seriously, that long blond stuff is Disney-princess quality.

"You are Frances LaFont's daughter, though, aren't you?"

"Frances LaFont gave birth to me, but the truth is she hasn't been a mother to me for years."

"What is your reaction to her announcement that she plans to run for mayor?"

"I'm super confused. I mean, my father was a decent mayor. Well, if you ignore the fact that he cut taxes for the top 1 percent and had an abysmal record of allowing Big Oil to totally screw up our environment—hello earthquakes in Oklahoma! Anyway, in spite of my father's Republican shortcomings, he was a career politician. He did his homework. He knew this city and its people. Mother was never, well, how should I put this so that it's not offensive ..." She paused, shrugged, and continued, "Never mind. I just realized that there's no reason for me *not* to be offensive. My mother has always been more concerned with shoes, cocktail parties, and appearances than law and government. And what

33

she just said proves she has a lot of homework to do before she could even begin to run this city."

"What do you mean?" Chera asked.

"Well, her first official announcement after her candidacy was that she plans to revoke the House of Night's *lease* on our school. Mother better check her facts. The House of Night doesn't lease anything. We own the property. Outright. No mortgage. She *can't* kick us out. Save your votes, people, for someone who deserves them. Toodles!" She blew a kiss at the camera, flung back her Disney-princess hair, and twitched off as cameras flashed and reporters called questions at her back.

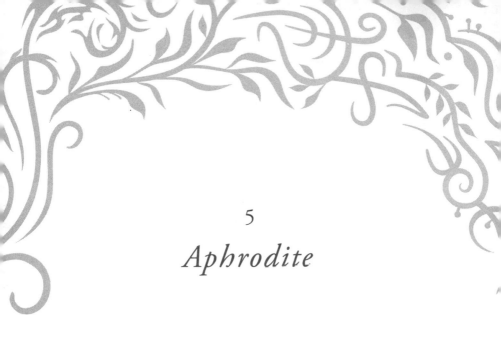

5

Aphrodite

Aphrodite walked away from the reporters and the cameras and the gawking people. Fast. She kept her head high and a purposefully blank but beautiful expression on her face—ironically, it was the expression her mother had schooled into her with stinging slaps and cutting insults. But it had worked. Even now. Even when her heart ached with every beat and her embarrassment was monumental—the cool, aloof, untouchable expression remained.

She could hear Z and Stark and Darius pushing through the crowd trying to catch up with her, but the reporters had realized there were "real vamps" in their midst, and then suddenly Chera recognized Zoey and the media circus went into full swing, closing a circle of mics and cameras around the three of them.

Aphrodite slowed a little. Darius would be frantic, but probably not willing to shove aside a bunch of human reporters to display his superhuman strength, especially not when there were cameras pointed in his direction. If she stayed within view, he wouldn't freak.

She could hear Zoey saying, "No, the House of Night doesn't

have a comment on next year's mayoral elections—especially because it's not *next year* yet."

She was sorry she left Z to clean up her mess. Well, more precisely, her mother's mess, but she had to get away from all those watching eyes before they saw through her thin facade—before they saw her hurt.

If they saw it they would film it. And then her mother would see it.

A normal mother seeing her daughter's pain and embarrassment would feel sorrow, remorse even—and would probably try to make things right. Or at least that's what Aphrodite supposed normal mothers would do—should do. She wouldn't know. She'd never had a normal mother.

Her mother—the ice queen socialite—would use her daughter's pain. She'd figure out some way to exploit her. Again.

"She'd *try* to. I'm not a scared kid anymore who wants her mommy's love and approval." She spoke slowly, emphatically, tasting each word. "She might still be able to hurt me, but she can't use me."

Aphrodite had come to the corner of Twenty-First and Peoria. She paused, unwilling to turn left toward the Tulsa Rose Gardens and step out of Darius' view. She looked back. The group was dispersing. Darius was striding so fast down the sidewalk to her that Z and Stark almost had to jog to keep up.

Aphrodite drew several deep breaths—in for four counts—out for four counts. She willed herself to relax. Darius was her Warrior. They shared a bond through which he could feel her emotions, and the last thing she wanted was for him to feel how badly her mother could still hurt her.

Aphrodite refused to give Frances LaFont that much power.

Darius rushed up to her. He said nothing. He simply pulled her into his arms and held her close. Aphrodite allowed herself to cling to him—to inhale his warmth and his scent—to be immersed in his unconditional love.

"Are you okay?" Z was panting as she hurried to Aphrodite, gently touching her shoulder and brushing back her hair.

"I'd forgotten what an awful bitch your mother is," Stark said, not unkindly. "That musta sucked for you."

Aphrodite tilted her head, her chin resting against Darius' chest. "It did. But, not surprisingly, it's far from the worst thing my mother has done to me."

"You stood up to her," Z said. "You were totally adulting. I'm so proud of you."

"We're all proud of you," Darius said.

"You sounded super smart, too. Damien couldn't have done better," Stark said.

That made Aphrodite's lips lift in the beginnings of a smile. "Promise me you'll tell him that."

"Oh, I won't have to," Stark said. "Between the cameras and the cell phones that recorded every second of that, *everyone* is going to see you putting that ice bitch in her place—over and over again."

"Hey, want to make a fake Facebook account? We could pretend to be a good ol' Republican Okie named Billy Bob Johnson. His profile pic will, of course, sport the stars and bars. Every time someone posts a video from tonight we'll share it with your mom. It'll drive her crazy," Z said.

"That does sound like fun. We could also share cute cat memes with her. She hates cats." Aphrodite's smile became real.

"That's it. She officially has no soul," Z said.

"Oh, that was official a long time ago." Aphrodite tiptoed to kiss Darius before stepping out of his arms. "Okay. I'm better now."

"Sure?" Z asked.

"Sure." Aphrodite glanced behind them. "What's taking them so long to leave?"

"Did you see all those cameras?" Z shook her head. "I don't get how your mom's ridiculously early announcement could pull that much press. And why did she stage it in the park? I mean, she wasn't even far from Neferet's …" Z's voice trailed off.

"Do you get it now?" Aphrodite asked.

"I do not. Please explain," Darius said.

"She's coming after the House of Night. Her comment about revoking our lease wasn't prompted by me. She's running on a platform of fear."

"And the best way to create fear is to give it a target, and then make up a bunch of bullpoopie and put it out there on the Internet."

"Not a good time for Neferet to be stirring," Stark said.

"Like there's ever a good time for that?" Aphrodite said.

"Well, yeah. A good time would be several hundred years from now after Z and I have peacefully died curled up together in our sleep and are frolicking in Nyx's Grove in the Other World," Stark said.

"So, you mean when she's someone else's problem," Z said.

Stark kissed her on her forehead, smack in the middle of her crescent moon. "Yep. Exactly."

"Can't say I disagree with that," Darius said.

"I hear ya, handsome." Aphrodite took Darius' calloused hand in hers as they turned and began down the sidewalk that framed Peoria Street. "But first, let's stop and smell the roses."

(

"Hey, I meant that rose comment to be metaphoric. I admit I'm crappy at figurative language, but not *this* crappy." Aphrodite was staring, dumbfounded, at what should have been deserted, winter-sparse gardens with rose bushes all tucked in mulch for a frigid sleep.

Instead, old people (OP)—obviously members of the Tulsa Garden Center—were milling around the bushes that stretched along the side of the gardens that bordered Woodward Park, muttering and staring at flowers that were in full bloom.

"This is really weird," Z said. "We've had a hard freeze already. The roses shouldn't be blooming."

"Huh?" Stark said.

"Roses don't bloom after a freeze. They go dormant. Like the koi in the water features. I know because I used to help Grandma prune her roses and then wrap them up for the winter. We always did it after the first hard freeze. But it looks like those roses are blooming."

"I have a bad feeling about this," Stark said.

"Stay here. I'm going to go ask one of those OP what's going on," Aphrodite said. When Darius started to go with her, she touched his shoulder gently, saying, "No, you stay here, too, handsome. You're a big, scary vampyre Warrior, remember? Things are better between vamps and humans right now, but there will be a lot less gawking and question asking if I'm not being escorted by you."

Darius nodded tightly. "I'll be watching from here. I'll know if you need me."

Aphrodite winked and hummed Sting's "Every Breath You Take" as she headed for the closest old man.

"Excuse me, sir." Aphrodite put on her sweetest girly-girl smile.

The retiree should have smiled. Men *always* smiled when she turned her charm on them, but this OP barely glanced in her direction as he mumbled, "Garden shop's closed."

"Oh, thank you, sir, but I don't want to shop. Well, not at this moment I don't," she added automatically. "I was just wondering what's going on with the roses. Isn't it weird that they're blooming right now?"

"It is, young lady. But it's weirder even than that. Apparently we are the victims of a rose thief."

"Rose thief? I don't understand." *I didn't even know there could be such a thing*, she added silently.

He did look at her then, and his annoyed expression lightened. "We don't understand either. But someone stole all of the roses from the beds bordering Woodward Park, and replaced them with these. They're not even a true rose." He pointed with disgust at a bush not far from them. Aphrodite followed his finger, and felt a jolt of shock when she realized what she was seeing.

All of the rose bushes that framed this side of Woodward Park were in full bloom, even though their leaves were shriveled and their stalks twisted and spindly.

Each rose was completely black.

These roses had an almost liquid look that made them glisten in the wan streetlight.

Aphrodite felt a sharp spear of fear. "When did this happen?"

"That's the strangest part of all of this. It had to have happened this afternoon—only a few hours ago. But no one saw anything until it was too late."

"What did you mean when you said they aren't even true roses?"

"There is no such thing as a true black rose. A rose doesn't have the correct genes for the color black."

While the old man talked, Aphrodite moved closer to the rose bushes, *really* looking at them. She put out a tentative finger, barely brushing one of the blooms.

And jerked her hand back fast.

Aphrodite stared at the roses. The blossoms were all wrong— they felt slick and cold—like no rose she'd ever known, but it was the bushes themselves that caused her breath to catch in fear. The stalks of the bushes—every one of the bushes—weren't actually twisted like they'd looked from a distance. Closer up it was obvious that they were bent, curling sinuously toward the ground in a snakelike fashion, giving the appearance of tendrils made of darkness and thorns …

"So, though they can be manipulated—watered with ink, sprayed with paint, etcetera, a black rose is genetically impossible to create at this time," finished the old gardener.

"Were these watered with ink or sprayed?" Aphrodite asked, the sickness in her gut already answering her question.

"Neither. We're completely befuddled about what's gone on here, but we are sure a crime has been committed."

"Thank you, sir. I hope you find your rose thief." She hastily turned away, hurrying back to her friends.

"Well? What's going on?" Z asked.

"It's bad. Come on, let's get into the park away from all these Garden Center people. They do not need to overhear this."

Aphrodite led the way up the wedding cake–tiered Rose Garden levels to the pebbled path that emptied into Woodward Park. Vintage-looking street lights illuminated soft yellow bubbles that the four of them passed quickly through, moving into the heart of the park that used to be filled with old-growth oaks and huge mazes of azaleas.

Last year's fire in the park had destroyed much of that, but the city—with the financial backing of Zoey Redbird's new North American High Council—had replanted vigorously all during the past year. Now the park had a fresh-faced look, even in the winter.

"Hey, no one's around. Tell us what was going on back there," Z said.

"Not yet. We're not there yet." Aphrodite kept walking. She had to. She was *compelled* to. As soon as she understood that she was being led, her palms started to get sweaty and her stomach roiled as her headache began to build. *I don't want it to happen out here in the middle of the park!* Her mind shrieked, but Aphrodite didn't give voice to her internal misery. She was used to it.

It was all part of being a Prophetess of Nyx.

Finally, they came to the stony ridge that looked down on the pool and grotto where Aurox's sacrifice had entombed Nyx.

Everything appeared deceptively normal.

The wall had been finished in the middle of the summer. Made of the same rock as the ridge and the grotto, it looked more like a natural formation than a barricade to keep out stupid humans who thought leaving tokens and lighting candles around the sealed cave was a good idea.

Good idea?

Just the thought of anyone worshipping Neferet made Aphrodite sick.

If Neferet ever managed to escape, those same humans—the ones who considered it romantic and tragic what had happened to the "Goddess of Tulsa," which is what a cult following on the Internet had dubbed Neferet—those worshippers would be the first to be eaten by the Tsi Sgili and her tendrils of Darkness. Morons and idiots, the lot of them.

So, with the help of the House of Night, a wall had been built around the grotto. It began at one end of the rocky ridge, grew to a height of ten feet, and formed a sinuous half-moon shape, which curved back toward the ridge, attaching beside the stone stairway.

The landscape architect had added a pergola topping it, and covered it with fast-growing, tenacious wisteria. Now, even in the winter, the vines, interspersed with thick cedar planks, almost completely obscured the view of the sealed grotto. In another year or so, it would be impossible to glimpse the tomb that rested silently beneath it.

Aphrodite looked around for the iron bench she remembered, and went to it. She sat and then gazed up at her confused friends.

"First, the roses. The OP at the garden believe someone ripped off their normal rose bushes and traded them for super weird, twisted roses that are in full bloom right now. In the middle of winter. Um, and the thief did all of that this afternoon at roughly the same time Z was being warned by Kalona that something bad was in the works. But no one saw a thing."

"Wait, they think someone ripped off a bunch of rose bushes? This afternoon? Why would anyone do that?" Z asked.

"*Anyone* didn't. If the OP actually thought about it they'd realize that it's impossible for someone to dig up *hundreds* of rose bushes, in daylight, and replace them with crazy roses—all without being seen. But they're distracted because of the color of the blooms—a color that is genetically impossible for a rose to produce."

"What color? It was hard to tell from a distance," Z said.

"Black. Each bloom was completely black."

"Magick. Someone has to be using magick," Stark said. "But why?"

"Sadly, I think I know why. The roses aren't just black. They're slick and cold. I touched one. It was like you'd imagine touching a snake would be—except snakes aren't cold and wet and disgusting."

"I don't like where this is heading," Z said, looking as pale as Aphrodite felt.

"I hear you, and that's not the worst of it. The bushes themselves are awful. Their stalks are all misshapen so that they curl and bend toward the ground, looking exactly like dark, thorn-filled tendrils."

"Oh, Goddess," Zoey gasped. "Neferet's children! The tendrils of Darkness."

"Did you get a sense of sentience from them?" Darius asked quickly. "Did you see or feel them move at all?"

"No. But you saw how long I stayed." She searched for and then met Zoey's gaze, speaking formally. "High Priestess, I believe Kalona was right to warn you."

"That is bad," Stark said.

"It is, but as Nyx's prophetess reminds us, this time we have been forewarned," Darius said. Then his eyes narrowed on Aphrodite. "My beauty? You look ill."

"I'm not sick." With a trembling hand, Aphrodite wiped at the sweat beading her brow, automatically flinching from the pain spearing through her temples. "I'll be okay. Just get me back to the House of Night as soon as possible. Call a black car Lyft. I can't bear to think about riding in another Prius or Corolla. It's just barbaric. And keep in mind that I don't think it's a problem to mix Xanax and wine." *Two months,* she told herself. *In two months it would have been a year since my last vision. Nyx, I don't mean to complain, but sometimes—most of the time—visions suck ass and—*

Aphrodite collapsed, covering her pain-seared eyes with her hands and pressing her palms into them, trying to keep them from exploding as the vision took her and pulled her under, submerging her in dark currents of semiconsciousness.

Then Aphrodite was no longer in her pain-wracked body. There was a terrible ripping sound, like a giant had torn a house-sized piece of cloth apart. She opened her eyes and was immediately overwhelmed with feelings of terror, despair, and loss.

And all around her, blood bubbled from an enormous tear in the ground, and with the geyser of blood figures emerged— swimming up—hooking hands with long, clawlike fingers into the earth and pulling themselves out of what looked like a bloody pit in the ground.

The feet of the body she inhabited began to stumble back.

Focus! She ordered herself. *You're not part of what's happening. You're just an observer.*

She blinked, trying to clear her eyes of the tears cascading down her face. She knew her shoulders shook with sobs, and she was making a strange keening sound.

But it's not me! Snap out of it, girl! Get your shit together and figure out what's going on!

This time when she blinked she also rubbed at her eyes, and she noticed the body she inhabited dropped something.

Aphrodite forced her gaze down. There was a yellow candle at her feet.

Yellow candle? Air. With a start, she realized who she must be inhabiting. *Damien!*

She tried to maintain control over the vision, and over the terror that was drowning Damien, but because she was experiencing the events with him, his fear was debilitating. And that single fact was the biggest problem with Aphrodite's visions. Because she didn't just see them, but actually *experienced* whatever was happening in them—which usually included a horrible death—the emotions her host felt tended to screw up the fact-gathering she tried desperately to do.

Just let me look around and see where the hell we are, and what the hell is happening!

For a moment—just a sliver of a breath—Aphrodite controlled Damien's body. She made it stand still and she looked around, trying to decipher where he was.

The place was familiar. Rocks, winter brown grass, more rocks—but everything was covered by the expanding torrent of blood, turning it alien and nightmarish.

"Get out of there! RUN!"

Z's voice! Aphrodite tried to make Damien turn his head so she could look at Zoey, but his gaze was trapped by the things emerging from the scarlet geyser.

Oh, my Goddess! They're red vampyres! But they weren't like any red vampyres or fledglings Aphrodite had ever seen. These creatures seemed barely human. They moved with a feral, hunched stride, growling and hissing softly at one another. As she watched through Damien's eyes, the creatures turned their heads to face him. Like a hunter who had just caught sign of his prey, their red eyes seared into Damien and they began to stalk toward him.

"*RUN!*" Zoey's voice again.

Yes, Damien, for shit's sake, RUN! Aphrodite agreed. But then the truth hit her as one more figure emerged from the tear in the ground. This circle hasn't been closed. If Damien runs, that disgusting blood fountain is going to keep vomiting those zombie vamps!

Just then Damien was, indeed, unfreezing and scrambling backwards, rushing blindly for the stone stairway behind him. Aphrodite blinked frantically along with Damien, trying to clear his vision. And it worked. Damien's vision cleared—just in time to see a terrible familiarity in that last emerging figure. The creature stood and his head swiveled, beast-like, to focus on Damien.

"*Jack!*" Aphrodite thought the name at the exact moment as the body she was in shouted it.

Then Damien ignored Zoey's screaming to run, and Aphrodite's mental screaming to stay and close the damn circle. He ignored his own terror. He knew only one thing, and Aphrodite knew it with him—Jack was standing before him.

With a movement that was definitely more predator than lover, Jack rushed at Damien, weeping tears of blood.

As soon as Jack was close, Aphrodite was hit by the stench of him. It was sweetly sickening and disgustingly familiar. Inside Damien's mind Aphrodite was shrieking, *Never mind with the circle closing—run, run, RUN!* But her body didn't move. Shock froze her in place.

Until Jack tilted his head back as if to gaze lovingly into Damien's eyes and claim their reunion kiss. Instead of the kiss, Jack opened his mouth impossibly wide, exposing bizarrely sharp teeth, and with a feral growl, Jack Twist tore huge hunks of flesh from his lover's face and neck.

Like a rocket, Aphrodite's roving spirit shot up and out of the body as it collapsed. Awash in terror, hovering above the city, she gazed down at Tulsa as the red tide of bizarre vampyres spread, and the shrieks and death wails of the doomed echoed all around her.

(

Aphrodite knew what those things were—and they were so, so much more than normal red fledglings or vampyres.

"No! Oh, my goddess! No, Damien!"

"Aphrodite! It's okay. You're back. You're safe." Zoey's voice came to Aphrodite, finding its way through her panicked gasps and pain-filled sobs.

Keeping her eyes pressed tightly closed, Aphrodite reached out, searching. Darius was there. Darius would always be there. He grabbed her hands, holding them tightly in his.

"You're safe, my beauty. All is well. The vision is over." Darius spoke softly, soothingly. "I have called the black car. It is five minutes out."

"What was it? What did you see?" Stark's voice intruded.

Aphrodite didn't need to see Darius' reaction. She could feel it. He stiffened and turned, putting himself between Aphrodite and Stark, as if to protect her from his questions.

But Aphrodite was a Prophetess of Nyx. She didn't need protection. She needed to do her job.

"Zombies. I saw zombies. I saw them set loose on Tulsa, infecting everyone—killing everyone." Into the shocked silence that followed her announcement, Aphrodite felt heavy, wet flakes begin to fall on her hair, face, and body. Unbidden, she heard herself speak the last words of Kramisha's poem.

"Sometimes it
      just
         needs
            to
               snow."

6

Zoey

"I know it's super tempting, but we can't keep this from Damien," I said.

"Okay, I hear you," Aphrodite said. "But I saw what I saw. Damien was the focus of their zombie rage, and Jack killed him. Scratch that. I'm pretty sure Jack killed him. I left while Jack was still eating his face, so one can only assume. If we're going to tell him—and I agree that we should—we need to tell him the truth. Face-eating boyfriend zombie and all."

"That's so gross," I said.

"You think hearing about it's gross? Trying living it. Or dying it." She shrugged and took another sip of champagne. "I think both are correct." Aphrodite grimaced and pressed her hand over the damp washcloth that Darius had wetted and folded across her bloody, weeping eyes while she reclined on the gold-trimmed velvet chaise lounge in the sitting room off her bedchamber. Like me, after we established our new High Council, she'd relocated from the girl's dorm to the castle-like stone building that housed the professors' quarters, dining hall, and, on the first floor, the House of Night administrative offices. Also like me, she'd totally redecorated her living area. Unlike me, she hadn't let Damien spearhead her project, but had hired a team of very chic and very expensive designers and told them to "turn these antiquated, depressing rooms into something that oozes bordello chic mixed with Louis XIV." They'd done an awesome job, even if all the gold they used did sometimes blind me and give me a headache.

Just kidding.

Sorta.

"We have to tell him," I repeated.

"It's going to hurt and confuse him, Z," Stark said.

I sighed. "I know that, but we're not kids anymore. *We're* the ones making adult decisions for *all* the North American vampyres. And by 'we,' I mean my Council, and that includes Damien. Of course it's going to hurt him, but we know what happens when we keep secrets from each other."

"Disaster. And, let me add that disaster is what I saw in that vision—of the zombie apocalypse kind. Damien caused it. I don't mean on purpose, but he ran instead of closing the circle." Aphrodite turned her face in my direction, aiming her blind frown at me. "You told him to. Uh, Z. Just by-the-by, if zombies are pouring out of a blood fountain or whatever, and you've cast a circle that let them in—*close the damn circle before you start screaming at people to flee.*"

"I'll definitely keep that in mind," I said, trying not to be offended that she was basically telling me that I'd messed up as bad as Damien.

Suddenly Aphrodite sat up straight, holding the gold wash-cloth tightly against her closed eyes. "Holy shit! I just realized where I was."

"You mean during the vision?" I asked.

She started to nod vigorously, then stopped with a moan, clutching her temples as the bloody washcloth fell from her face to expose the tracks of scarlet tears that still seeped from beneath her closed lids. "Fuck, that hurts. But yeah, during the vision. It was Woodward Park—by Neferet's grotto. I recognize it now that I'm out of all that panic and confusion. Damien was backing for the stone stairs when Jack pulled himself out of the bloody, disgusting fountain thing." She shuddered. "He was below where we were standing when I had the vision. Right by the wall."

"Damn, this keeps getting worse and worse!" Stark cursed.

"Did you get any sense of Neferet? Tendrils of Darkness? Anything slithering around at all?"

"No, but I think that was covered before the vision. Those rose bushes were definitely tendril-like. As for the actual vision? Unless Damien noticed I probably wouldn't have. Plus, you have to remember the state of panic he was in, which means I was in the same state of panic. It's really hard to think when your body is filled with adrenaline, hysterical and dying."

"You have no idea why Damien and I were at the grotto?"

"None at all, except that I'm about 95 percent sure that you two had cast a circle."

"Was anyone else there?" Stark asked.

"No. Well, maybe. Sorry. I can't say for sure."

"This could have to do with what Kalona was warning me about," I said. "Aphrodite's visions aren't always literal. Maybe this was one of the more metaphoric visions, initiated by whatever Kalona sensed. It could have been symbolic for something. Could you tell?" I asked her.

She started to shake her head, and then grimaced in pain, holding herself very still. "No. But I can tell you that it felt just like it does every time I have a death vision. I'm inside the person who's dying. It's confusing, terrifying, painful, and not particularly helpful because I have to try to sift through all of those awful emotions quickly, before the person I'm attached to either dies or I'm sucked out of them again."

"What's your gut say—literal or metaphor?" Stark asked.

"Literal. It didn't have the feel of one of my dreamlike visions," Aphrodite said. "Except I'm confused about Jack. He's dead, right? I mean, there's no way he could be lurking around the depot tunnels as a salivating, stinky, feral red fledgling, could he?"

I shook my head. "No, or at least I don't see how that could be possible. I'll fill Kramisha in when she's done teaching and see if she can give us any insight. She's totally redone those tunnels. I was there just a couple of days ago. They're nice. Really nice, and filled with the red fledglings being bussed back and forth from there to here for school. It's actually crowded enough that Kramisha and I were talking about getting Stevie Rae to open up some of the tunnels she sealed off last year next time she's in town. I just don't see how there could be any zombielike creatures creeping around down there."

"And, I have to say, the Depot Restaurant is surprisingly fantastic," Aphrodite added. "It's about time Tulsa opened a high-end vegan restaurant."

I couldn't help but smile. The restaurant had been Kramisha's brainchild. She'd created the business plan and presented it to our High Council. It got a unanimous yes vote. Every one of us loved the layers of irony—vampyres running a meat-free restaurant smack in the middle of bible-belted cattle country! And now we love that the restaurant is a resounding success. At first Tulsans might have gone to the restaurant to gawk at and be waited on by beautiful fledglings, but pretty soon it was apparent that they were returning because the food was totally awesome.

"Yeah, it'd be tough for anyone to lurk around that busy place unnoticed. Especially if that someone smelled like dead things rotting in a basement and acted even worse than the first red fledglings used to."

"Plus, there's Aphrodite's sacrifice. The one where she lost her Mark and became, well, whatever it is she is now," Stark began.

"Which is an amazingly attractive Prophetess of Nyx," Aphrodite interrupted.

"Yeah, that. But once you made the sacrifice of your humanity, you saved Stevie Rae *and* you gave all red fledglings the ability to choose between Light and Darkness. We knew Jack. Dead or undead, there's no way he would have chosen Darkness over Light."

"I apologize for the insensitive way this sounds, but we saw Jack's body burn on the funeral pyre. He could not have been resurrected as a red fledgling," Darius said.

"Which gives me hope that at least some of Aphrodite's vision was metaphoric," I said.

"Yeah, it does seem that we can't take the part about Jack literally," Aphrodite said. "Still, it's going to be rough to tell Damien that he's the focus of a zombie attack on Tulsa led metaphorically by his dead boyfriend."

I sighed. "So much for my birthmas surprise."

"She knows about that?" Aphrodite said with disgust. "Good job, Bow Boy."

"I had to tell her after that damn Kalona dream. She was going to call everyone here anyway, and she was already freaking about not being able to reach her circle," Stark said.

"When is everyone getting here? We need to call a Council meeting, ASAP," I said.

Stark took his phone from his pocket and tapped the screen. "They'll be here within half an hour. They met at the tunnels last night and were to stay there until the party tomorrow, but I sent an emergency group text. Everyone's coming here instead. Stevie Rae and Rephaim just landed—they were the last to get in."

"Damien's already here?" I asked.

"Yep. Got here yesterday afternoon. He's already been to Ihloff Salon for a mani-pedi."

I frowned. "He's been to Ihloff, but hasn't been here to see me?"

"Hey, genius," Aphrodite said. "It was supposed to be a *surprise*."

"Oh, yeah," I said.

"And aren't you totally used to having a crappy birthday, so a ruined surprise party is actually above the norm for you?" She added.

"There is that," I agreed. "Okay, let's start gathering the Council. Are you going to be okay enough in thirty minutes or so to join us?"

"Absolutely, if Darius releases his stranglehold on my Xanax bottle."

I looked at Darius. He shook his head.

"I could feel that," Aphrodite said.

"Is that some weird gift from Nyx?" Stark murmured to me as we left Aphrodite's room.

"Is what?"

"Her bizarre ability to know what's going on around her even when she's blind."

"Um. No. I think that's a selective gift sent by the pharmaccutical gods."

Stark grinned as he slid his arm around my shoulders. "You're a funny girl."

"Hey, I'm totally serious."

"Which makes you even funnier." He kissed my ear, making me squirm and laugh.

I pulled him to a stop and looked up into his gentle brown eyes. "Thank you."

"You're welcome. But for what?"

"For my almost surprise party."

"You don't think it was Stevie Rae's idea?" he asked.

"I'm pretty sure she was in on it with you, but I recognize a Stark idea when I see one," I said. "So, thank you. And, in case you've forgotten. I love you. Always."

"I'll never forget. Always."

Stark kissed me then, and for a moment his touch, taste, and the current of love that flowed between us drowned out everything else—every scary, sad, crazy thing else.

(

"Ohmygood*ness!* I've missed you so much, Z!"

Stevie Rae flew into my arms. If I hadn't been expecting it, she would have knocked me over. Not that I minded. Seeing my BFF again was definitely worth being knocked on my butt.

"Stevie Rae! It's like I haven't seen you for years!" I held onto her tightly, not caring that she was squeezing the breath out of me. When we finally were able to let each other go, I saw that tears were pouring down her cheeks. "No! Don't cry! You'll make me start and I'll turn into a snot-and-mascara disaster site."

"You will not stop her. She's been crying since the plane circled Tulsa to land." Rephaim pulled me into a quick hug, kissing me on top of my head (which reminded me of just how tall he was).

I hugged him back and then met my BFF's liquid gaze. "You've been bawling since then? What's going on with you?"

She sniffled and wiped at her cheeks, trying to smile through her tears. "I just—I just, m-miss home."

"Awww, come here." I opened my arms again and, sobbing like someone had taken her favorite cowboy boots (which wasn't true because she was wearing them), she clung to me. "Hey, if you're that homesick we can talk about bringing you back here. Stevie Rae, I didn't mean for you to be miserable up there in the north."

"What about me? I'm semimiserable in the east. New York City has been in the deep freeze since mid-November. I'm so over it." Damien spoke as he entered the Council Chamber, holding out his arms and grinning at me.

"Damien!" Stevie Rae and I said together.

"Group hug!" she said, and we shifted so that Damien could join our hug fest.

"Me, too! Me, too!" Shaylin rushed into the chamber, clapping her hands, with Nicole close on her heals.

"Oh, no, no, no. No one's group hugging without fire!" Shaunee blazed into the room.

"And me. Unless my star power is too much for you guys to handle."

"Erik!" I grinned happily as Erik Night made his grand entrance—last, of course. "OMG, is it *really* you, Dracula?" I gushed in my best tween-boy-band-concert voice. Erik was the current megastar of a new Joss Whedon–directed cable series called *Fantasyworld*—a fantastic addition to the insanely popular *Westworld* and *Futureworld* series. He plays, of course, Dracula. A super-sexy robot version of Dracula—complete with seminude sex scenes realistic enough to make me blush. They filmed the series in NOLA, and Joss was so awesome that he kept a private jet on standby for when Erik was called to fulfill his Tracker duties—which is why he could be a megasuperstar.

Stevie Rae, Shaylin, and Damien all followed my lead. They began swooning dramatically and begging "Dracula" for his autograph.

"And could I have a little ol' lock of your hair? I'm making an Erik Night doll for my Erik Night shrine. Not that that's creepy at all," Stevie Rae said, giggling through her tears.

"I want to have your babies!" Damien gushed.

"I can hardly speak. Your handsomeness has done me in." Shaylin fanned herself.

Erik frowned. "Okay, Shaylin just jumped the shark. She doesn't even bat for my team."

"Nope, she's totally on my team." Nicole made kiss noises at her Consort.

"Jumped the shark?" Stevie Rae asked.

"I'll explain later," Damien said.

"Is this better?" Shaylin put the back of her hand against her forehead and launched into a fairly good imitation of Scarlet from

Gone with the Wind. "Your virility has changed me. I shall nevah eat pussy again!"

"I hate that movie," I said. "It goes on, like, forever."

"And it's racist," Shaunee added.

"Everything back then was racist," Damien said, sotto voce.

"Please don't use that word. It makes you sound like a peasant." Aphrodite walked slowly into the room, holding on to Darius' arm.

"Racist?" Damien said.

"Pussy," Aphrodite said.

"Ohmygood*ness.* Your eyes." Stevie Rae went to Aphrodite and touched her face gently. "You just had a vision. Are you okay?"

"I will be. And it's good to see you, too."

"Wait, that's why the surprise was foiled?" Damien said. "Aphrodite had a vision." His eyes met mine. "And it's bad enough that we all needed to get here right away."

"Yeah," I said.

"On the good-bad scale, with there being for-real unicorns discovered as good, and Kenny Chesney permanently losing his voice as bad—how bad is it?" Stevie Rae asked.

"It's Kenny-Chesney-was-never-born, off-the-scale bad." Stark said.

"We all need to sit down," I said as Lenobia and Kramisha entered the room with the Poet Laureate closing the Council Chamber door firmly behind them.

"Ah, hell," Stevie Rae whispered, sounding disconcertingly like me.

7

Zoey

"Okay, so you guys all have copies of the poem Kramisha brought to me just as I was waking up from the Kalona dream." I'd quickly explained the dream to everyone while Kramisha passed out copies of her prophetic poem.

"I think we all also need copies of Neferet's journal," Lenobia said. She was officially part of our school's High Council and not the North American Council, but we all respected her wisdom—so she was always invited to our meetings. "Let us read it carefully. Kalona has a point. If we have to fight Neferet again, knowledge will be our second greatest power."

"Second greatest?" Stark asked.

Lenobia smiled seraphically. "Why, Stark, I'm surprised you have to ask." Her distinctive gray eyes found mine. "Zoey Redbird, what is our greatest power?"

"Love," I said automatically. "Always, love."

"Indeed," Lenobia said.

"May I ask something?" Rephaim raised his hand like a good little student.

"Of course. And you don't have to raise your hand," I said.

"Are you sure Father visited you in Capri?"

"Well, yeah. I've been there before, and he's been there before—I mean, in my dreams. Believe me, those visits are seared into my memory."

"Because of their negative nature?" Rephaim asked.

I cleared my throat, uncomfortable with the memories this conversation was unearthing. "Yes. Because of their negative nature."

"And it was Father who caused the negative parts of the old dreams?"

"Rephaim, if you have something to say, just say it. I'm not sure what you're getting at," I said.

"I don't mean to offend," he said, looking as uncomfortable as I felt.

"Oh, for shit's sake! We don't have time for tiptoeing around each other's feelings. Just get to the point, Bird Boy," Aphrodite said.

He glanced from Aphrodite to me, and I nodded. "Then here's my point: Father visits my dreams often, but never in a place from the past that has negative associations for him. I asked him about it once—why he only enters my dreams when they're set in new places where he and I have not been before. He said that he cannot bear to relive any memory from when he was lost to Darkness."

"Wait, you're telling me that over the past year Kalona has never, *not once* visited you in a dream in a place where he had done something bad?" A really awful fear frosted up my spine.

"That's exactly what I'm telling you," Rephaim said. "With the addition that Father explained it to me. His exact words were …" He paused, thinking, then he quoted Kalona, "Son, I will *never* revisit the past. I cannot bear the remembrance of what I allowed Darkness to do."

"Rephaim, can you, um, call Kalona or something and ask him why he visited me on Capri, even though that place was definitely from a time he was filled with Darkness?" I asked.

Rephaim grinned, suddenly boyish. "I don't call him. I send prayers to him."

"Just a moment. Are you likening Kalona to a god to whom you pray?" Damien said. "That doesn't feel right to me."

"Father is definitely not a god, but he did die. Damien, do you not believe our dead loved ones can hear our prayers?"

I watched Damien's face blanch white, and then flush a bright, happy pink. "I'd always *hoped* so, but …" Damien left his chair and went to Rephaim, hugging him as he said, "Thank you so much for that." He smiled and wiped his eyes, returning to his place at the round table.

Stark, Aphrodite, Darius, and I stared mutely at Damien's happy expression. I knew what my friends were thinking, and I hated, *hated* that I had to be the one to take that joy from him.

But, like I'd said earlier. We aren't kids anymore. We're the High Council. Adulting often sucks—right now it super sucked.

"So, after the Kalona dream and Kramisha's prophetic poem, Stark, Aphrodite, Darius, and I decided we needed to go to Woodward Park and be sure nothing weird was going on with Neferet," I said. "Aphrodite, fill them in on what you found when we cut through the rose gardens."

Aphrodite quickly recounted her talk with the old rose-garden guy, describing the bizarre black roses and their tendril-like canes.

"That is highly disturbing," Lenobia skewered Aphrodite with her sharp gaze. "My guess is you had a vision not long after that."

"Smart lady," Aphrodite said. Then she looked to me. I nodded.

"All right. Here's what I saw. Damien, I want to say that I'm sorry about this first."

"About what?" Damien asked.

"About how hard this is going to be for you." Aphrodite's gaze flicked to mine and I nodded. She sighed and continued. "I'm going to tell it like I felt it. I'm not sugarcoating anything."

"Blame me," I said. "This is too important for any details to be lost, even if not losing them hurts you."

"I don't like where this is going," Damien said.

Without me asking them to, Stevie Rae, Shaunee, and Shaylin got up from their places around the table and went to Damien. They surrounded him, physically and emotionally, with the elements they embodied as well as their love.

Damien drew a deep breath. "All right. I'm ready now. Go ahead, Aphrodite. What did your vision show you?"

(

Aphrodite shared her vision without leaving out details. She spoke with little emotion, as if she was reading a news story about something bad that had happened on the other side of the world. It was awful, but there was a sense of detachment that allowed for us to be aware of the elements of her vision and possible dangers we might be facing, without freaking out.

Damien didn't speak. He listened intently, only showing emotion twice. First, when Aphrodite described Jack emerging from the bloody fountain. His eyes widened and filled with tears, which he brushed from his cheeks impatiently with a hand that trembled slightly. Then, when she told how he'd rushed to his lover, only to be met with teeth and death, Damien's face lost all color and he clutched his hands together as if in silent prayer.

Stevie Rae was crying silently. She placed one hand on Damien's shoulder.

Shaunee looked like she was going to be sick, but she, too, rested her hand on Damien.

Shaylin's hand shook, but she placed it beside fire and earth, firmly on air's shoulder.

There was a long silence when Aphrodite concluded after adding, "Zoey wanted to know if my vision was metaphoric, like some of my dream visions have been. My answer is the same then as it is now—it didn't feel symbolic at all. It felt real—like when I dreamed of Z getting her head chopped off. That real. The only thing dreamlike in the vision was the appearance of Jack. I honestly don't know what to make of that."

"Damien," I spoke gently, glad my voice didn't sound as trembly as I felt. "If you need to step out—wash your face—take some time for yourself, we completely understand."

"No," he started to speak and his voice broke. He paused to clear his throat, and began again. "No. I need to be here. I need to help you figure out what this is about."

"Are you sure?"

"Completely." Damien wiped his eyes with a tissue from a box of Kleenex Stark slid across the table for him. When he spoke again, there was no weepy emotion clinging to his voice. Damien was all business.

"As much as I want it to be true, I know what you all know. Jack can't be alive," he said. "Let's consider this thing logically. Aphrodite, you said your vision felt literal, though at least part of it must be metaphoric because of that one important fact—Jack can't be alive," he repeated.

"Yes. It's confusing—even for one of my visions, which are always confusing to some extent."

"I have a hypothesis," Damien said. "What if the vision was both—figurative and literal?"

"Can you explain?" I asked.

"I'll try. From Kalona's warning and the strange roses, it appears as if Neferet must be stirring. Or, at the very least, she's found a way to influence the mortal world from within her prison. What if the vision was meant to be taken as both—a literal warning that Neferet is exerting her influence on the world, much as she exerted her influence on dead fledglings, turning them into the red fledglings that were once devoid of goodness—hence the red fledglings emerging from a fountain of blood situated near her prison. *And* figurative—by including the resurrection of Jack in a vision, Nyx could be alluding to our loved ones being in danger from Neferet's awakening influence."

"It feels logical," Lenobia said. "Disturbing, but logical."

"Though I still wonder about Father's part in this. I'll be interested to ask him why he chose to appear to Zoey in a place so riddled with negative memories," Rephaim added.

"And that's a good next step," I said. "Rephaim, how long does it usually take Kalona to answer your, um, prayers?"

"Not long," he said.

"He's really turned into a good daddy," Stevie Rae said. "I mean except for the part about him being dead and all."

"Okay, while Rephaim sends up his prayer request, I strongly believe we need to take action," Damien said.

"What are you thinking?" I asked.

"I think we should proceed as if Neferet has discovered some way to exert her influence, even from her prison. And when someone's worried about a prison break, what is the logical step for the wardens to do?" he asked.

"If I was a warden, I'd dang sure hire more guards," Stevie Rae said.

"Exactly," Damien said.

"Huh?" I asked.

"You need to do what a warden would do, Z," Damien continued. "Be sure Neferet's prison guard is increased."

"Aurox sacrificed his immortality to trap Neferet. Unless you know an immortal who doesn't mind joining Aurox, I have no clue what to do," I said.

"Wait, don't think so literally," Shaunee said. "We don't need another immortal. Neferet hasn't escaped. We don't need to retrap her. We just need to boost what's already holding her."

"Like a protection spell!" I said, feeling a flutter of hope. "I can do that—*we* can do that."

"Hells to the yes!" Shaunee said.

"And once the additional protection is set, if the black roses go away, along with Aphrodite's vision and Kalona's dream visits—then we'll know that's the answer," I said.

"Partially," Lenobia spoke over the relieved sounds my friends were making.

"Partially?" I asked her.

"If the problem is that Neferet has found a way to exert influence over the mortal world, then a protection spell is just the first part of the solution to the problem, unless you cast a very special protection spell—perhaps one that is linked specifically to you, Zoey."

"Why would Zoey want to do that?" Stark asked the question that was buzzing through my mind.

"I don't think it's so much something that Zoey *wants* to do, but rather something she *needs* to do," Lenobia explained. "If the spell is linked to Zoey, then if it begins to be breached, our High Priestess will know."

"Hopefully, that means I'll also know how to fix the breach." Under the table I started to pick nervously at my fingernails.

"You will, Z." Stevie Rae's voice was filled with a confidence I wasn't feeling. "All you need to do is to call us, and your cavalry will arrive to save the day."

"The Herd of Nerds rides again," Aphrodite said, only semisardonically.

"You're part of that herd," I said.

"The most attractive part," she quipped.

I rolled my eyes, feeling more and more normal. We had a plan—and that was a relief. And I had my circle around me—that was a blessing.

"Okay, so here's what we need to do. First, everyone needs to read Neferet's journal."

"I'll make copies," Shaunee said.

"I'm going to the media center to research protective spells," I said. "I'd appreciate any help you want to give me."

"No problem," Damien said. "My specialty is research."

"Awesome, so we all know what to do. Let's break until after dinner." I glanced at the clock on the wall. "It's not quite midnight. When's sunrise, Stark?"

"Tomorrow it'll be at 7:36 a.m."

"Okay, how about we meet in the media center at 4:00 a.m. Oh, Lenobia, would you please make an announcement that the media center will be closed to students until further notice?"

"Of course," Lenobia said.

"Hopefully, we'll find the perfect spell quickly and then we can—"

Aphrodite's purposeful throat-clearing interrupted me.

"Problem?" I asked.

"Potentially," she said. "Sorry, Damien. Again. But as Nyx's prophetess I'm going to insist on this. Damien cannot represent air when you cast the circle for the protective spell."

"Of course I have to represent air! I *am* air," Damien practically sputtered. "And I absolutely have to be there when the spell is cast."

"Why?" Aphrodite asked, meeting his gaze steadily.

"Because I'm air," Damien said stubbornly.

"I can stand in for you," Aphrodite said. "You can't be there."

"I must be there!"

"Why?" she repeated the question in a calm, reasonable voice.

"Because I have to be!" Damien shouted.

Into the after-shout silence I spoke to him softly, kindly. "Jack won't be there, Damien, but Aphrodite's vision was clear about one thing. We don't know why, but your life is in danger."

"But it could be a metaphor," he said miserably.

"Could be isn't enough," I said. "Take Jack out of the vision, and you'd know that."

Damien hung his head. "I—I don't know what to say."

"Say that you'll help Z find the perfect spell," Stevie Rae said, squeezing Damien's shoulder.

"Say that you understand we can't let anything happen to you," Shaylin said.

"Say that you know how well-loved you are, even though Jack isn't here," Shaunee said.

Damien lifted his head. His eyes were bright with tears. "I think all I can say right now is thank you, my friends. Thank you."

"That's a good start," Aphrodite said. "Would you also say you forgive me?"

I was surprised by Aphrodite's question until I remembered the agony in her voice as she'd come out of the vision—how she'd screamed Damien's name over and over. Sometimes it's easy to forget that Aphrodite feels things deeply, personally—even though she doesn't often feel safe enough to show her feelings.

"There is nothing to forgive, my friend," Damien said.

I watched the last of the tension relax out of Aphrodite's shoulders.

"Thank you," she said. Then she turned to me. "I'm coming to the media room with you."

"I thought you hated research," I said.

"I hate sitting and waiting more."

"Well, okay then."

"We're gonna put our suitcases in our rooms, then we'll meet you there, too," Stevie Rae said.

"Rooms? Don't you mean your visiting professors' quarters?" I asked.

"No, um. Well. That was another part of your birthday surprise," Stark said.

"Jesus effing Christ, Bow Boy!" Aphrodite exploded. "Do you have to give away all of it?"

"WTF?" I asked.

"Please don't," Aphrodite said. "Cuss or don't cuss. But give up the abbreviations."

"Oh, just tell her!" Shaunee said.

"I'll tell her." Stevie Rae skipped over to me, grinning like a crazy person. "We're gonna be staying in our old dorm room. Well, at least for the next few nights we are. That was part of Stark's gift to you. He had our room done up like it used to be."

"He did?" I looked from my BFF to Stark. "You did?"

"Yep."

"You mean, my dorm room—the one I shared with Stevie Rae—looks like it used to?"

"Yep again. You two can slumber party to your heart's content. Surprise!"

I turned to him. "James Stark, that is the nicest birthday gift I've ever been given." I kissed him then, like no one was watching.

"Ugh. Get a room," Aphrodite grumped.

"She can't! She's sharing it with me, me, me!" Stevie Rae giggled.

"I hope this doesn't mean I have to stay in the dorm, too," Shaunee said as everyone began shuffling for the door.

"Goddess, how I hope that's not what it means," Damien said. "I'm loving the guest rooms at the tunnels. And that restaurant—delicious."

"I only fixed up Z's room," Stark said, his arms still around me.

"Thank the Goddess," I heard Shaylin whisper to Nicole. "I'm so done with twin beds."

I hung back, keeping Stark with me until we were the only people left in the Council Chamber.

He waggled his brows at me. "Want to make out?"

"I'd usually say yes, but right now something else is on my mind. Here's what's bothering me." I kept my voice low, even though we were definitely alone. "Kalona said Nyx didn't think we should be worried, which is why he visited me without her knowing. But real soon after his stealthy dream visit, Aphrodite was given a vision—and her visions are *always* from Nyx. So, someone isn't telling the truth."

"Do you mean Kalona, Nyx, or Aphrodite is lying?" Stark asked.

"I'm afraid I do."

8

Zoey

"It's okay. Go ahead and teach your archery class. The school needs to stay as normal as possible for as long as possible. Hopefully the fledglings won't even know anything weird is going on because the protection spell will work so well. That's why I didn't call Kramisha out of her poetry class." I tiptoed and kissed Stark at the media center door, then gave him a little push down the hall. "Remember, normal. As far as the fledglings and most of the other professors know—everything is normal."

"Got it. I'll meet you back here as soon as my class lets out."

"Text me first. It'll be time for dinner and if we're still working you can stop by the dining hall and give them an order to be delivered to the media center."

"How 'bout we be really bad and order from Andolini's?"

I grinned. "Stevie Rae will want to kiss you for that."

"Well, she'll be out of luck, because I prefer gorgeous brunettes."

"Right answer!" I blew a kiss at him before heading into the deserted media center, which was an awesome mixture of cutting-edge modern technology and ancient, Dewey Decimal–

filed books that are sooooo out of print that some of them just have the names of the vampyre authors who wrote *and* created the single and only copy of the book.

It was to those books—the ones that were off-limits to fledglings—that I headed.

Damien was there already and had several of the old tomes open around him. He didn't notice me, which had way more to do with his ability to concentrate than my stealthiness, but it did give me an opportunity to study him.

His adult Mark still moved me with its beauty. It spread from the sapphire crescent moon in the center of his forehead to frame his eyes with wings. And they weren't just any wings. They looked distinctively Egyptian. When the light caught the tattoo just right the center crescent seemed to be Isis turning her head in profile as she unfurled her mighty wings. It was a perfect Mark for the personification of air, and it was, quite simply, exquisite.

Damien was the first male to be accepted on a High Council. He was also the smartest person I knew. But at that moment I noticed how tired he looked. His tattoo almost, but didn't quite, hide the bruised circles under his eyes. And he looked thin.

I cleared my throat and his gaze shot up to meet mine.

"Hey, you got here fast," I said.

He shrugged. "I figured there was a lot of work to do, and my research skills have gotten pretty rusty this past year. Who knew administration could be so ..." he hesitated, looking at me for help.

"Boring? Tedious? Time-consuming?" I offered.

"All of the above," he said with a slight smile.

I joined him at the table after grabbing a notebook and a handful of number-two pencils.

"Is Adam enjoying his visit home?"

Damien didn't meet my eyes. "Adam's not here."

"Huh? He stayed in New York? I figured he'd for sure come with you. Neither of you have been back to T-Town for almost a year."

"Actually, he has been. A month or so ago, I think. I just didn't come with him." Damien drew a deep breath, then did meet my gaze. "We broke up three months ago."

"What? Oh, Damien, I'm sorry."

He moved a shoulder restlessly. "It's okay. Really. We were just at different places in our lives."

"OMG, he's a commitment-phobe? He has no idea how lucky he was to be with you! Do you want me to call him? I have words for him. Seriously."

"Um. No. Thank you. Really. But, it's fine."

"But you didn't say anything! I would have come out to New York and fed you ice cream and watched old movies with you."

He rested a hand over mine. "I know you would have, but we didn't break up because Adam was a commitment-phobe. Adam was completely committed. It was me."

"You broke up with Adam?"

"Well, according to Adam, I iced him out." Damien lifted his shoulder again. "And I can't disagree with him. He's a great guy, but he's not *my* great guy." Then he seemed to deflate. "My great guy is dead."

"Oh, honey!" I held his hand in both of mine. "I understand. I really do. When Heath was killed, it shattered me—literally. But I made it through."

"Because you had Stark."

"I'm not going to say having Stark didn't help. It did. It still does. But the truth is that I pulled myself together because Heath wanted me to be happy again. That's one thing you can always count on with someone who really loves you—they want you to find happiness, even when you can't imagine it for yourself."

"It feels like part of me is missing." Damien hung his head. "I thought this terrible empty feeling would go away. Maybe not completely, but enough so that I could feel normal again. But it hasn't. I tried to fill it up with Adam, and I'm sorry I did. I hurt a good man, and the hole is still inside me. How did you get over Heath?"

"I didn't," I said honestly. "It's not about getting over Heath. I have that place inside me, too. The place only Heath can fill. I've learned that I can be happy *and* miss him—and one more thing—the hardest thing of all. I had to give myself permission to be happy without Heath." I touched Damien's chin, lifting his face so that he had to look into my eyes. "Give yourself permission to be happy without Jack."

"It feels like a betrayal."

"I know. But where is Jack?"

Damien looked confused by my question, but he answered. "In the Other World with Nyx."

"Do you think he's happy?"

His haunted expression softened into a smile. "I'm sure he is."

"Even though you're not there with him?"

"Yes. Even though I'm not there with him. Okay, I get your point. It would be terrible if I thought Jack was unhappy and unable to go on without me. It just seems different because I'm the one left alive."

"Will you try to give yourself permission to be happy? If not for yourself, for Jack?" I asked.

"I will." He sighed. "But it's odd timing for all of this to be happening, isn't it? Especially with Jack and me in the middle of Aphrodite's vision."

"It is. I don't understand it at all. But this isn't the first time I don't understand evil."

Damien paused and tapped a finger on a thin stack of papers that I realized was a copy of Neferet's journal. "I think we need to keep in mind that according to her own words, Neferet didn't begin as evil. I'm not even completely sure she realized that she was turning to Darkness. It seems she was simply looking for a savior, and then power so that she would never be in a position of needing to be saved again."

"How do we move forward keeping that in mind?" I was glad Damien was a fast reader, and that he'd voiced thoughts that'd been circling around in my mind since I read Neferet's journal, too.

"I'm not sure yet, but I have a feeling we need to remember Neferet was courted by Darkness well before she was Marked."

"Okay, well, I'll keep that in mind." I turned a couple of the old books Damien had spread around him, checking their spines. "Did you find a good protection spell yet?"

"I've found several already. I marked some pages here, here, and here." Bookmarks feathered out of the books he slid over to my side of the table. "Any of them would do, but you don't need a so-so spell. You need one that speaks to you specifically."

"But how do I know what should speak to me if I don't really know what I'm protecting against?"

"Well, Z, that's why we're here!" Stevie Rae rushed up to our table bringing her familiar positive attitude, her bright, shining smile, and Shaunee, Shaylin, and Aphrodite in her wake.

"You're looking better," I told my BFF as she slid into a chair beside me while Aphrodite took the chair on my other side.

"I feel better, too," Aphrodite said.

I rolled my eyes. "I was talking to Stevie Rae, but you do look better."

"What does the bumpkin have to feel better about?" Aphrodite squinted her eyes at Stevie Rae. "You and Bird Boy have a tiff?"

"No," Stevie Rae said. Then she looked at Damien. "What's a tiff?"

He answered without looking up from the text he was studying. "Tiff—a petty quarrel, especially one between friends or lovers."

"Oh. Thanks. Like I said—no. Rephaim and I are just fine. I've been a little homesick, that's all."

"Homesick? You're in Chicago still, right?" Aphrodite asked.

"Yep."

"*That's* a city. Not quite New York, but still decidedly better than Tulsa, which is really just an oil slick on steroids," Aphrodite said.

"I love Tulsa," Stevie Rae bristled. "And it's not some dang oil slick. It's home."

"Trade ya," Aphrodite said.

"Any day!" Stevie Rae shouted.

"Uh, how about we redirect this energy into something positive—like trying to help me find the right protection spell. Later we'll talk about making some moves." I could feel everyone's eyes on me. "Hey, are *all* of you homesick?"

Damien sighed. "I love New York. It's true that it doesn't sleep. That's part of its charm and its neurosis."

"That didn't answer my question," I said.

"I'm homesick," Damien said.

"I'm loving NOLA," Shaunee said. "But I'm not a Tulsa native like you guys. And I know this is shocking, but for a fire girl I've decided that I really like living close to the ocean."

"So, your nonhomesickness doesn't have anything to do with the fact that Erik Night happens to be filming in New Orleans?" Shaylin waggled her brows at Shaunee.

"Maybe a little."

"You two are really a thing?" Aphrodite said. "Exclusively?"

"Apparently," Shaunee said.

"Our boy Erik isn't sampling all the young starlets on set?" Aphrodite pushed.

Shaunee pierced Aphrodite with her dark eyes. "*Your* boy Erik messed around. *My* Erik doesn't. I'm not even sure why he doesn't. I've given him his freedom. Told him no damn way am I gonna spend my energy worrying about whether or not he can keep his pants zipped. But he insists I'm who he wants. I don't even think about it anymore. He comes home to me after shooting everyday. And, let's just say his *enthusiasm* for coming home to me is obvious. Starlets? Apparently they can't compete with a mixture of brown sugar and fire, baby."

"Huh. Well, that's a surprise," Aphrodite said. "And you're

totally right about the brown sugar thing. White boys definitely need to broaden their dating horizons. I'm not as sure about the fire part, but it's obviously working for you." Then she added, "I'm happy for you two."

Shaunee blinked in surprise, but she smiled at Aphrodite. "Thank you. I'm happy for me, too. And I'm perfectly content in NOLA."

"What about you, Shaylin? How's San Francisco treating you?" I asked.

"The weather's weird. It's cold in the summer and nice in the winter. But I'm getting used to it. And I really, *really* like the fog. Plus, there's a big queer community. Nicole and I feel at home."

"Good to know," I said. "Damien, Stevie Rae, when we get this new mess figured out, how about you two stick around Tulsa for awhile. We'll talk about making some changes."

"I'd appreciate that," Damien said.

"So would Rephaim and I. He doesn't say much about being homesick, but I think that's mostly 'cause I've been so miserable and he doesn't want to heap any more shit on the turd truck."

"If she comes back here can we do something about those bumpkin analogies?" Aphrodite asked.

"No!" Stevie Rae and I said together.

"Where is Rephaim? Sending up a prayer call to Kalona?" I asked.

"No, he's takin' Stark's archery class. His daddy only visits him during the day while he's in crow form. Rephaim said it's something about the fact that his human consciousness, which is what Kalona communicates with since he's not, well, a bird, rests during the day. Basically, that's when the human part of Rephaim sleeps. So that's also when Rephaim and his daddy visit. I think it's real nice."

"Can't he speed up the conversation by going to sleep right now?" Aphrodite asked.

Stevie Rae opened her mouth to answer Aphrodite, but I spoke up first. "I don't think there's any reason to send up some frantic emergency call to Kalona. I mean, he said he appeared to me in Capri because he thought I'd like it. That's probably all there is to it. No need to make a big deal over it."

Aphrodite shrugged. "Yeah, well, it's not like Nyx isn't on top of whatever-the-hell's going on. She double-teamed it by sending Kramisha a poem and me a vision."

"And now it's time we did our part," said a voice from over by the media center door. I spun around, happiness filling me, as my friends and I all shouted her name together.

"Grandma Redbird!"

With steps that were light and filled with energy that belied her age, my grandma hurried to me, pulling me into her arms.

"Grandma! I thought you were in Maui!"

"Oh, u-we-tsi-a-ge-ya, did you really think I would miss your birthday? And not just any birthday, but a rite of passage?" She cupped my face between her soft, warm hands and kissed me on the forehead. "Maui can wait. You only turn eighteen once."

"I'm so glad you're here!" I said.

"So am I! And when can I get my hug?" Stevie Rae said, practically dancing on her toes.

"Come here, sweet girl, and give Grandma a hug." She opened her arms.

"Me too!" Damien said.

"And me!" Shaunee pushed back her chair and hurried to Grandma.

"I want in on this," Shaylin said.

"Oh, for shit's sake. Me too," Aphrodite said.

Grandma's laughter was joyous and pure. "All of you, then. Group hug!"

For that moment we were just a circle of friends surrounded by laughter and joined by love.

Then Grandma kissed each of my friends and shooed them back to their places around the table as she retrieved the picnic basket she'd left by the door.

"I brought serious fortification—lavender chocolate chip cookies. Let's get to work," she said.

Like the smart group we are, we did what Grandma said.

9

Zoey

"So, none of the most powerful protection spells will work because—
like the spell Thanatos used to trap Neferet in the Mayo—they're
always tied to the High Priestess who casts them," I reasoned aloud.

Damien nodded. "Yes, and that's bad because we need something that's permanent."

"Is there no way for Zoey to relegate a part of her subconscious
mind to holding the spell?" Grandma asked.

"I could try, but eventually the spell will end."

Grandma looked confused, so I continued.

"When I die. I mean, that's not going to happen for possibly
several hundred years, but still. Not good for whoever is here
after me."

"And there's more to it than that. Linking Zoey to the spell will
drain her, no matter if she's actively aware of it or not," Damien said.
"And if Neferet is indeed stirring and decides to start pushing and
testing the spell, Zoey might very well end up like Thanatos. Dead."

"No. We will not allow that," said my grandma.

"What if we take turns?" Stevie Rae asked. "We're all High

Priestesses. Z can start by casting the spell. She can hold it for, I dunno, however long she feels comfortable holding it—then we circle again, and I take a turn."

"And when you get tired it's my turn," Shaunee said. "And so on and so on. Would that work?"

"I don't think so." Everyone turned to Aphrodite. "I know I'm not the bookworm Damien is."

"I prefer the term scholar," Damien said.

"Of course you do. Anyway. I don't know all that Damien does, but I am a Prophetess of Nyx, and taking turns holding a protection spell doesn't feel right. Too much could happen to mess it up."

Stevie Rae sighed. "Is it like when my mama says there're too many cooks in the kitchen?"

"This time I understand your bumpkin analogy, and yes. I think that's it," Aphrodite said.

"So, the core problem seems to be a stability issue," Grandma said. "If the spell passes from priestess to priestess, there is no stability. And in a protection spell stability is paramount."

"Well, then, Z needs to choose one of these other spells." Shaunee pushed a stack of spell books toward me.

I looked at the books and sighed. "I've already gone through them. Nothing fits. Nothing at all. They're either too dark, or too light and happy. Or they're for, like, protecting your garden against pests. Or being protected against migraines—"

"Hang on. I need that one," Aphrodite interrupted, snatching a book from me.

"Or ill wishes. Or clumsiness. I didn't even know that was a thing," I said. "Or warding off annoyances, like flat tires or bird poo landing on your head."

"Seriously? There's a spell for that?" Stevie Rae asked.

"That'd be a good one for you to have," Aphrodite said, then she dissolved into giggles, which the rest of us ignored.

"Yeah, there are spells for a bunch of minor things. There are spells for major things, too. Spells that don't keep the High Priestess who casts them connected to the protection, but ... I don't know. I just ..." My words trailed off and I just sat there staring at the giant pile of books and a bunch of cookie crumbs, trying to figure out what it was that wasn't right. As if that made sense.

"U-we-tsi-a-ge-ya, I think the answer is within you. You simply have to let it out."

"Okay. How?"

"Show me one of the protection spells that almost feels right."

I shuffled through the books until I found one of the spells I'd marked earlier. It was an old protection spell against ill wishes.

"Here's one." I handed it to her.

"Protection against an Ill Wish," she read. "That does sound promising, and I see you even marked the page. But you rejected it. Why?"

"It just didn't feel right."

"Why?" she asked.

"Well, it wasn't big enough," I said.

"Big enough? What does that mean?" Aphrodite asked.

"If Neferet's stirring she's going to be up to a lot more than an ill wish or two. She's a killer. I just didn't think it was big enough."

"That makes sense. But, Zoeybird, what if you changed some of this spell and made it bigger. Would that work?"

"No." I glanced through the spell again. "Yes." I kept reading. "No." I sighed. "Even if I change some of the wording, it still doesn't feel right. None of these do."

"Why?" Grandma prodded again.

Beginning to feel annoyed, I blurted, "Because they're not mine! They're just some random, generic spells created by vampyres who are probably dead, but even if they're still alive they don't know me. They don't know my circle. They don't know Neferet. They don't even know Tulsa. These just won't work."

Grandma's face split into a dazzling smile. "And there you have your answer!"

"Huh?"

"Your grandma's right!" Damien cried, coming around the table to give Grandma a hug.

"I don't get it," Stevie Rae said. "But I'm real glad someone does."

"Time to fill the rest of us in," Shaunee said.

"It's so simple I can't believe we all overlooked it," Damien said. "Zoey, you have to create the spell yourself."

"Oh, but not *by herself*," Grandma said. "In order to make it powerful, but keep it from linking only to our Zoeybird, her circle must help her create the spell. Then all of you will have a part in it."

"And if it's linked to anyone—it'll be linked to all of us," Damien said.

"Is—is that okay with all of you?" I asked.

"Yes," Damien said.

"Of course, Z," Stevie Rae said.

"Absolutely," Shaunee said.

"One for all—all for one!" Shaylin grinned.

"And the Herd of Nerds rides again," Aphrodite said.

"Yes, isn't it glorious?" said my wonderful, wise grandma.

"If you mean Andolini's Pizza, yep, it most definitely is glorious!" Stark shouted from behind the tower of pizza boxes he was carry as he, Darius, Rephaim, and Nicole poured into the room in a wave of cold air and warm pizza smells.

"Is it still snowing?" I asked.

"Yep, but no ice. So the roads shouldn't get too bad," Stark said.

"He says that like he's unaware of how Oklahoma drivers lose every bit of their minds as soon as one flake of snow falls." Shaunee shook her head in disgust. "They need to check out a Connecticut winter. I got some snow for them up there."

"Hey there, Grandma Redbird!" Stark went to her and picked her up in a giant hug. "How's my second-best girl?"

"Oh, tsi-ta-ga-a-s-ha-ya. Such a charmer." She patted his cheek and gave him a grandma kiss. "Now put me down. We just figured out Zoey's protection spell and if we work fast, she can cast the spell tonight."

I almost choked on the piece of pizza I was shoving into my face. "Wait, tonight?"

"Seems perfectly timed. It's snowing, which means the park will be deserted. And it's still two hours before midnight. If you hurry, you could time the casting of the spell for midnight. Correct me if I'm wrong, Damien, but isn't midnight the perfect timing for a protection spell?"

"It is, Grandma," he said. "But, Z, can you be ready by then?"

I pushed aside my nerves. "Yeah, probably. If you guys help me. So, my intent is going to be specific. I'm going to protect against any tears in Aurox's seal. It's his sacrifice that's keeping her in there. I figured it'd be smart to give him a boost."

"Logical," Damien said. "And what do you need from each of us?"

"Bring me something that symbolizes each of your elements. Something that means protection to you. I'll write the items into the spell."

"Ya mean like somethin' you can touch?" Stevie Rae asked.

"Yes. Let's be as literal as possible. It'll make the spell simpler."

"Z's right. The simpler the spell is—the less chance of confusion," Shaylin said. "Or at least that's what I found out when I tried to cast a happy spell over the opening of the new House of Night in San Francisco. I used symbolism. It, um, didn't turn out as I expected."

Nicole giggled. "Yeah, she used our relationship as her symbol for happiness when she cast the spell, which was very sweet. But it also made every girl at the event suddenly have the hots for girls."

Shaylin let out a long-suffering sigh. "Whether they were gay or not."

Nicole's giggles made her snort, but she managed to say, "*Especially* the girls who weren't gay. It definitely turned into an interesting night."

"And there was a lot of happiness. Just, um, not what I'd imagined."

"Shaylin, that lotta happiness wasn't what a whole bunch of those straight girls imagined," Nicole said.

"Is it misogynistic to say that I wish I'd been there to witness that?" Erik asked, using all of his vast acting skills to sound and look innocent.

"Nah, boy. Doesn't sound misogynistic. Sounds typical. And you know how I feel about typical," Shaunee said, aiming a lazy, sexy smile at Erik.

"I hear and I obey. I don't need a room full of pretend lesbians when I have my own Nubian Princess." Erik bowed to Shaunee with a flourish and kissed her gracefully extended hand.

"How'd she do that?" Aphrodite whispered to me.

"No clue," I said, watching Erik drool over Shaunee.

"Black girl magick," Stevie Rae said. "I gotta get me some."

"Ditto," I said. Then I thought about the fact that I couldn't even get a tan anymore, and decided to change the subject before it got depressing. "Okay, I'm going to start with air. Damien, as soon as you've figured out what you want to use to symbolize air, step into my office. Bring pizza." I grabbed my notebook and headed for a table that wasn't piled full with books, cookie remnants, pop cans, and pizza.

I didn't have to wait long. I was still chewing the end of my pencil and trying to decide what the heck my spirit symbology would be when Damien *and* Aphrodite took seats across the table from me.

I raised my brow questioningly.

Damien looked at Aphrodite. She sighed. "Go ahead. You tell her. You're better with words."

"Correct, but you talk more," Damien said.

81

"True. I'll go. Okay, Damien and I got together on the air symbol. I came up with the idea of the athame. It's often used to slice through the air during Ritual, and it's a symbol of power, which I think is important," Aphrodite said.

"And I thought of the rest of it, which is what you should do with the athame. What's the most powerful symbol in the vampyre lexicon?" Damien said.

"Is this a test?" I asked, only half kidding.

"If it is, I hope you pass, u-we-tsi-a-ge-ya." Grandma took the seat beside me.

"Z's a good test taker," Stark said between bites of pizza as he sat at my other side.

"No pressure at all," I muttered. Then I smiled. What was wrong with me? Of course I knew the answer to that question. "It's a pentacle!"

"Correct," Damien said. "After Aphrodite presents you with the symbol for air, I think it would be perfect if you used the athame to draw a protective pentacle within the circle."

"That's an excellent idea," I said.

"Fantastic!" Damien said. "I'm going to go to Nyx's Temple and choose an athame."

"I'll come with you. We might as well get the ritual candles while we're there," Aphrodite said.

I smiled as they hurried off. *This might just be easier than I thought it was going to be.* "Okay, Shaunee, fire is up next."

Shaunee was chewing pizza when she slid into the chair across from me. "Do you know what a tetrahedron is?"

"This *is* a test," I grumped. "Sounds like something mathy. Which means I have no clue."

"It's a solid, four-sided pyramid," Shaunee said.

"Yep. Definitely math," I said.

"Geometry, actually," Stark corrected.

"Yes," Shaunee said. "A *fire* tetrahedron is a geometric representation of the four factors that are necessary to create fire: fuel, heat, oxygen, and an uninhibited chain reaction. Voilà! You have fire."

"Makes sense. I think," I said. "So, your symbol is?"

"Z, stay with me. My symbol is going to be a tetrahedron."

I blinked blankly at her.

She sighed. "In other words, I'm going to make a pyramid for your spell. You can put it in the center of the circle. It'll be a focus for fire protection."

"Oh, like the pentacle I'm going to draw with Damien's athame! Your pyramid thingie is just another focus for protection."

"Exactly. And now I'm gonna search this room for something cool to make the tetrahedron out of. It's a school, right? We should have construction paper, scissors, and some glue."

"Well, yeah, but the scissors might have those obnoxious rounded ends," I said.

"Let's hope not," Shaunee said with a sad shake of her head.

"Water! Your turn," I called.

Shaylin came to my table, reached into her purse, and pulled out a rock. She put it down on the table in front of me. "This is my symbol. It's weird, but I've been carrying it around in my purse since I found it when Nicole and I were taking a walk in Golden Gate Park. It was in the water feature by the Japanese pagoda. It's perfect."

I picked up the rock. It was nothing special. About fist-sized, made of some kind of brown stone. It had an indentation on the top side of it that was kinda wavy. I gave her a question-mark look. "Sorry, I don't get it."

"Oh, here. It's easier to see from this direction." Shaylin spun the stone so that I was looking at the indented design from the opposite angle.

"It's a heart!" I said.

"Guess what made it?"

I traced the wavy indentation that had made an almost perfect heart, and suddenly got it. I grinned up at Shaylin. "Water!"

"Yep! Water is so powerful that it can even change stone. I think that's powerful protection energy."

"I think you're right," I said.

"Oh, and your aura is looking very bright and shiny," Shaylin said. "So's yours and yours," she told Stark and Grandma. Then she lowered her voice. "But Damien's is looking sad. I think he might be depressed. And Aphrodite's is definitely stressed."

"I'm not surprised," I said.

"What about mine?" Stevie Rae asked as she joined the table.

Shaylin studied her. "Your aura is muted. Not as badly as Damien's, but you're not 100 percent."

"Does it look homesick to you?" she asked.

"Definitely."

"Which we're going to fix," I said. "Thanks, Shaylin. I agree with you. Your rock is perfect. Ready, earth?"

"Yepper!" Stevie Rae said, plopping into the seat across from me. "I know exactly what my symbol is, but I'm not sure where we're gonna get one at this time of night."

"What is it?" I asked, intrigued.

"Well, the most powerful earth protection comes in the form of trees. And the rowan tree has special powers. It rules communication between the worlds. It's known as the Quickening Tree because it can quicken your psychic abilities. I think it's the perfect symbol for earth protection, but I don't have one."

"Stevie Rae, do you need an actual sapling, or would just a part of the tree work?" Grandma asked.

"Any part of the tree would work just fine. I can make it grow. Do ya have a rowan twig or somethin', Grandma Redbird?"

"I do not, but I'm sure a rowan wand wouldn't be difficult to find here at the House of Night," Grandma said.

"There are tons of wands and such in the Spells and Rituals classroom, back in the supplies cupboard," I said.

"That'll work!" Stevie Rae said. "I'll go find something rowan."

"Four down, one to go," Stark said. "So, what's gonna be your spirit symbol?"

"I have no clue," I said.

"Then it is good that you have your Grandma here with you, u-we-tsi-a-ge-ya." Grandma went to her picnic basket and reached into its mysterious, fragrant depths to pull out a single red feather. She brought it to the table and handed it to me. "This is your symbol, Zoeybird, and the symbol of the spirit of your people."

"Oh, Grandma! It's perfect. Thank you."

"That's it then. You have all the elements of your spell," Stark said.

"I do. What time is it?"

He checked his phone. "Ten thirty. Looks like we're going to make the midnight deadline."

"Looks like it," I said.

"That's gotta be a good sign," Shaylin said.

"Yep. Okay, give me a few minutes to put all of this together in a spell form. By that time, Aphrodite and Damien should be back with the athame and candles, Shaunee will have made her fire-pyramid thing, and Stevie Rae will have found a rowan wand. Then we go to Woodward Park."

"How are you feeling about the spell overall, Zoeybird?" Grandma asked when Stark went to fetch us some more pizza.

"Pretty good," I said. "I mean, it's really a simple spell. There's not much that can go wrong."

I saw a shadow pass over Grandma's expression, but before I could ask her anything she brightened. "Exactly, u-we-tsi-a-ge-ya. Let's go put an end to Neferet's nonsense. Again."

10

Zoey

Winter in Oklahoma is a mixture of anticipation and expectation—you know the ice and snow are coming. You just don't know when, where, or how much. I should have been sick of winter weather, what with the icepocalypse that had shut the city down for weeks last winter, but as we walked through deserted Woodward Park with fat flakes of snow drifting lazily down from an ominously clouded sky I couldn't help but feel the same sense of wonder and excitement I'd felt every school day of my life when the weather report hinted at snow. Seriously. What's more awesome than a snow day? (Okay, yes, I hear you. Summer vacation. But I'm talking about *surprise* days off from school.)

Mature or immature, the snow had all of us in a positive mood. And there, tromping through leaves salted with shimmering white flakes, surrounded by the people I loved most in this world, I was filled with optimism. Neferet and Darkness felt like a half-remembered bad dream. The kind that you wake from crying, but as soon as you're fully aware it fades into vague remembrances and forgotten fears.

"I like the replanting," Stevie Rae said. She was walking beside me, gazing around at the snow-silent park. "It's gonna be weird in the spring and summer—without most of the ginormous oaks and those huge azalea bushes everyone likes to take pictures in front of—but I can already see that it's gonna be real pretty once everything grows up. Maybe even prettier than it used to be."

"That's what we're hoping for. The House of Night poured a bunch of money into the renovation, and it was one of our landscape architects that created the new planting grids. She even added a gorgeous water feature over there by the Peoria side of the park, which we filled with koi."

Stevie Rae shot me a look. "I hope I'm here to see it."

I snagged her hand and made her slow with me until we lagged a little behind the others. "You'll be here to see it if you want to be here. Stevie Rae, I didn't know you've been unhappy. I'm really sorry."

"It's not your fault."

"Sure it is. I'm the one who set up our new High Council and had the semibrilliant idea of sending everyone scattered out like that."

"It's a good idea, Z. I just miss home. Too much I think. My heart's here." She glanced at where Rephaim walked beside Stark and added, "So's his."

"So's Damien's," I said softly, glancing to where he was walking beside Aphrodite.

"Yeah, I don't see Adam anywhere. What's up with that?" she asked.

"They broke up. Damien's not over Jack," I said.

"Oh, man, that sucks. But I'm not surprised. Maybe being home will help him put Jack to rest."

"I hope so. I am a little weirded out by Aphrodite's vision, though. Jack featuring predominately in it is pretty crazy, and feels more than coincidental what with Damien being so homesick and sad."

"Maybe that part's not supposed to be literal. Maybe Nyx decided we do need some extra protection on the grotto, and she took the opportunity to make a point about not letting go of the past."

"Meaning that it'll eat you alive if you can't make peace with it." I nodded. "I can see that. But then there's Kramisha's poem. No clue how that works into it."

"Well, there's a snow metaphor throughout it, with a reference to snowflakes joining by finding themselves again. That could play into Aphrodite's vision, too. It could be for Damien, symbolizing that he really needs to heal so that he can love again. You did say he and Adam broke up, right?"

"Right."

"I'm guessin' the breakup had more to do with Damien than Adam?"

"Right again," I said. "But I should let Damien tell the rest of it."

"No worries, Z. I don't want to be all in his business. But it does seem like a bunch of this could be about Damien moving on." She lowered her voice. "He looks rough. And Damien *never* looks rough."

"Yeah, he needs to be home. I wish I'd known—about him as well as you. Hey, make me a deal. Promise you'll never keep things from me like that again."

"Z, you're so busy with the new Council and integrating the North American Houses of Night. I didn't want to bother you. I'll bet Damien felt like that, too."

"Sure, I'm busy, but I'm *never* too busy for my friends."

"I can't just leave Chicago, you know. There's too much to do up there. The city's just starting to relax enough to let a few human art students attend classes at the House of Night. I gotta go back and be sure everything runs smoothly."

"What if you go back *temporarily*. Just long enough to train your replacement. I really could use you here. The depot tunnels house the only House of Night for red fledglings. You'd be a better High Priestess to them than me."

"Really?" Stevie Rae's blue eyes sparkled happily.

"Really," I said. "What with Stark and Kramisha added to the staff here, I have a few extra priestesses. I'm sure one of them would love to check out Chicago."

"What about Damien? New York can't be any easier to integrate than Chicago."

"Damien finished the yearly professor evaluations at his House of Night early," I said.

"'Course he did," Stevie Rae said with a grin.

"Yeah, he's super organized. He gushed about one young High Priestess in particular. I think I remember that her name is Monique. Anyway, in his evaluation he went on and on about how skillful she is at brainstorming creative answers to dead-end problems. Perhaps Damien should groom her to take his place in New York." *And then return to T-Town and help me organize the administrative mess I've buried myself under.*

"Z, you're gonna make three people real happy this holiday!"

Feeling lighthearted, I linked my arm with my BFF and, like giggling preteens, we skipped to catch up with the rest of our group.

Everyone was waiting for us at the rocky ridge that looked down on the walled, concealed grotto prison.

"All right, does everyone remember their parts?" I asked.

Aphrodite, Shaunee, Shaylin, and Stevie Rae all nodded. I met Damien's sad gaze. "Honey, I need you to stay up here with Stark and Rephaim."

"But I really wanted to be part of the circle, even if I can't call air," he spoke quietly, miserably.

"I don't think it's safe. Aphrodite's vision took place down there." I pointed to the place beside the grotto wall where I'd decided to cast the circle and set the new protection spell. "You were killed, Damien."

"But by Jack, and that's impossible," he insisted.

"Seriously, Damien? You're going to argue about what's possible and what isn't after everything that happened last year?" Aphrodite said, though she spoke kindly. "I don't understand the vision Nyx sent me. I do understand I was in a body that died. And that body was holding your yellow candle. It's not safe for you down there. Hell, I don't even like the fact that you're going to be up here. My vote was for you to wait back at the House of Night with Grandma Redbird and Nicole."

Aphrodite's gaze met mine. I'd vetoed her vote and allowed Damien to come with us. I just couldn't bear the misery in Damien's eyes. He personified air and had been part of my circle since the first time I'd cast one so long ago. I couldn't leave him behind.

"I won't run. I'll close the circle if something crazy happens. That wouldn't change whether Damien was here watching or not," I told her firmly.

"What does that mean?" Damien asked.

"Nothing!" Aphrodite, Darius, Stark, and I all said together. Yeah, the four of us had decided to leave some of the details out of the vision she retold to Damien. He didn't need to know his breaking the circle had let the tide of zombie things loose on Tulsa. I'd been forewarned. My running wouldn't happen until *after* my circle was closed. I could say that for sure. But if there was even the slightest chance something to do with Jack might happen, none of us believed Damien would be in any shape to make the right decision—the safe decision.

"It means that whatever happens tonight we're all going to be clear-headed," I said. "That's why Stark and Rephaim are going to wait up here with you, Damien."

"To make sure I don't do something idiotic," Damien said sadly.

"No. To make sure the circle stays safe," Stark said—only semilying.

"Hey, I'd rather be down there with Stevie Rae," Rephaim said. "But I don't want to distract her."

"Damien, we have a perfect view up here. If anything goes wonky, we'll know it and we can warn Z and the circle. I can cover them easily from up here." He patted the full quiver of arrows strapped to his side.

"Yeah, Stark and I are glad for another set of eyes to watch with us," Rephaim added.

"And I'll go down to ground level with the circle," Darius said. "If you see anything—yell. I'll get them out."

"Sounds good." I turned to Shaylin, taking an instant to admire her adult vampyre tattoo. Hokusai's Great Wave looked amazing in scarlet. The tattoo was layered, with wave upon wave, giving it the appropriate effect of having an aura. "Shaylin, could you please check each of the five of us out before we cast the circle and set the spell? Our intentions have to be solid. I need to know for sure that we're all ready."

"Of course, High Priestess," she said formally. Then Shaylin studied each of my friends. It didn't take long. Her skill at reading auras had definitely gotten quicker during the past year. "We all look good. And I do mean me, too. I checked myself out in a mirror before we left the House of Night." Shaylin paused, sending me a questioning look. I nodded slightly, and she continued. "Damien, your aura is usually like a summer sky—all bright and billowy with stuff that looks like cumulus clouds swirling in it. But right now your sky colors look bruised and thunderstormish."

"What does that mean?" he asked, sounding uncharacteristically hesitant.

"Nothing awful," she assured him. "Just that you're stretching yourself thin. Even if Aphrodite hadn't had that vision I would be recommending to Zoey that you sit this circle out. I'm sorry."

"Don't be sorry for telling the truth. It's okay." Damien made an effort to smile, which was only a so-so success. "I'll stay up here with Stark. I do feel tired."

"I'm going to take care of that when we're done here. I have an idea," I said. "An outstanding idea."

"Great. *That's* never gone wrong before," Aphrodite muttered.

"Be nice," I said.

"It's hard to be nice *and* honest," she said.

I ignored her.

"Okay, do all of you have your props?"

My four friends nodded. I lifted my hand and felt for the redbird feather Grandma had woven into my hair just before we left. "All right, remember our intention. It's simple and clear—protection against Neferet. That's it. That and calling your element are the only things you need to be thinking about down there. Got it?"

"Got it!" they echoed.

I led them down the wide, winding stone stairs that emptied beside the new stone wall surrounding the grotto.

"Oh, for shit's sake. Look at that. Talk about morons." Aphrodite pointed at the wall and we all looked closer. Tucked into small cracks and natural niches in the stone were offerings. I saw everything from coins to crystals and beads, and even several votive candles—not lit at the moment.

"Those need to go," I said. "After we cast the spell and close the circle, let's throw all of that crap away. And for a while I'm going to have the Sons of Erebus send a Warrior to stand guard twenty-four-seven."

"Noted, High Priestess," Darius said. "Shifts will begin at dawn."

"The last thing we need is for Neferet to feed off idiotic human worship," Aphrodite said.

I nodded agreement, and thanked Darius, but shoved the general public's idiocy from my mind. "Focus, everyone. Remember our intent." Then I moved several yards from the wall to stand in the center of a nice flat section of ground. "All right, circle around me."

My friends found their directions easily: air–east, fire–south, water–west, earth–north. All circled around me, personifying spirit, in the center. I carefully put down the tall purple ritual candle at my feet. Spirit was always the last element called to the circle, and the first to close the circle. I pulled the box of extra-long wood matches from where I'd snuggled it inside my awesome black bomber jacket (that had WILD FEMINIST printed in bold white letters on the back—I love me some Wild Fang!). I closed my eyes and drew three long, deep breaths—in and out, in and out, in and out, while I focused my thoughts on my intent.

Protection against Neferet.

When I felt ready, I opened my eyes and walked directly to where Aphrodite stood at the east side of the circle. I'd written the calling of the elements and the spell itself with a focus on protection. My words and my voice mirrored the power that I was determined to invoke.

"Oh, winds of storm, I call for you. Cast your mighty blessing upon the magick I work here. Air, come forth!" I touched my match to Aphrodite's yellow candle. It lit instantly, and Aphrodite's hair lifted, whirling in a gust of wind so wild that had she not covered her candle, it would have gone out. "Air, what is your offering for this spell of protection?"

Aphrodite pulled the ritual dagger from somewhere inside the fur trimmed cape she'd swathed herself in. "I offer an athame. May it cut through anything that stands in the way of our spellwork tonight."

I bowed formally to her before taking the athame and tucking it into a belt loop on my jeans. Then I made my way clockwise to the south and fire.

"Oh, fire of lightning, storm bringer, magick worker I call for you. Cast your mighty blessing upon the magick I work here. Fire, come forth!"

I didn't need to touch a match to Shaunee's red candle. It blazed into life on its own in a burst of heat so great it made me flinch. "Fire, what is your offering for this spell of protection?"

Shaunee lifted the hand not holding her ritual candle and gave me a perfect pyramid made of crystal. I blinked in surprise.

Shaunee's grin was fierce, making her facial tattoos, which were twin phoenixes rising from flames, seem to glow from her internal flame. "I offer a tetrahedron—the physical manifestation of the elements that create fire. It is my wish that it burns away anything that stands in the way of our spellwork tonight. I found it in one of the old trophy cases. Perfect, right?"

"Perfect," I agreed. I bowed and took it. The pyramid rested, cool and smooth, in the palm of my hand before I put it in the pocket of my jacket. I moved to the west, and Shaylin's personification of water.

"Oh, drowning torrents of storm-wrapped tornado rain, I call for you. Cast your mighty blessing upon the magick I work here. Water, come forth!"

It took Shaylin's candle an instant longer than necessary to light, but when it finally did I held my breath as, for just a moment, I swear I felt as if I'd been transported to the middle of the ocean. Shaylin giggled gleefully.

"Water, what is your offering for this spell of protection?"

Shaylin handed me the fist-sized stone, water-etched with a heart. "I offer proof of my element's power. It is my wish that it flood anything that stands in the way of our spellwork tonight."

I bowed to Shaylin and water, and put the rock in my other pocket. It felt heavy and solid—and I thought how perfect it was, as well.

Moving to the top of the circle, I stood before Stevie Rae, who dimpled at me.

"Oh, earth—solid, mighty survivor of every storm ever created, I call for you. Cast your mighty blessing upon the magick I work here. Earth, come forth!"

Stevie Rae's green candle lit easily and I was instantly transported to a mighty mountain range. I felt it all around me, and knew earth would support our protection spell with unparalleled power.

"Earth, what is your offering for this spell of protection?"

"I offer this rowan. It's a magickal gateway as well as a protector. It is my wish that it serves as a doorway for our spellwork tonight."

Clutching a wand, Stevie Rae lifted her hand. It suddenly reminded me of a scene from Harry Potter, which made me smile as I bowed to my bestie and took the slender, graceful offering. I turned and walked to the center of our circle, kneeling beside my purple spirit candle to complete its opening. "Oh, strong and powerful, all-knowing spirit, I call for you. Cast your mighty blessing upon the magick I work here. Spirit, come forth and complete my circle!"

An exquisitely familiar feeling swallowed me, reminding me how much I'd missed circling. Quickly, I made a silent promise to myself that I wasn't going to let work keep me from the pleasure of circle casting. Then I reached up and released the braid that held my redbird feather.

"I offer this feather—the spirit of my people—free and strong. It is my wish that it fills our circle and focuses our intent for our spellwork tonight."

I stood then, and let my eyes follow the glowing silver thread that bound my friends, the personification of the elements, together in a perfect circle of power, shining with intent. Feeling full, happy, powerful, I began emptying my pockets and arranging the items carefully on the soft, snow-sprinkled ground.

I worked backwards. First I held out the rowan wand. Speaking slowly, carefully, I began casting the spell of protection. I'd decided that there hadn't been time for creating the rhyme and meter that usually went into the words of a spell. Instead, I focused on intention and power—lots of power.

"I begin with earth's offering, the rowan. I return it to earth, blessed by the elements, and infused with power. May it grow strong and long—so mighty that it can withstand any negative influence." I pressed the raw end of the wand into the ground, planting it firmly. Then I took Shaylin's rock and placed it on the west side of the rowan twig, saying, "Next comes water. I place it beside the rowan where it can nurture its growth through life-giving waters, like blood through our bodies." My hand found the pyramid, which I placed on the opposite side of the twig. "I move to the manifestation of fire, symbolized by the four sides of this pyramid. May its heat warm the rowan, even when the cold breath of Darkness threatens to stunt or destroy it." Finally, I held the athame high. The light from our joined circle glinted off its blade, and its fierce beauty made me smile. "And now, air! With this athame I will mark a pentacle within our circle, to create a power-filled pentagram, infused with the might of the elements and our combined intent." I moved deliberately because in order for a pentacle to manifest a circled pentagram fully, it must be drawn by a single line, with the spirit point up.

I'd drawn four of the five lines when it happened.

"I'm sorry, I'm going to insist you leave. This area of the park is closed for a private event."

Darius' voice—deep and firm—broke through my concentration. I glanced up, squinting as I tried to look through the glowing thread of power that held our circle together. There was a small group of people. I could see that one of them was carrying a camera, and that they were following a woman, who was striding quickly toward our circle.

"This is a public park. It cannot be closed for private events." I was struck by the familiarity of the voice, though my mind, which was still trying to focus on the spell I was almost done casting, felt fuzzy—slow.

I heard Aphrodite gasp just before the woman spoke again.

"Just as I suspected! The vampyres are trafficking with Satan! Look at that unholy circle! And the vampyre in the middle—she's drawing Satan's mark, the pentagram! Fox News, are you getting this? When I am elected mayor of Tulsa I will put an end to this kind of dangerous blasphemy against our good Christian community."

"Oh, for shit's sake, Mother. Go away!" Aphrodite shouted.

11

Zoey

I blame myself for what happened next. The thought was only in my mind for an instant, but I should have controlled it. I should have ignored everything outside my circle and held firm to my intent. An older High Priestess would have. A wiser High Priestess would have.

I'm not old or wise, and I messed up.

If a zombie apocalypse caused Aphrodite's mom to be eaten, I think I'd consider it #winning. As my mind registered the thought, I drew the last line of the pentacle—and something happened. Something terrible. My grip on the athame slipped midstroke. My hand slid awkwardly down the handle of the ritualistic yet razor-sharp dagger—cutting a deep gash across my palm.

From my position on my knees, I stared at my hand. The athame was so sharp that I didn't register any pain at first. All I felt was a rush of heat and warmth as blood dripped from my palm, spattering the rowan twig and the ground in the center of the sacred pentagram.

Then time seemed to fast-forward, and everything happened with blinding speed.

A great inrush of power knocked me from my knees. I rolled so hard I would have broken the circle had Shaunee's strong arms not caught me.

"Z, are you okay?" She stared at my bloody hand as I scrambled to my feet.

"I—I'm not sure." I pressed my hand against my waist. I could feel the wetness soaking through my shirt, and I played a child's game with myself. *If I don't look at it, it can't be that bad.* "I feel weird. Dizzy. Tired. I don't know what's—"

"Oh, Goddess, no!"

Aphrodite's cry had me staggering around to face the center of the circle. The rowan was no longer a twig. It had shot up to form a fully grown tree. But this wasn't like any rowan I'd ever seen—and I'd seen a lot, both on the Isle of Skye and in the Goddess' Grove in the Other World. This tree's delicate, frond-like leaves weren't the verdant, healthy green of a young tree. Nor were they the vibrant red of a rowan in the fall. This tree's leaves were twisted and long, curled like arthritic fingers, and they were the dark rust of old blood. Its branches were misshapen, and not the magickal way healthy rowans bend and shape themselves, often twining with another rowan or, as I often saw in the Goddess Grove, a mystical hawthorn. This tree's limbs moved restlessly, wrapping around and around itself in a bizarre, serpentine fashion. The trunk of the tree began to quiver, expand, pulse—as if it was breathing—then with a great tearing sound, the rowan broke open and a fountain of blood geysered from beneath it.

As if washed up by a crimson wave from the bowels of the earth, bodies began to appear. The first one lifted his head. His red-eyed glare roved around the circle in obvious confusion before he hauled himself from the broken tree to crouch, staring around as if he had no idea where he was. More creatures followed him, vomiting from the center of the circle. They all seemed disoriented, falling over one another to crouch together with uncertainty as more and more of them swam up from the bloody fountain.

I shook my head, trying to shake off a deep, pulling exhaustion. It felt like I was running a marathon, only I was standing there—dizzy, breathing heavily, unable to ground myself.

"Goddess, I don't know what's wrong with my head." Behind me Shaunee sounded as dazed and drained as I felt. I glanced at her, and right away noticed that the flame of the red candle she was still clutching was burning so low it was in danger of being put out by the snow.

But Shaunee is fire. She never has a problem keeping a flame lit.

I looked quickly around my circle. Shaylin, Stevie Rae, and Aphrodite were all staring gape-mouthed at the red vampyre things that continued to pour from the tear in the ground. Shaylin looked so pale it seemed she'd turned ghostly. Stevie Rae rubbed at her eyes as if to try to clear them. Aphrodite stumbled, like she might fall over.

And I understood what was going on.

"Zoey, get out of there!" Stark shouted from the ridge above us.

"No one gets out of here until I close this circle!" I yelled.

"Those vampyre zombie things are siphoning the power of our circle," I told Shaunee. "I gotta close it and cut off their power."

"Do it, girl! I'll hold on until you release fire."

I nodded. "Shaylin, Stevie Rae, Aphrodite! They're draining our elements. Hang on till I get to you and release them!"

Piercing screams drowned their responses, echoing from the group of humans surrounding Aphrodite's mom, though none of them moved—none of them bolted for their cars like they should have. They all stared at the creatures pouring from the bloody fountain—and I could see the red recording light was still blazing as the Fox camera filmed everything.

Aphrodite planted her feet like she was part of the Broken Arrow Tiger's defensive line. I saw her draw a deep breath, and with a herculean effort, she cupped her hands around her mouth to shout, "Mother! Get out of here! Now! Our circle is all that's holding them, and we're closing the circle!"

More screams came from the group of journalists, but Aphrodite's mother stood firm in the middle of them, her eyes huge as she stared at the creatures.

"You summoned demons!" she shrieked at her daughter. "And now the world will see for themselves the aberrations vampyres create!"

"They're not vampyres, Mother. They're zombies. We didn't summon them, but they're going to eat your skinny ass if *you don't get out of here!*"

"Go! Close the circle!" Shaunee told me. "Hurry!"

I forced my feet to move through the fear, seeming as thick and deep as quicksand, toward the center of the circle and my spirit candle. The increasing mob of creatures swiveled their heads in my direction, and I stumbled to a halt, unable to breathe as they trained their glowing eyes on me.

Some still looked muddled, shaking their heads and rubbing their heavy lids—a lot like the four members of my circle.

But others stilled—their scarlet glares piercing through heavy snow.

I was running out of time.

Frantically, my eyes scanned the blood-soaked ground, trying to find my candle. It was there—beside the twisted rowan—and it was on its side, flame already extinguished. I breathed a quick sigh of relief, saying, "Spirit! I release you from my circle!"

Staggering into an awkward sprint, I made a wide sweep, hugging the inside of the circle as I ran, counterclockwise, to get to north and earth.

"I got your back, Z. I'm not moving until you send air away." Aphrodite called as I ran past her.

"Not moving either!" Shaylin's shout sounded high and weak, but unwavering.

"Standing strong!" Shaunee said grimly.

I stumbled to a stop in front of Stevie Rae and paused only

long enough to blow out her candle and say, "Earth! I release you from my circle!" I grabbled Stevie Rae's arm as the element released her, and she almost fell.

"I've got you, Stevie Rae!" Rephaim was suddenly there, beside Stevie Rae, putting a strong arm around her waist to support her, and brandishing what looked like little more than a pocketknife in his other hand.

Great. Had no one but Stark brought real weapons? I already knew the answer to my question. No one had expected our well-intended protection spell to turn into the zombie apocalypse. We were woefully unprepared for everything that happened next.

"Follow me!" I told Rephaim.

With Stevie Rae and Rephaim, I staggered to Shaylin.

"Water! I release you from my circle! Stay with us. Hang on to Rephaim if you can't walk. We're getting Shaunee and Aphrodite!"

Shaylin nodded and grabbed Rephaim's arm. We lurched to Shaunee.

"Get out of the way, boy! You're messing up the camera's shot."

I glanced over my shoulder. Aphrodite's mom was screaming at Darius, who had taken a stand between our circle and the group of journalists. He'd drawn a sword (thank Goddess for the training of the Sons of Erebus Warriors)—obviously ready to protect them if the zombie things started to attack.

"He's all that's standing between you and death!" Aphrodite said.

"He's all that's standing between me and showing the truth to the world!" Francis LaFont shouted back.

"Fire! I release you from my circle!"

But Shaunee wasn't even looking at me. She was staring over my shoulder at the middle of the circle. She pointed a trembling finger, saying, "Fledglings! Oh, Goddess. There are fledglings puking out of that mess."

I barely took time to look, but what I saw fueled me with

enough adrenaline to push me around the circle. With Stevie Rae and Shaylin clinging to Rephaim, and Shaunee hanging on to me, I closed the last yards to Aphrodite.

"Air! I—"

"*JACK!*" The cry overpowered my words with the force of its agony. I looked up at the ridge. Damien was there beside Stark. Stark was holding his arm as he struggled to get free, his eyes huge with shock he stared behind me at the center of the circle.

"Don't look. Just finish closing the fucking circle!" Aphrodite said.

"Air! I release you!" I blew out the yellow candle, and with a small sizzle, like a snuffed-out flame, the glowing thread that held our circle together extinguished. The five of us reeled as we were released from the terrible drain that had usurped the power of our circle from us.

A heartbeat after, there was another terrible sound—only this one was less a ripping than an explosion. I turned to see the twisted rowan had been sucked into the ground. Nothing remained of it or the ritual symbols I'd placed beside it. All that remained was a circle of gore filled with salivating, hissing monsters that had definitely been released from whatever confusion had contained them.

At the middle of that circle stood Jack Twist, looking pale and confused. In the center of his sallow forehead was the outline of a red crescent moon.

"We are free!" cried one of the creatures whose face was Marked with the fully formed tattoo of an adult red vampyre. "Devour them!"

Then all hell broke loose. Literally.

The red vampyres began pouring out of the circle. Half of them closed on us, while the other half faced off with Darius, who was still standing between them and the group of humans.

"Get up here! Now!" Stark shouted. I glanced up as arrows rained down on the creatures. Damien was lying in a crumbled heap at Stark's feet.

"Go! Go! Go!" I said. "Get up there!"

Stevie Rae, Shaylin, and Shaunee ran for the stone stairs. Rephaim was backing away more slowly, his knife raised against the hissing horde, but the creatures had paused as they batted at the arrows fired one right after another from Stark's deadly bow.

With a sick stomach, I realized that none of the creatures were mortally wounded. Sure, they'd paused, but they were simply pulling the arrows from their bodies and throwing them to the ground—like they were annoying insects.

"Stark! It's not working! Add intent!" I yelled to him, then I grabbed Aphrodite's arm. "Come on!" She shook me off and started forward.

"Not leaving Darius," she said firmly.

"Hell yes, you are!" I shoved her into Rephaim. "Get her out of here!" Rephaim nodded, hooked his arm around her slender waist, lifted her, and as she kicked and screamed he kept backing to the stairs.

"Darius! Time to go!" I yelled, retreating to follow Rephaim as, finally, one creature shrieked and fell to the ground. Stark's arrow had caught him through the throat, burying itself to its feathers. A bloom of metal and blood sprouted from the back of his neck.

Darius was fighting a closing half circle of creatures. Most of them were running after the journalists who had finally stopped listening to Aphrodite's mom and were rushing with a lot of hysterical screaming to a line of cars parked illegally on Twenty-First Street. Aphrodite's mom hadn't followed them. She was cowering behind Darius, whose sword was singing in a loop around them, catching a random creature's arm as they hissed and circled.

"Sever their spines! That's the only way to kill them!" Stark shouted. "Zoey, get your ass up here!"

"Getting!" I yelled. "Darius, grab LaFont and let's go!"

Darius did exactly that. In one motion he picked up Frances LaFont and flopped her over his shoulder in a classic fireman's carry. With his free sword hand, he plowed through the snarling creatures, taking off the nearest vampyre's head. The creature crumbled, twitching spasmodically, but it definitely didn't get up.

And just like that, the red vampyres scattered. Later, when I had time to think, I remembered that they'd been hissing words of encouragement to each other, but after Stark and Darius figured out their weakness, those whispers changed. It seemed the creatures shared a brain and, Borg-like, the horde scattered, fading into the snowy darkness.

"Come on, Darius!" I called to him.

Hefting LaFont, Darius jogged across the circle, and ran right into Jack.

Jack hadn't moved. He hadn't followed any of the adult vampyres. He was still standing in the blackened ruins of what used to be a twisted rowan tree. Darius staggered to a stop not three feet from him.

"Jack?" he said, taking a step closer to the boy.

"I—I can't." Jack had his arms wrapped around his chest, like he was trying to hold himself together. His voice was his own, and not his own. It hit me hard when I realized who it reminded me of—Stevie Rae. When she was a red fledgling. Before Aphrodite's sacrifice. When she had little to no control over her feral urges.

"Darius, don't—" I began the warning too late.

"Can't ... Need to feed!" Jack hissed and gathered himself, obviously ready to leap on Darius. The Warrior's eyes widened in understanding. His raised sword wavered, and for a horrible second I thought the Son of Erebus Warrior was going to get eaten by sweet, zombie Jack.

From the ridge above us, Damien screamed Jack's name.

Jack hesitated just long enough for Aphrodite to run past me and jab him with something that had him collapsing to the ground in a jerking, spastic fit.

She looked over her shoulder at me. "Taser. I came prepared."

She made an impatient gesture at Jack and told Darius, "Well, put her down and grab him. Mother can walk."

The instant LaFont's feet touched the ground she whirled on Darius, lifting her hand to slap him hard across the face.

"No!" Aphrodite was on her in a heartbeat, grabbing her raised arm and getting right in her face. "He just saved your life."

"My life wouldn't need saving if you hadn't summoned demons!" LaFont spat the words at her daughter.

My anger boiled over. "Your daughter didn't summon anything. I did. Accidentally. I was trying to protect Tulsa. You interfered. *You caused this!*"

"Lies! You monsters killed my husband and took my daughter from me. Now you've loosed a plague on Tulsa!" Her slit eye gaze lit on Aphrodite. "May you rot in hell with the vampyres you love more than your own people!"

"Mother. Once and for all. I. Am. Not. Human."

Aphrodite didn't yell. She didn't do anything except stand up to her bat-shit-crazy mom. But she shimmered with power in a way I'd never seen until that moment, as if Nyx had sprinkled glitter over her.

Mrs. LaFont shrank back from her, staggering several steps before turning and rushing off toward Twenty-First Street.

Darius started to follow her, but Aphrodite's cool voice stopped him.

"Let her go."

The Warrior paused. "But the creatures are out there. They could kill her."

Aphrodite nodded tightly. "Yes. They could. And that would be exactly what she deserves."

"You might want to rethink—" I began, but she stopped me.

"No. I might not. Let's go, High Priestess. We have an emergency situation to deal with, and saving my mother is not part of it."

"All righty then," I said. "Let's go."

Like he didn't weigh much more than a child, Darius picked up the unconscious Jack, and we headed up the stone stairs to join our friends.

Aphrodite pulled on my sleeve as we crossed the bloody circle. "I was wrong about the vision," she told me, speaking softly and quickly. "It wasn't Damien's death that I witnessed."

I gave her a question-mark look. "I don't understand."

"Nyx sent me a vision of my own death."

I felt the jolt of shock and stared at her. "What the hell does that mean?"

"It means whatever this cluster fuck is, it isn't as simple as us getting rid of zombie red vampyres and making sure Damien doesn't lose his damn mind over zombie Jack. It means I'm at the heart of this mess, *not* Damien. And if a Prophetess of Nyx is being targeted, we could be looking at something much darker than we thought."

"Ah, hell," I said.

12

General Dominick

There was a dark, feral intelligence that went with the horde. It wasn't a community consciousness, though they did share thoughts, as their psychic gifts were vast. At the moment they were released from the spell that rent the fabric of their world, transporting them to an alternative reality, two thoughts were foremost in their minds—*feed* and *flee to the tunnels!*

Dominick led them. He'd been the first to enter the strange opening, drawn by the scent of the blood of a High Priestess and by her intent as well. He felt her. He heard her. Dominick was well used to listening to the commands of a High Priestess. He was, after all, her second-favorite general.

As soon as the Warriors realized how to kill them, Dominick ordered his small army to flee. It was obvious where they were— Woodward Park in Tulsa. Only this Woodward Park was drastically changed from the one he knew, and not only because everything was carpeted with snow. The park looked off. Where were the old oaks? The mounds of huge azalea bushes?

Dominick pushed aside such inconsequential thoughts.

He was a Warrior. A leader of the Red Army. He had one job—to do his High Priestess' bidding. He had only one desire beyond that: to feed.

And as this strange summons had awakened him and this small portion of his army in the middle of their coma-like sleep, so his need to feed was strong—so strong it even surpassed his confusion at where or *when* he really was.

He'd ordered his unarmed men to flee the barrage of arrows and the deadly sword the Son of Erebus wielded against them—against them! They must be part of a rebel pack. How had they captured the High Priestess? Where was her Red Guard? More importantly, where was she?

Dominick shook himself. Search for the High Priestess later. They must get to safety. They must find weapons. But first, they must feed.

Huddling beneath the snow-shrouded arched bridge that was east of the area they'd materialized, Dominick paused, trying to order his thoughts. It was difficult. Even he—the leader of the Red Army—had trouble concentrating when the hunger filled him.

"Feed!" hissed the pitiful few of his army that pressed close around him.

"Quiet!" he barked at them. They cringed away from him, well aware of what would happen should they become the focus of his wrath. "Wait here," he commanded. Then he stepped out from under the concealment of the bridge.

The vampyres whose circle had drawn him here were gone.

The humans were not. Foolishly, they were leaving the cars they'd fled to earlier, and had returned to the bloody circle.

Dominick whistled once. The sound split the snowy air. He saw the humans pause and glance around nervously.

But they were human. Their night vision was inadequate, even if the darkness hadn't been shrouded in thickly falling snow. And soon they continued to gather the equipment they'd dropped, oblivious to their own danger.

Dominick waited until the shadows stirred and the second half of his people joined him. They grouped around him, whispering their hunger. One of them approached.

"General, where are we? What has happened?"

Dominick recognized the lieutenant immediately. Lieutenant Heff was the youngest red fledgling to ever have been Marked—and was also the youngest to have gone through the Change. Barely sixteen, he was also one of the red vampyres who maintained some self-control over the hunger that overwhelmed the vast majority of the Red Army.

"We answered the call of the High Priestess. We are home, but not home. We must feed and get to the tunnels. Gather our weapons. And keep watch for the High Priestess. I believe she may have been taken by the rebels."

"The High Priestess? Do you mean the one who closed the circle, trapping us here?"

"No. I did not recognize that priestess. We need to find Neferet. She is our only High Priestess."

"It will be as you command, General. But the soldiers must feed."

Dominick snarled and backhanded the lieutenant. "Lieutenant Heff, never presume to tell me about my men!" He pointed to the group of humans in the distance. "We feed there." He faced the milling, whispering horde. "Quietly. Quickly. Feed on the humans. Then we flee to the tunnels from where we will begin to search for our High Priestess." *And we will try to figure out where the hell we are,* he added silently to himself. "Lieutenant, you watch our rear. If the rebels return, we have nothing but our teeth and hands to protect ourselves."

"Our teeth and hands are stronger than theirs," the lieutenant said.

Dominick backhanded him again. "But they are *not* stronger than arrows or swords. Do as I command or I will sever your head from your body myself."

Lieutenant Heff cowered. "Yes, General."

"Follow me!"

Dominick darted out of the concealment of the bridge and the deep shadows surrounding it, followed closely by those who had been pulled from their sleep and wrenched into this changed world with him. They were almost completely silent. The snow aided them in that, though stalking humans was a simple thing. They had ears, but they did not use them to hear. Just as they did not use their eyes to see into the night.

The red vampyres and fledglings attacked silently, too.

The humans were not silent, though their screams did not last long.

His men were so ravenous that they fell to the feeding, rending arms and legs from living bodies with their bare hands. They did not notice one of the humans had escaped. She actually made it to the van that waited beside Twenty-First Street.

"Do not let her leave!" Dominick growled as he tore hunks of flesh from a warm body.

Five of his men darted after the woman. She started the van. It lurched forward as the vampyres swarmed the roof. They broke the driver's window and pulled her from behind the wheel as the van ran headfirst into a truck that had just come over the hill at the top of the street. Both vehicles burst into flame. The man behind the wheel of the truck exploded through the front window, which was lucky for Dominick's men. It gave them someone else on which to feed.

Dominick stood and wiped the blood from his mouth.

Lights were already going on in the homes that bordered Woodward Park. In his world humans knew their place.

This was not his world.

He whistled again. Instantly his small army regrouped.

"Enough! We need to get to the tunnels. Now. We stay as a group as long as we're not attacked. Should an attack come, scatter. Those of you who are strong enough will make it to the tunnels.

Those of you who are not should not be in my army. Understood?"

His men hissed and nodded as they finished gulping down the last of the human flesh. Dominick searched the group and found the lieutenant.

"Heff, stay with me. But if we're attacked, get as many men as you can to the tunnels. I name you my Second. If I fall it is up to you to complete this mission. Find the High Priestess. She called us here. As always, we live to serve her will."

"We live to serve her will …" whispered the horde.

Lieutenant Heff nodded solemnly. "Yes, sir."

"Cloak yourselves with shadow. We run!"

(

Heff

Kevin Heffner ran, though his mind was in tumult. He'd been asleep, as had the rest of the soldiers, and had awakened as he was wrenched from his bed and spewed in a bloody tide with his brother soldiers into this strange version of Woodward Park.

But that wasn't why his mind was in tumult. That was just strange. It was the priestess. The one who had closed the circle. He'd recognized her. Of course he'd recognized her.

But how could it have been her? She's dead!

"Lieutenant, wake the hell up and pay attention! One of the soldiers just took off after a woman in the alley. Get him back here!" The general barked, pointing down a dark side street.

"Yes, sir!" Heff did as he was told. He raced into the street to find one of the more feral of the soldiers bent over a well-dressed, middle-aged woman. He'd already taken a bite out of her shoulder and she was screaming hysterically. He grabbed the red vamp, and tossed him aside. "You heard the general! We get to the tunnels. Now. No stopping."

111

The vampyre gnashed his teeth, but cringed when Heff raised his fist, threatening to beat him into submission. "Yessssss, ssir," he hissed.

"Go!" Heff pointed at the rear of their group, and the soldier sprinted after them. Heff turned to the woman.

"No! Get away from me!" she screamed. She tried to stand and run from him, but she slipped on her own blood and fell heavily to the snowy street.

Heff met her gaze, locking it in his own. *"No more screaming,"* he commanded her. She instantly complied.

"No more screaming," she repeated mechanically.

He considered feeding from her. He wouldn't rip and tear, as the feral vampyre would have. Heff didn't do that. He never did that. And she was under his mind control, so he could taste her, just a little, and she wouldn't protest. He wouldn't even hurt her much more than she'd already been hurt. He was still hungry. He was always hungry. But one glance at the disappearing column of soldiers had him racing away. *There will be more feeding later. There will also be time to try to understand how my sister could be alive …*

(

Zoey

CRACK! We automatically cringed as an enormous explosive sound echoed throughout the night.

"Oh, shit! Was that a transponder?" Shaunee said.

"Seems like it," Shaylin said. "And it's not even icy."

"Dang, the snow *was* pretty. Now it's super cray," Stevie Rae said.

"Oklahoma weather," Aphrodite grumbled. "It. Sucks."

"Hurry, Stark," I said, trying to peer through the SUV's tinted window. The snow was falling so fast it had already covered the

112

lines in the road. And now the wind had picked up, causing whiteout conditions.

"Doing my best," Stark said without taking his eyes from the street.

"He's a red fledgling! Why is he a red fledgling?" Damien was turned completely around, staring back at Jack, who was still unconscious, trussed like a roped goat, and seat belted between Darius and Rephaim in the rear of the school's new Escalade. Aphrodite, Stevie Rae, and I were in the second seats. Stark was driving and Damien was in the passenger seat. Shaylin and Shaunee were smashed into the back like groceries.

"No clue," I told Damien. "Can't you go faster?" I asked Stark.

He gave me a *look* in the rearview mirror. "Have you noticed the snow? I'm doing my best, but Utica is already a mess."

"Sorry," I said. "I just can't tell where we are. Um, because of the snow."

"He's still unconscious. What did you do to him?" Damien asked for the umpteenth time.

"I already told you. I tazed him," Aphrodite said. "And it's a good thing I did. He was either going to eat one of us or get dead. Again."

"Jack would never hurt any of us!" Damien insisted.

"Honey," I touched his shoulder gently. "You have to remember that this isn't your Jack. Your Jack is dead. This Jack is like those things that came out of the bloody tree fountain. I know it's hard. Of course you're emotional, but—"

"He recognized me. He was attacking Darius, but he stopped when I called his name," Damien insisted. "And I'm not being overly emotional."

Aphrodite snorted.

Damien skewered her with his eyes. "What if it was Darius? What if Darius had been killed last year, and suddenly appeared out of nowhere—changed, but alive? What would you do? Or rather, what *wouldn't* you do?"

Aphrodite met Damien's gaze. "My heart would break. I don't know how else to answer your questions. Damien, we're only trying to keep you from getting hurt, or worse."

"Don't," Damien said. "I'm not a child. I don't need protection. I need answers and I need your trust."

"But can we trust you not to put yourself in danger?" I spoke gently. When he didn't answer, I added, "We're your best friends. We love you. We want Jack back, too. But we're not as emotionally involved as you are. We see with more than our hearts, and what we see is a kid who is, and isn't, Jack. Can you please trust that we're not patronizing you?"

Damien's shoulders slumped, though he didn't take his gaze from Jack. "I hear you, Z. I hear all of you. My mind understands, but my heart doesn't. Not at all."

"Let us help you," Shaunee said.

"We're all here for you," Stevie Rae added.

"He's breathing okay," Rephaim said. "He'll be fine when he wakes."

"He smells wrong," Darius said.

"He smells like I used to," Stevie Rae said.

"And me," Stark added. He glanced at Damien. "And you know what that means."

Damien nodded jerkily. "He's a red fledgling who has not retained all of his humanity."

"Or maybe any of it," Stevie Rae said. When Damien opened his mouth to respond, she lifted a hand, cutting him off. "I know more about this than you do. So does Stark. You gotta listen to us."

"I know. Forgive me. I'll listen to you."

"There's nothin' to forgive," Stevie Rae told him gently. "We get it. We all get it."

"It's why he's *not* dead," Aphrodite said.

"You saved him for me?" Damien's eyes spilled over as silent tears tracked down his cheeks.

"Of course," Aphrodite said. "Stevie Rae and Stark found their humanity, maybe—"

Jack jolted awake, struggling against the zip ties that kept him tightly bound as he hissed and snarled.

"Jack! Jack, it's okay! Everything's going to be okay! It's me—Damien."

Jack turned his red-eyed glare on Damien. I saw it. I saw the flash of recognition. Then Jack's lip curled. "Dead! You're dead!" His voice was bizarre—a terrible dark twin of Jack's sweet softness. It shocked us all into silence.

Well, all of us except Aphrodite.

"Who the hell are you?" she asked him.

His eyes turned to her. "Priestess?"

"Well, sure. You can call me Priestess. Who are you?"

"You know me. I am Jack. Why do you cover your Mark?" His words were short, hard, clipped—as if speaking took too much effort. "I must feed!" He twisted his head, obviously checking out Rephaim's neck.

Aphrodite raised the Taser. "Um, no. You won't be eating anyone. We'll get you a nice blood smoothie when we're home."

"What did you mean by dead?" I found my voice again. "Were you talking about Damien?"

Jack stared at me. "Yes. And you. Dead."

"Shut the fuck up!" Stark snapped.

Jack's eyes flew to where Stark was fighting against the blowing snow. "General?"

I saw Stark's startled reflection in the rearview mirror. "My name is Stark. Do you know me?"

"We all know you, General. You lead the Blue Army. But your Mark is wrong. Why is it red?" His gaze searched the SUV. "Where is the High Priestess?"

"Well, there are several of them in this car," Stark neatly avoided Jack's question about his Mark. "Which one are you looking for?"

"Neferet, of course," he said.

"Fuck," Aphrodite said. She turned all the way around in her seat so she could face Jack. "Do you mean High Priestess Neferet, or Goddess Neferet?"

Jack looked confused. "There is only one Neferet. She is our High Priestess. Our only High Priestess."

"But you called me 'High Priestess.'"

"No. I called you 'Priestess,'" he said.

"Okay, so, Neferet isn't an immortal?" I asked.

Jack stared at me. Then, very deliberately, he pressed his lips together and stopped speaking.

"Jack?" Damien spoke gently to him. "What's wrong? Why don't you answer Zoey?"

Jack refused to look at Damien. When he spoke his voice was flat—emotionless. "You are rebels."

"We're rebels? What kind of rebels?" Damien said.

Jack didn't answer.

Damien tried again. "Talk to me, Jack. Please."

Jack's gaze lifted reluctantly to find Damien. I saw it again. Saw the shock of recognition flash through his red-tinged eyes. "You are dead," he repeated stubbornly.

Damien's throat moved spasmodically as he swallowed several times, obviously trying to collect himself. Finally, he said, "But I'm not. You see me. You hear me. I'm alive. And I love you."

Jack shook his head. "Not enough to live."

"What? I don't understand," Damien said.

"My Damien killed himself six months and two days ago. He didn't love me enough to live for me. You aren't my Damien."

Damien gasped, his hand going to his throat. He opened and closed his mouth, though no words came out.

"We're at the gate," Stark said. "How about putting our, uh, guest in one of the basement rooms under the Field House? I could rig a lock on one of them pretty easily."

"Gate? Field House?" Jack looked frantically out the window. "No! Not here. This is not where I belong. Take me to the tunnels. I belong in the tunnels."

A terrible foreboding wrapped around my stomach and squeezed. "You mean the tunnels under the depot?"

When he didn't speak, Stark shouted, "Answer her!"

"Yes. The depot tunnels. You all know it. It is where the Red Army lives."

"Double fuck!" Aphrodite said. "That's probably where the rest of those things took off to."

"Ah, hell!" I said. "The restaurant!" I didn't have to check the time. The Depot Restaurant, run by the House of Night, was open all night—every night. It was still several hours before dawn, which meant it was still open and still serving late-night Tulsa diners, along with any vampyre or fledgling who wanted to splurge on fine dining. I scrambled for my phone. "No service! Does anyone have service?"

Everyone frantically checked their phones—no one had service.

"It's the snow. It probably knocked out the downtown cell tower about when it hit that transponder," Damien said.

Stark slid to a stop beside the Field House entrance. "I'm getting to a landline and calling the restaurant. Darius, gather the Sons of Erebus. I'll meet you in the basement." I was out of the door and running through calf-deep snow before Stark shut off the SUV's engine.

Please let me be in time ... please let me be in time ...

13

Skye

"Goddess, you'd think the crappy weather would've kept people home. But, no. Why are we so busy?" The young waitress' etched silver name tag read SKYE.

"Girl, you better not let Kramisha hear you talkin' like that. All these folks are a good thing. Keeps us busy, and that's a good thing, too. I don't know 'bout you, but my mamma and daddy disowned me the second they saw this." The young waitress pointed the center of her forehead, where the outline of a red crescent moon stood out against her pale skin. "The House of Night gives us room and board and such, but not a lot of spending money. Tips are good here. Check your attitude."

Skye didn't actually check her attitude, but rather checked the volume of her voice. "Sorry, Xena. I guess I just need a night off. I have a serious test tomorrow in Spells and Rituals, and I haven't had one second to study."

"Hey, I'll finish up your last two tables, and take the rest of your shift. I have section D tonight," Xena said.

Skye grimaced with understanding. "Worst section ever.

Someone needs to talk to Kramisha about it. That big community table thing just doesn't work in Tulsa."

"Right?" Xena said. "Like we're New York City, or something?"

"Hey, thanks. I really appreciate it."

"No big deal. I have my eye on a designer bed for my Pita cat, so I appreciate the extra tips."

"Thanks again. Um, your cat is cray. You know that, right?" Skye frowned as the phone began ringing.

"Your mom's cray," Xena shot over her shoulder as she headed into the kitchen to check on her orders. "And answer the damn phone."

Still frowning, Skye picked up the phone that was a reproduction of a brass cradle rotary dial. It totally fit the rest of the Depot's décor as the restaurant was decorated in 1920's art deco classic club style—right down to their flapper waitress, and tuxedoed waiter uniforms. "Depot Restaurant, how may I help you?"

"This is Zoey Redbird. Who is this?"

"High Priestess!" Skye automatically stood straighter. "This is Skye Summers. Your table is open. Can we expect you—"

"Is Kramisha there?"

"Well, no ma'am. Or, yes, but she's somewhere downstairs in the—"

"Listen carefully to me. Do exactly what I tell you. Go to the front doors. Lock them. NOW. Then get all of the guests downstairs and into the tunnels. Close and bar the entry behind you. Then have Kramisha call me."

"But, um. They're not done eating. And there are a lot of humans here. They won't want to go into the tunnels."

"I don't give a crap about what they want! There is an army of creatures on their way to you. They will kill everyone in their path. Put the phone down *right now* and lock that front door. Then get everyone into the tunnels and call me back on the landline down there."

"Y—yes, High Priestess." Shakily, Skye set the phone down and started toward the big double glass doors at the entrance of the restaurant.

She didn't make it.

The doors exploded open. On a tide of snow and frigid air, ravenous creatures flooded into the depot. Skye saw their red Marks. She saw their glowing eyes and flashing fangs. She heard the shrieks of the restaurant patrons as they bolted from their tables, only to be tackled as the horde mobbed the dining room and began ripping, tearing, and eating the flesh from the humans.

"Skye!" She heard Xena's shout, and she tried to retrace her steps. Tried to make it back to the kitchen and the trapdoor that opened to the tunnels below.

Instead a red-eyed demon blocked her way.

"Ooooh, pretty," he hissed.

Skye screamed until he ripped out her throat, and then, blissfully, she knew no more.

(

Zoey

"Oh, Goddess, no. No, no, no, no, no!" I could hear everything. "Run!" I screamed impotently into the phone. "Get into the tunnels!"

The line went dead.

"Think, Zoey!" I punched three numbers into the landline, 9-1-1.

A busy signal beeped like a harbinger of doom.

"Seriously?" I shouted into the phone. My hands were trembling so badly that I had a hard time putting in the security code to my phone. Still no service. I got into my contacts and found Kramisha's landline number. We'd had a landline installed in the tunnels during their renovation. No matter how hard we tried, none of the cell phone providers could come up with a plan that gave us reliable service down there.

The phone rang. "Come on, Kramisha!" And rang. And rang. Then her archaic answering machine kicked on. "Messages is lame. If you under forty, I know you feel the same. I seen your ID. But I ain't here. Just re-call me."

"Oh my god. Oh my god. Oh my god!" I hung up and scrolled to Detective Marx's desk number and somehow managed to punch it correctly into the landline. *Please ... please ... detectives have to work weird hours. Please be there.* He answered on the second ring.

"Marx, it's Zoey. Just listen. Get a lot of cops to the Depot Restaurant. Now. Something happened in Woodward Park tonight. Red vampyres and fledglings from somewhere else got through to our world. They're killers. And they're at the depot."

"How do we tell the difference between good and bad red vamps?"

"If it smells off, like something dead mixed with your grandma's moldy old basement, it's a bad guy. Oh, and you have to sever their spines to kill them."

"Sounds like old-school vampyre stuff."

"More like old-school zombie stuff, but you're not wrong."

"Is Neferet loose?"

"Not that I know of."

"Did she do this?"

"We didn't see any sign of her."

"The mess on Twenty-First—in front of Woodward Park—that wasn't a simple car accident?"

"Nope. And there's more. Look by the wall around Neferet's grotto. It's bad. Also, keep an eye out for Frances LaFont."

"LaFont? What does she have to do with this?"

"Well, let's just say she was her usual charming self and interrupted some spellwork tonight, which let those red vampyre zombie things into Tulsa. She took off, but I have no clue if she made it home, or if one of those creatures got her."

"Noted," he said.

"And I'm sending Sons of Erebus Warriors to the depot to help in any way they can. Darius will lead them, and they are all blue vampyres."

"Roger that."

"How bad is the weather?"

"Apparently we're being slammed by a major winter snowstorm. It was just supposed to be a couple of inches, but something changed in the weather pattern an hour or so ago. It's going to be bad. Stay safe. Touch base with me later."

"Thank y—" He hung up before I could finish.

I wiped a shaky hand across my sweaty forehead, drew a deep breath in, let it out, and made the decision I thought would keep the most people under my protection safe. Then I pressed the INTERCOM button and spoke with a pretense of calm.

"Students and faculty, this is your High Priestess. I've just spoken to the Tulsa Police Department about the weather, and they advise everyone stay off the roads. Due to the unexpected treacherous conditions, I'm calling the school day immediately. Faculty, please see that your students make their way back to the dorms as soon as possible, and please help your human students call their parents—using landlines because the cell towers are out—to let them know that the police have advised we do not run buses on these roads, so their students will be our welcome guests at the House of Night until the weather clears. Thank you, and blessed be."

I clicked the intercom button off and picked at my fingernails. Had I made the right decision keeping human students on campus? But if I hadn't and they'd run into those red creatures ... I shuddered, not even wanting to think about it.

"Zoeybird, what has happened?"

I looked up to see Grandma standing in the doorway to the administrative offices. "Come with me, Grandma. Maybe you can help us figure it out."

(

Zoey

In the basement under the Field House, the Sons of Erebus Warriors kept their massive stash of weapons. Some were simply lethal. Some were lethal and jewel-encrusted. I'd first discovered the priceless room full of swords, knives, bows, and whatnot when we were battling Neferet, and needed to keep the red fledglings safe in our basement. Over the year I'd assumed the role of Leader of the New North American High Council, I'd been sure Darius—current Swordmaster of the Sons of Erebus—had supervised the cataloging and sorting of all the stored weaponry. We'd found out that the House of Night was sitting on a fortune of weapons, and we'd begun loaning some of the more ancient ones to human museums. The Philbrook was currently displaying a gorgeous collection of samurai swords that dated back more than one thousand years.

We'd also cleaned and reorganized the basement, dividing off a section of it and building out half a dozen cozy guest rooms for any visiting red fledglings or red vampyres. Regular vamps find the sun uncomfortable, but bearable. Red fledglings and vamps find it impossible to tolerate. Exposed too long and they incinerate like one of the ever-fabulous Anne Rice's fictional vampires. Hence the reason they rest most comfortably underground.

Grandma and I hurried down the stairs that spilled into the huge basement that stretched the length of the Field House. Right now even its vastness was crowded with very large, very well-armed Sons of Erebus Warriors.

Darius and Stark came to my side immediately. Darius raised one hand and the murmurs of the Warriors silenced.

"Get to the Depot Restaurant. It's too late. They've already attacked. I can't get anyone to answer Kramisha's landline in the tunnels. 9-1-1 was busy, so I called Detective Marx's desk. He's sending TPD there right away, but from what I overheard when I called the restaurant they're going to be walking into something as awful ..." I swallowed hard before I could continue. "Something as awful as when Neferet and her tendrils slaughtered the people at the Boston Avenue Church."

"They're going to blame us." Stark's look was dark and tense.

"That's gonna be hard to do when they find out those red zombies killed our people, too," I said.

Aphrodite moved through the crowd to stand beside Darius. "You mean those kids who waited tables at the restaurant are ..." her words trailed off.

I nodded tightly. "Sounded like it."

"What about Kramisha and the rest of the red fledglings and vamps who live in the tunnels?" Aphrodite asked.

"I don't know. I tried to warn them. I just don't know."

"Then we need to move and move fast," Darius said. "Sons of Erebus, those of you I've already chosen will come with me to the depot. The rest of you remain here under Stark's command. Protect the school. We don't know exactly what we're dealing with yet, but we do know they're familiar with our city, and the only way they can be stopped is to sever their spines. Take off their heads."

"And we will know what we're dealing with soon. We have one of them. We're going to get answers," Stark said grimly.

"Which you won't know about unless the cell service comes back on," I added. "So, be careful."

"This is going to sound strange, but don't let them bite you," Aphrodite said.

"What do you know?" I asked.

"Nothing for sure. Yet. But my gut is telling me something, and I know what I saw in my vision. A red tide covered Tulsa, and there just weren't that many of them that came through whatever the hell that was in the park. I put two and two together. Don't let them bite you. Period."

"Better to be safe." I lifted my hands and the Sons of Erebus bowed their heads. "May Nyx's blessing fill you with strength and courage and wisdom—and may you return here safely to give your thanks to our goddess. Blessed be."

"Blessed be," the Warriors replied.

I grabbed Darius before he could follow his Warriors from the room and hugged him. "Stay safe. No one could stand Aphrodite if you weren't here."

"I will, High Priestess," he said.

Then Aphrodite was in his arms. She kissed him thoroughly and pulled the gorgeous blue, black, and white Burberry scarf from where she'd draped it around her neck, wrapping it high up on his bicep and tying it there securely.

"My beauty? Do you think my arm will be cold?"

Her smile was trembly. "No, and it's silk anyway so it's not exactly warm. You're my Warrior. My knight. Swordmaster of the Sons of Erebus. It's right that you should carry your prophetess' favor into battle."

"I suppose you expect me to bring it back to you unharmed and unstained?"

"You suppose correctly. And the only stains I'll tolerate are *other people's* blood. Not yours. I'll know the difference." She kissed him again, and he followed his Warriors up the stairs.

"I think we should post lookouts all along the wall," Stark said.

"I agree," I said.

"U-we-tsi-a-ge-ya, did you not tell me you had the city designate the House of Night as a storm shelter?" Grandma said.

"I did. Crap!" I just realized the implications of what Grandma had said. "If the snow's bad enough to knock out cell service it's just a matter of time before the electricity is out. Our gaslights and our gas heat won't be affected, so the humans in the neighborhood might start straggling here. Don't mistake them for the red zombie vampyre things."

"Good point," Stark said. "Thanks for reminding us, Grandma Redbird."

"And I need someone to stay at the phone in the admin office," I said. "Keep calling Kramisha's landline. We need to know what's going on down there."

"Nicole and I can do that," Shaylin said. I smiled my thanks to her as she hurried from the basement.

"Warriors, divide yourself into shifts according to squads," Stark was telling the Sons of Erebus. "First Squad, begin patrol immediately. Second Squad, relieve them at dawn. I'll brief you on what we learn about these creatures ASAP." The Warriors saluted him, bowed to me, and filed up the stairway.

We were facing a scary, dangerous unknown, but I felt safe knowing that our Warriors were standing guard—and I knew, no matter how awful it was out there—Darius would bring his Warriors back.

Was I being naïve? I hoped not. I hoped I was being a High Priestess who had faith in her Warriors.

"Tell me what has happened, Zoeybird," Grandma said.

"It's easier to show you. Where is he?" I asked Stark.

"We put him in the last bedroom. It was the smallest, and has a steel door with a lock." He jerked his chin in the direction of the far corner of the basement. Now that the group of Warriors was gone, I could see Damien was sitting on a chair just outside the closed door to the little guest room. Rephaim and Shaunee stood on either side of him.

"Okay, time for answers," I said. "How are you holding up?" I asked Damien as I approached him.

He looked up at me with haunted eyes framed with dark, puffy circles. His face was too thin. His skin was too white. He looked awful.

"He's alive. That's all I've been able to really take in."

I nodded. "I can't say I understand how you feel, but I can imagine how it would be if Heath or even Aurox suddenly showed

126

up here—alive, but not really themselves. It'd be hard. Really hard. What can I do to help you through this?"

"All of us," Aphrodite spoke up from beside me. "What can all of us do to help you?"

Damien wiped his eyes and attempted a smile. "Just be here with me. I—I don't think I should be alone right now. So, even if I tell you to go away, please don't."

"Oh, boyfriend, you can definitely count on us to be übernosy and all up in your business," Shaunee said.

"That's right," Stevie Rae said. "Heck, I don't even need an excuse to be in your business. I like it. I'm naturally übernosy."

"Sadly, that's too true," Aphrodite said. "But you can count on us. We're the Nerd Herd. Shit can't tear us apart."

"One for all—all for nerd!" Stevie Rae shouted.

"Th-thanks," Damien said, wiping more tears from his face. "Okay. I'm ready for whatever."

"And I do not understand," Grandma said.

"Stay back by Stark," I told Grandma. "We're going to open this door. Jack's inside. But he's not *our* Jack."

Grandma's startled expression cleared quickly. She moved to Damien's side and gently touched his shoulder. "I see. And I am here for you, too, child."

Damien squeezed her hand. "Thank you, Grandma. That helps."

"Remember, be careful," I said. "It's tough, but we don't really know this kid—and he's a different kind of red fledgling."

"A zombie kind," Aphrodite said.

"No! I can't believe—" Damien began, but my raised hand stopped him.

"Damien, we don't know what he is. We do know we're going to keep you—and the rest of us—safe. Don't be defensive. Remember we're all on your side and we want to be on Jack's side, too. We just don't know what side he's on."

Damien nodded brokenly.

Grandma rested her hand on his shoulder. "I will stay with you, child."

"Let's do this," Stark said, and opened the door.

Other Jack startled, hissed at us. I noticed his eyes weren't red, though, and he stopped his hissing when none of us tried to come into the room. He was sitting on the edge of a very comfy queen-sized bed, clutching a tall glass that was empty, but my awesome sense of smell told me that Aphrodite had made sure he'd gotten a blood smoothie first thing.

"Hi, Jack," I said. "Want more of that?"

"Yes."

"I'll get him some more," Shaunee said, hurrying away.

"We need to talk to you," I said. "It's important."

"I don't have anything to say to rebels."

"We aren't rebels," Stark said.

"I don't know what's going on with you, General. But you're not a red vampyre. You're Neferet's right hand—leader of the Blue Army." He made a brisk gesture that took in Stark's adult red vampyre tattoos that were in the shape of arrows.

"Okay, here's the thing." Stark took one of the chairs from outside the room, turned it around, and nonchalantly sat in it, like talking to red fledgling dead/undead Jack was an everyday occurrence. "Something happened in Woodward Park. We don't know why. We don't know how. We do know you aren't from here because the Jack who was a part of this world died several months ago."

"How?" Jack's voice was faint. His eyes flicked back and forth from Stark to me.

"Let's table that until later," I said.

"No." Damien got up from his chair and moved into the doorway with us. "No. We're telling him the truth. All of the truth. If we don't, how can we expect him to trust us?"

"Damien has a good point, u-we-tsi-a-ge-ya," Grandma agreed.

"Okay, but just the basics for now. We're under a time crunch,"

I said. "Jack, your death was made to look like an accident, but we're pretty sure Neferet killed you—or at least caused your death."

"But how?" he asked, sounding so much like *our* Jack that my heart squeezed.

"It was a sword," Damien said. "You fell off a ladder and landed on a sword."

"What was I doing on a ladder?"

"Decorating," Damien said.

"Oh. That makes sense," Jack said.

I almost smiled. "Um, Jack, where are you from?"

He looked surprised. "Tulsa."

I reconsidered and changed my question. "*When* are you from? What year is it?"

"2017. Well, it's almost 2018."

I sighed and muttered, "That didn't help."

"How about this—you're obviously a red fledgling," Stark said.

Jack nodded.

"And those others who came through with you into Woodward Park—they were mostly red vampyres, correct?"

"Yes."

"But they're not—you're not—like the red the fledglings or vampyres we're used to," Stark continued. "So, what are you?"

"I don't understand the question."

"Look at Stark. He's a red vampyre. The kind we're used to," Aphrodite said, moving so that Jack could see her. "*Really* look at him. And smell him."

Jack actually did as she asked. He even sniffed in his direction.

"He's like the blue vampyres," Jack said.

"But I'm not. I'm a red vampyre."

"Does your bite Mark others as red? Do they rise again?" Jack asked.

There was a long pause, and then Stark said, "You're going to have to explain that question better."

"No."

I sighed. "We don't have time for this."

"Jack, you say that in your world there is a war going on?" Damien asked.

"You know there is," Jack said, not looking at Damien.

"And the Tulsa House of Night—what is it?" he asked Jack.

Jack did look at Damien then. He shrugged. "I guess it can't hurt to answer that. Everyone knows. The Tulsa House of Night is Neferet's stronghold for her Blue Army. Like the Tulsa depot tunnels are a stronghold for her Red Army."

"So, basically, this House of Night is a fortress for Neferet," I said.

"Yes."

"And you were just here? Like, earlier today?" I continued, understanding what Damien was setting up.

"Yes. I was at the House of Night earlier this evening. Then I returned to the tunnels just before sunrise. That's where I was when we were pulled into Woodward Park."

"All right then, come with me. I want you to see our House of Night. If it's the same as yours then you'll know you're right. We're rebels or whatever, and we've captured you—even though I don't have a clue why we would. If it's nothing like your House of Night, well, then I hope you know you can trust us," I said.

"Fine." He stood. "I'll go with you."

"Tie his hands," Aphrodite said. Damien started to say something, but Stevie Rae interrupted.

"She's right, Damien. I've been where I think Jack is, and the one thing I can tell you for sure is that it's not safe to trust him."

"How do you expect me to trust you if you don't trust me?" Jack asked.

Aphrodite took several steps into Jack's room. Jack's reaction was instantaneous. His eyes began to glow and he actually started salivating. He crouched, his body taking on a predatory pose. Stark started to move, but Aphrodite raised the Taser, pointing it at Jack.

"Do not make me zap you. Again. And look at yourself. You're slobbering and snarling like an animal at me. Tell me why."

He didn't say anything and she stomped at him, raising the Taser a little higher.

"It's your blood! It smells so sssssweet," he hissed the last word.

"Point made," Aphrodite said. "Keep his hands tied and stay away from his fangs." She turned to Damien. "You know that vision I had—the one where I thought I was seeing your death at his hands?"

Damien nodded.

"I realized tonight that I'd gotten it wrong. He didn't eat you. He ate the person who was standing in for you tonight. He ate me. And if it hadn't been for me being forewarned enough to bring this,"—she hefted the Taser again—"tonight he would have either been killed or eaten one of us for real. I know this is hard on you, but you gotta get a handle on your shit, Damien. This isn't your Jack."

Damien's gaze flew to Other Jack, who stared back at him with glowing, rust-colored eyes.

"I hear you," Damien said. "And I understand. Tie his hands."

As Stark bound Jack's hands in front of him, Grandma came to me, speaking low for my ears alone. "U-we-tsi-a-ge-ya, I have an idea. Do you mind if I go to my room and work on it?"

One of the first things I'd done after being put in charge of the Tulsa House of Night was to turn a wing of the student dorms into guest rooms for family members, and one of those rooms I gave to Grandma—permanently. "Sure, Grandma. No problem."

She kissed me on the cheek and hurried off. And I faced Other Jack, wishing I had a better plan—or any plan—about how to get him to talk.

And then I realized I was overcomplicating everything. When in doubt, go with the absolute truth, and that's exactly what I did.

14

Zoey

"First, before we go up there I want you to take a look around," I told Jack. Stark had tied his hands behind his back and was keeping ahold of the end of the length of rope he'd used. I'd paused just before the stairway and turned, pointing at the neat basement and the cozy guest rooms. "Does your House of Night have all of this?"

Jack looked around, then he shrugged. "I wouldn't know. I've never been down here. I didn't even know there was a basement under the Field House."

"Well, that's not unusual. We didn't know about it, either, until last year," Damien said.

"I agree, but I'm making a point. Remember this, Jack. This will just be the first of a bunch of differences."

He nodded slightly and we went up the stairs, turning into the hallway that connected the Equestrian Center and the Field House with the main House of Night building.

"Hang on." The hallway was deserted, but when I peeked through the window into the school's beautiful courtyard, I noticed students were still straggling to their dorms. And by straggling, I mean they were messing around making snow angels and having snowball fights—as they moved in the general direction of the dorms. "Stark, give Jack your hoodie." Stark frowned at me. "Do you want someone to recognize him? We don't have time to answer questions right now, and we don't need a bunch of gossip going around the school."

Stark sighed, but he quickly untied Jack's hands, pulled his hoodie off, and tossed it to Jack, who put it on.

"Pull the hood up and cover as much of your face as you can," I told him, which he did without complaining. "Okay, what do you want to see, Jack?"

Jack looked surprised.

"I don't want you saying that you only saw what we wanted you to see, or any other garbage like that. So, where do you want to go?"

"Where I was just a few hours ago—the auditorium. Neferet spoke to the Red Army. I'm only in the beginning of my Warrior training, but they let me attend her speech before I went to my fencing lesson in the Field House."

"Does our Field House look the same?" I asked as Damien said, at the same moment, "Warrior training? You?"

Jack gave Damien a look that was hard for me to read. I thought he looked sad, and even a little scared, and very much like he might want to say something to Damien, but his expression flattened to become as emotionless as his voice. "Yeah, I'm in Warrior training like the rest of the red fledglings. And I guess the Field House looks pretty much the same, but the stuff is put up."

"Stuff?" Stark asked.

"The weapons. They're usually out and hanging all over the walls of the Field House. But now they're down in the basement."

"Let's go to the auditorium," I said.

We started walking in silence. I could feel Damien staring at Jack. I knew he couldn't help it, and my heart ached for him. What would I do if Heath suddenly showed up?

We were about halfway to the auditorium when Jack stopped. He stared out the hallway window to the courtyard where fledglings and human students still played around in the snow while House of Night cats frolicked about them. And by frolic, I mean they twined around their legs and caused fledglings to trip over their own feet. I saw Maleficent yowl at a kid like she'd just had her fat, fluffy tail tromped on and broken into a million pieces—the unsuspecting fledgling shrieked and lunged back, falling on her butt, while Maleficent groomed herself smugly. (I sighed internally—making a note to myself to get back on the intercom and tell the fledglings to get to their dorms, and *take the cats with them*.)

"If you have humans to use as refrigerators, why do I have to drink stale blood from a glass?" Jack's voice was hard—almost mean, which sounded super strange coming from him.

"Do not ever call them refrigerators." I shared a look with Aphrodite, knowing she'd take over from there. There's nothing quite like the righteous indignation of someone who has made mistakes and learned from them.

"They're students, *people*, and they take classes here," Aphrodite said. "We *never* call them refrigerators."

"And we don't *ever* let fledglings or vampyres—no matter what color—feed from 'em. That crap ended when Z took charge," Stevie Rae said.

"Yeah, grow some compassion and get a clue, Other Jack," Aphrodite finished.

Other Jack was blinking in disbelief at the mixed group of fledglings and human teenagers rolling snowballs to make a giant something that might be a dragon—or a dog. Or possibly a big-snouted cat.

"Human teenagers can take classes at the Tulsa House of Night," I explained. "We're mostly working with the art departments at Tulsa Public, BA, Union, and Jenks. It's only been in place for a semester, but the classes are already full for next year and Bixby and Coweta have shown interest in joining the program."

"And we're expandin' our human transfer program nationwide," Stevie Rae continued. "It makes for great PR. I mean, prejudice feeds on ignorance and fear. If the only interaction humans have with vamps is on the big screen, or when they buy a piece of our art—well, that doesn't make for much give and take, or understanding, right?"

Jack had gone from gawking at the kids outside to staring at Stevie Rae. "You're telling me humans are free here?"

"Uh, yeah. That's exactly what I'm tellin' you, but I don't know why I need to tell ya that. It's just normal stuff. Sheesh," she said. "Tell him, Rephaim."

"I've never even heard the word refrigerator used for a human," Rephaim said. "That's just wrong."

"Who are you?" Jack said.

"He's Rephaim. He and our Jack were friends," Stevie Rae said.

"He used to be a Raven Mocker. He still turns into a bird from sunrise to sunset," Aphrodite said. At Jack's startled expression, she just grinned. "Exactly my reaction to Bird Boy."

"None of this is normal," Jack said.

"All of it is," Damien said softly, and I wondered how such a sweet, sad voice could cut so deeply. "You're the one who isn't normal, Other Jack."

Jack shook his head slightly and closed his mouth.

"Ready to continue?" I asked.

He nodded. We continued down the hallway, and Jack continued to shoot bemused glances out at the kids playing together in the snow. My mind raced as I thought about what he'd revealed. Humans weren't free wherever he came from. And Neferet controlled two armies. None of that sounded good.

The hallway emptied into the entrance to the main House of Night building with the administrative offices on one side and multiple entrances to the auditorium on the other.

"Hang on." I opened the door to the admin offices and stuck my head in, calling to Nicole and Shaylin. "Did anyone answer yet?"

"No, sorry," Shaylin said.

"Keep trying." I rejoined my group. "Okay, let's go in the auditorium." I opened the door and stepped to one side. "After you and Stark."

Jack marched into the auditorium like he knew exactly what to expect—and stopped like he'd run into a brick wall. He stared— with an even more shocked expression than he'd had when he gawked at the human kids. Damien started to step forward, but I silently raised my hand, staying him. Jack needed to figure out the truth on his own. It was the only way we'd have a shot at getting the information we needed from him.

Finally, Jack turned to face me. "Those portraits. Where did they come from?"

I glanced into the dimly lit auditorium. I knew what he was asking about. Lining the walls were huge original oil portraits of famous vampyre actresses, actors, and singers who were from Oklahoma, like Brad Pitt, Alfre Woodard, Blake Shelton, Megan Mullally, and Kristin Chenoweth—just to name a few. You see, people don't really get that Oklahoma seems to breed talent. Sure, a bunch of it leaves. But still. Talent. It's a serious mistake to under-estimate any Okie.

"They're commissioned by the school. They're not from one artist. The star gets to choose his or her favorite artist. Don't tell Erik, but if he wins the Golden Globe he's nominated for, the Council is going to vote that he be the subject of the next portrait."

"I'm going in there." Jack walked straight up to the closest portrait. It was an older one of Blake Shelton, commissioned in 2011 after his album *Red River Blue* went platinum. (I only know that because the dates are on each of the plaques—I'm not the country music expert. That's Stevie Rae's thing.)

I was standing there, thinking about how much I heart one

of Blake's classics, "Honey Bee," even though I'm more of a Zayn kind of girl, when Jack lifted his tied hands, grabbed the bottom of the ornate gold frame and tried to tug it off the wall.

"Hey! He's tryin' to mess up Blake's picture!" Stevie Rae shouted.

Stark shoved Jack away from the painting saying, "What the hell?"

"They're bolted to the wall," Jack said.

"Uh, yeah. Just like they've always been," Stevie Rae said as she marched to the portrait and studied it to be sure he hadn't damaged it.

"And those museum-light things are bolted above them, too, in case you want to get a ladder and check them out," I said.

"But your luck on ladders isn't good," Aphrodite said. "I'd skip that part, if I were you."

"Aphrodite!" Damien gasped.

"What? It's the truth. And, anyway, it wasn't this Jack that fell off the ladder. This is Other Jack, not *Jack* Jack. You really need to keep them straight, Damien."

Other Jack walked slowly back to the rest of us, still hanging out in the doorway. He was thinking so hard I could practically see the little gerbils scurrying around inside his head.

"Those portraits can't just be taken down and put back up in a few hours," he said.

"Nope," I said. "This is how the auditorium—*our* auditorium—looks. I'm assuming it's different than the one you were in just a few hours ago?"

Jack opened his mouth to answer, but no words came out. He was staring over my shoulder, open-mouthed. His already pale face had lost every bit of color it had almost had.

"Zoey—there you are. I need an update on what went on at Woodward Park. And what's happening at the restaurant? Travis and I tried to change our reservation and—"

"Lenobia! You're alive!" Jack tried to run to her, but Stark kept a tight hold on the rope that bound his hands in front of him.

Lenobia's beautiful gray eyes went wide with shock. "Jack? My Goddess! Is it really you?"

"Not out here," I said. "Let's go in the auditorium and shut the doors."

We all filed in, with Lenobia still gaping at Jack. As soon as the doors were securely closed, words spilled from Other Jack.

"But they killed you! I saw it. You and Travis. And your horses." Other Jack had to pause then and look away from her to collect himself. But it was like he couldn't stop looking at her because his gaze found her again right away. "I didn't tell on you. I swear it. You were my favorite professor. I would never have told on you."

Lenobia was still staring at Other Jack, but she spoke to me. "Zoey, who is this, why does he smell so foul, and what the hell is he talking about?"

"Remember Aphrodite's vision?"

"Of course."

"Well, it wasn't metaphoric. This is Other Jack. He came through the bloody fountain thing. Along with a horde of really creepy, dangerous red vampyres. They all smell bad—like Stevie Rae and the other red fledglings used to before Aphrodite sacrificed her humanity for them. You can't reach the Depot Restaurant because they attacked it. Aphrodite tased Other Jack. That's why he's here. We're trying to convince him that he's not in the same world he was in earlier today—a world where Neferet is High Priestess and is in charge of two vampyre armies, a red one and a blue one. And, apparently, humans are used as refrigerators in his world. There. You're pretty much caught up."

"You were part of the rebels," Jack repeated, looking a little less shell-shocked than he had when Lenobia had first appeared. "Is—is Persephone still alive?"

"Um, yeah," I said. "I rode her yesterday."

He deflated, sitting heavily on one of the cushy velvet theater seats. "I'm glad. I'm really glad. And the rest of the horses, like Bonny, Mujaji, Anjo. They're all okay?"

"Of course," Lenobia said.

"Could I see them? Not this second. But would you mind if I visited the stables? Even if Stark keeps my hands tied."

Lenobia looked haunted. "In the world you're from, someone killed all of my horses."

She didn't ask it, but Jack answered. "Yes. I'm so sorry. Someone turned you in. You and Travis tried to escape. You—you didn't make it. Neither did the horses."

Lenobia's gaze fell and she closed her eyes. I could see her lips move as she whispered an almost silent prayer. When she raised her face her eyes swam in tears that tracked down her cheeks. "I don't know anything about rebels, or an army, be it red or blue, Jack Twist. In this world we fought to get rid of Neferet before her poison ruined us. I will tell you, though, that if I lived in a world where Neferet was in charge I swear on my life that I would step up and join anyone rebelling against her. My Travis would follow me. My horses would follow me. No matter the cost."

"Truth," Aphrodite said.

"Yep. No question 'bout it," Stevie Rae agreed.

"We're with Lenobia," Rephaim said.

"Absolutely," Damien said. "If a rebel is someone who fights against Neferet, then I'm a rebel."

"Definitely," Stark said. "We battled that bitch once and won. We'd do it again."

"But we don't have to," I told Jack, meeting his gaze steadily. "Neferet isn't in charge of anything here. She tried to take over the world and we stopped her. And there is no war against humans here because we stopped her."

"There is no Neferet here," Jack said slowly. "No armies, either?"

"None," I said firmly. "There are only the Sons of Erebus Warriors, and their job is to protect the House of Night and its priestesses. They also protect the humans of our community. Like right now if you look out on the wall you'll see Warriors patrolling. Those Warriors will allow *any* human who wants sanctuary into the school. We aren't at war against anything except whatever those creatures are who came into this world with you."

Other Jack got up and walked to me. Stark came with him, fully on alert.

"I'm convinced. This isn't my world."

I let out a long breath in relief. "Good. We have questions. A lot of questions."

He nodded. "I'll help you. Would you help me, too? Please?" Red-tinged tears spilled from his eyes.

"I don't know if I can get you back to your world," I said.

"I don't want to go back. Ever. And I don't want to lose myself and turn into a red vampyre. Please. Please. Help me."

15

Zoey

"Of course we'll help you!" Damien gushed. Moving forward he stepped in front of me to take Jack into his arms. He managed to reach Jack and even embraced him awkwardly.

I saw the change happen as soon as Jack's face got close to the soft skin on the side of Damien's neck. His eyes glowed. He pulled his lips back in a snarl and opened his mouth impossibly wide, showing teeth dripping saliva and a too-red tongue.

"No!" Stark shouted, wrenching the two of them apart, and shoving Jack down into a seat. Then he rounded on Damien. "Have you not been paying attention? This is *not* your Jack. Damnit, Damien! Sniff him."

"Would you care how Zoey smelled?" Damien said.

"No. Yes." Stark sighed. "No, I wouldn't care because I'd still love her, but yes, I would pay attention to her scent because it means something's wrong."

"Listen to him, Damien," Jack said. His voice was rough. His eyes still glowed red. "You have to stay away from me. Your blood isn't as sweet as a human's, but I can't always control

141

myself, especially when I get hungry."

"How often do you get hungry?" I asked. I mean, he'd just sucked down a big blood smoothie back in the basement.

"All the time," Stevie Rae answered for him. "Right, Stark?"

Stark nodded solemnly. "She's right. We understand how he feels. He might try—emphasis on the might—but it's still hard to control his thirst for blood."

"Not just blood," Jack spoke slowly, as if forming the words had become difficult. "Living meat. I crave it, too."

"Ohmygoodness," Stevie Rae gasped. "You're cannibals?"

"Not vampyres or fledglings. Not if we don't have to. Humans. We eat humans."

"Like that's any less disgusting?" Stevie Rae said.

Jack's hand was shaking as he wiped away the red tears that stained his cheeks. "I need—I need to feed. Can't concentrate."

"Rephaim, go find Shaunee. She was supposed to be bringing him another smoothie. We're going to take Other Jack back to his room in the basement. Get the blood—a lot of blood—and take it to his room down there. Now."

Rephaim shot out of the auditorium. I faced Jack. "We're going to get you more blood. Actually, we'll keep you in all the blood you can drink, but not flesh. Not human flesh. Never. Do you understand?"

He nodded.

"Can you control yourself enough to walk back to the basement?" I steeled myself and continued in a hard voice totally devoid of emotion. "Because if you can't Aphrodite is going to taze you unconscious again and Stark will carry you."

"I can do it."

"Do not think I'm kidding. You threaten my people and you will be stopped."

"I understand."

"Do you? I'm holding the Taser and I'm the closest to a human in this room. You look sideways at any of us, and I'm going to zap you. Sorry, Damien," Aphrodite said.

Damien hung his head and wiped his eyes with a shaky hand. I knew what Jack had just done—just said—had shaken him to his core. I had to be strong for him. We all did.

"Yes. I understand perfectly," Jack said.

"Good. Let's go. We have a lot of questions and we need answers right away," I said. "Aphrodite and Stevie Rae, please gather the professors in our dining hall and update them on everything we know so far. Lenobia, please go to the infirmary and warn them that there is a probability that they're going to have incoming."

"On my way, High Priestess," Lenobia said, hurrying from the auditorium.

"Hey, don't you want me to come to the basement with you? You might need me to deal with the cannibal." Aphrodite gestured at Jack with the Taser.

"Thanks, but I think Stark, Damien, and I can handle it."

"Want to take this with you?" She offered me the Taser.

"Nah, she has me," Stark said.

"So, you want to take this, right?" Aphrodite said, rolling her eyes at Stark.

I stifled a grin. "Keep it. You never know when you might need it."

Totally serious, Aphrodite nodded. "You're right about that. And here's a little secret: I enjoyed the hell out of using it."

"Oh, Aphrodite," Stark said. "That's no secret."

(

Jack sucked down three full glasses of blood before his eyes stopped glowing.

"Why so much?" I asked. "You seemed okay after just one glass before."

Jack wiped his mouth delicately on the back of his sleeve,

grimacing at the bloodstain on his shirt. "My hunger is more intense because I'm not eating flesh."

"Is that how it is for all red fledglings?" Stark asked.

"Yes. And red vampyres."

I glanced at Damien, whose hand was poised above the pad of paper on which he was supposed to be taking notes on the answers Other Jack was giving us.

"Damien, if this is too much, I can call Stevie Rae down here and she can take notes," I said gently.

Damien shook his head. "No. I can do this. I want to do this." He pulled his eyes from Jack and started writing.

Stark and I shared a look. He shrugged. I'd given everyone a task that took them out of the basement—except Stark and Damien. Stark refused to leave, of course. He still thought Other Jack might try to eat one of us. And I refused to make Damien leave. I hoped I hadn't made a bad decision. Again.

"Okay, then let's hurry and get these questions answered. Jack, I can tell you that we'll probably have more questions later."

"I understand," he said.

"Okay, first, we have red fledglings and vampyres in this House of Night world, but they're different. As you can see by Stark. Um, I don't mean to offend you, but you and the others—though mostly the others—seem very … uh …" I paused, struggling to find a word that wouldn't completely alienate him.

"Blood-crazy and feral like zombies," Stark said.

"Well, yeah, that's one way of putting it." I gave Stark a you're-not-helping look. "Another way is that your people seem much more driven by the blood feeding frenzy than our red fledglings and vamps."

Other Jack nodded. "There are different levels of the feeding frenzy, but it does mostly control us reds."

"So, you don't retain your humanity once you're Marked red?" Damien asked.

Other Jack's eyes were shadowed by sadness. "By the time we

make the Change, the feeding frenzy rules our lives. Some red vampyres can control it enough to function. They're made officers in the Red Army. The rest are soldiers."

"That sounds like all red fledglings make the Change to vampyre," Stark said.

"They do."

"So, you always make the Change to adult vampyre if you're a red fledgling. Okay, what other rules apply to you? Like, can you go out in daylight?" I asked.

"No, we can't be exposed to the sun. Not as fledglings or vampyres. It burns us up."

"What else?" I prompted.

"Well, between sunrise and sunset red fledglings are unconscious. Red vampyres can function, but they're very weak."

"Wait, you mean you literally can't stay awake?" Stark asked.

"Yes. I can feel it right now. Sunrise isn't far away, and already my mind is getting sleepy."

"Okay, we need to hurry up then. What else is different about you and blue vamps and fledglings?" I asked quickly.

Looking more and more exhausted, Other Jack started to tick points off his fingers. "We have to be invited inside a private dwelling to enter. Some red vampyres can use mind control, but they are the same vamps who are officers in the army. Regular red vamps can't concentrate on anything except feeding, so they can't control minds. We heal from wounds quickly, but we have to feed to do so. Oh, and of course, a red vampyre's bite is contagious. I think that's it."

"Rewind," I said as my stomach felt heavy and sick. "What do you mean by contagious?"

Other Jack gave me a surprised look. "You know, if a red vampyre bites a human that human will die within three days, and then within another three days if their body isn't beheaded or burned they rise as red zombies."

"You're going to need to explain that better," Stark said when all I did was stare at Jack.

"That doesn't happen here?" Jack asked.

"No," I said. "Being a vampyre isn't contagious. It's a gift from Nyx, whether you're Marked blue or red."

"Oh, well, being a vampyre isn't contagious in my world, either. That's why we call them zombies. They rise within three days, but they're not human and they're not vampyre. They just lust for blood and living flesh, and then they die. For good this time. Usually within a week or so. Oh, their bite is contagious, too."

"Zombies. Literally," I said.

Other Jack nodded. "Yep. Literally."

"You said you heal from wounds quickly, but I noticed the red vampyres hardly flinched when my arrows struck them—until I shot them through the neck. What's that about?" Stark said.

"We can only be killed by severing our spines or by being burned. Oh, we can starve to death, too, but that takes some time and it's terribly painful. It's how the Red Army disciplines soldiers. They starve them to make them do as they command." Other Jack shuddered delicately, reminding me so much of our Jack that I had to look away from him so he wouldn't see the tears that pooled in my eyes.

"And Neferet is the leader of both the Red and Blue Armies?" Stark asked.

"Yes."

"Um, who exactly is she fighting?" I asked.

"It's more like who *isn't* she fighting," Jack said. "Her armies have taken control of the middle of the US. Rebel and human strongholds are on the east and west coasts. As soon as she defeats them, she's going to take over Europe, but she has to do away with the High Council, first. And that's proving harder than she thought it would be."

"What do you mean by 'taken control of the middle of the US'?" I asked.

"You know, humans are refriger—ur, I mean, they are used to

feed from. Some of them do it willingly. They try to get a blue vampyre to choose them to use as, ur, their private feeder. At least that won't kill them. Well, not if the blue vamp is careful. The rest of the humans are feeders for the Red Army."

"Which is a death sentence," Stark said.

Other Jack nodded.

I felt shaky and sick. What he was talking about wasn't our world, but it was close enough to us—to what might have happened had Neferet gained power—that it was frightening. "Jack, you said Neferet is a High Priestess. What happened to the rest of them?"

"There are no other High Priestesses." Jack shrugged uncomfortably. "I don't know what happened to them. When Neferet created the two armies, and they began to gain control of different states, well, they either renounced their positions, swearing that Neferet was the only High Priestess, or they just disappeared." He cleared his throat before adding, "Or they were made examples of."

"What does that mean?"

Jack's eyes lifted from where he'd been staring at his hands, clenched together on his lap. He met my gaze. "They were beheaded and tied to crosses outside their House of Night."

I shuddered. "Just like she did with Professor Nolan and Lauren Blake. Only here she blamed it on humans so she could start a war. Are you sure Neferet is still mortal?"

"You asked me that before, and I don't know what you mean. She's a vampyre. I don't know anything about her being anything else."

"Is Kalona in your world?" Damien asked suddenly.

"Kalona? What's a Kalona?" said Other Jack.

"A winged immortal—ancient consort of Nyx—but, well, he Fell and caused a bunch of problems for humans for a long time," I explained. "He hooked up with Neferet and then she figured out how to become immortal."

"There's no one like that around Neferet. I'm sure of it."

"Well, that's good," Stark said.

"Where is Nyx?" I blurted the next question burning my mind.

Jack sighed heavily. "Neferet says Nyx is with us. All of us vampyres, whether red or blue. But she's stopped the monthly rituals and circles. She says she worships Nyx privately and then tells her armies what the goddess says. The rebels say that's bull. They say Nyx is firmly on their side."

"I say so, too, and I'm not even in that world," Damien said softly, without looking up from his notepad.

"So, if the depot tunnels are sealed and the red vamps from your world can't get down there, what would be their Plan B? Where would they go to escape the sun?" Stark asked.

"In this world, it's hard to say. In my Tulsa, under downtown and midtown there is a complex system of tunnels. Many are linked. But there are entries to them all over so that no red vamp is ever stuck outside."

I looked at Stark. "They can't enter any private homes or buildings. And we don't have a huge system of tunnels under the city—or at least not yet we don't."

"So we need to take Warriors to the public buildings that do have entrances to tunnels," Stark said.

"Let's try to narrow it down," Damien said. He looked at Other Jack. I could see that he was working hard to keep his face as expressionless as possible. I hated to think about how difficult it must be for Damien—to have Jack back, but to not *really* have *his* Jack back.

"Okay, how?" Jack said.

"We have tunnel entrances in just a few downtown buildings." Damien paused, considering, then listed them. "Besides the system under the depot, there is the section that connects the Philtower to the Philcade. The Atlas Building, the Mid-Continent Tower, the Kennedy Building, and the Exchange Tower, all on Boston, are connected. And then there's a system under the Crowne Plaza and the PAC. Are any of these main entrances to tunnels in your world?"

"Neferet has an apartment in the Philtower building, so those tunnels are busy. There are even cots in those because of officers visiting Neferet. Also, the Atlas Building has a club in it that red vamps go to. A lot." Other Jack paused, looking uncomfortable. "'Cause that's, um, where the officers feed pretty often, so they have cots down there, too."

"I'll bet that's a real happy place," Stark said sarcastically.

Jack's head snapped up. "It makes me sick."

"Oh, really? Sick like when you tried to bite Damien when he hugged you?" Stark stared him down.

Other Jack's cheeks flushed red. "I fight it. I try. But the hunger—it's like a wave that keeps breaking over me. That and the terrible anger that goes with it—it's *awful*. And I know I'm going to drown. It's inevitable that someday I'm going to be a fully Changed red vampyre and the Jack that is me will be gone—or mostly gone. I hate it." Red-tinged tears leaked down his flushed cheeks. "I hate every second of it." His bleeding eyes found Damien. "I don't want to hurt you, but if I'm hungry enough I will. I know you're not my Damien and I'm not your Jack, but I'm so, so sorry."

Damien's head bowed and his tears fell onto his pad of paper, making damp splotches run the ink. "I know. I just don't know what to do."

"Well, the first thing we're going to do is to send Warriors to the Philtower and the Atlas Building," I said, handing Jack and Damien crumpled tissues I dug out of the bottom of my pocket. "We're going to take care of this red vampyre zombie plague, and then we're going to figure out how to fix Other Jack."

Jack held the crumpled tissue against his chest, looking at me with big, familiar eyes. "Really? You're really going to try to fix me?"

"Really." I said it with complete conviction, even though I had no clue how I was going to manage it. "Stark, let's see what's going on with Darius and Marx, and how bad it is at the Depot. I'll send Shaunee down here with more of her blood smoothies."

"I can—" Damien began, but I cut him off.

"No, Damien. You can't be alone with Other Jack. Not until we figure out how to help him control himself. I'm sorry, but it's the way it has to be."

"I understand," Damien said faintly. He stood and went to where Jack was sitting on the end of the bed. "I'll be back. When I can."

Hesitantly, he reached out and rested a hand on Jack's shoulder. I felt more than saw Stark tense at the same time Jack sat up straighter and gripped his hands together, as if to keep himself from touching (*Touching? Or biting? Tearing? Ripping?*) Damien.

"I can't tell you how good it is to see you, Jack. Even under these peculiar circumstances."

Other Jack looked up at him, and my heart squeezed as he smiled a totally Jack smile at Damien. "You sound just like Damien."

"I am Damien." Other Jack's gaze lowered back to his clutching hands. "No, I meant *my* Damien."

"I understand exactly what you meant." Damien spoke so softly I could barely hear him. Then he handed me his notebook and left the room without looking back.

I sighed, feeling heartbroken for both of them. "Other Jack, can you think of anything else we need to know?"

"Yes. Kill them. Kill all of the red vampyres. They're contagious and they're full vampyres. They won't change. I think I remember seeing two officers come through with me, and some fledglings, but mostly it was just soldiers. Red soldiers are vicious—I mean, *real* mean. The only thing you can predict about them is that they live to feed, and they prefer human flesh."

"But they'll eat vampyres, correct?" Stark asked.

"Yes. They'd rather not, though. Like, when they fight the rebels. They just kill them. Drink their blood, and mostly leave their flesh. They don't like the taste."

"Okay, that helps." I smiled at Other Jack. "You did good. At least we know what we're up against. Shaunee will be down soon with your blood. I'll have her put some in your minifridge, too. And you do have cable down here, plus Netflix."

He smiled back at me, looking just like our Jack. "Thanks. I'll be out of it real soon anyway. I can feel sunrise. But I'll need to feed as soon as I wake up, so blood in the fridge is a good idea."

"Is there anything else I can get you?"

"A cure."

"I'm going to try my best," I said.

"Will you let me stay here, in this House of Night world, if you can cure me?" His voice sounded fragile, as if my answer might break it.

"Other Jack, I have no real clue how I opened the passage between our worlds, so doing it again is gonna be difficult."

His gaze never left mine. "But there's a difference between me staying here because you can't send me back, and me staying here because you're letting me."

"You're right. There is. So, let me be clear once and for all. You're welcome here, Other Jack. Very welcome here."

His shoulders slumped in relief as red tears filled his eyes. "Thank you. Thank you so much."

"We'll make this work," Stark said.

"It's going to be okay," I said.

"Promise?"

"Yep. Pinky swear." Automatically, I held my hand out, little finger extended—just as I would've done had it been our Jack.

Other Jack dimpled and hooked his little finger around mine before Stark could step between us. "Totally pinky sworn," he said.

Stark and I left then. We had to, and not just because of the stupid zombie apocalypse we had to prevent. We had to leave because that Jack had touched a raw place in my heart that still belonged to our Jack. It was either leave or dissolve into snot and tears and bittersweet memories ...

16

Zoey

Stark and I hurried into the administrative offices. Shaylin, Nicole, and Grandma Redbird were looking grim.

"Please tell me Kramisha's okay," was all I could make my mouth say.

"She is safe," Grandma said.

I plopped into a chair and tried to prepare myself. "What's the rest of it?"

Shaylin and Nicole stared mutely at Grandma. She came to me and took my hand. "All of the fledglings who were working tonight at the Depot Restaurant were killed."

My hand started to tremble, and Grandma squeezed it tightly.

"One of them managed to get to the trapdoor in the kitchen and close it, bolting it behind her and warning the others before she died of her wounds," Grandma continued.

"Did they get into the tunnels?" I asked.

"No. Thanks to the heroism of that young fledgling," Grandma said.

"Humans?" I held my breath.

Grandma shook her head. "They are all gone, u-we-tsi-a-ge-ya."

"Oh, Goddess," I breathed the word as a prayer. "How many?"

"Seventy-eight humans."

"Holy crap, that's a lot of people." Stark looked as sick as I felt.

"The restaurant was almost filled with people celebrating the holidays," Shaylin said.

"How many fledglings and vampyres?"

"All of the waitstaff. There were seven of them. They were all fledglings," Grandma said sadly. "So, young. They were all so young."

"There was also a bartender. He was a blue vampyre," Shaylin said.

"Derek," Stark's voice was thick with sorrow. "I knew him. He was a better bartender than archer, but a good guy."

"The chef, a sous chef, a line chef, and two dishwashers. All of them dead," Nicole said. Her voice shook like my hands.

"Chef Zachary? He's dead?" I kept shaking my head back and forth, back and forth. And then a terrible knowing skittered across my skin. "I have to talk to Darius. And Marx. They have to behead or burn the human bodies."

"Zoey, what is this about?" Grandma asked.

"The red vampyres from the other world are contagious. It's something in their bite. When they bite humans, they infect them. If they aren't beheaded or burned they rise in three days."

"Oh, Great Earth Mother!" Grandma gasped.

"Are they vampyres when they rise?" Shaylin asked. She and Nicole were sitting with their chairs pressed together as if to share the shock.

"No. It's bad. They're mindless things that have to feed. And their bites are contagious, too. Then they die, for good, in another week," I explained.

"But not before they infect a bunch more people," Stark said.

"It's the zombie apocalypse. In Tulsa. Unfuckingbelievable."

We turned to see Aphrodite standing in the doorway. She looked at me. "Don't worry. Stevie Rae and I clued all the professors in on

153

what's going on. Well, we didn't know about this latest horribleness, but still. Stevie Rae went to say, 'Bye, bye, Birdie,' before Rephaim flies away … Holy shit, this sounds bad. How's Other Jack?"

"Fine. Except for his hunger and the fact that he's going to turn into a contagious, zombie-plague-spreading, nearly mindless red vampyre eventually. Fine," I said.

"Seriously?" Shaunee said, peeking her head into the office. "Other Jack's a zombie?"

I sighed. "No. But the bite of an adult red vampyre from his world turns humans into something like zombies. Speaking of Other Jack, could you please grab a bunch more blood and take it down to him? He needs enough to drink now, and a bunch for his minifridge for when he wakes up after sunset. Oh, and don't go down there alone." I let my gaze take in the whole room. "No one goes down there to see him alone. Do not trust him. He looks like our Jack. Sometimes he even sounds like our Jack."

"But he's not," Stark said firmly. "He has a hunger that only Stevie Rae and I fully understand. Believe us. He can't control it."

"I'll get Erik to go with me. He's FaceTiming Joss about the new *Fantasyworld* episode."

"Take this." Aphrodite handed her the Taser. "But I want it back."

"Okay, no problem." Shaunee left, calling over her shoulder, "Hey, a bunch of SUVs just pulled up out front. I think the Warriors are back."

We didn't even have time to get out of the office when Warriors rushed into the building, bringing frigid air, snow, and a terrible sense of bleakness with them.

"Get the men fed. We have a job left to do." Darius spoke somberly to the Warriors with Detective Marx standing beside him looking equally as grim and unnaturally pale.

Aphrodite got to Darius first. She flew into his arms and then stepped back quickly. "Is any of that blood yours?"

"No."

"Are you okay?"

"No. It was—" he shuddered. "It was horrendous. Almost as bad as the Mayo."

"Where's Kramisha?" I asked.

Darius met my eyes. "She chose to stay in the tunnels with the red fledglings. She's leading them in casting a circle and sending up prayers to Nyx for those who were killed." He shook his head. "I cannot imagine the carnage that would have happened had we not installed those heavy, bolted doors. Those creatures couldn't get in, though they did dent the steel trapdoor so badly that it will need to be cut off its hinges to be removed."

"That's probably a good thing. No one should go into that kitchen until it has been cleaned," Marx said.

"But they're okay? Kramisha and the rest of the students who weren't working at the restaurant?" I asked.

"They are shaken, but physically they are well," Darius said.

"Okay, come into the office," I told them. "Shaylin and Nicole, please get Darius and Marx something warm to drink." Both men were covered with snow. Red snow. I tried not to look too closely at their clothes.

"I shall bring these two young Warriors some towels. Perhaps they would feel better if they could dry off," Grandma said.

"Yes, thank you, Grandma," I said. Then I faced Darius and Marx. "Okay, this is going to be hard to hear, so I'm going to say it fast. Here's what we've found out from Other Jack."

Before I could begin, Marx interrupted. "Who is Other Jack?"

"He's from an alternative House of Night world, which is where those other red fledglings and vampyres came from," I said. "He's a lot like our Jack. Remember? The one who died about a year ago in that freak accident when he fell from a ladder and landed on a sword."

Marx nodded quickly. "The accident you didn't think was one, but never were able to prove otherwise?"

"Right," I said. "Here's what he's told us about his world."

I put it all out there for them. Told them everything—adding the part about the tunnels and that I was going to try to figure out a way to save Other Jack from his impending doom. When I finished there was a long silence, then Darius turned to Aphrodite and put his hands on her shoulders.

"I know it's something bad. Just say it fast," she said.

"Detective Marx got a call from St. John's emergency room. Your mother staggered into the ER not long ago. She's been bitten, Aphrodite. By a red vampyre."

Aphrodite wobbled a little, like the ground beneath her had shaken. Then her gaze found mine. "She's infected."

"She is," I said.

"And Other Jack says she's going to die. For sure. Within three days."

"Yes."

"I am so sorry, my beauty," Darius spoke quietly to her, pulling her into his arms.

I could see her blue eyes, bright with unshed tears.

"All of those humans. The ones killed at your restaurant. They're going to have to be decapitated or cremated, correct?" Marx spoke into the silence.

"Yes. That's what Other Jack said."

"And you trust him?" Marx asked me.

"I do. He wants sanctuary here, so he has every reason to tell us the truth," I said.

"Then they need to be cremated," Marx said, sounding a lot older than his years. "I'll tell the families myself." He looked at Stark. "How long until sunrise?"

"An hour and a half," Stark said.

"And you said you're pretty sure you know where that goddamned horde went? It's blizzard conditions out there since the wind picked up. We couldn't track those monsters."

"I would've thought you could track their blood trails," Stark said.

156

"That's what we thought at first, too," Darius said. "But they took care of that."

"Huh? How?" I asked.

"They rolled in the snow. Like animals. And then they scattered, all in different directions. We can't even get canines out there because of the damn weather. They can't track in a blizzard."

"We think we know where they are," I said. "Other Jack told us where they'd go to ground in their world. They're all red fledglings or vampyres. That means they have to get under cover before sunrise, or they'll be dead."

"Even if it keeps snowing and hides the sun?" Marx asked.

"I don't know if they're more sensitive than we are," Stark said. "But I would have trouble being outside during the day for long, even under cover of snow."

"So, they have to find shelter," Marx said.

"And it has to be in a public building. They can't enter a private residence without being invited," I added. "We need to go to the Philtower tunnels and the tunnels under the Atlas Building. But first we need to send Warriors to the entrances to the other tunnels. Have them be showy. They need to stand where they can be clearly seen by anyone sneaking around outside looking to get in."

Marx nodded. "Limit their safe places."

"Act like we do not know that they'll target the Philtower and the Atlas Building," Stark said. "Then close in after sunrise and wipe them out."

"I'll get my men right on it," Marx said, but I put a hand on his arm, stopping him.

"It needs to be Warriors. They can't be turned into, well, for lack of a better word—zombies," I said.

Marx sighed. "Okay. Yeah. I get it. Your Warriors will take the lead on this one."

"But the Warriors will need to look like TPD," Stark said. "If they think they're only dealing with humans, they'll get sloppy.

They have no idea that vampyres and humans work together in this world."

"Good point," Marx said. "I'll get dispatch on the horn and put the word out to have someone get the hell over here with a bunch of uniform trench coats and hats."

"Also, be sure all your cops know not to get bitten by any of those creatures," Stark said.

"Put out another word," I said. "Tell Tulsa to stay inside. *All* of Tulsa. Don't even let the snowplows go out there. We have to keep humans safe from this infection."

"I'll call the mayor's office and brief him. He'll put out an emergency bulletin telling everyone to stay inside because of the blizzard. But you know Okies."

"We stand outside and watch the tornados come. I know. Let's hope we show better sense in the winter," I said.

"One can dream," Aphrodite said as Marx started to head back to his truck to radio the really terrible news back to the station.

He paused at the door and looked at me. "Do you know how they got into this world?"

I made the decision quickly. He deserved the truth. Tulsa deserved the truth. "Kalona warned me through a dream that danger was coming." Marx's eyes widened at the mention of his dead friend, but he stayed silent, letting me finish. "He thought it might have something to do with Neferet, so we were casting a protective spell over the grotto just in case she was trying to stir up trouble."

"I thought you said Neferet wasn't behind this." I wouldn't have thought it possible, but Marx blanched even paler.

"We haven't seen any sign of Neferet, but she is alive and well in the zombie world," I said.

"Figures," he muttered. "If it wasn't something Neferet did, what happened?"

"My mother showed up and screwed up our spell," Aphrodite said.

"Actually, I think I messed up our spell," I said. "It was because

158

Mrs. LaFont was screaming at us, and I shouldn't have let her get to me, but I did." I drew a big breath and then told on myself. "My hand slipped. I cut myself. And at the same time I remember thinking that if a zombie apocalypse happened in Tulsa it wouldn't be such a bad thing if they ate Mrs. LaFont." Miserable, I stared at Aphrodite. "I'm so sorry. I really didn't mean it. And this is all my fault."

Aphrodite stared back at me, and then she started laughing. It began as a soft giggle, and grew until she had to lean against Darius, who looked utterly confused and more than a little worried.

"Uh, I'm going to get the ball rolling on warning people," Marx said, throwing Aphrodite a concerned sidewise glance as he left.

I went to her. She was wiping her eyes. Her laughter had dissipated to soft giggles interspersed with snorts. "Hey. I'm so, so sorry. Truly."

"Oh, Z. It wasn't *all* your fault. I was basically thinking the same thing you were," she said.

Shaylin cleared her throat and our attention shifted to her. "Um. Me, too."

"Me, too, what?" Stevie Rae asked as she hurried into the office, holding Rephaim's hand.

"When Mrs. LaFont showed up at the park I wished she'd drop dead," Shaylin said.

"Oh, yeah," Stevie Rae nodded, making her blond curls bounce. "I was wishin' she'd go away and stop pesterin' Aphrodite—for good."

"And I'll bet if we ask Shaunee, she'll say she was thinking something about the same," Aphrodite said. "Don't stress, Z. My mother has that effect on people. Lots of them have wished she'd die. They just didn't have the power to make the wish come true. Our circle does."

Ah, hell ... I thought as I pulled Aphrodite into my arms, hugging her fiercely.

17

Damien

On autopilot, Damien made his way from the basement under the Field House to the room that had been assigned to him in the guest wing of the professors' quarters. He walked slowly, gazing out at the snowy predawn morning, noting that all the students, fledgling or human, seemed to finally have retired to the dorms.

He envied them.

Sometimes he wished he could go back to being one of them. Actually, lately he'd wished it a lot more often than not.

The truth was Damien felt empty and alone. Adam had tried diligently to get him to shake off this terrible melancholy, but all of his attempts—be they romantic and sexy, or, toward the end, angry and confused—had only served to make Damien feel more alone.

It was like there was something wrong with him.

His parents used to say that he thought too much and didn't go outside and play enough. Well, one good thing about being an adult vampyre—he didn't have to suffer through his parent's pathetic attempts to pretend like they wanted him around.

Actually, after he'd been Marked, they had pretty much stopped being his parents. Though they used to send the same sports-themed birthday gifts every year. But this last year, after he made the Change, the gifts stopped. The sporadic calls stopped. The visits—not that there had been many of them to begin with—stopped. Period. It was a relief. Or, at least that's what he told himself.

He'd reached out. Not long after he'd moved to New York. He'd called. Their phone number had been changed. The email he sent them had bounced back undeliverable. He'd sent them a postcard—a gorgeous shot of the Statue of Liberty—letting them know he'd been transferred to New York, inviting them to visit any time. It had been returned with a handwritten note refusing delivery. That was the last time he'd tried to reach them.

He had friends. A lot of them, actually. At the New York House of Night he'd been welcomed eagerly—as had most of the changes Zoey's new Council had initiated. Basically, things were going well. Really well.

Except he missed everything about Tulsa. Even the moronic redneck Bubbas and Bubbettes. At least they were Okies, and *his* redneck morons.

His homesickness was his guilty secret. His new friends were great—smart, well-traveled, interesting, and a lot of fun. There definitely was a *lot* of fun to be had in the Big Apple.

Yet, still, Damien found himself alone in his very hip condo on the New York House of Night campus pulling up Tulsa's midtown real estate sites and looking at houses for sale—just so he could see the old neighborhood that surrounded the House of Night. Home. Just so he could see home.

There was definitely something wrong with him.

Damien reached his room and entered the spacious, luxurious suite. He went straight to the kitchenette and began brewing a pot of tea, and while it brewed he held the delicate porcelain teacup in his hand and stared at nothing.

When the electric pot beeped, he jerked and shook himself. He put the tea service on a tray and placed it on the coffee table. Then he easily located his carry-on and suitcase where one of the fledglings had put them on the luggage holders just outside the closet. Inside his carry-on he found the book he'd grabbed at the airport, *Last Seen Leaving* by Caleb Roehrig, and went to the plush velvet settee. While he added almond milk and cubes of sugar to the cup, he lifted the school's landline and pressed 9 for the administrative office.

"House of Night, Tulsa. This is Shaylin," she said after one ring.

"It's Damien."

"Hi! I heard all about Other Jack trying to bite your neck, and the zombies and such. Are you okay?"

"I'm fine. I'm in my guest suite, but with the cell service still out I'm not sure how to find Zoey."

"Oh, she's in and out of the office. I can tell her to call you next time she comes in," Shaylin said.

"That'd be nice. Thank you. She's planning to send Warriors downtown to trap the other red vampyres, isn't she?"

"Well, yeah, that seems to be the plan."

"Would you let her know I'm ready to go with her if she needs me?"

"Absolutely. Hey, are you sure you're okay. You sound a little—I don't know—off. No offense."

"No offense taken. I am off. Probably more than a little—what with Other Jack and everything. But I'll be fine. Just let her know I'm here if she needs me."

"Will do. Damien?"

"Yes?"

"Remember we're all here for you. All of the Nerd Herd. We love you."

Damien's head bowed as he fought against tears. "Thank you," he managed to say faintly before hanging up.

Damien wiped his eyes and tried to sound cheery. "Okay. Well, Z knows I'm here, and she'll call if she needs me. I'll have a pot of chamomile tea, read a little, and then maybe even nap. Actually, napping sounds like a good idea." His shoulders slumped and he stared at the closed cover of the book he had been looking forward to reading.

He missed Jack. *His* Jack. But his Jack was dead. Other Jack, as Aphrodite and everyone was calling him, was downstairs. Alive. He wasn't *his* Jack, but he looked like him. He even sounded like him sometimes. And any part of Jack was better than the horrid gaping hole that was his absence.

"What would happen if I went back down there—to his room—and just sat with him?" Damien murmured to himself. He glanced at the clock on the mantel of the unlit fireplace. It was a few minutes after six, so he had about an hour and a half until Jack was unconscious.

"No. I have to stay away. I have to remember he's dangerous, and he's *not mine*." Damien pressed his hand against his mouth, trying to stifle a sob.

There was a soft knock on his door.

Damien cleared his throat and wiped at his eyes. "Who is it?"

"Grandma Redbird. Might I come in, please, Damien?"

Surprised, Damien hurried to open the door. She was standing there with a small picnic basket held in the crook of her arm, smiling up at him and looking sweet and familiar and so filled with grandma-love that he wanted to put his head on her shoulder and cry himself to sleep.

Instead, he said, "Of course. It's really good to see you. Would you like some chamomile tea?"

"I would, dear," Grandma said.

He motioned for her to have a seat on the settee while he went to the cupboard for another cup.

"These guest rooms turned out beautifully," she said. "Zoey told me you did most of the redecorating work on them. You're really very talented, Damien."

"Thank you. I enjoy design. Before I was Marked I planned on going to SCAD. That's the Savannah College of Art and Design. They have a program located in Lacoste, France. I was going to try for a study-abroad semester there. It's why I started learning French in middle school. Would you like almond milk and sugar?"

"Just a little milk, please. Well, you're certainly a gifted decorator." Grandma's face wrinkled into a cherubic smile. "Though I believe decorator is probably the wrong title for something this grand." With a sweeping gesture, she took in the beautiful suite.

"The more official title is interior design, but I don't think it's offensive to call it home décor, or home decorating. Of course I also don't have a degree or a career in the field, so I could definitely be wrong."

"Ah, semantics. They can certainly bog us down, can they not?"

Damien nodded and sipped his tea before asking, "Can I do something for you, Mrs. Redbird?"

"First, you can promise never to call me Mrs. Redbird again. I'm Sylvia or Grandma, whichever you prefer."

"I prefer Grandma," Damien said.

"As do I, dear," she said. "I came here not because I need you to do something for me, but because I would like to do something for you."

"Me?" He stopped the motion of his cup midway to his mouth.

"You," she said firmly before opening the lid of the small picnic basket. Carefully, she pulled out a bundle wrapped in a brightly colored scarf. "I see your sadness, wahuhi."

"Yes, I'm sad. Jack is downstairs. But he isn't. Jack is alive. But he isn't. I think being sad is a correct response."

"I was not admonishing you, child. I was only acknowledging the depth of your grief." Grandma Redbird touched his cheek gently. "But you and I know this sadness has nothing to do with Jack."

"I don't know what you mean." His words denied it, but the fact that he spoke them in a voice pitched much higher than usual revealed the truth.

Grandma said nothing. She simply watched him with knowing eyes and a kind expression.

Damien bowed his head, unable to meet her gaze any longer.

"You have no reason to show shame. Sometimes our spirit weeps. When it does you must work at comforting it, and then healing it."

"Can—can you do that for me?" he asked hesitantly.

"No, wahuhi, no one can do that for you. That is something you must do yourself. I can help strengthen you, though, so that you may begin the job of healing."

He lifted his head. "What if I can't heal?"

"Then you will either live miserably, or you will die. It is your choice—and only your choice." Grandma cocked her head to the side, studying him. "But I believe you will choose wisely. I have always sensed much wisdom and kindness within you, though you rarely use either for yourself. May I ask you a rather impertinent question?"

"Yes."

"Do you want to heal? Do you want to live embracing joy and all the messiness it brings with it?"

Damien opened his mouth to give an automatic reply, but Grandma Redbird lifted her hand in an imperious gesture. "Do not answer by rote. Many people do not want to embrace joy—not in this lifetime. If you are one of those people, have the courage to speak your life path in truth. I will not judge you—that I swear."

"Why would someone not want to embrace joy?"

"Because a life filled with depression—sadness and stress and the tumult and drama that comes with such a life—can be addicting. After you live with it long enough, you only feel normal if you are mired in darkness. No, I do not mean the Darkness that is accompanied by evil. I mean the darkness that is an absence of joy, of lightness of spirit, of happiness. Depression is an abyss—a pit from which it is difficult to emerge. You must truly want everything that the absence of sadness brings with it—all the victories and defeats of a life lived open to the endless possibilities of love and light and laughter."

"In other words, a life where I could get my heart broken. Again."

"Yes, child."

"Or I could be disappointed by friends and family."

"Or, in a life lived fully, embracing joy, you could choose the wrong career path or make decisions that hurt others even though you do so with the best intentions, and so, so many other mistakes you would not make if you retreated within yourself and closed off those possibilities. Or if you ended your life. So, think before you answer me. Do you want to heal?"

Damien felt his eyes well and then overflow, but he didn't look away from Grandma Redbird's knowing gaze. Finally, he whispered, "What if I'm not brave enough to open myself to that kind of pain?"

"Then you will not know that kind of joy, either."

"I want it, though. I want joy," Damien whispered desperately.

Grandma leaned forward and spoke earnestly. "Then believe in yourself. Believe you are brave and worthy of such joy."

"Yes." The word came out as a whisper and Damien stopped, cleared his throat, and began again—this time in a voice that filled the room. "Yes. I want to heal. I want to live a life filled with joy."

Grandma's smile was like the full moon beaming on a winter-white field. "Of course you do, child. And you shall. Now, let us begin."

She opened the folded cloth, pushed the tea set aside, and began placing items on the table: a large shell, two smudge sticks, a dove's feather, a purple candle which she lit, and a handful of turquoise that he realized was a long necklace.

"I thought you said you couldn't heal me," he said.

"I cannot. But I can cleanse your spirit and wrap you in protection so that you might begin to walk the path that will lead you to joy," she said as she lit the purple candle.

"All right. I'll do whatever you say I should," he said, sitting up straighter.

"I say you must make your peace with Jack."

"Jack's dead."

"Jack is in a quaint little room under the Field House."

"That isn't my Jack, Grandma. That's Other Jack."

"Does it truly matter whose Jack he is supposed to be?" Grandma spoke as she held a thick smudge stick of white sage to the flame of the purple candle. "Isn't he, in any form, eternally your Jack? Would you not love him in any body—male or female?"

"I would." Damien felt a rush of emotional shock as he realized his automatic response was actually the truth. *I would love Jack no matter what body he returned to me in—male, female—it just wouldn't matter. He would still be my true love.*

"And couldn't you understand that his spirit—that essence that is truly Jack—might be the same, even though the body it houses, the personality that goes with it, could be somewhat different because of different life experiences?"

Damien nodded thoughtfully. "Yes, Grandma, I think I could."

"So you believe you could learn to love Jack again, even if he'd been reborn into a totally different body. Perhaps a lovely Asian man who has never known a vampyre or even a fledgling? Or a woman whose only experience with the gay community is her homophobic family railing against what they call sinners?"

"It would still be Jack in there somewhere. Yes, I would want to be with him. Or her."

"Then learn to love him again in his own body."

Damien jerked back as if she'd slapped him. "Oh, Goddess, Grandma! I didn't think of it like that." He felt a sudden, amazing lightening of the rubber band of stress that squeezed his chest. "I was so wrapped up in him being Other Jack that I couldn't see the truth. It *doesn't* matter. If he's not my Jack at this instant, I know he can be, will be, *my* Jack again."

"That is right, wahuhi. Follow that path. Hope will lead you to joy."

"We fell in love once. We can fall in love again."

"Of course you can, child. Of course you can." Grandma reached for the long strand of turquoise beads and lifted it, settling it around Damien's neck so that it draped down his chest. Then she took the smoking sage bundle in her left hand and the dove feather in her right. "Please stand."

Damien did as Grandma asked, stepping a little to the side of the settee so that she could easily move around him. Then she began smudging him, rhythmically moving in a tight, clockwise circle, using the dove feather to waft the smoke as she sang a heartbeat of a song in Cherokee.

She circled him four times and then rested the smoking sage bundle on the oyster shell. Still singing and moving her feet rhythmically, she lit the long braided strand of sweet grass and began the process all over again.

When she finished her four rotations, she motioned for Damien to bow his head so that she could rest her hand on it, blessing him.

"Oh, great Earth Mother, help this soft-hearted wahuhi to always speak the truth, to listen with an open mind, to remember peace must always first be found within. Protect him as he walks his life path, open to joy, speaking the truth, and believing in carrying peace within."

Then, she tiptoed and oh, so gently, kissed the filled-in crescent moon in the center of his forehead. "Nyx, I seal my blessing with a kiss from me to you."

"Thank you, Grandma." Damien felt as if he stood taller, and as he moved he seemed lighter. He started to lift the turquoise beads over his head to return them to her, but her hand stayed him.

"These are yours now. I strung them for you, singing each bead into place with a protection prayer. I don't want you to take them off until after the next full moon."

"You mean, wear them all the time? Even in the shower?"

She smiled and nodded. "Yes, child. And to bed as well. They will help you on your new path. They will also help Jack."

"Jack?"

"I understand that as he is now he has trouble controlling his impulse to feed."

"Yes, Stark and Zoey don't want me to be alone with him because of it. They're probably right."

"They are concerned for your well-being. We all are. But it isn't Jack's hunger from which you need to be protected. It is the illness of his spirit. I felt it as soon as I saw him. His spirit is steeped in Darkness." Grandma Redbird pressed her palm against the turquoise beads. "Darkness is pained by this sacred stone's protective powers. It will weaken the Darkness in Jack's spirit enough that he will be able to control his terrible hunger for a time."

"That's amazing, Grandma. Thank you so much!"

"Child, this isn't a cure for Jack's illness. I do not have that power—neither do these stones. Neither do you. Remember that. Be wise. Go to him now. Talk with him. Get to know this Other Jack who is just another version of your true love."

"I will." Damien's sense of relief was overwhelming. He ran a trembling hand through his hair. "How much time will these beads give me with him?"

"You should be safe until he sleeps with the rising of the sun." She closed and handed him the small picnic basket. "Take this with you. I packed it with a little something for you both."

"It's a lot smaller than your normal picnic basket, Grandma."

"Oh, I have many such baskets—each the correct size for its purpose."

Damien peered inside to find a thermos, which was warm to his touch, and two beautiful crystal wine glasses. Damien raised his eyebrow at Grandma. "Coffee?"

She smiled knowingly. "Blood. Warm and fresh. Shaunee got it for me." Damien blinked in shock, which had Grandma giggling and looking like a precocious girl. "Do you think I do not know you drink blood, wahuhi?"

"I, well, yes. I suppose I did know you knew. But I didn't expect you to be so comfortable with it."

She lifted one shoulder. "It does not shock me. Do you know my people used to eat the fresh, still-bleeding livers from the animals killed to feed the tribe? It was done with respect and appreciation for the life given. This blood was donated, not forced, and it was accepted with respect and appreciation. I see no fundamental difference in the two."

"Thank you." Before he closed the lid of the basket, Damien slipped in the book he'd been planning to read—just in case Jack was sleepier than he anticipated. He could, at least for a little while, sit in his room and watch him while he slept.

"And, Damien, I want you to take someone with you to see Jack." Grandma interrupted his thoughts.

"But I thought you gave me this so that I could be alone with him," he said, gently touching the beads. They felt cool and soft beneath his fingers, and they seemed to vibrate slightly with every beat of his heart.

"This someone is special. She's waiting outside your door. You'll find a little something for her under the thermos and the wine glasses." Grandma waved her hand dismissively at him. "Go, now. I will tidy this and show myself out. You don't have long until sunrise."

Damien smoothed his shirt, glancing around for a mirror.

"You look perfect. Just go. He is alone down there. He is frightened. And he is struggling against Darkness that has a deep, firm hold on his soul. Go to him. He needs you as much as you need him."

"I will. Right now. Thank you, again." Damien bent and kissed her gently on her soft cheek, and whispered, "I love you, Grandma."

"I love you, too. Never forget how very much you are loved in this lifetime. Wahuhi, a family isn't made from blood. It is made from spirit. The spirit of your House of Night family is very strong."

Damien went to the door, but before he opened it he looked back at Grandma. "What does 'wahuhi' mean?"

"Owl. I decided if Stark is a rooster, then you must be an owl."

"I like it," Damien said. Then he opened the door slowly and peered out. "Hello?" he said to the empty hall.

Woof!

He looked down to see the blond lab sitting prettily, tail wagging as if she'd just been given her heart's dream. "Duchess! OMG, it's fabulous to see you! I've missed you so much!" Damien went on his knees and she practically crawled into his lap as he laughed and rained kisses on her sweet, familiar face. "Hey, want to go see Jack?"

Woof! Woof! The tail wagging increased to an almost maniacal level.

"Okay, let's go then!" Damien had to force himself not to jog. Duchess stayed at his side, wagging happily and doggie-smiling up at him. He rested his hand near her head so that he could touch her reassuring warmth. "Jack's going to be different," he told her earnestly, and the lab fixed her intelligent gaze on him, listening carefully. "He's going to smell different. A lot different. And he might not know you. But, please don't let that scare you. Be nice to him. Please. For me."

Woof! Woof! Woof!

Damien hoped three barks meant yes.

18

Damien

Damien paused outside the door to Jack's room, nodding to the Son of Erebus Warrior who had been stationed there as a guard. Thankfully, the Warrior was there to keep Jack in—not to keep people out.

Damien was nervous. Very nervous. Duchess sat beside him, tongue lolling and tail wagging happily.

Perhaps I should be a dog, he thought. They seem to find happiness easily.

He raised his hand to knock, and then couldn't do it.

Duchess looked up at him and whined.

"Okay. I know. Okay." He drew a deep breath and knocked.

"Come on in," Jack said.

Duchess' ears pricked instantly at the sound of his voice.

"That's right. It's Jack," Damien whispered to her as he keyed the numbers into the deadbolt lock on the door. "Ready?" When she wagged and danced around enthusiastically, Damien decided a little decorum might help. "Sit, Duchess," he told her. "And wait."

He opened the door.

Jack was sitting on the bed, watching TV. He had a half-finished liter of blood in his hand. He'd taken his shoes off and had his feet tucked cross-legged under him. His eyes went to Damien first. He opened his mouth, and then Duchess whined and his gaze snapped down to the big, blond lab sitting beside Damien.

"A dog? Really?" Jack's voice broke adorably, reminding Damien so much of his true love that he wanted to weep.

Instead he forced himself to smile. "Yes, indeed. A dog. Really."

"I used to love dogs. I mean, I know we're supposed to all be cat people, but I can't help it. Plus, I don't think there's anything wrong with loving dogs."

"Right? That's something we've always agreed on. Do you recognize her?"

"Her?"

Damien nodded and patted Duchess on the head. "The dog's a her. And her name is Duchess."

"She's beautiful."

"She certainly is. So, you don't recognize her?"

Jack tore his gaze from Duchess to meet Damien's eyes. "No. There aren't any dogs at the House of Night."

"She's not with Stark?"

"General Stark? No. Or if she is, I've never seen or heard about her," Jack said. "Wait, she's Stark's dog?"

"Yes, but he shares her. With us."

Jack's eyes got huge. "Are you being serious?"

"Ask her."

Jack swallowed visibly and shifted until his legs dangled over the side of the bed and he faced the two of them. He put the liter jug on his bedside table and then rubbed his hands nervously together. "But cats hate us. All of us. Don't dogs, too?"

"Us?"

"All red fledglings and vampyres," Jack explained.

Damien thought quickly. He remembered that Stark hadn't

wanted Duchess to be around him when he was struggling with his own humanity as a young red fledgling. He looked down at Duchess and the lab gazed back at him with eyes filled with unconditional love and acceptance. And he *knew* Duchess wouldn't reject Other Jack. Like Grandma Redbird, Duchess would see within him to the Jack they loved.

Then he looked at Jack, who was staring with longing at Duchess.

"Ask Duchess. She knows you. She'll accept you," Damien said, and registered the flush of surprise and brief expression of raw happiness that passed over Jack's face.

"Duchess? Would you come here, pretty girl?"

Duchess glanced quickly up at Damien. "Go on," he told her with a grin.

She bounded to Other Jack, wiggling joyously as he petted her and told her how soft and special and beautiful she was.

So like his Jack. So very much like his sweet, lost Jack.

"Hey, are you okay?"

Damien hadn't realized he'd been standing there with tears flowing down his face until Jack spoke.

"Oh, yes." He swiped at his cheeks. "Sorry. It's just ..." And his words trailed away because the truth was that it was just too painful to put to words.

"I know," Other Jack spoke softly. "Would you like to come in and sit down?" He motioned to the chair beside the little desk under which the TV was mounted. "Or maybe that's not such a good idea."

"I would like to come in. But how do you feel? Do you think you can control yourself?"

Jack kept petting Duchess with one hand while he reached for the jug of blood with the other and took a long gulp before answering. "Yes. I've had a lot to drink, and sunrise is close enough that I'm feeling sleepy already."

"Well, then, I'll come in for a little while." Damien took the chair from the desk and moved it beside the bed. Not too close, but not as far away as it had been, either. He set the picnic basket beside him, wondering when would be the right time to share what was inside with Jack.

They sat there in silence while Jack drank from his blood jug and petted Duchess. Finally, Damien said, "You have Netflix down here, you know." He jerked his chin at the television.

"Oh, good. Movies," Other Jack said, picking up the remote. "Do you want to watch something with me?"

"Sure. It'll need to be something short, though, if you're going to pass out pretty soon."

"Um, do you have a series here called *Make the Date*?"

"I don't think so. What is it?"

"OMG, it's awesomesauce. It's about these two guys—gay, of course." Jack paused.

"Of course," Damien said automatically. Just as he had said so, so many times before. He blinked fast, not wanting to spoil the moment with tears. "What about the two guys?"

"Well, it's a dating reality show. Only the gays run the whole thing—who's fixed up with who, what they wear, how their hair and makeup look, where they go on the date. They even get to choose if the couples have another date together, or they can trade them for another contestant on the show. At the end of each season there is *at least* one proposal. And drama. So much drama. You'd love it."

"It sounds divine, but I'm sure we don't have it here. We do have a show I'm 100 percent sure you'll love. It's called *Project Runway*. Ever heard of it?"

"Nope."

"Okay, good. Give me the remote and I'll find the latest season for you. Wait till you see Tim Gunn. He's fantastic. I actually met him recently at a House of Night party in New York, and he's as fantastic in real life as he seems on the show." Damien leaned forward, his arm extended and hand held out for the remote.

Without any hesitation, Jack gave him the remote.

Their fingers touched. Their eyes met.

Slowly, ever so slowly, Damien splayed his fingers so that even though the remote was between them, he could still feel the warmth of Jack's skin.

When Jack's eyes began to turn rust colored, Damien released him and leaned back in the chair as if nothing had happened.

"Okay, let's see. Oh, here's the button." He was punching in P-R-O-J-E-C-T when Jack's words tore at his heart.

"I missed you so much. You left me. All alone. In that terrible, terrible world. You left me."

Damien put the remote in his lap and turned his chair to face Other Jack.

"In this world, it was *you* who left me."

"Not on purpose, right? Zoey said my death was made to look like an accident, even though she thinks it had something to do with Neferet. But whether it did or not, I for sure didn't go on purpose. You did. You killed yourself."

Damien drew a deep breath and let it out slowly before he could speak. "How? How did I kill myself?"

"You ran a bath and slit your wrists. I found you like that. Dead. Cold. Bloody. It was the worst thing that has ever happened to me. Not even this," he gestured violently to the outline of the red crescent on his forehead, "is worse."

"I'm sorry, Jack. I'm so sorry." Then, slowly, Damien began to tell Other Jack what he had never told anyone ever before. "But I understand your Damien. I've felt that same depression—that same hopelessness."

"In this world, too?"

Damien nodded.

"But only after I died, right?"

Damien sighed heavily. "No. Before. A long time before. I've felt sad and broken for as long as I can remember. It's why I've always been into books and studying. It helps me escape. And my depression got better when I was Marked and came here. I was accepted here. I wasn't bullied anymore, or not much anyway. Well, not at all after Erik Night made me his roommate, but that's another story. Then you were Marked, and we fell in love. And I thought the terrible sadness had gone away, but it hadn't. It was like it was sleeping and waiting."

"For what?"

"For a quiet time. A normal time. A time when I wasn't newly in love, or busy helping Z save the world. Basically, it was waiting for life to go on. And then it woke up, and I've been trying to put it back to sleep ever since. It's just today, just a few minutes ago, that I realized there is no putting it to sleep. I have to fix it, heal it—heal myself."

"How?"

"I'm not really sure, but I do know coming down here and being with you is a step toward healing. I also know I have to talk about my feelings. Have to admit I need help." Damien held out his hand. Hesitatingly, Other Jack took it. "I love you, Jack Twist. In any world. In any form. I love you, and if it is within my power, I will never, ever leave you. I want you to know that."

"I love you, too, Damien. All I want is you. You're all I've wanted since the day I met you."

Damien couldn't help himself. He didn't want to help himself. He wanted Jack. He pulled on Jack's hand, bringing him closer. Carefully, moving deliberately so that Jack was aware of what was coming, Damien drew him closer and closer—until their lips were only a breath apart.

"Please kiss me," Damien murmured.

Jack did. It was a sweet, innocent kiss. Their lips barely rested on one another's.

Damien blocked out Jack's smell and focused on the way his lips felt. They were the same—still soft and full. He still had no stubble, only a sweet smattering of peach fuzz that tickled with beloved familiarity. Damien reached up and let his hand caress Jack's hair. And it was Jack's hair—soft, slightly curly, and a little too long—or too short, depending on your sense of style. But either way—perfectly Jack. With a moan, Damien deepened the kiss, finding Jack's tongue.

Jack's arms went up to wrap around Damien's shoulders.

And then Duchess started to whine at the exact moment Other Jack's hand slid from his shoulders toward Damien's neck.

Damien felt the change within Jack instantly.

The kiss hardened—became painful.

Jack's hand that had been so gently resting on Damien's shoulder was suddenly viselike, holding him in place so that he couldn't move when Jack wrenched his lips from their kiss. Jack snarled, baring his teeth—and then his free hand was snaking around Damien's neck—

"Aaah!" Other Jack shrieked, jerking his hand away from the slim strand of turquoise it had found.

Damien stood so fast that he overturned his chair. Duchess moved quickly, too, positioning herself between Jack and Damien, though she didn't growl and she didn't threaten. She simply sat there, looking at Jack as she whined pitifully.

Other Jack cradled his hand against his stomach and used his legs to push himself backwards on the bed. "Go. And take her away, too. I don't want either of you to see me like this." His voice was rough, and Damien could see the red glow of his changed eyes.

"No."

"Go on! I'm a monster! And I can't help myself even though I'm sorry. I'm so, so sorry," he sobbed brokenly.

"I'm not going anywhere." Damien took the blood jug from the bedside table and tossed it to Jack, who caught it with the preternatural speed of a predator. "And you're not a monster. You're sick. That's all. And I believe we're going to figure out a way to make you well."

"You should stay away from me until then. I can't control myself." He unscrewed the cap of the jug and downed the rest of the liquid thirstily.

"Jack, you *did* control yourself."

Jack swallowed, wiped his lips, and then looked down at his hand, which was red and blistered, but was already beginning to heal. "What was that?"

Damien righted his chair and sat down, petting Duchess reassuringly. "Turquoise infused with the love of a grandma."

Jack looked at Damien. His eyes were already beginning to fade from red back to hazel. "It hurt me."

"Not you. It hurt the Darkness inside you that's making you sick. Do you really want us to leave?"

"No," Jack's voice was muted, broken. "But you should. I don't want to hurt you."

"You won't. We won't let you—Duchess, Grandma, and me."

"You really won't leave?"

"Not unless you truly want me to," Damien said.

"Please don't," Jack said so faintly Damien almost didn't hear him. "I'm so tired of being alone."

"Then I won't leave." He bent and opened the picnic basket, taking out the thermos and the two cut-crystal wine glasses.

"Ooooh, those are so pretty!" Jack said, sounding more and more like himself.

"They are lovely, aren't they? Here, one is for you." He offered it to Jack, who hesitantly scooted to the edge of the bed to take it. Then Damien opened the thermos and poured them both full glasses of the warm red liquid that filled the room with the enticing fragrance of fresh blood.

Damien watched Other Jack carefully. His eyes began to change color, but as soon as he drank from the glass they faded again. Remembering what Grandma had said, Damien felt around in the bottom of the basket and found a fresh Himalayan chew, which he tossed to Duchess. She caught it neatly, then jumped up on the foot of Jack's bed, circled a few times, and with a happy sigh, lay down and began to chew.

"I really, *really* like her." Jack spoke in a hushed voice, as if he was afraid of startling Duchess, but all the big lab did was wag her tail.

"You always have," Damien said. Then he looked back in the basket, and pulled out the copy of *Last Seen Leaving*. "You know what else you've always liked?"

Jack sipped from the wine glass before saying, "No, tell me."

"You've always liked it when I read to you."

"You've never read to me before."

"Seriously?"

Jack nodded. "Yep. You were too busy studying or writing papers and such."

"Well, I'm not too busy now. Would you like me to read to you?"

"Yeah, I would." Jack took the thermos from where Damien had put it on the night table and refilled his glass. "But I'm going to fall asleep as soon as the sun sets. I can't help it."

"Then I'll sit here and read you to sleep."

Jack's eyes were shining again, but this time with unshed tears. "Will you be here when I wake up, too?"

"Always," Damien told him firmly. "Always, my love." Then he opened the book and began reading, "*Last Seen Leaving* by Caleb Roehrig. Chapter One. 'Into the darkness they go, the wise and the lovely.'—Edna St. Vincent Millay. There was a corpse in my neighbor's front yard …"

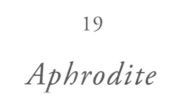

19

Aphrodite

The Escalade pulled up in front of Aphrodite, the newly applied chains on its tires making a god-awful sound against the blowing snow as it slid to a stop. The passenger's door opened and Darius peered out at her in the gray light of a predawn blizzard.

"You are not going to walk. I do not care what you say, and I do not care that you have that electric gun. I am taking you. I am picking you up. Get in."

Aphrodite sighed, but climbed into the SUV. "You sound pissed."

"I sound annoyed."

"Nope, pissed. I know pissed. I do it well." She leaned across the seat and kissed his cheek, nuzzling him intimately. "But thank you."

Darius caressed her hair back from her face and kissed her properly. "You are welcome." Then he started slowly forward, picking his way carefully through the parking lot, heading to the school's gate that opened to Utica Street.

"How did you know I was going to walk to the hospital?"

"Zoey told me. And I could feel you. I knew you were up to something."

"You know me well," she said.

"Are you certain it is a good idea for you to visit your mother?"

"Actually, I'm pretty certain it isn't a good idea. But she's going to die in three days. I think that means I have to visit her. Those are the mother-daughter rules."

"I believe that rule holds only when a mother truly acts like one," Darius said.

"Well, she's the only mother I have, so she's going to have to do. Plus, I'm not going to see her for her sake. I'm going for me. I don't ever want to be sorry that I didn't when I could." Aphrodite studied Darius' profile as he concentrated on the snow-covered road. "I've never asked you about your parents. What are they like?"

"They are dead," he said without taking his eyes off the road.

"Oh. I'm sorry."

He glanced at her, his lips lifting slightly. "It was a long time ago. My father was born in 1902. My mother was born in 1910. They were good people. They didn't understand what was happening when I was Marked, and I only saw them twice afterward. The world was different then—smaller. Simpler."

"Holy crap. When were you born?" Aphrodite stared at her lover and mate. He looked like he was, maybe, twenty-five at the oldest.

"1929. It was a very good year."

"Oh, good Goddess! You're eighty-eight!"

Hi smile widened to a grin. "I am."

"Good thing I've always like older men," she said.

"Good thing," he agreed.

"Hey. I should have asked you about your parents before now. Darius, I am sorry I can be so selfish. I'll work on it."

"I believe in your goodness, and your goodness is greater than your selfishness, my beauty."

"I'm real glad you think so."

"I know so."

Darius glanced at the clock on the dash, which read 6:22 a.m.

"Sunrise is in about an hour. Do you want me to stay here with you, or come back and pick you up?"

"Neither. I need to see Mother alone. I'll wait until sunrise, then I'll walk back to the school." Before he could argue with her, Aphrodite barreled on. "No! I'll be fine. Other Jack said his people are even more sensitive to the sun than our red vamps. They won't get me. Plus, you know I have this." She lifted the Taser from her silver-studded Saint Laurent bucket purse.

Darius snorted.

"All you need to focus on is getting rid of the bad guys." She pointed to her scarf, which was still wrapped around his bicep. "And remember, only other people's blood gets on that."

Darius pulled into the St. John's ER entrance and turned to her. "Are you sure you do not want me to be with you?"

"I'm sure. Are you sure you're going to stay safe out there?"

"I am sure."

She'd already unclicked her seatbelt, so he reached over and easily pulled her from her seat into his arms so that he could kiss her thoroughly. She wrapped her arms around him and held on, kissing him passionately.

"Do not let her hurt your feelings too much," he said as they parted.

"I'll do my best. Don't you let anyone hurt you at all."

"And I shall do my best, as well. Be well, my beauty, and know you carry my heart with you. Always."

"I will. And I love you, too."

Aphrodite closed the door to the SUV firmly, and then ducked her head against the onslaught of wind and snow, and trudged into the ER. She paused before she made her way to the nurses' station, stomping the snow off her Sorel snow boots. She looked around to be sure no one was watching her before she slid her hand into the pouch of her purse and quickly took two Xanax from the ever-present bottle, swallowing them dry.

"There. That's better. And now that I'm girded for battle …" She approached the nurses' station. "Hi, I'm Aphrodite LaFont. My mother is Frances LaFont. I'd like to see her, please."

"ID?" Aphrodite showed it to her and the nurse nodded and tapped her mom's name into the computer. "She's been moved from the ER to the ICU. That's odd. Her wound wasn't that serious." The nurse's brow furrowed as she read the comments on the screen. "Miss LaFont, I can page Dr. Ruffing for you."

"No, that's okay. I know her prognosis. Does Mother?"

The nurse read the notes silently for a few more breaths before saying, "No. It looks as if Dr. Ruffing was waiting for family to get here to tell her the worst of it. She is in isolation, though, due to the contagious nature of her wound."

"So she doesn't have a clue why she's isolated or in the ICU?"

"I'm not certain. As I said, I can page the doctor."

"No, don't bother. I won't stay long. But if I need him I'll have them page from upstairs. What floor is the ICU on?"

"Third floor. You must stop at the nurses' station, but your mother is in room 820."

"Will do." Resolutely, Aphrodite headed into the elevator. The hospital was eerily quiet for such a blizzardy day. "Guess the action won't pick up until after the Okies wake up and try to take their trucks to Albertsons to get them some disaster supplies—yuck, yuck." She quipped in a really bad Okie accent. Then the doors opened to the antiseptic scent of the ICU. Aphrodite lifted her chin and marched to the nurses' station. "Hi. I'm Aphrodite LaFont, Frances LaFont's daughter. The ER nurse told me she'd been transferred up here." Aphrodite held out her ID for the nurse to check.

"Yes, Miss LaFont. Your mother is in room 820, but she is under isolation protocol. No human is allowed to see her alone. I can page the doctor, or a security guard to accompany you."

"Nope, that won't be necessary. I'm not human." When the nurse gave her a disbelieving look, Aphrodite stifled an eye roll.

"Seriously. I used to be a fledgling. Then I became Nyx's prophetess. It was in all the papers when my Dad was killed about a year ago. Remember?" She started to pull her phone from her purse. "I can Google the *Tulsa World* article if you want."

The nurse's eyes widened as she stared at Aphrodite. "Oh, that's right. I remember now. No, the article won't be necessary. Are you certain you can't be infected? You don't have any Mark on you, fledgling or vampyre."

"Yeah, I know. And yeah, I'm sure. I don't look it, but I'm not human. May I go into my mother's room now?"

"Yes, but perhaps you should prepare yourself. She isn't being very …" the nurse paused, chewed her cheek, and then finished, "pleasant."

"My mother has never been very pleasant. I'm used to it. Thanks."

Aphrodite found room 820 easily. It had a big orange BIOHAZARD—INFECTIOUS sign on it that was impossible to miss. She knocked on the door twice.

"Yes, yes—come in," her mother said irritably. "I hope you have my nightgown and my overnight bag. And do not tell me again that it is snowing too hard to drive. Get one of your CNA mo-mos to walk there. My housekeeper lives in the carriage house. She knows where my emergency overnight bag is kept and she can—" Her mother's tirade halted when she looked up from the hand mirror she was using to study the bite on her shoulder. "Oh. It's you."

"Yep. And I didn't bring a spare mo-mo to go schlep your stuff."

"Of course you didn't."

"How are you feeling, Mother?"

"My shoulder hurts and I will have a scar, but I'm fine. No thanks to you. I am pleased they finally moved me to a private room, even though I am annoyed the only bed available is in the ICU."

Oh, so that's what they told her, Aphrodite thought. There was one metal chair in the room and she sat in it, glad that it wasn't any closer to her mother's bed. She studied her mom—noting that she was unusually pale and that the bite, which was in the curve between her mother's neck and shoulder, looked red and weepy.

Her mother narrowed her eyes at Aphrodite and hastily reapplied the bandage over the unsightly wound.

"Why are you here?"

"You're my mother and you're in the hospital. It's my job to be here," Aphrodite said.

"Ah, familial duty. You've never been much for that. Why the sudden change?"

Aphrodite shrugged. "I don't know. Maybe it has something to do with the fact that I'm partially responsible for those creatures getting into this world."

"Partially? I'd say you and your group of freaks are wholly responsible."

"Well, you would say that."

"Why aren't you out there catching them? My God!" Frances shuddered delicately. "Those things are monstrous! And their smell—horrid!"

"Our Warriors are working with TPD to catch them. They have a plan. It'll be fine." Aphrodite drew a deep breath. "Mother, about your wound. There's more—"

"Let's not talk about me. Let's talk about you."

"Me? You want to talk about me?" Aphrodite was honestly shocked. Since when had her mother wanted anything to do with her?

"Yes. I've been thinking about you. About us. Since I announced my plans to run for mayor."

"*Us?* You've been thinking about us?" Aphrodite felt slightly dizzy, like she'd taken three instead of two Xanax.

"Oh, don't sound so surprised. And stop gaping with your mouth open like that. It's unattractive. Yes, I've been thinking about us, and about how you can help me with my campaign."

"You want me to help you campaign for mayor?" Aphrodite

couldn't help it. Her heart beat faster and she felt her face flush. Was her mother really asking for her help? Finally? Just days before she was going to die?

"Yes, definitely. I've been paying attention, you know. To you. I admit I might have been hasty in severing our ties after your father was murdered by vampyre scum."

"Mother, he was murdered by Neferet. She wasn't a vampyre when she killed him. She was an immortal and our enemy."

LaFont waved her hand dismissively. "Oh, stop nitpicking. And stop pretending like you're one of them—though I do admire that you have used your brains and not your twat and figured out an angle that has made you invaluable to the vampyre scum. Pretending to get visions and be a prophetess. I may not have done better myself. Well done, you."

"Mother, I'm not pretending."

"Nitpicking. Again." With a grimace LaFont sat up a little straighter, rearranging the pillows behind her. "Ask me about my plan for us."

"I don't think you understand that—"

As usual, Frances LaFont talked over her daughter. "My plan is to win this election by rallying the *righteous* People of Faith," she said sarcastically, "into a frenzy over getting rid of the vampyre scum amongst us. Like I'm the first politician to get elected by stirring up a little xenophobia?" She laughed softly—a deceptively sweet sound that sent chills over Aphrodite's skin. "Actually, your little escapade at Woodward Park has worked right into my plan. Didn't I hear something about those same creatures attacking that abomination restaurant at the depot?"

Aphrodite swallowed down the nausea threatening to choke her. *She hasn't changed. She'll never change.* "Yes, Mother. The creatures killed everyone who was at the Depot Restaurant last night."

"Perfect. Where was I? Oh, I know. As soon as I'm elected I'm going to initiate a hefty tax on anything vampyre. Want to eat at a vampyre restaurant? Expect to pay more. A lot more. Want to buy a vampyre piece of art? Get out your platinum credit card. Want to attend one of the ridiculous farmers' markets on the House of Night campus, or take one of their inflammatory classes? Better be prepared to pay at least double the price you would if you were supporting your *own kind.* Yes, I am going to make Tulsa strong again."

Aphrodite shook her head. "I don't get it. Why do you care so much? Vampyres and humans are *finally* coming together. We're all getting along. It's good for vampyres *and* humans."

"Not all humans," LaFont said with a sly glint in her eyes.

"Oh. I do get it. There's something in it for you."

"That took you long enough. I think the scum you've been hanging around with has addled your brains—though you were never exceptionally bright to begin with—pretty enough, but not too bright. It's simple, really. Even you will understand it. There is a faction—a minority, but a very rich, very powerful minority—who wants to begin putting people in political power who will hear their voices and act on their ideals. They don't like much that isn't human, white, and upper middle class."

"What?" Aphrodite felt nauseous. Her mother was literally on her deathbed, scheming like a super villain. It would be hilarious if it were a scene in a movie. But it was real. Too, too real.

"I said, human, white, and upper middle class. You know— people who make just enough money to think they have money, so they start donating to political campaigns. Anyway, it's a very good thing that we are human, white, and rich. Truly rich and not nouveau riche. They're useful, but so, so tacky." She patted at a strand of her hair before continuing. "Anyway, as I was saying before you interrupted—you by my side during the campaign would be perfect. It can be as if you've risen from the dead—the prodigal returned to your mother's bosom after realizing the error of your ways and denouncing the monsters among us. The voters will love it."

"You're mixing your metaphors."

"You get the point."

"I do. Mother, whether it is convenient for you or not, I am not human."

Her mother waved away Aphrodite's words. "What does that matter? You look it. Play your cards right and you can pass."

"Pass?"

"For human, you idiot."

Aphrodite felt herself go very still inside. She stared at her mother, perhaps really seeing her for the first time. *She is a monster.*

"You're a monster." The words slipped from Aphrodite's mouth before she knew she'd spoken.

LaFont's laughter was edged with spite. "That's ironic coming from you."

"No, what's ironic is that you are *literally* a monster. Or you will be one very soon. Mother, you were bitten by a red vampyre from an alternative world. In that world the bite of a red vampyre is infectious. You will die in three days. Then you will rise in three more, but you will be one of them. *A monster.* And there is nothing you can do about it."

"Liar!" Her mother spat the word at her. "You've always been such a liar!"

"No, Mother. That's one of the many things you've always been wrong about. I don't lie. It's one of my strengths and one of my faults. So let me tell you something else, *honestly.* Not only will you rise a monster, but you will also die a monster. Your puny *human* body can't tolerate the Change. It'll burn out. You will die. The end. And you know what? If I had the power to heal you—*I would not.* You don't deserve it. The world is better off without you. Goodbye, Mother. I won't be seeing you again."

Aphrodite stumbled blindly for the door as her mother screamed obscenities at her.

"Miss LaFont?" The nurse rushed from the nurses' station, sending concerned glances at the closed door through which her mother's tide of obscenities could still be heard. "Is everything all right?"

"No. She knows she's going to die. As is typical for my mother, she doesn't take bad news well. She probably needs to be sedated."

The nurse touched Aphrodite's arm gently. "I meant with you. Is everything all right with you?"

Aphrodite blinked fast. *I will not cry.* "Again, no. But I'm used to it. My mother poisons everything she touches. Though she might be right about one thing—me thinking that she had changed even a little probably means I am an idiot."

"No, it doesn't," she said kindly. "It means you're the daughter of an unpleasant woman."

"Maybe it means both. Excuse me."

Aphrodite fled for the elevator and punched the button for the ground floor. Before the elevator doors opened, she'd fished through her purse and found the flask she kept there. She pulled it out. It was a beautiful thing—silver, monogrammed with an ornate *A*. Aphrodite unscrewed the cap, lifted the flask to her lips, and drank deeply, grimacing only slightly at the peaty taste of the twenty-one-year-old single malt scotch.

20

Zoey

"Okay, Darius and his Warriors are all in place. There's only fifteen minutes until sunrise. Time for us to go!" Stark shouted at me as he held open the door of the Escalade. I bolted from the warm, dry House of Night through the stinging snowy wind with my head ducked and my eyes half closed. He ran around to the driver's side and climbed in.

"It's getting bad. Real bad," Shaunee said from the back seat.

"Which is the only reason I'm letting Stark come with us at all," I said.

Stark shot me his cocky, half grin. "Z, I'm driving. It's you who is coming with me."

I shook my head at him. "I don't like this. It's going to be sunrise in half an hour."

"I told you that I'll be fine. There is no way the sun can shine through this mess, and I have this." He lifted his hoodie and winked at me. "I won't fry. Promise."

"I'll be real pissed if you do," I said. "Not to mention if I see your skin even starting to look a little red, I'll drag your butt back to this very heavily tinted SUV, throw you in the back seat, and cover you with blankets while I floor this thing to the school."

"*You* driving in a blizzard? Now *I* am scared," Stark said.

Shaunee snorted.

"Hey, that's not funny," I said.

"It is, Z," Shaunee said. "Everyone knows you're a shitty driver."

"No, everyone knows I can't parallel park. Hardly anyone can parallel park. That doesn't make me a bad driver." I turned to look at Shaunee before we left campus. "Hey, are you sure you don't want to stay here? This weather is awful."

"I heard Marx telling you they have flamethrowers ready. No damn way I'm going to miss that."

"It is a good idea to have fire with us," Stark said.

"Okay, yeah, I get it. I just haven't been able to stop worrying since Kalona showed up in my dream and mentioned the N word."

"Z, get real. You haven't stopped worrying since you were Marked," Stark said.

I sighed. "You're probably right. I just, I dunno. I just keep feeling like something is going to happen. Something really awful."

"You mean something more awful than the zombie apocalypse?" Shaunee said.

"Sadly, yes," I said. We'd come to the gate that opened to Utica. I glanced down what I expected to be a totally empty street to see …

"Hey, that's not Aphrodite staggering down the middle of Utica, is it?" Stark said.

"Ah, hell, it is. Hang on. I'll get her."

Stark's hand on my shoulder stopped me. "Not without me you won't. You don't know why she's staggering."

"Are you being serious?" Shaunee said. "If Aphrodite's stumbling we all know why. She's either drunk or high."

I sighed and added, "Or both."

"Normally, I'd agree. But right now we have zombie vampyres loose in Tulsa, so I'm not taking any chances." He grabbed his bow and notched an arrow. "Shaunee, slide up here. If any of those creatures show up—run them over."

"Totally doable," Shaunee said.

Stark and I got out of the SUV, braced ourselves against the wind and snow, and plowed our way to Aphrodite.

"What happened? Are you okay?" I hurried to her side while Stark stood guard, his keen eyes scanning around us looking for danger.

"Zoey! Stark!" Aphrodite stumbled and fell against me. "Two of my fave peoples!"

I caught her and got a huge whiff of her boozy breath as I helped her get upright. "You're drunk."

"And super high! Took two, no wait, *three* Xanax. Xanaxes? Xanaxie? Ah, whatever." She lifted the sliver flask she was holding loosely and turned it upside down, shaking it. Nothing came out. "Well, shit. And looks like I'm out of single malt. Again."

"You gotta stop mixing drugs and alcohol," I said, catching her as she swayed drunkenly. "You're going to kill yourself someday."

She snorted. "Again I say, 'Whatever.'"

"Did you see your mom?" I asked.

"Yes, I abso fucking lutely did. Do you know she's a monster? Literally?" She proceeded to giggle hysterically as she tried to suck nonexistent scotch from her flask.

Something inside me snapped. I grabbed her flask from her and threw it into the ditch.

"Hey! That was expensive!"

"Enough!" I got in her face. "You have to stop this. It's self-destructive. And it's not the way adults act, especially adults who are in the service of Nyx."

"Maybe I don't want to be in anyone's service! Maybe I don't *deserve* to be in anyone's service! Maybe that's what my vision was really about. I'm not human. I'm not vampyre. I'm nothing except an idiot who isn't even good enough for her mother to love."

I grabbed her by her shoulders and shook her. Hard. "Snap the hell out of it! Your mom is awful. She's always been awful. So stop letting her fuck with your head."

"Ooooo, you said hell and fuck. It really must be the zombie apocalypse." She giggled some more.

"It's not funny." I let her go so abruptly that she almost fell. "And I'm serious. What if I needed you right now? What if we all needed you right now? You're a Prophetess of Nyx. We're in a time of crisis. And what did you choose to do? Get so messed up that you can hardly walk. That's total bullpoopie, Aphrodite, and as your High Priestess I'm telling you—no, I'm *commanding* you—to sober up."

"Hey, my monster of a mom is dying. Then I'll be an orphan. I have the right to get messed up."

"No, you don't. What you have is an obligation to yourself and to the people who care about you to *deal with the issues in your life!* You're acting like you're the only one of us who ever lost a parent. Or who ever had a crappy parent. Bingo and bingo for me and for a bunch of us. Grow the hell up, Aphrodite, and realize you have a problem."

Aphrodite narrowed her eyes at me, switching from giggly drunk to mean drunk in an instant. "What *problem* are you talking about?"

"Get real, Aphrodite." Stark spoke without taking his eyes from the street around us. "Everyone knows you have a major alcohol and prescription drug problem."

Aphrodite stopped swaying. Her face flushed bright red. "Fuck you, James Stark! And fuck you, too, Zoey Redbird! Fuck all of you. You peasants don't know who the hell you're dealing with. Command me? *Command me?* I didn't ask for any of this, and you, *High Priestess,*" she sneered, "don't have the brains or experience to *command* the correct spell to enter a circle, let alone *command* me. *I quit!*" She shoved past me, bumping me so hard she almost knocked me on my butt and repeating, "I fucking quit!" Over her shoulder she continued to spew anger.

"Tell Darius we're out of here as soon as the airport opens. Queen Damien hates New York? Well, I love it, so mark him off and pencil me in. I'll do a better job than he's been doing anyway—all he's been doing is boohooing. Yeah, New York City. That's where I'm going. As soon as possible."

I started to follow her, but Stark caught my wrist.

"Let her go."

"But she's—"

"She's drunk, full of pills, and mean. And she's currently walking onto campus. She'll be fine."

"Walking? Don't you mean stumbling?"

"No." He pointed at her. "Look. She's not stumbling at all now. And she's already through the gate. Let's get back in the car."

We fought against the wind to the car.

"Let me guess—she was majorly fucked up," Shaunee said as she climbed into the back seat and Stark took her place.

"Totally," I said.

"You know, the amount of drugs and alcohol she ingests on a regular basis would kill a normal person," said Shaunee. "And I don't think she ever eats anymore. I mean, I haven't been around for a while, but I've only seen her drink her meals since I've been back."

"I'm aware of that." I watched as Stark pulled the SUV onto Utica and Aphrodite disappeared into the snow. "She's getting worse and worse. We're going to have to tell Darius something."

"But not what she really said. Not right now," Stark said. "He doesn't need to worry about that while he's battling soldiers from a different world."

"Just tell him she got drunk after she saw her mom," Shaunee said. "Z, Darius lives with her. He's her Oathbound Warrior. He has to know she has a serious problem."

"It's going to tear them apart if she doesn't get a handle on it." I spoke the words aloud I'd been thinking for some time now.

"We've all known that, Z," Stark said. "But get your head back into the game. You can figure out what to do about Aphrodite after we solve the zombie apocalypse problem."

"You're right. I'm in the game. Promise."

"Where are we going?" Shaunee asked.

"I'm going to park down the street from the Philtower. No one got past any of the Warriors at the entrances to the other tunnels, so it's looking good for the bad guys to be either there or the Atlas Building. Marx radioed that his men found tracks outside both buildings. They made sure all the street level doors were unlocked, but locked up everything on the first floors except the entrances to the tunnels. They should be trapped."

"With flamethrowers!" Shaunee practically squealed from the back seat.

"Don't be so gleeful. That's gross," I said.

"Oh, yeah. Sorry. I wasn't actually being gleeful about burning people up—just about burning in general."

"Okay, so we're going to the Philtower while Darius is taking the Atlas Building?" I asked.

"Yeah. TPD has officers in the upper floors of both buildings waiting until the sun rises. Then they're going to join our Warriors, and we'll open the doors to the two tunnels at the same time. Z, I want you to wait in the Philcade Building."

"Huh? I'm not staying there. I'm going with you to the Philtower."

"No, you're not. And Shaunee is going with you."

"Double huh?" Shaunee said.

"Look, Darius described to me what those creatures did at the depot. They ripped people apart. They ate hunks of flesh from their bodies. I won't take any chance that you're going to get hurt. So, Fire can wait with the Leader of the North American High Council, my Queen and my Consort, *in the adjoining building where it's safer.*"

"No," I said firmly. "Fire and the Leader of the North American High Council, your Queen and Consort, are going to wait in the gorgeous lobby of the Philtower. I get that you don't want me in that cramped basement with you—I'd just be in your way when you start to fight, but I won't be banished to across the street."

"Fine," Stark said. "But I'm going to station a flamethrower and a cop there with you."

"That and my fire will be plenty to keep our Zoey safe," Shaunee said. "Wait, isn't there a tunnel that connects the Philtower to the Philcade Building? Doesn't it run almost directly under Boston Street?"

"Yeah. There's also a metal door to that tunnel that's locked with a crazy old-time weight-and-pulley system that can only be opened from the Philcade side of the tunnel," Stark said.

"So, they're really trapped."

"Yep, really."

"Hey, you did tell everyone that the fledglings are harmless when the sun's out, right?" I reminded Stark. "Other Jack said they'll all be unconscious."

"Yep, everyone knows not to burn up anyone who is sleeping. We'll just tie them up and bring them back to the House of Night. When you cure Jack, you can cure them, too."

"*If* I cure Jack," I muttered.

"I heard that," Stark said.

"Well, I have no clue how to help him."

"You will," Stark said.

"Yep, Z. You always figure it out," Shaunee said.

I sighed and kept my mouth shut, but I had a bad feeling about this—about all of this. Something was going to go wrong. I just knew it.

21

Aphrodite

Aphrodite was pissed. Really, really pissed.

What fucking right did Zoey Redbird have to speak to her like that? Especially after all Aphrodite had done for her and for the entire damn Nerd Herd. It was bull*shit*. Not bullpoopie. BULLSHIT.

"This fucking snow. I'm so done with this snow. With this city. With this *everything*," she mumbled to herself as she trudged to the front door of the school. "Goddess, I need a hot spiced wine and another Xanax." She pulled on the door. It didn't budge. She tried it again. Nothing. "Fucking locked? You have got to be shitting me. We never lock anything." *Just my damn luck. This is ridiculous.* Aphrodite banged her fists against the door, but with the wind and the muffling effect of the falling snow, the sound didn't travel at all. She peered in through the side window. "Hello! Anybody in there?"

Not a single person stirred.

"This sucks. This sucks so damn bad." Aphrodite plowed her way around the side of the building through the calf-deep drifting snow to the little courtyard that held the fountain and outdoor seating for the fledgling dining hall. There she paused, weaving only a little, and stared in through the semi-frosted-over window. "Not one damn person in there, either. Shit. Alright. To the back entrance I go."

She got to the entrance to the turret-like tower that housed the Council Chamber and the media center, and was also an entrance to the professors' quarters.

"Whew. Finally. Home. Or, temp home until Darius and I get the hell out of this backwards, bumpkin city." She put her hand on the doorknob, turned and *pushed*. It opened right away. Then it hit her. "Oh, for shit's sake—the front door wasn't locked. I was *pulling* instead of pushing." She started to laugh and laugh. And laugh some more, until she was leaning against the arched wooden door frame, barely able to remain upright.

There was a flash of light from behind her as the wind stilled and the snow paused at the moment the sun lifted over the horizon. Its reflection caught in the long, rectangular windows that framed the hallway beside the door. Aphrodite blinked, wiped at her eyes, and stared.

Caged in the beveled glass, the rising sun created an aura of silver and gold around Nyx's Temple, with the goddess, arms raised and cupping the crescent moon, seeming to glisten in the strange, changing light of a snowy dawn. Aphrodite stood still, superimposed on the reflection. As her eyes focused on her own face, the odd light lent a sepia affect to her image as if she were looking through a time camera.

And Aphrodite truly *saw* herself—saw what she was becoming.

Her thick blond hair was a mess, trailing dank strands across her face and over her shoulders. She was thin, yet she looked puffy—bloated. Her eyes were shadowed, their expression flat—almost dead. She looked hard and mean and much older than her twenty-one years yet so, so familiar.

With a trembling hand, Aphrodite touched her face and the familiar stranger in the reflection did so too.

"Mother?" she whispered. "I am my mother."

The reflection began to sob brokenly. Aphrodite turned away from it, unable to look any longer—and found she was staring directly at Nyx's Temple, alight with dawn and snow and the love of a benevolent goddess.

Still sobbing, Aphrodite stumbled across the courtyard to the door of the temple. She pushed it open and staggered inside. Instantly she was surrounded by silence and the peaceful scents of vanilla and lavender. Aphrodite didn't pause. She made her way to the main altar of the temple where a gorgeous statue of Nyx stood as the focus of the room. All around it were tokens of love: brightly colored beads, crystal gemstones, handmade jewelry, candles, chalices filled with wine, bowls of honey, and fresh fruit.

Aphrodite crumpled at the feet of the goddess. She covered her face and wept inconsolably—wept for her dead father; wept for her hateful, absentee mother who would soon be dead; wept for her lost childhood; and finally, wept for herself. Scenes she hadn't thought about for years flooded her memory.

She remembered when she was six and so glad to see her father come home from work that she'd climbed up on his lap, wrapped her arms around his neck, and kissed him sweetly on the mouth. Her mother had grabbed her by the arm and yanked her painfully from him, tossing her to the floor, saying she was too old to kiss men on the mouth—that only certain kinds of girls did that to certain kinds of men—said it like she thought her daughter was dirty and disgusting. After that day Aphrodite didn't remember her father ever kissing her hello or goodbye again.

She didn't try to remember her mother kissing her. She had no memory of that happening. Ever.

Aphrodite remembered when she was eight and had put on her first two-piece swimsuit. It'd been white and yellow, dotted with daisies. She'd run out to their pool where her mother had been sunning to show off her "big girl suit," as young Aphrodite had called it. Her mother had given her a disdainful sideways glance and said, "If you're old enough to wear a two-piece suit, you're old enough to start holding in that gut of yours."

She'd been eight. She hadn't been fat, or even chubby. But from that day forward she'd worried about her weight and skipped meals.

Aphrodite remembered when she was eleven. A boy from down the street had stopped by to ask if she could play kickball with him and some of the other neighborhood kids. Her mother had said no and told their maid to close the door in his face. Aphrodite had cried. Her mother had slapped her. Hard. And called her a little slut.

She hadn't known what slut meant until that day. She'd googled it, but had still not really understood. She'd never even kissed a boy—never even held a boy's hand. But her mother had told her she was a slut. So, she believed it. How could she not?

Over and over the memories deluged her, and as they played across her mind's eye, her tears dried. Her sobs quieted to hiccups. She lifted her face from the marble floor and sat, looking up at the serene goddess, and it was as if the scales fell from her eyes, her mind, her heart—and she was finally able to understand the truth.

"I'm not the problem."

Aphrodite spoke to the statue of her goddess. At first her voice was trembly, choked with tears and emotion, but as she kept speaking, kept reasoning through a past that had kept her shackled to self-loathing, her words became clearer, stronger, and wiser. Much, much wiser.

"It's not that I'm not good enough for my mother to love. No one—no child, no husband, no job—would ever be good enough for her because she wasn't ever good enough for herself. Her life disappointed her over and over again, because it was broken. It was broken because *she* was broken. She *is* broken." Aphrodite brushed her damp hair from her face and wiped her nose. "I can't fix her. I can't make her love me. I can only fix myself—love myself. And I have to let Mother go, and let the pain she created in my life go with her, or I will become her. I have to let her go."

She put her face in her hands and began to weep again, but this time her tears were an outpouring of relief and release because it was at that moment Aphrodite LaFont truly began to live her own life.

"Daughter, I have been waiting to see if you would choose healing or self-destruction. I am infinitely pleased that you have chosen wisely."

Aphrodite lifted her head from her hands to look up at the statue—which was no more. Instead of a marble replica of Nyx, the goddess herself stood before her, wrapped in gossamer silver and gold. Her dark hair cascaded around her waist, and over it was Nyx's headdress of stars that glistened so brightly Aphrodite had to lower her eyes, which she did immediately, pressing her forehead to the cool marble in supplication.

"Forgive me, Nyx. I've been vain and selfish and cruel—to myself and to the people who love me. I don't deserve it, but please forgive me."

Aphrodite felt the goddess' touch on her head and she was filled with love so complete, so unconditional, that she gasped aloud.

"I do not require your supplication, daughter. I understand you. I've understood you from the moment you were Marked. I was simply waiting for you to understand yourself. Rise, Prophetess! Behold your future!"

At Nyx's command a bolt of pain splintered Aphrodite's forehead sending shards of white-hot agony across her face. But in the span of a breath, the pain was gone.

Aphrodite lifted her head to see the goddess smiling down on her. Nyx made a graceful, sweeping motion with her hand, and a silver-framed mirror appeared before her, catching Aphrodite's reflection. Feeling as if she was moving through a fantastical dream, Aphrodite lifted her hand. With trembling fingers she watched her reflection trace the incredibly beautiful tattoo pattern of exploding blue and red fireworks that framed her eyes in a perfect mask.

"W-what is this? I don't understand." Her voice trembled with so much emotion she could hardly speak.

"This is the part of my prophetic gift to you that had to wait until you were wise enough to wield it."

"Forgive me, Nyx, but I still don't understand."

"Daughter, you have no need to continue to ask for my forgiveness. You have no way of understanding without my explanation."

Aphrodite pulled her gaze from her incredibly changed reflection to look into the eyes of her goddess. "What am I?"

Nyx's smile was sunlight and moonlight married in one harmonious blaze of joy. "Just as Zoey Redbird bridges two worlds—the ancient one of the first of my children, and today's hectic, mad, modern world—so, too, do you bridge worlds." The goddess flicked her wrist and the mirror disappeared.

"Worlds? You mean the human and the vampyre worlds?"

"No, daughter. I mean the worlds of my red and blue Marked children. From the moment you sacrificed a piece of your humanity to save Stevie Rae and my children Marked in red, you have been on this path. I hoped that you would be strong enough to heal your past and wise enough to seek a new future—my hope has come to fruition today."

"So, I'm a bridge?" she said, sounding more like herself.

Nyx laughed and the stars in her headdress twinkled with impossible brilliance. "*Yes, but you are also truly a vampyre—fully Changed.*"

Aphrodite pressed her hand against her mouth. She felt so filled with happiness that she thought she might explode. The goddess waited with seemingly infinite patience while she sifted through her emotions, savoring a sense of peace and fulfillment that she had never before known. Finally, when she was able to speak again, she lifted her face to her goddess once more.

"Thank you. Those two words aren't enough, but they are all I have. Thank you, Nyx. I won't let you down. I won't be my mother, and I won't let her hurt me anymore."

"I know you won't, Daughter. But do you not wish to know the extent of your prophetess gifts?"

"There's more than this gorgeous Mark and those visions I get?" Aphrodite gave the goddess a cheeky grin. "Please tell me you took away the bloody tears, pain, and blindness that goes with them."

"No, Daughter. I cannot tell you that, for with every gift comes a price, and the price for your visions is pain. There is a price for your new gift, too, though I believe you will find it more and less painful than your visions."

"Now I'm really confused," she said.

"Then I shall clarify. In these modern worlds where blue and red vampyres collide, I require a Prophetess of Judgment—someone whose past has taught them that not everything that is beautiful is good—and not everything that is plain is bad, for darkness does not always equate to evil, just as light does not always bring good."

Aphrodite nodded. "My mother and Neferet are beautiful, and both are filled with Darkness. The black bull could easily be seen as a bad guy, but really he is pure love, pure Light. I get it. But what does that have to do with me and with judgment?"

"I do not like to interfere in the life choices of my children because I believe that free will defines humanity. Take free will away, and humans become a race of puppets who will never evolve to find their fullest potential. And yet the events surrounding Kalona's fall and Neferet's curse shook me to my core. I realized I was wrong. There are times when divine intervention is not just necessary, but merciful—especially when worlds collide, as they are doing at this moment. You, my wise, witty, irreverent Daughter, are my divine intervention."

"You know about the zombie apocalypse from the other House of Night world?" Aphrodite shook her head. "What am I saying? You're our goddess. Of course you know about it. But now I'm scared *and* confused."

"Then I shall reassure you and explain. I have granted you the gift of humanity and second chances. There are times when someone who seems unredeemable becomes worthy of an opportunity for redemption. I have given you the power to gift humanity to those who have lost their own so that they might have a second chance."

Aphrodite gaped at the goddess and blurted, "I don't want that power!"

"And that, mixed with your past, is why I have chosen you to be my first Prophetess of Judgment. No one worthy would want this power."

"But how will I know if someone deserves a second chance?"

"You will know."

"How?" The word came out as a squeak and Aphrodite cleared her throat before continuing. "I'm not really that smart, and I screw up *and* hurt people's feelings. Constantly, actually. Even when I don't mean to."

"Yes, you are very human. That is part of what I appreciate about you. And you speak your mind clearly with very little niceties. I find that essential in a prophetess. You have a unique wisdom that I appreciate. Depend on that wisdom and depend on your heart."

"My heart?"

"*When you know it here,*" the goddess touched Aphrodite's forehead gently. "*As well as here,*" her hand rested briefly on Aphrodite's breast, over her heart. "*Then the answer you seek will be the correct one.*"

"Okay, I'll try. I'm not sure how good I'll be at this, and I'm pretty sure I'm going to screw things up sometimes, but I will try. I give you my promise."

"I shall keep your promise, Prophetess."

"You said every gift comes with a price. What's the price I pay for this gift?"

"Each time you give someone a second chance, you give away a piece of your gift of judgment. You'll see it happen, for part of your Mark will fade until finally, one day, it will disappear completely leaving you as you were before."

"Before?"

"Before you were Marked at all. When your tattoo is gone, so too will your term as my prophetess be gone, and you may live out the rest of your life as a human mortal, revered and loved by every House of Night in this world and any other you choose to touch until you die peacefully, surrounded by your children and loved ones, and you return to me."

Aphrodite felt hot and cold at once. "Children?"

"Many—and grandchildren as well as great grandchildren. You will be beloved by generations of your blood. Your life will be so filled with love and Light and laughter that it will drown out the sorrow of your past. So I have spoken—so shall it be."

Aphrodite brushed the fresh tears from her cheeks. "I can save Other Jack."

"You can. You also can save every red fledgling and vampyre who crossed into this world. But, will you, Prophetess? Are they worthy of a second chance?"

She stared at the goddess, her mind whirring. "I—I don't know. How do I know if they're worthy? The only one of them I know is Other Jack, and I don't really know him well. Holy shit, I have no idea what to do!" Then she shook herself and amended, "Sorry about that. I don't sound very prophetess-ey."

"Think with your mind and feel with your heart."

"Well, I know Other Jack and the rest of them are from a crappy world where Neferet's managed to start a war. A world with no Stevie Rae or Zoey, so there was no one to basically manipulate me into giving my humanity up so that the red fledglings and vamps could choose for themselves whether they followed Light or …" her words faded as her heart agreed with her mind. "I know what to do."

"What is your decision, Daughter?"

"They never had a choice, so they all deserve a second chance."

"Does it matter to you how much of your gift you will lose by saving all of them?"

Aphrodite drew a deep breath and let it out slowly. "No. I don't think I can let it matter. It's not about me. It's about them." She hesitated, and then added, "How much of it will I lose?"

The Goddess answered her question with a question. "And what of your mother? Will you gift her with a second chance?"

Aphrodite jerked back in shock. "My mother? What does this have to do with her? She's not a red or blue vampyre."

"Your gift isn't limited to fledglings and vampyres—your gift is for humanity, and you are all humans, though some of you would like to debate that."

Aphrodite stood and began to pace back and forth, back and forth in front of the Goddess. She wrapped her arms around herself, as if to keep herself from breaking. Finally, she stopped and faced Nyx. Fresh tears flowed down her face and her voice was filled with despair. "My heart and mind say the same thing. My mother doesn't deserve a second chance."

Nyx stepped from the dais and went to Aphrodite. Gently, the Goddess took the young prophetess into her arms and held her close while she sobbed. Nyx stroked her hair and murmured wordless comfort until Aphrodite's tears dried.

"Thank you," Aphrodite said, stepping from Nyx's embrace. "I'm better now. And my answer is still the same. My mother does not deserve another chance. My heart and mind told me that. They also told me that I can't fix her, and that I have to let her go. So, that's what I'm doing."

"You are wise. Frances LaFont has been given many chances for redemption during her life. Selfishness and self-loathing prevented her from taking them. But no child should be made to choose whether their parent deserves redemption. My final gift to you, Prophetess, is twofold. The humanity will be restored to the red fledglings and vampyres from the other world. That gift comes from me. You will not pay a price for it. I also gift your mother with a second chance. So mote it be!"

The Goddess waved her hand, causing a ripple in the air around them that reminded Aphrodite of a stone being thrown into a still pool of clear water. Reality pressed against her, shifting, changing … making it difficult for her to breathe.

Then, just as suddenly as it had begun, the strange shift in reality lifted. Aphrodite gasped and was able to draw breath again.

"Is that it? Is it done?"

"It is, Daughter. I am proud of you, and my pride is truly of a mother for a favorite child. And now I wish you merry meet, merry part, and that we merry meet again." Nyx's form faded until only her headdress of stars was all that remained, and then it, too, faded in a glittering rain of diamond sparks.

"I am worth a mother's love," Aphrodite whispered.

From the air around her rang the Goddess' loving words. *"Of course you are, my sweet, wise daughter. And may you always blessed be."*

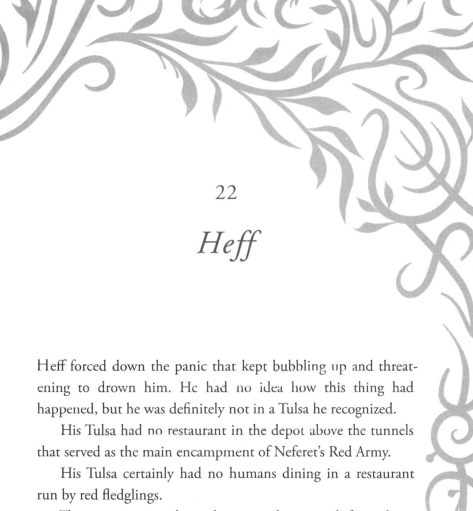

22

Heff

Heff forced down the panic that kept bubbling up and threatening to drown him. He had no idea how this thing had happened, but he was definitely not in a Tulsa he recognized.

His Tulsa had no restaurant in the depot above the tunnels that served as the main encampment of Neferet's Red Army.

His Tulsa certainly had no humans dining in a restaurant run by red fledglings.

There were no trapdoors that opened at a touch from above so that they could drop into the safety of the depot tunnels from several places along the deserted railroad line and between the depot building and the heart of downtown. Heff knew. He and General Dominick had split up and tried every trick entrance to what should have been their army's stronghold.

None of them worked. There was no sign that there had *ever* been trapdoors leading from street level to the tunnels.

There was a lot about Tulsa itself that was wrong—even though the city slept under a whiteout blizzard.

Festive garlands wrapped with lights decorated the downtown

streets, swaying in the wind as if they were dancing with glee at being there—at being allowed there.

In Heff's Tulsa, humans were no longer allowed to decorate the streets for Christmas. Neferet had declared that holiday obsolete.

And now human police officers—*humans*—made their presence very obvious outside the entrances to several buildings that provided tunnel sanctuaries beneath them. It was the second-oddest thing Heff had ever seen.

The first was his sister—alive and well and a fully Changed vampyre—closing the circle that had drawn them to this upside-down world. He tried to compartmentalize his confusion and his hope. Tried to use the mental tricks that had helped him stay sane during the past year, but like this world, his emotions were turned upside down.

"With me, Lieutenant," General Dominick snapped as he brushed past Heff.

"Yes, sir." Heff followed the general through the rubble and remains left by the homeless who had the poor luck to have chosen to pull apart one of the boarded up windows of the abandoned Sinclair Building to try to weather the storm. The general had ordered his vampyres to break into the building so that they could regroup. The homeless within? They had been what the general called "before-bedtime snacks."

"Nothing is right." General Dominick rubbed his hands together and braced himself against the wind and snow as they closed the plywood opening to the broken window. The two of them stayed close to the side of the building—taking refuge from the blizzard, as well as concealment from roving humans. "This is not our world. It cannot be."

Heff said nothing. He knew better than to call too much attention to himself or to accidentally provoke the general.

"Sunrise is close. Too close."

"Thirty minutes," Heff said.

Dominick's red gaze blazed at him. "I know that as well as you do!" The general turned his attention back to the snow-covered street. "I still see no one outside the Philtower, and there is no movement by the Atlas Building, either. Even with this snow covering the sun, we can't take a chance at staying above ground."

"But this building's obviously been abandoned for awhile. There are public auction flyers posted that it's selling next month. With this snow, I don't think anyone except the homeless will be coming in here, and not even them if we barricade that loose board."

The general didn't answer with words. Instead he backhanded Heff. The force hurled him against the side of the building, his ears ringing as his head smacked a crumbling limestone pillar.

"It's not your job to think. Take the fledglings and a squad of the vampyres. Go to the Philtower tunnels. I'll take the rest of the vampyres to the Atlas Building. After sunset we meet here and decide how to find Neferet and get our orders. Now."

"Yes, sir," Heff repeated, rubbing the back of his head. He kept a tight rein on his emotions. He'd learned this lesson well. *Draw no attention. Do as I'm told. And hold on. Always try to hold on to who I am. I am Kevin Heffner. I am surrounded by monsters, but they do not define me.*

Heff did as he was told.

Their evacuation of the abandoned building was fast and efficient. No one had to tell any of them how close it was until sunrise. Like shadows within shadows, they slipped soundlessly from the Sinclair Building. Heff brought up the rear of his squad of ten adult vampyres and almost the same number of fledglings. He paused, waiting for the general to move far enough down the street with his soldiers that the blowing snow obscured his sight. Then he carefully repositioned the plywood barrier, using a broken piece of tile he'd found within to quickly pound the nails into place, securing it as if it had never been breached.

I might need this later, and that is something Dominick doesn't need to know.

He caught up with the fledglings easily. They were already

becoming sluggish and were almost sleepwalking when they came to the ornate entrance to the Philtower lobby.

"Stay here until I whistle. Then, come to me quickly," Heff told his group, leaving them huddled together in the darkness just outside the arched entrance.

He sprinted to the double doors and slipped within.

He saw little differences between this Philtower and the one that housed Neferet. But those little differences were significant. There were no red Warriors stationed at the entrance and the elevators. There were no blue Warriors marching in to relieve them. There were no Warriors present at all. The lobby was completely deserted.

It was still ornate, with Gothic arches and huge light fixtures. But this Philtower had clusters of expensively upholstered circular seating arrangements, and the fixtures bathed the Gothic carving with a soft, rose-tinted electric light.

Neferet's Philtower had no seating arrangements. And she had replaced the electric lights with flickering gaslights.

Though the flesh on the back of his neck prickled with a sense of unease, Heff jogged to the door that opened to plain, industrial-looking stairs leading down to a basement that housed the tunnels. The thick double metal doors were the same, only they were closed and barred, though it was easy enough for Heff to open them.

He peered into the complete darkness of the tunnel. Heff left the door open as he hurried within; his glowing red eyes didn't need the light.

The peeling green paint was the same. The arched tunnel was the same, except for the absence of cots.

And the door that should be open to the adjoining Philcade system was closed.

Heff ran his hand over the familiar rounded side of the tunnel. He held his breath until his fingers found the slight indentation he hoped was there.

It was. He could feel it ready to give under his palm. He let out a long sigh of relief. At least they wouldn't be trapped. Then he jogged up the stairs and through the deserted lobby, opened the door and whistled sharply.

It was close enough to dawn that the fledglings were staggering badly, so he and his squad had to support them down the stairs and into the tunnel.

Heff shut the metal door behind them. Without speaking, the fledglings curled up on the floor in a tight nest and fell asleep instantly.

He ordered the adults to rest close to the entrance.

Kevin Heffner didn't join them. Instead, he trudged to the rear of the tunnel, picking his way around already sleeping fledglings and sat, propped against the cold side of the tunnel near the rear door, and as sunrise pressed down on him, pulling him into a fitful semiconscious state, he thought about his sister.

Was she truly alive? Had he really seen her, or had that been just another trick of this strange world?

Heff thought he'd forgotten how to let himself hope, but as sunrise forced him into sleep, he surprised himself by discovering he still knew how—Kevin Heffner still knew how to hope.

If only … If only it was true, and Zoey was alive and safe and a High Priestess. Could she help him? More importantly, *would* she help him?

(

Zoey

"They split up. A group of red vampyres went inside the Atlas Building. Just minutes ago a second group—this one mostly made up of fledglings—went into the tunnels in this basement," Marx reported to Stark, Shaunee, and me from the second-floor Philtower office that the TPD had commandeered.

"So, they're really trapped?" I said.

Marx nodded grimly. "They are. We blocked all exits from the Atlas tunnel. They have to go out the way they came in. And we double-checked the door between the Philtower and Philcade. It's been locked for years from the Philcade side, and it's definitely still secure. That's the only exit from the short Philtower tunnel system. Again, they have to go out the way they went in."

"It's sunrise," Stark said, wiping a weary hand across his face and sitting in a chair as far away from the picture windows as possible.

"Close those blinds, please," I said, squinting at the wall of windows.

"Sorry, Zoey. I wasn't thinking." Marx motioned for a uniformed officer to do so. "You okay, Stark?"

Stark nodded. "I'll be fine. The cloud cover is thick enough that I can walk outside, with this over my head." He tugged on his hoodie. "It's just not comfortable."

"How long are we going to wait before we move in?" I asked.

Marx spoke into the portable radio he pulled from his belt. "This is Marx. Ready to go at the Atlas?"

"Roger. Ready to go," came the crackly response.

Marx glanced at the mixed group of TPD officers and House of Night Warriors. Several of the cops held dangerous-looking equipment that, given Shaunee's obsessive staring, could only be flamethrowers. The rest had shotguns. Really big shotguns. The Warriors were armed with the ancient weapons we preferred—swords of different sizes and from different eras, as well as bows and long, evil looking lances.

"Ready to go?" he asked them.

As a group they nodded.

"Okay, briefly, we coordinate our attack with our people at the Atlas. We go to the tunnels at the same time. Give them an opportunity to surrender. If they don't take it—we take them out," Marx said. "Whatever happens, if you are human, do *not* let any of those creatures bite you."

"You said the fledglings are all here in the Philtower tunnel?" I asked.

"Yeah, we're pretty sure only full vampyres entered the Atlas. The fledglings were pretty easy to tell from the vampyres. They were staggering by the time they got inside."

"That's because they can't stay conscious after sunrise," I said.

"Stark and Darius already briefed us. We understand." Marx eyed his men. "There will be a bunch of fledglings passed out inside the tunnel. They can't wake while the sun's out. They're harmless. Ignore them while we deal with the vampyres. Then we can secure the fledglings." He glanced at me. "You want them taken to the House of Night, correct?"

"I do."

"All right. I talked to the chief. He's fine with the House of Night locking up the fledglings, but they are part of that vampyre group that killed eighty-four humans. He's going to need to know how they're punished."

"I understand," I said with confidence I didn't feel. *How the hell were we going to punish fledglings that everyday were losing more and more of what is left of their humanity?* I decided now was not the time to worry about that. Now was the time to get dangerous fledglings and vampyres off Tulsa's streets. "And I'm ready."

"All right, let's do this."

With military precision, the men moved out. We didn't use the elevator. We made our way quietly down the two stories to the door that opened to the lobby. Then we moved across the gorgeous space to another side door that opened to a drastically different-looking Philtower, morphing from Gothic and ornate to industrial and rather boring in the space of just a few feet.

"Okay, this is where you wait," Stark told me.

"Brownston, stay with the High Priestess," Marx ordered one of the men holding a flamethrower. "Be sure nothing gets to her."

"Will do, detective," Brownston said.

"And you back him up," Stark told Shaunee.

"No problemo. Z will be fine," Shaunee said.

"Leave that door open," I said. "I want to hear what's going on down there."

Stark nodded. The men moved silently down the first set of stairs. I heard Marx speaking quietly into his radio.

"On my mark counting down. Going at one. Starting—now. Ten, nine, eight, seven, six, five, four, three, two—engage!"

I paced while Shaunee and Brownston took positions near the open door.

Except for muffled footfalls, there were no sounds at first. Then there was what seemed like a forever pause, followed by the groaning of old hinges swinging open.

And then it was chaos.

"Red vampyres inside the tunnel! This is the Tulsa Police Department and the Sons of Erebus Warriors from the Tulsa House of Night. You have trespassed on a world not your own. You are trapped. We have flamethrowers and rifles trained on you. Adult vampyres—come out slowly with your hands open and raised. If you surrender, you will not be harmed. This is your only opportunity to save yourselves."

Marx's voice echoed up from the basement.

"Engage! Engage! Engage!" a voice shouted—one that seemed weirdly familiar to me, and I wondered briefly if some other vampyre who doesn't exist here anymore might have slipped from their world into ours.

Then I didn't have time to wonder about anything. Deafening shots echoed against the carved walls, filling my ears with ringing that almost, but not quite, covered the screams and curses of the men below us.

"No flamethrowers!" I distinctly heard Stark's shout. "You'll fry the fledglings!"

That had me running for the open door. Shaunee caught me as Brownston blocked the way to the basement with his body.

There were more shots—and more screams.

Then Stark again. "What the hell?" A pause. "They're getting away!"

And shoes pounded against tile as Stark surged through the open door.

"What's happening?" I shouted.

"They opened the door! They're in the Philcade! Brownston, come with me! Shaunee, stay here with Z!" The men sprinted to the door.

Shaunee looked at me.

"No, we will damn well *not* stay here," I said.

"Yaasss!" Shaunee said with a grin that was really just bared teeth.

We ran after the two men.

Moments ahead of us, Stark shoved open the doors to explode out onto a deserted, whitewashed street. He ducked his head and pulled his hoodie down over his face as he raced across the street to the Philcade with Brownston beside him.

The building was locked. Stark grabbed the flamethrower and hurled the butt end of it against the glass-fronted doors. They shattered and he reached in to yank open the door before disappearing into the T-shaped lobby.

"Go back!" Stark glared at me as Shaunee and I caught up with them.

"No!"

"This way!" Marx blew past me, rifle in his hand, pointing to his left. The five of us sprinted over the sleek marble floors, running past beautifully veined columns that held up the gold-leaf domed ceiling.

The men were ahead of me as I rounded the corner that fed into the decorative entrance to the tunnel system.

"Halt! If you do not stop, we will shoot!" Marx shouted.

I saw him lift his rifle and aim at the same instant Brownston flipped the safety off the flamethrower, and Stark, who was suddenly at my side, notched an arrow in his bow.

A long, evil hiss pulled my gaze to the end of the hall as the group of red vampyres, fangs bared, hands lifted like claws, and eyes glowing the red of old blood, converged on us.

"Steady. Fire as soon as they're in range," Marx told Stark and Brownston.

From the corner of my eye I saw Shaunee drawing deep breaths to center herself, and I knew she was evoking her element.

My gaze flickered to the group of red-eyed demons closing on us—and all the breath left my body.

Leading the group—eyes glowing red, fangs bared, full adult tattoo blazing scarlet against his skin—was my little brother.

"Ready, fi—"

"No!" I screamed, plowing my shoulder against Stark so hard that he fell against Marx. Stark lost his grip on his bow and almost dropped it. Marx's rifle wavered. "Don't shoot!" I yelled at him.

"Detective?" Brownston said, backing away with his finger on the trigger of the flamethrower.

At the same instant, Marx and I shouted together:

"Fire!"

"That's *my brother*!"

I heard Shaunee's shocked intake of breath, and then she moved with blurring speed to stand between the flamethrower and Kevin. The flamethrower engaged with a nauseating clicking sound. Shaunee lifted her hands, palms out. The tongue of flame simply licked against them harmlessly. She twisted her wrists, aiming her palms up, and the flame ricocheted off them to blast the ceiling.

There were glowing eyes everywhere.

Stark grabbed me, trying to pull me behind him. I turned as the horde raced past us.

"Kevin!" I shouted.

The lead vampyre stumbled. He whirled around to face me.

"Zoey!" His voice was rough—like he had a pack-a-day smoking habit—but it was *his* voice.

"Don't run! It's okay! Come with me back to the House of Night! I won't let anything happen to you!"

I saw him waver. I saw a flash of desire in his eyes so keen that

I swear they stopped glowing for a moment.

And then, with a feral cry, he spun back around and raced after the other vampyres.

"Go!" I screamed at Stark. "Don't let them kill him!"

Stark sprinted after Kevin, with Marx and Brownston right behind him. I tried to make my legs work. They wouldn't.

Then Shaunee grabbed my hand and pulled. Hard. "Come on!"

I unfroze and ran, retracing our path to the lobby. I got there to find Marx and Brownston standing in the middle of the street, staring impotently around them. Stark had run halfway down the block, but he'd stopped. The blowing snow made him barely visible, but I could see him turning in a slow circle, breathing hard.

Nothing. Kevin was nowhere, and neither were any of the other red vamps that had been with him.

"Where is he? Where'd he go?"

Marx shook his head. "Gone. Disappeared into the snow. Gotta call the Atlas." He keyed his radio. "Atlas, report!"

"All done here. Got 'em," came the reply.

"Did they surrender?" Marx asked.

"No, sir. They attacked. We defended. There are no survivors."

My gut felt hollow and my legs gave way. I was suddenly sitting on the cold marble floor.

"What's our casualty count?"

"Zero."

"Roger. Get the bus here to collect the fledglings. A group of adults escaped. Last seen headed east on Fifth Street. They're on foot."

"Roger! Be right there."

Marx rounded on me. "What the hell was that about? You could've gotten yourself killed and us worse."

I looked up at him. "That was my little brother. That was Kevin. That red vampyre in the lead. Kevin. *My little brother.* I—I couldn't let you kill him." And then I started to sob.

23

Damien

Sobbing and two sharp barks woke Damien. At first he didn't remember where he was, and then he saw Duchess. She was on Jack's bed. *Jack's bed? Jack's bed!* And reality chased away all vestiges of sleep.

Damien sat up straight—fully awake.

He'd fallen asleep in the chair beside Other Jack's bed. *Last Seen Leaving* was open on his lap. He hardly remembered it, but he knew he hadn't lasted long after sunrise when Jack had suddenly closed his eyes and gone completely still. As in *dead still.*

Duchess barked again and Damien was up and moving toward the bed before his thoughts had time to catch up with his feet.

Other Jack was crying.

No, that was wrong.

Jack was *sobbing*. He had his arms around Duchess' neck and his face was buried into the soft fur of her shoulder, and he was sobbing so hard that his whole body shook.

Damien felt a rush of concern and confusion.

Could I have slept the entire day in that chair? I must have.

"Jack?" He approached the bed cautiously as Duchess whined and gave him a doggy look that clearly conveyed worry. "What's wrong?"

Other Jack raised his head. Tears streamed down his face. "L—look at the time."

Completely confused, Damien glanced at his watch. He blinked. And blinked again.

"That can't be right."

"Wh—what does it say?" Jack hiccupped between sobs.

"It says that it's 8:25 a.m. On the morning of the twenty-fourth of December. But that can't be right. That means sunrise was less than an hour ago, and you definitely shouldn't be awake."

"Not shouldn't," Jack sniffled. "*Couldn't.*"

Damien went to the desk and grabbed the box of Kleenex, offering it to Jack. Jack blew his nose and wiped his eyes. Then he stared at the Kleenex.

"Jack? I don't understand what's going on."

Jack raised his face to look at Damien, and his eyes were shining, but not with red hunger and mindless anger. Jack's eyes were shining with joy.

"My tears. They're not bloody. Not at all." He held up the tissue, but Damien didn't need to see it for proof. Clear tears tracked their way down Jack's cheeks.

"Your tears." Damien's knees gave way and he sat heavily on the edge of Jack's bed. "They're clear. How do you feel?" he asked urgently.

Jack's smile was innocent and sweet and full of happiness. "I feel like myself."

"Like yourself?"

Jack nodded. "Yep! Exactly like myself. Before I rejected the Change. Before terrible, awful hunger woke me and I was a red fledgling, drafted to enter the Red Army. Damien, *I feel like myself.*"

"Come here," Damien said.

Eagerly, Jack lunged across the bed and into Damien's open arms. Their lips met and there was nothing tentative or hesitant about their kiss. It was deep and long and hot.

Damien forced himself to pull back a little. He was holding Jack against his chest and Grandma Redbird's rope of turquoise nestled between them—pressed as firmly against Jack as was Damien.

"The turquoise isn't burning you." Damien felt breathless and dizzy.

"And I don't want to bite you!" Jack touched Damien's cheek. His hand followed a light, caressing path down the side of his neck, where it lingered for a moment, before it slid down to Damien's chest where it rested, palm pressed against the turquoise beads. "Well," Jack smiled with shy flirtation. "I may want to bite you, but I don't mean to hurt you."

"How could this be?"

"I don't know. But I am so—"

The door slammed open and Aphrodite rushed into the room. She came to a stop beside the bed. Her Taser was in her hand, raised, and ready to shoot, but her eyes studied Damien and Jack. She lowered it.

"It really did work. Hey, Other Jack. You feeling fine?"

"I feel like *myself!*"

"Well, good. Excellent, actually."

"*Oh my holy shitfuck what happened to your face?*" Damien shouted, almost dropping Jack off the edge of the bed.

One corner of Aphrodite's mouth lifted. She raised her chin and shook back her uncharacteristically messy hair. "I made the Change. Times two. Oh, and Other Jack's totally fixed. You are welcome." And she twitched away.

Damien looked at Jack. Jack looked at Damien.

"Aphrodite is weird in any world," Other Jack said.

"I have zero trouble believing that." He pulled Jack into his arms. "Welcome home."

Their lips met, and they clung to each other as if they were human lifelines. Because that was exactly what they were.

(

Zoey

"No, Stark, we're getting you home. The sky is clearing. You know you can't stay out here in the sunlight." I turned around and stared out of the front window of the Escalade. "Ignore him and drive, Shaunee."

"Whatever you say, High Priestess." Shaunee gave me her version of a salute and pulled out into the snow-covered street while Stark huddled in the back seat, covered with a blanket against the sunlight that had suddenly decided to break through the low-hanging clouds and turn Tulsa into a glistening snow-globe scene. Yeah, it was beautiful. It was also deadly for red vampyres and red fledglings.

"Shaunee, go east down Fifth until you get to Detroit, then take a left. Let's go up over the overpass and make a loop around the Brady District. They might have found places to hide around Guthrie Green." Stark's voice was muffled but insistent.

"Well?" Shaunee cocked a brow at me.

"I'm fine back here, and you need to look for your brother."

"Without you frying," I said. "Which is why we're going back to the House of Night—right after we make that loop around the Brady District and Guthrie Green. But I'm doing the looking. Shaunee is doing the driving. And you keep your head covered."

"Deal," Stark said. "Hey, can you think of anywhere your brother would go? Any place that's special to him downtown?"

"No! I don't know him that well!" Then I drew a deep breath and started again. "Sorry. I don't mean to seem so crazy, but I'm—um—I'm pretty freaked out right now."

"When's the last time you talked to your brother?" Shaunee asked.

"The day I was Marked. I have a sister, too. Her name's Barbara, but I like to call her Barbie. She's a freshman at OSU—majoring in beer, cheerleading, and hot guys. Kevin is a sophomore this year at Broken Arrow. He's doing okay, but his teachers say his grades aren't great."

No one said anything. I sighed again. "What? Just because we don't talk doesn't mean I don't check up on them. Since Mom died I wanted to be sure they were okay. They are. The step-loser adopted Kevin. He didn't adopt Barbie, but she's over eighteen, so whatever."

"You didn't call them or anything?" Shaunee asked—not unkindly.

"I didn't know what to say. And the step-loser is a problem. He hated me. Well, hates me. I'm sure it's a present-tense thing. I didn't want any of that to rub off on them, plus Barbie has never wanted much to do with me. She was always perfect. She looked way more like Mom than Kev and me." I paused, thinking about what I really meant. *We all had the same bio-dad, but Barbie looked super white—she was even blond without too much help from her colorist at Ihloff Salon. Kevin and I looked like Grandma. We were brown—brown hair, brown eyes, brownish skin.* I shrugged. "I thought I was helping them by staying away. And most fledglings and vamps break from their human families. If not when they're Marked, when they Change." I squinted out at the uber-bright snowy morning, trying to catch a glimpse of something— anything—that might be Other Kevin.

"Hey, I'm not judging," Shaunee said. "My family totally has nothing to do with me. When I got Marked they basically dumped me."

"Mine, too," Stark said. "Z, we didn't mean to come down on you. We're just trying to help."

"I know, I know. I was just so shocked. *Am* just so shocked. I mean—Kevin. My annoying little brother who is totally into video games and smells like a teenage boy."

"Eww," Shaunee said.

"Yeah, he was *that* little brother. But now he's a killer red vampyre who can spread a zombie plague throughout Tulsa. I just … I just … I just have no words."

"We'll help, Z. Your Nerd Herd is all in one place again. We'll handle this. *You'll* handle this," Stark said.

I had no clue why his vote of confidence made my stomach hurt.

"This is a lot of snow. I'm glad you put chains on these tires," Shaunee said as she expertly steered us out of a nasty slide.

"Hey, you are good at snow driving," I said.

"Yep. I learned in Connecticut. Twenty inches of snow in a winter is considered mild."

"Slow down!" I said. "I think I saw something over there by the Brady Theater."

Shaunee braked and made a left turn the wrong way down a one-way street which was, thankfully, deserted. The Escalade barely crawled as we circled around the Brady Theater block.

"No, it was just that banner from Mexicali Grill flapping all weird in the wind," I said. "Maybe we should go inside the Brady, though, just in case."

"No," Stark said firmly. "Zoey, I'm your Warrior. You need to listen to me. It is not safe for the three of us to go into the Brady. Call Marx. Tell him you think you saw something. He'll be here with backup to check it out."

"You're right. I know you're right. It's just so bizarre. *It's Kevin.*"

"Yes. And Damien thought Other Jack was just Jack. If we hadn't been looking out for him, what would have happened?" Stark said.

"Other Jack would have eaten him," I said miserably. "Okay, I'm calling Marx. Keep driving, Shaunee. Circle around by the west edge of the railroad tracks. There are some overpasses there. They could be hiding under them."

"Okie dokie," Shaunee said.

I reached for the portable radio Marx had given us because the damn cell towers were still down—and my cell phone scared the crap out of me by exploding in vibrations and my "Eye of the Tiger" ringtone. I snatched it out of the side pocket of my coat.

"Hello."

"Zoey—Marx. The fledglings are awake."

"What? You mean fledglings at the House of Night?" Marx had agreed to escort the bus filled with the unconscious red fledglings to school, which is—sadly—where they had to be taken since the depot was still a crime zone, meaning the tunnels were off-limits.

"No. The ones in the bus. We're not at the school yet. What the hell's going on?" Marx said.

I looked at the face of my phone. It was 8:25 a.m. "I have no idea, but we'll meet you at the House of Night. Be sure you keep those fledglings covered and pull into the entrance by the Field House—the one that's covered. Cell service is obviously back, so I'll call the school and be sure they know you're coming in with red fledglings. Oh, and I might have seen something by the Brady Theater. Could you send some cops to check it out?"

"Will do." He hung up without another word.

"Shaunee, we need to—"

"Already heading back," she said. "Hang on."

"What was that about?" Stark asked.

"The red fledglings are awake," I said as I scrolled through my recent calls to find Lenobia's number, but before I could punch it, my phone rang again. The caller ID said APHRODITE. I stifled a sigh and answered. "Aphrodite, I don't have time for this right now."

"I'm sorry I was an awful bitch," she said.

"Oh. That's okay. Apology accepted."

"No, it's not okay, but I'm working on it. And you need to get back here."

"You sound sober."

"That's because I am sober. And there's something you need to see. Well, you need to know about it, too, but seeing it's important. Or at least I think it is. It really is beautiful, though I don't know why I'd expect anything less—what with Nyx doing it and all."

"You're babbling. Are you sure you're sober?"

"Positive."

"Okay, I'm on my way back. But Marx and a big TPD mobile prison van thing they call a bus is going to beat me there. It's supposed to be filled with passed-out red fledglings from the other world, but—"

"But they're awake," she said.

"How did you know that?"

"Come home and see for yourself. I'll tuck the fledglings in. Bye."

"Bye," I said, staring at the phone.

"Now what?" Stark asked.

"Aphrodite is sober. And she apologized to me for being a bitch."

"Are you sure you weren't talking to Other Aphrodite?" Shaunee said.

"I didn't see any other Aphrodite come through the fountain thing," I said.

"Well, neither did I, but apologizing for being a bitch doesn't sound like our Aphrodite."

"And yet she just did. She also knew the fledglings were awake. She said I need to see something. Or know about something. Or both, I guess. She's confusing me. Hell, this entire day is confusing me."

"Let's get home," Stark said, and Shaunee floored it.

24

Heff

Five of the vampyres made it out alive with him. Kevin ran. He led the remnant of his squad directly to the sewer grate he'd noted earlier. With their strength, they tore off the grill-like covering and dropped below in less than the time it took their pursuers to race out of the buildings after them.

The six of them were breathing hard, gasping with panic and adrenaline. He motioned for the soldiers to move through the sewer line, away from the grate as he whispered, "Quiet. Move this way." They followed him without question, crouching in the narrow, fetid space. Kevin was relieved that these five were coherent enough to actually follow orders—much of the Red Army's soldiers could only be pointed in an enemy's direction and set loose to rip and tear and bite and kill.

Kevin shuddered.

He was different. He'd always been different.

From the day his sister died—the day the dreams had started—the day he'd been Marked as the youngest red fledgling in history. And a scant two months later, the Change had altered him again—making him the youngest red vampyre in history.

Well, in his world's history anyway.

Sounds echoed from above, mixing eerily with the whining of the wind and the *drip, drip, drip* of water from somewhere behind them. The six of them huddled together, waiting.

Kevin's mind was a maelstrom of thoughts and emotions trying to sift their way through the incessant hunger and anger that shadowed his every moment since he'd picked up the phone one night and heard an emotionless voice report that his sister, Zoey Redbird, had been found dead—decapitated and nailed to a cross outside the House of Night. He'd put the phone down and turned to tell his mom the horrible news when he'd collapsed, only to struggle to his feet a moment later as his mother started screaming ... over and over ... pointing at the red crescent moon tattooed in the center of his forehead.

Think. Reason. You can do it. What do I know for sure?

Zoey was alive, even though he knew she was dead. The morbid pictures had been in the *Tulsa World*. Zo's death was the third decapitation outside the House of Night, and the backlash from the vampyres against humans had been swift and decisive.

Neferet's armies had been victorious. They were still victorious.

But there was no sign of Neferet or her soldiers here.

Humans and vampyres—red and blue—worked together here.

Zoey was alive. His sister was alive. She'd recognized him. She'd saved him from being fried.

The men who attacked us aren't lying. This really isn't my world.

"What are our orders?"

Kevin shook himself and refocused on the present. One of the soldiers was watching him closely—the red glow in his eyes present, but dim. *If we stay awake, we will have to feed.*

"Sleep," Kevin told him. "I'll stay on watch."

"At sunset. What orders then?" the soldier asked.

"At sunset we go to the rendezvous point and meet the general,"

Kevin said automatically, though he sincerely doubted the general would show.

The people of this world were on to them, and the general had fallen into their trap. Kevin would have been trapped, too, and killed, had it not been for Zoey.

"Sleep," Kevin repeated. "Then we rendezvous and feed."

That got through to them, and the soldiers formed a nest-like group together and slept.

Kevin struggled against that pull. It would be good—so good to curl up with the others—to share their heat and their heartbeats—to sleep mindlessly and then wake with nothing but hunger on his mind.

No. I do not want that. I do not want to lose myself. And I do not want to lose my dreams.

Adrenaline and panic gone, exhaustion took their place. Kevin walked heavily to stand closer to the grate. He had to cover his eyes and squint against the suddenly strong light of the sun, and he was careful to avoid the slatted rays that filtered down between the grate. Sounds of the men above became more distant and irregular. The street seemed to have quieted. Kevin sat and leaned his head against the cold, wet side of the sewer pipe.

What am I going to do now?

His thoughts were shifting back to Zoey and the wide-eyed look of shock that had frozen her in place before him when it happened.

It was like he had been holding his breath for too long, and all of a sudden, he was able to draw air—clean, sweet, life-giving air. He gasped aloud—and heard his gasp echoed by the five soldiers. They sat, blinking and looking around as if they had no idea where they were. Their gazes turned to him as one.

"Lieutenant?" The soldier who had spoken before was the first to say anything. "What just happened?"

The other men shook their heads and rubbed their eyes as if they'd just stepped inside out of a ferocious rainstorm.

Kevin drew a breath. And then another. "I—I'm not sure. How do you feel?" he asked the soldier.

"My name is Marc—Marc Haimes. And I feel normal. I feel absolutely normal."

"So do I," said the guy next to him. "I'm Ben."

"Yeah, I'm good, too. And I'm Ethan."

"Got a headache and it smells bad down here, but I'm cool. My name's Dave."

"I'm Justin. Where the hell are we?"

Kevin stared at them. "You can think again."

The five of them nodded. They didn't look much different except there was no sign of redness in their eyes and their faces were animated with emotion—emotion that wasn't anger or insatiable hunger.

"We've been healed," Kevin said slowly.

"What do ya mean, healed?" Marc said. "I'm fine. Or, I *was* fine until just the other day when I woke up with that damned red crescent Mark on my ..." his voice faltered.

Then Kevin watched as they remembered.

Silently, the five of them stared, slack-jawed, at one another. Kevin saw it. He saw the realization of what they had become—the memory of the things they had done—flood into minds that were no longer poisoned. He understood then for the first time the answer to the question he had been unable to ask safely back in his world. *Am I the only red vampyre who still remembers what it's like to be human?*

Yes. The answer was yes. Kevin Heffner had been the only red vampyre in his world to remember what it was like to be human—to mourn for it, to miss it, and to be disgusted by what they had all become. But now these other five—they, too, remembered their humanity. And they couldn't bear it.

"No." The word wrenched from Marc on a sob.

"I couldn't do those things. Really. I'm serious. I couldn't," Ben said as tears washed down his cheeks.

"No, no, no, no, no, no, no, no, no, no," Justin repeated the litany as he shook his head back and forth.

Marc forced himself to his feet and stumbled to Kevin. He went to his knees and stared into Kevin's eyes. "We have torn people apart with our teeth and hands. We ate them. People. Innocent people."

"Yes." The word hovered in the air around them, condemning them—taunting them—hurting them.

"I've got to get outta here!" Marc lurched toward the grate, only pausing to grimace in pain when the slats of sunlight hit his body.

"Stop!" Kevin shouted, lunging for him. But he was already in the sunlight. Kevin recoiled, expecting Marc to burst into flames.

Instead Marc jumped back—staring down at his body. He was wearing a T-shirt and his exposed forearms were striped with a nasty sunburn that was already blistering. "I didn't die."

"We have been healed," Dave said, scooting over closer to them as he gaped at Marc.

"Will it go away? Will we turn back into those—those *things* we were?" Marc asked.

"I don't know," Kevin said.

"How could this be? Who did this to us? I can't—I can't bear the memories. I can't." Ethan put his face in his hands and sobbed.

"No, no, no, no, no, no ..." Justin babbled as he stared up at the grate.

"Do you remember what they shouted at us when they trapped us? They said we'd trespassed on a world not our own," Kevin reasoned aloud. "I think they were right. We're not in our world anymore."

"It could be a trap. A rebel army trap," said Marc.

"No. This isn't our world. Since when have humans been allowed to decorate the streets for Christmas?" Kevin said. "And what about the depot? There was a restaurant there where *humans* were being waited on *by fledglings—red fledglings.*"

"That's impossible," Dave said.

"Exactly. And that vampyre—the blue one in the tunnels who

232

stopped the others from killing us—she's my sister. In our world, my sister died the day I was Marked, more than a year ago."

"What does all of this mean?" Marc asked.

"I know who might help us figure this out," Kevin said.

"Who?" Davis said.

"My sister. She tried to tell me. She said not to run. Zoey will help me. She'll help us. I know it."

"She can't help this." Ben stood and lifted a trembling finger to press it to his temple. "She can't help the memories stop here."

"No, but she can help us figure out how to go forward from here," Kevin said.

"There's no going forward after what I've done." Ethan stood shakily beside Ben.

"But we have to," Kevin said.

"No, no, no, no, no." Justin repeated the word as he stood with Ben and Ethan.

The three vampyres shared a long look.

"Justin has it right. No," Ben said. "No, we don't have to go forward."

"And we won't," Ethan said.

Together, Ben, Ethan, and Justin charged forward, knocking David off his feet and throwing Marc into Kevin. Caught off guard, Kevin scrambled to get out from under Marc and gain his footing. When he did it was too late. Ben had shoved the sewer grate aside and crawled through the opening, with Ethan and Justin following him.

Kevin lunged for Justin's leg. He managed to snag his ankle, but Justin kicked him, sending Kevin back on his butt. By the time he regained his feet for the second time, the three red vampyres were already running clear of the grate.

Yanking his shirt up so that it covered his head and part of his face, Kevin pulled himself up in time to see Ethan, Ben, and Justin, bodies smoking in the winter sunlight, shouting incoherently at the group of uniformed men who had been getting into black

SUVs. The men turned. Kevin heard them order, "*TPD! Halt or we'll shoot!*" The three didn't pause.

"Do it or we will eat you!" Ben's anguished shout carried down to them.

The man with the flamethrower turned it on them.

Kevin pulled the grate back over the manhole and fell heavily to the ground as their screams died in flames and sunlight and blood.

Marc hurried to him, pulling him back out of the splotch of sunlight.

"I couldn't stop them," Kevin said between heaving breaths. "I tried. But I couldn't stop them." He stared up at Marc and David. "Are you going to do it, too? Are you going to commit suicide?"

"I can't promise that I'll be able to live with my past, but I need answers," Marc said. "I'm coming with you, Lieutenant."

"I'm with you, too. I won't pretend that I can handle this, but I also need answers," David said.

"So, our plan?" Marc asked as he sat beside Kevin.

"Wait here until dusk and then go to the House of Night and ask to see my sister."

"What if they kill us?" David asked.

"Then we're dead and we don't have to figure out how to live with our memories," Kevin said.

"Good point," Marc said. "I'm in."

"That'd solve one problem for us. I'm in, too," David said.

(

Zoey

There was just enough room for the Escalade to fit beside the TPD transport bus and still be under the covered entrance to the Field House. Shaunee hadn't even put it into park yet and I was out of the SUV and halfway through the door to the school, with Stark and Shaunee scrambling to catch up with me, when I ran into Aphrodite. Literally. Knocking her smack on her butt.

Well, technically *I* didn't knock her on her butt. The door I'd pushed open did. But still, she fell with an ungraceful *smack* on the tile floor.

"Ouch! Damn, Z. I thought you said my apology was accepted." She was rubbing her butt as she stood. She tilted her head up to give me a scrunch-faced look and there it was—the most incredible Mark I had ever seen.

"How? Wh—? I don't—I've never seen anything like that!" I blurted when I finally managed to regain control over my mouth.

"Fuck me running, Aphrodite's a vampyre!" Shaunee said as she slid to a stop behind me.

"Red and blue. Red *and* blue?" Stark babbled. "How could it be red and blue? And you weren't even a fledgling anymore."

"Right?! It's crazy cool, isn't it?" Aphrodite said. She shook back her hair so that we could get a better look.

I'll admit it. I gawked.

Her Mark was spectacular! It looked like one of the handmade, vintage Mardi Gras masks sold in the gorgeous boutiques in Venice— the kind exquisite women held to frame their eyes after their hair was piled on top of their heads and their boobs billowed out of the bodice of their seventeenth-century reproduction gowns. Stark was right—the Mark was in red *and* blue, and it looked like delicate, glistening fireworks exploding in beauty across her flawless skin.

"I don't understand," I said.

"Neither do I," Stark said.

"Yeah, it's cool and all, but what the hell are you?" Shaunee asked.

Aphrodite lifted one perfect brow. "I am a bridge."

"Huh?" I said.

"That's what Nyx told me. That was pretty much my reaction, too. At first."

"But why did this happen?" I still couldn't wrap my mind

around it. "Are you still a Prophetess?"

"Uh, yes. Squared. At least. And it happened because I finally let it go," Aphrodite said.

"Damn, girl. You know we have no clue what *it* is," Shaunee said.

"*It* is a lot of things—but mostly my mother and all the crap she's done to me. And by letting her go I mean I finally got it. I finally understood that no matter how much I want her to love me and to be a good mom—hell, even an average mom—however much I want that, it's out of my control. It doesn't matter what I say or do. I can't fix her. I can only fix how I react to her—or I'm doomed, *through my own decisions and my own actions* to repeat her bullshit awful life. That's it. Then Nyx showed up and this happened and a bunch more."

"Well put, Aphrodite. Zoeybird, that nice Detective Marx said that you needed to speak with me." Grandma appeared from the hallway that led to the Field House.

"I do." I drew a deep breath and blurted, "You know how Other Jack came through from the other House of Night world?"

"Yes."

"Someone else we recognize came through from that world. It's Kevin, Grandma. He's a red vampyre."

"Oh, dear. Oh, oh, dear." She swayed a little and Stark rushed to take her arm.

"Steady, there, Grandma. It'll be okay. We're going to find him and bring him here. Just like Other Jack is here."

"Is he like those poor young fledglings? They are all so upset. It's just terrible what they're going through."

"I don't know what he's like, Grandma," I said. "I only saw him for a second, but he called my name. He definitely recognized me."

"Zoey, there you are!" Marx rushed up from the Field House side of the entrance. "I'm getting crazy reports from downtown. Seems a few red vampyres, the same ones that were in our tunnels, committed suicide."

"Oh, Goddess, no!" Grandma's legs buckled and only Stark's

strong arm around her kept her from falling to the floor.

Marx moved to Grandma's side. "No, no, not your grandson! I'm sorry, Mrs. Redbird. I should have led with that. One of the officers who saw Kevin in the tunnel earlier was there. He said none of these vampyres were your brother." "Committed suicide? What the hell?" Stark said.

"I know what the hell," Aphrodite said. "It goes along with this." She pointed to her incredible Mark. "And to why the red fledglings from the other world are awake and aware. Come on inside. I'll tell you everything. Oh, and don't expect Damien to join us anytime soon. He and Other Jack are having a *thing*." She held up her hand and "*shh, shh, shh'd*" me when I tried to get more info about the *thing*.

"Boy-on-boy action. That's all I'm gonna say because I'm pretty sure they won't let me watch. Even though I'm pretty sure I'd like to watch. So, to tell you more, I'd have to make up the details, and my brain is busy." She shrugged. "Anyway, come on. I have some unbelievable shit to tell you."

"This should certainly be interesting," Grandma said, already sounding more like herself.

"Would you do me the honor of taking my arm, Sylvia?" Stark held his arm out for her, looking every bit the gentleman. Grandma smiled at him and took it, the color coming back into her smooth cheeks.

I loved him so much at that moment that it was difficult for me to breathe.

25

Zoey

"Wow. Just wow." I couldn't stop staring at Aphrodite's Mark. We were all in the conference room attached to the administrative offices, and everyone—Stark, Shaunee, Marx, and Lenobia—was gawking at Aphrodite, too.

"Let me make sure I have this straight—the vamps and fledglings from the other world are cured, for lack of a better word," Marx said.

"They are," Aphrodite said. "Well, a better way of putting it is that they have been restored. Their humanity, that is."

"And that is why they began committing suicide—because their humanity has been returned and they cannot live with the things they've done," Grandma said. "That does make a terrible sort of sense."

Stark touched her shoulder gently. "Hey, that doesn't mean Kevin will commit suicide."

"I understand that, child, but it does mean he is suffering."

I looked at Marx. "We need to find him."

"I have all of TPD combing downtown looking for places he could be hiding. Give me a sec and I'll radio that they are to hold their fire and not let them commit suicide by cop like those other three just did."

"U-we-tsi-a-ge-ya, I must leave."

"Grandma? You can't go back to the lavender farm. There's just too much snow," I said.

"Oh, no, Zoeybird. I must leave this room and go to Nyx's Temple. There I will cleanse and then begin the prayer vigil for Kevin. That is—if I have your permission to do so."

"Of course, Grandma! If you need anything just ask one of the priestesses in the meditation chamber." I went to her and took her hand. "Are you okay?"

"I will be when we bring Kevin home." She patted my hand and then kissed my cheek. "You do your part, and I will do mine." Then, slowly, as if her age had suddenly caught up with her, Grandma shuffled from the room.

I went to the phone on the admin desk and punched the number for Nyx's Temple. The priestess answered on the second ring. "This is Zoey. My grandma's on her way to the temple. Give her anything she needs and keep an eye on her. Not stalker-ish, though. Just be sure she's okay. Call me if she needs anything at all. Thank you." I put the phone down and took my seat again. "Okay, where were we?"

"I'm assuming you want your brother and any other red vampyre we find brought here right away?" Marx continued.

"Yes. Please," I said.

"Okay, no problem." He started to step out into the hall to do so, but paused and looked back at Aphrodite. "Is their bite still infectious?"

"No. They're like regular red fledglings and vampyres now," she said. "Hey, uh, Marx, could you do something for me, please?"

"If I can."

"Would you go to St. John's and tell my mother she's been cured— or there's been a mistake and she was always okay—whatever. Just let her know she's not turning into anything and not dying."

"You went to the hospital? To see that horrible woman? Really?" Shaunee said.

"Is your mother crazy?" Aphrodite shot the question at Shaunee.

"No. She's just apathetic."

"Then don't talk to me about going to see her. I'm not proud of the things I said to her, and I won't do it again. But I'm not going to pretend like I'm sorry. I'm not. I'm just sorry I let her hurt me for so long." Her gaze went back to Marx. "Will you talk to her for me?"

"Are you sure you don't want to? I'd go with you," he said.

"I am absolutely sure. Actually, one of my new goals is never to talk to my mother again in this lifetime."

"All righty then. I'll stop by St. John's on the way downtown. If you'll excuse me. My men need to be briefed on the latest."

He left the room and we went back to staring at Aphrodite's Mark.

"So, what now?" she asked.

"Are you sure you don't want to go to the hospital with him to tell your mom she's going to be okay?" I asked.

"Yes. Let's change the subject. How do you feel about your brother being a rogue red vampyre?"

"I feel like my head might explode," I said honestly.

"Makes sense," she said. "Are you going to go out and look for him?"

"Of course," I said.

"You could stay here," Stark said. "And get the new red fledglings situated. I'll go out there for you. If Darius and I can't find him—no one can."

"You're not going out there. It's way too sunny," I said.

"You're not going out there. It's way too dangerous," Stark said.

"I hate to break up this cute little prelude to an argument, but someone—someone who is a red vampyre—needs to stay here and calm those new fledglings down. They're pretty freaked," Aphrodite said.

"That's no surprise," Shaunee said. "They ate people. *Literally.* That can't be good for your self-esteem."

"Aphrodite's right," I said. "Those fledglings are going to have a tough time. Where's Stevie Rae?"

"In the basement with them already. It's too bad you missed her reaction to seeing my Mark. It was a classic bumpkin explosion of "Ohmygood*ness*" and a disturbing metaphor that had something to do with a speckled pup—what the hell ever that means. Anyway, she's down there. So are Shaylin and Nicole, but the new fledglings are all guys, and I think they'd feel better with a guy to talk to. Or whatever males do when they bond."

"I'll go back out there with Z. The red vamps aren't dangerous anymore, but if anything happens fire will light them up." Shaunee made a little flourish with her hands.

"Just because they have their humanity back doesn't mean they aren't dangerous," Stark said. "Three of them already committed suicide by cop. We don't know what the rest of them might do."

"I can handle myself. And I'll stay with Shaunee."

"And Darius," Aphrodite added. "Where is my man?"

Finished with his call, Marx stuck his head back in the room. "Darius is returning to the House of Night. He's escorting the coroner's van here with the remains from the tunnels—not that there's much left. Should I wait for him to get here?"

"No, go ahead. He has a radio, right?" I asked.

"Yeah."

"Good. Shaunee and I will go out with him and start searching. We'll coordinate with you through the radio."

"We've already started searching a grid. Darius has been briefed. And be careful out there. The city is still under a state of emergency and I haven't let the plows go yet."

"We'll take the Escalade. It has chains."

"She'll also fill the Escalade with Warriors." Stark gave me a dark but resigned look.

"Okay, I'm out of here," Marx said. "Aphrodite, want me to give you a call and update you on how your mom's doing?"

"No thank you," she said.

I watched Aphrodite. She was definitely not drunk or high anymore, but that wasn't a surprise. Vampyres metabolized alcohol and drugs differently than humans, so in order for her to be drunk she'd have to drink, like, a case or so of booze—which I wouldn't put past her, but she clearly hadn't had the time. Yet. I had no clue if Xanax was still going to work on her at all, and I wondered how she was going to handle her new powers—and her new attitude about her mom—sober. For as long as I'd known her, Aphrodite hadn't handled much of anything sober.

"You are staring."

"Sorry. Your Mark is really pretty."

"I know, right? But you weren't staring at me with a your-Mark-is-really-pretty stare."

"Well, it's a lot to take in," I equivocated.

"Guys, could we get some help downstairs?" Shaylin rushed into the conference room looking wide-eyed and wild-haired. "Those new fledglings are crying. Seriously. I mean, bawling with snot and everything. Damien and Other Jack are trying to comfort them, but they're super freaked. And by-the-by, their auras are all over the place."

"Someone needs to knock them out," Aphrodite muttered.

That gave me an idea. "Hey, what if we moved them from the basement to the boy's dorm. The windows are securely draped and they'd be safe from sunlight, but it's harder for red fledglings to stay awake if they're above the ground."

"That's a good idea," Stark said. "And you're right."

Shaylin smacked herself on the forehead. "Sheesh, I used to be a red fledgling. You'd think I would've remembered that."

"Okay, I'll help move them," Stark said.

"And be sure they're safe," I said. "And I mean even from themselves."

"How about assigning one of our fledglings to each of them?" Aphrodite said.

"I like that. Where's Lenobia?"

"In the basement, very awkwardly trying to get a bunch of boys to stop crying," Shaylin said. "At this moment I'm pretty sure she hates her job."

"I'm pretty sure you're right. So, have Lenobia make a list of students she thinks would be good partners for the new fledglings. Then you guys start pairing them off to the dorm."

"Okay, will do!" Shaylin said. Before she disappeared down the hallway, her eyes focused on Aphrodite. "Your Mark freaks me out. It's beautiful and all, but still. Freaks. Me. Out."

"Thank you," Aphrodite said. Then her eyes brightened and she was on her feet. "There's my man!" She glanced around the room and rolled her eyes. "Why do we not have a mirror in here?"

"Uh, it's a conference room. A student conference room," Shaunee said.

"And your point is students don't want to look good? That's just ridiculous." She came to me and peered into my face like I was a mirror. "How do I look?"

"Well, your Mark is gorgeous."

"I know."

"And your hair is very cray."

"If Erin were here she'd say it looks like a fart," Shaunee said.

"No words. I have no words for you and that awful comment," Aphrodite said to Shaunee.

While Shaunee cackled, I told Aphrodite the truth. "Hey, stop stressing. Darius is going to think you're beautiful. Because you are beautiful and because he loves you."

"You're absolutely right. Thanks, Z."

Then Darius walked into the room, with a wall of Sons of Erebus Warriors at his back.

"This is gonna be good," Shaunee whispered.

Aphrodite turned. I saw Darius' face go blank, as if he couldn't process what he was seeing, and then his eyes widened and his face flushed. He went to Aphrodite and knelt on one knee and bowed his head.

"Marx said something happened. He said you are why the red fledglings woke and why the red vampyres committed suicide. My beauty, my High Priestess, my Consort, and my love—it is my lifelong honor to be your Oathbound Warrior. Do you accept my pledge?"

Aphrodite knelt in front of him. She took his face between her hands so that he looked into her eyes. "Always, Darius. Always. I haven't deserved you. But I give you my oath in return that I'll work harder to be worthy of you. Now, please stand up and kiss me."

Darius did as his High Priestess commanded, and the Warriors behind him cheered.

"That was super sappy," Shaunee said under her breath.

"What Shaunee said." Stark kissed me quickly. "I'll go help with the red fledglings. I have my phone with me, but if the cells go out again, be sure you keep radioing in back here. I want constant updates. Okay?"

"Okay." I kissed him back. "Thank you. By the way, just in case you even wonder—you are my definition of awesomesauce."

He grinned his cocky James Stark smile, tapped the end of my nose with his finger, and whispered, "I love you, too, my Queen."

(

Zoey

I was beyond frustrated. We'd been searching downtown on a grid, and hadn't found Kevin or any recent sign of him or any other red vampyres.

Oh, we'd found where they'd broken into the old Sinclair

Building on Boston. They'd eaten some poor homeless people who'd had the bad luck to think they'd found safety from the blizzard, but the red vampyres hadn't returned. And now it was 5:00 and almost sunset, and I could only think of one thing to do.

"Let's return to the House of Night. I'll get Stark and Stevie Rae and Rephaim, and we'll come back out and keep searching."

"Z, not sure that's such a good idea. It's starting to snow again," Shaunee said.

"It'd be bad if you got stuck out here in another blizzard. Especially bad as there are red vampyres, probably panicked and dangerous, that are going to emerge from wherever they're hiding in just a few minutes," Darius added.

"I have to keep looking. He's my brother." What I didn't want to admit aloud is what had been circling around and around inside my head all day—that I couldn't let Other Kevin down. I'd already let one Kevin down. I'd basically abandoned him, leaving him to deal with my step-loser and high school peer pressure by himself.

"We get it, Z. We just want you to be safe," Shaunee said.

"I know. Sorry if I seem short." I rubbed the bridge of my nose. I had an awful headache and my eyes were stinging from staring out at sun-drenched snow all day. I needed food and rest, but when I thought about Kevin out there huddled somewhere dark and the pain and fear and confusion he must be going through—well, I had to keep looking. "I appreciate you guys."

"We'll find him." Darius spoke with a lot more confidence than I felt.

I stared out at the milky grayness that signaled the beginning of sunset as the SUV crawled its way home. It had started to snow again. Thankfully this time the wind was being still and fat flakes lazily feathered their way to the ground.

Sometime in the middle of the day, the electricity had gone out across most of midtown, and as we approached the House of Night, it was lit up by flickering gaslight flames, making the campus look as if it had been frozen in the past.

Stark met us as we walked through the door. He hugged me tightly and I gave myself a moment, resting my cheek against his chest while he wrapped me in his arms, surrounding me in love and warmth.

"Thanks," I whispered to him. "I needed that."

"Me, too. You okay?"

"If I said yes would you believe me?"

"Not for a second."

"Well then, let's get something to eat and talk about our plan for the night."

"That sounds like a great idea. I'm starving," Shaunee said. "And where's—"

Erik Night rounded the corner. The instant he saw Shaunee his face lit with his megawatt movie-star smile. He covered the few yards that separated them in two strides and lifted her into his arms, twirling her around.

I waited, trying not to cringe, for her to zap him with a spark or, at the very least, order him to put her down. Instead, she giggled.

Giggled.

"There's my hotness!" He nuzzled her neck and gave her a mischievous little bite. "Do you know what I've been doing all day while you were out gallivanting with Z?"

"Running lines while you gazed lovingly at yourself in the mirror? Again?" she said impishly.

"No, smartass. I've been babysitting red fledglings."

"Did they not settle down and sleep?" I tried not to stare at the two of them. I mean, they make a gorgeous couple, but I just wasn't used to Shaunee being all girly about a guy. *Or* Erik being so infatuated that he didn't care whether he looked cool or not.

Erik put Shaunee down. "About half of them did. The other half are touch and go. It was a good idea to pair them with our

246

fledglings, though. That did help. One kid won't stop crying. At all. Shaylin said his aura is very dark and messed up. I don't think anyone knows what to do about it."

"I do." Aphrodite emerged from the hallway that led to the Field House. "We give him time. We let him talk. And we get him a dog." She went to Darius and started to wrap her arms around him before realizing he was covered in fat snowflakes. With a grimace, she brushed the snow from his shoulders, grumbling, "Ugh. Snow. It always reminds me of that awful scene from *The Breakfast Club* when Ally Sheedy's Goth character makes that picture with dandruff snow. It scarred me for life." Then she pulled him to her for a long, lingering kiss.

"Wait, did you say a dog?" I asked.

"Yes. I think we need to invest in PTSD service dogs for the new fledglings. The cats don't want anything to do with them. It's weird, actually. But they came from another world, so I suppose cats being repulsed by them isn't really that weird. Anyway, Duchess was downstairs with Damien and Other Jack. She didn't mind the fledglings at all when they showed up hysterical and dirty. You know—that's just another difference between dogs and cats, who I think are much better judges of character. Dogs accept practically anyone. Cats are more discerning."

"Do not disrespect my dog, Aphrodite," Stark said.

"Oh, don't get your panties in a wad, Bow Boy. I'm just mentioning a difference in the two—I'm not disrespecting. Duchess helped today. A lot. So, let's get more dogs."

"Seems like an easy fix to me. And I like dogs. Let's contact the Tulsa Humane Society and rescue a bunch of cool dogs for the fledglings. Totally a win-win," I said. "Do you guys all want to get something to eat and then I'll check on the new kids before I go back out there and keep looking for Other Kevin?" I glanced around. "Is Damien still downstairs with Other Jack? And where's Stevie Rae?"

"Damien and Other Jack were heading to our dining hall. I told him you wouldn't care if Other Jack joined him because he's technically dead and not a student here," Aphrodite said.

"Morbid, but correct."

"And Stevie Rae was helping us with the fledglings, but when it got close to dusk she took off to catch Bird Boy, or whatever it is she does to get him to fly back to her."

I rolled my eyes.

"She said she'd meet us in the dining hall with Rephaim. I assume after he exchanges feathers for jeans and a T-shirt."

"All righty then," I smiled at everyone, hoping if my face was happy, my mind would follow. "Who wants psaghetti?"

(

Zoey

I got a major flash of déjà vu when I stepped into the dining hall and saw Damien sitting at our table with Other Jack. The two of them were holding hands; their heads tilted toward one another. Jack whispered something into Damien's ear and his laughter was like glitter, floating around the room and leaving little pieces of it on all of us.

"He looks so much better," Shaunee said.

"Which one?" Aphrodite said.

"Both," Darius said as we walked to our table.

"Hi guys. Other Jack, it's really good to see you. I'd ask how you're feeling, but it's obvious that you are feeling great."

"Merry meet, High Priestess!" Other Jack stood, bowing to me formally.

"Hey, call me Zoey. You and I are going to be good friends. Again."

We slid into our large table and the waitress took our orders. I was surprised when Aphrodite ordered a salad to go with her usual glass (or five) of wine, and even more surprised when it came and she ignored the wine and dug into the food.

"There you are, u-we-tsi-a-ge-ya!" Grandma, whirlwind-like, rushed up to our table. "Might I have a plate of that spaghetti?"

"Absolutely!" Stark caught the priestess-on-duty's attention and ordered a plate for Grandma.

"I didn't find him, Grandma. But I will. We will. I promise."

"The Sons of Erebus will do everything we can to bring him home, on that you have my word, as well, Grandma Redbird," Darius said solemnly.

"Oh, you won't need to," she said.

"Huh?"

Grandma gave me a sly smile and Darius a wink. "I believe Kevin will find you."

"Z! Good! You're back. Rephaim has stuff to tell you." Stevie Rae and Rephaim rushed to our table. "Hi Grandma! Oooh! Psaghetti! Yum. I'll take some."

"Kalona wasn't in your dream!" Rephaim said without any preamble.

"Uh, yeah, he was. I was there. I saw him."

"It may have looked like him and sounded like him, but I promise you it was not my father. He swore on his love for Nyx that he did not enter your dream. Furthermore, he told me to relay to you that he gives you his oath that he will *never* come to you in a dream in a place from your past. It is just as I explained before, Father wants to distance himself from what he once was."

"If it wasn't him, then who the hell was it?" Stark looked as confused and upset as I felt.

"Father said that you should try to remember anything that might have been off about the dream. He also said it was very odd that the message had to do with Neferet's journal, as he believes he is the only person who knows about it."

I thought back. "It seemed like him. Well, an awkward

version of him, but I didn't think anything of that. I mean, he was showing up in my dream in a place he once stalked me—hence the awkwardness." I chewed my lip, thinking. "Wait, there were two things a little weird. I mentioned that I liked his white wings better than the black ones, and he seemed shocked."

"Shocked that you like 'em?" Stevie Rae asked between bites of spaghetti.

"No, shocked that they were white. Also, he made a comment that I didn't think much of then, but now it could be a big deal. I'm paraphrasing, but he said that he was warning me because, unlike Nyx, he'd spent time with all of us and he knew we could handle the worry."

I saw Rephaim startle. "Father would not say that. He would not even infer anything negative about Nyx."

"Ah, shit. I just had a thought. Could it have been Neferet, pretending to be Kalona?" Aphrodite said.

"I don't think that's possible," I said.

"Well, it might be if she has attained the ability to influence the world around her," Darius said.

"But it doesn't make sense that she would warn us about herself," I said. "And she would never show us her journal."

"Seriously, it's way too personal," Shaunee said.

"Yeah, no way. And whoever was pretendin' to be Kalona was right—we did learn a bunch of stuff about her when we read it," Stevie Rae said.

"Then who else has the power to manipulate dreams *and* has personal knowledge about Neferet?" Grandma asked.

I thought back, mentally sifting through the horrific memories recorded in Emily Wheiler's tragic journal—and a sudden coldness began to build and expand in the core of my body.

"There's only one entity who has that kind of power and that kind of knowledge—the White Bull," I said.

Into the awful silence, Other Jack raised his hand.

"Honey, you don't have to raise your hand to say something," Damien told him.

"Not even to ask a question?"

"Not even to ask a question," I said.

"Oh, thanks. That's nice of you. So, um, who's the White Bull?"

"Evil," Damien said. "The White Bull is pure evil."

"That's bad. Really bad," said Other Jack.

"You have no idea." I pushed my psaghetti away as I felt the puzzle pieces fall into place. "Of course the White Bull's behind this mess. All that crap about Neferet and bad things coming our way—none of that was true. That dream created all of this—all by simply making us think Neferet was up to something and then letting it avalanche from there."

"But why? What does he want?" Other Jack asked.

"Chaos and death—that's all the White Bull wants," Damien said.

"And that's exactly what he caused. Again," I said.

"Actually, u-we-tsi-a-ge-ya, this time that is not all he caused," Grandma added. "This time he caused Damien and Jack to be reunited, Aphrodite to be healed of her past and Marked as a special kind of vampyre Prophetess, and Kevin, our Other Kevin, to have his humanity returned to him. This time he believed he was causing chaos and working evil, but in truth love and Light shinned through his Darkness."

"Which means he's going to be really pissed that his nefarious plan didn't work," said Aphrodite.

Ah. Hell.

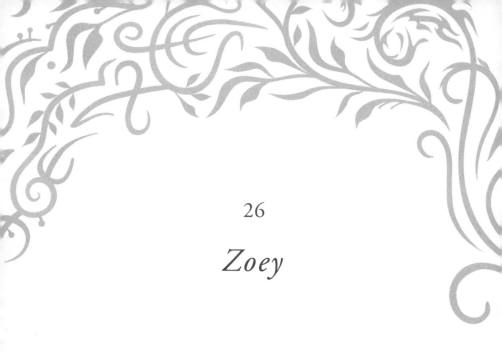

26

Zoey

I'd gone back to my room to wash my face and change my clothes before Stark and I and a bunch of Warriors headed out to keep looking for Kevin when I heard the Warriors who were pulling duty on the wall sound a warning. I rushed from my room and down the hall, meeting Aphrodite and Darius as we surged into the stairway.

"Do you know what it is?" I asked Darius.

"No." He looked grim, and I noticed as we jogged down the stair he was fitting throwing knives into his custom-made vest.

I mentally crossed my fingers and sent up a silent plea, *Nyx, let it be Other Kevin, and don't let him be too crazy.*

We rushed to the front of the building and were met by a Son of Erebus Warrior and Stark.

"What's going on?" I asked Stark.

"Three vampyres just climbed the Utica-side gate and entered campus," Stark said.

"Red?" Darius asked.

"Yes," said the Warrior.

Flanked by my Warriors, I went to the front door, trying to see through the darkness and the large, lazy snowflakes that didn't seem to ever want to end. I could make out three figures. They were moving slowly but deliberately, trudging their way through knee-deep snow, following the currently invisible drive that led directly to us in the rear of the building.

"They know where they're going," Stark said.

"They have to be from the other world. None of our Warriors are on foot," Darius said.

"Well, let's see what they want." Stark unslung the bow from his back and put his hand on the door.

Grandma's voice stopped him. "Just a moment, tsi-ta-ga-a-s-ha-ya. I do not believe you will have need for that bow."

"What do you know, Grandma?" I asked, still staring out at the approaching vampyres.

"I have a feeling, Zoeybird. And my feelings are rarely wrong."

I could hear more Warriors filing in behind us, but I didn't take my gaze from the vampyres. Silently, I cursed the snow, wishing for a bright, shining full moon—or at least a pair of binoculars. I was just opening my mouth to ask a Warrior to go find me some, when the leader of the group—the kid who was walking in the middle of the other two and kept helping them when they stumbled—did something that was so simple and so familiar that I knew beyond any doubt who he was.

Kevin cracked his knuckles. It was a thing he's done since he was a little kid. I remember Mom used to tell him to stop and that he'd make his knuckles big, but he always laughed and made a joke. And back then—back before our mom married John Heffner, the step-loser, and completely lost herself in being his perfect wife—Kevin could make her laugh at the silliest little kid jokes in the world. Barbie and I used to make fun of him—call him "mommy's boy" and force him to steal chocolate chips and ice cream from the kitchen because it was true. He was definitely Mom's favorite. If he was caught, he'd just make Mom laugh and we'd all eat chocolate chips and ice cream.

Now all I could see was that little boy—the one whose bangs had been cut too short by Mom's money-saving home haircut. I rushed out the door. Stark grabbed my arm, but I shook him off. "That's my brother. I know it is."

"Then wait here. Let him come to you where you'll be safe," Stark said.

"No, I—" Then I looked at my Warrior. His gaze was filled with love and worry.

"I don't want to keep you from your brother. I just want to keep you safe, Zoey."

I nodded and stepped back inside. And waited.

It seemed to take forever, but the three vampyres were finally close enough that I could make out their faces. I'd been right. Other Kevin was the one in the middle. He had his arm around the waist of the vampyre on his right, and his hand under the elbow of the one on his left. Both looked older than him, and both looked in worse shape than my brother.

As they approached the door, I saw Other Kevin's eyes scanning the crowd, and knew the moment he saw me.

He stopped. He said something to the men with him, and then he walked on while they stood where they were, heads tucked down against the cold and the snow, arms wrapped around themselves.

Other Kevin got to the door and I opened it.

We stared at each other. I felt happy and sad and I didn't know what to do. My little brother spoke first.

"Zo! You're alive!"

His face broke into a huge smile and he started toward me. I moved to him. We met just in front of the open door, and I hugged him so hard I heard the breath *whump* out of him. But Kevin didn't let me go. He didn't move back. He just stood there, hugging me, saying, "You're alive … you're alive … you're alive …" over and over.

Then Grandma was there, too, and Other Kevin exclaimed in happiness, pulling her into his arms with me. He pressed his cheek against the top of Grandma's head and burst into big, snotting man-tears.

(

Zoey

We took care of Kev's men first. He introduced them as Marc and Dave, soldiers in Neferet's Red Army. Darius took them to the basement rooms where Other Jack and Damien brought them a change of clothes and food. They spoke very little and moved slowly, startling at small sounds and shadows.

I knew they'd been part of the group that had killed humans and our fledglings. But as I watched them, I felt nothing but pity. They hadn't asked to have their humanity taken away. I was seeing them as they truly were, or rather had been before they'd been Marked red and Changed. It was clear that they were traumatized and barely holding on to what was left of their sanity. They were living a hell—and that was more punishment than the TPD or I could ever give them.

Kevin was different. He seemed less in shock and more in control. Grandma, Stark, and I waited outside the basement room we'd assigned to him. When he finally emerged, hair wet and sticking up crazily, face freshly scrubbed, wearing a pair of Stark's old jeans and a T-shirt that said OKLAHOMA IS OK in bold letters across it, I could hardly breathe. I could still see the cute, kinda annoying little brother I used to torment, but he was *so grown up.*

"You look better," Grandma said, reaching up to pat his cheek.

He grinned at her. "You didn't bring any of your lavender and chocolate chip cookies, did you?"

I spoke without thinking, my big-sister-ness taking over automatically. "Jeesh, you're such a garbage can."

255

"So you've always said, Zo."

My heart hurt when he called me that. In my world, Heath Luck, my grade school and high school sweetheart, had been the only person to ever call me Zo. Heath was dead and no one had called me that for almost a year.

"Of course I brought cookies. There might even be some left. I'll get them."

"We'll be in the dining hall. I imagine you'd like to eat more than just cookies, right?" said Stark.

"Right you are," Other Kevin said.

"I shall meet you there. With my cookies." And like he did it every day, Other Kevin bent down so Grandma could kiss his cheek before she hurried away, humming happily to herself.

"You got really tall," I managed to say with a smile.

"Thanks. Our tattoos look a lot alike."

"Right? It's weird," I said.

"And you have a bunch more of them than I do. Did an artist do that, or did Nyx?"

"Nyx did it," I said as Stark and I led Other Kevin from the basement up through our House of Night. "There was a time when a new tattoo from Nyx was the only way I knew I wasn't totally messing everything up."

"I can understand that. Wish she'd give me some tattoos when I did something right."

"Dude, be careful what you wish for," Stark said.

It was Saturday, so I didn't have to call classes, and fledglings swarmed the corridors, nodding respectfully at Stark and me and sending Other Kevin curious looks. They were also outside in the courtyard. A big group of the art students, humans and fledglings, were in the process of building an elaborate snow castle. I saw the shock pass over Other Kevin's face when he realized that, yes, there really were human kids out there playing with fledglings.

"Things are very different here," he said.

"So we've heard," I said.

"You're a priestess."

"Kev, she's our High Priestess, and the Leader of the North American Vampyre High Council," Stark corrected him. "And she has affinities for all five elements."

"Jeesh, Zo, that's freaking cool." He grinned cheekily at me. "Good thing there's no math test to qualify for that job, huh?"

Stark frowned like he'd insulted me, but I laughed. "Right? Or a parallel-parking test."

"That would've been a major fail," he said.

"The dining hall's through here," I pointed to the stairway that led up.

"Yeah, I know. Some things are the same in both worlds. Uh, are you sure it's okay for me to go up there? It's mostly off-limits to everyone but Neferet's elite." Other Kevin paused when we reached the polished wooden door.

"Stark's telling you the truth. I really am the High Priestess here. If I say it's okay—it's okay."

"Oh, I didn't think he was lying. I just thought, you know, that I might be completely insane and my break with reality transported me into a video game and if I open that door there will be a Balrog behind it who will eat me."

"So, there's *Lord of the Rings* in your world?" I asked.

Other Kevin looked at me like I was the crazy person. "Of course."

"Oh, yeah, of course." Stark muttered.

When Kev still hesitated I gave him a question-mark look.

"Marc and Dave—are they getting something to eat, too?" he asked.

"Absolutely," I said. "You don't need to worry about them. They're totally being taken care of. So are the red fledglings that came from your world."

"Pinky swear?" he looked at me with ten-year-old Kevin's eyes.

I held up my pinky for him to hook with his own. "Pinky swear."

"Okay, then. I am starving." We headed up the stairs and to our booth while Other Kevin's gaze never stayed still. "This place is cool. Is there a menu? Or a buffet or something?" he asked.

"Not tonight. But just tell them what you want and they'll make it," I said.

"Anything?"

"Well, yeah, within reason," I said.

The priestess appeared at our table and Other Kevin said, "I'd like macaroni, cheese, and sleaze, please."

I burst out laughing at the waitress' expression.

Between rolls of giggles I managed, "Tell the chef to do the special mac and cheese he does for me. The one with cream of mushroom soup, peas, and tuna added to it. And he'll also take a brown pop. Not diet."

"Whoa, the cheese and sleaze is perfect, but not your crazy brown pop, Zo. That stuff'll kill you. Could I get a big glass of blood? I like O neg best."

"Of course," said the unshakable priestess before she headed back to the kitchen. I made a mental note to give her some extra time off and speak to whoever is her mentor to let them know how calm she is under weirdness pressure.

"So. You're alive *and* High Priestess." Other Kevin abruptly brought my attention back to him. "And Neferet is, what, dead in your world?"

"That's more complicated than it seems." I glanced at Stark. "I think he needs to know."

"I can't see that it'd hurt. He's here, and his Neferet is in another world," Stark said.

"Hang on there—she's not *my* Neferet."

"Okay, here's the short version." I tried to order my thoughts, and finally decided—what the hell—and just threw it out there at him. "Neferet tried to start a war against humans here, too. My friends and I stopped her." His brows went up to his hairline, but he didn't interrupt. "It wasn't easy. Mostly because at first I was the only one who believed she was evil. Then because she was so powerful. And evil. And manipulative. A lot of people died. Human, fledgling, vampyre, and, um, other." That thought had me asking, "Hey, does Neferet have a mate or a consort in your world?"

Kevin snorted. "Yeah. A bunch of them."

"Sounds about right," Stark said.

Kevin folded his hands and sent Stark an appraising look. "You're one of them."

"What. The. Hell?" I said.

Kevin's lips quirked up. "Yeah. Everyone knows General Stark and Neferet have an on-and-off thing."

"Goddess, I may puke," Stark said.

"Ditto," I said. "And now I'm going to forget I ever heard that. Where was I? Oh, um, also Neferet was hard to defeat because she managed to become immortal."

"Seriously?"

"Heart attack–like," I said. "We did finally beat her, but she's not dead. She can't die. Right now she's entombed in that grotto in Woodward Park. You know, where you came through the disgusting blood fountain into this world."

"Did Neferet bring us here?"

I shook my head. "As far as we can tell, she can't influence anything outside the grotto. But her BFF, for lack of a better way to describe him, is the White Bull. Do you know about him?"

"No clue," Other Kevin said.

"That could be good," Stark spoke up. "Maybe good and evil are in balance in his world."

The priestess had brought Other Kevin his blood drink and he almost snorted it out of his nose. He swallowed, coughed, and finally said, "Um, no. Definitely no. Evil is out of control in my world."

I sighed. "Well, the White Bull is the physical incarnation of evil. His twin is a Black Bull—the physical incarnation of good.

The White Bull and Neferet worked together in this world and almost tipped the balance to evil. We think it's the White Bull who started the whole crazy chain of events that led to you being here."

"And when you entombed Neferet, you took her place?"

"Yeah, basically. My circle, my prophetesses, my Warriors, and me. It was Aphrodite, one of my prophetesses, who's responsible for you and your people getting your humanity back."

"So, that's what happened. Red fledglings and red vampyres lose their humanity. Makes sense. I'd like to thank her, if that's possible."

"It's possible. I'll introduce the two of you," I said. "Okay, your turn. Tell me how you were Marked and how you ended up here."

"Wait, first, am I here? At this House of Night in this world? I'd like to know before I run into myself. Man, that'd be freaky, huh?"

"You're here, but you're not Marked. You're a human kid going to BA."

"Really?"

"Yep."

"Are we close?"

I hesitated. *Tell him the truth.* "No. Not anymore. Not since Mom married the step-loser and our family basically fell apart."

"The step-loser sucks. I wish Mom would wake the hell up and get rid of that asshat."

I felt the blood drain from my face. "Mom's alive in your world."

"Of course she's alive. Not that she has anything to do with me. She was all, 'As if your sister didn't cause me enough grief, now you had to go and get Marked, too.' You know how she is now—blah, blah, God. Blah, blah, John. Blah, blah, church." Then Kevin shook his head and said, "Wait. Mom's not alive here?"

"No."

His expression sobered. "What happened?"

Stark told him when I couldn't make my mouth work. "Neferet killed her."

Other Kevin stared down at the table, obviously trying to compose himself. "Did—did she suffer?"

In my mind I replayed the scene. Neferet coming to Grandma's door, looking for the perfect sacrifice to make her Vessel of evil. Mom answering the door. Neferet slitting her throat. It had been quick, but there were some things Kevin didn't need to know. There were some things, many things, I wish I didn't know.

"No. Mom didn't suffer," I said firmly. "And she'd left the step-loser."

Other Kevin's eyes lifted to mine. "She was going to be Mom again?"

I nodded, not trusting my voice.

"Zo, what about Barbie?"

"She's at OSU," I said.

"Majoring in beer, cheerleading, and hot guys?" he asked.

That had me almost smiling. "Yep."

"Glad some things don't change. Okay, so, where was I? Marked. Well, I was Marked the day you died."

"This makes me very uncomfortable," Stark said.

"Join the crowd," I said. "But go on. I want to know how I died."

My brother hesitated. "I'll tell you, Zo, but it's pretty gross. Are you sure you want to know?"

"Kev, I'm here. I'm alive. That me isn't this me. It's fine. And I do want to know."

"All right, here goes. The official word from the House of Night was that you were the last in a string of murders. First two other professors, then you, were found decapitated, disemboweled, and nailed to our front gate with some stupid scripture bullshit hung around your neck. The cops never found the killers of the first two professors, and they didn't have a chance to bumble your case, either. Neferet held the People of Faith responsible. Zo, your death was what started the human-vampyre war."

27

Zoey

"I'd be worried about interrupting, but with the way Z looks I'm thinking she might need to be saved," Aphrodite said.

I felt dizzy and everything suddenly looked blurry. I'd told Kev it wouldn't bother me to hear how I'd died, but that was before I'd realized how absolutely violent and awful it had been. I blinked my eyes fast to clear my vision, and looked up to see Aphrodite and Darius standing beside our table. Her hands were on her hips and she was giving Other Kevin the stank eye.

"You're not interrupting. Sit down," Stark said. "Other Kevin just told Zoey how she was killed in his world. It—er—wasn't good."

"Well, of course it wasn't good, boy genius. She *died*." Aphrodite continued to glare at Other Kevin as he stood up and switched seats so that she and Darius could join us.

"Aphrodite, Darius, this is my brother, Kevin. Or Other Kevin." I glanced at my brother and he shrugged.

"I'm cool with being Other Kevin."

I nodded and continued, finding that a simple thing, like an introduction, was better to focus on than my decapitation and disembowelment at Neferet's hands. "Kev, this is Aphrodite, the prophetess who returned the humanity to you and your guys."

Other Kevin held out his hand for the traditional greeting and Aphrodite's eyes narrowed at him, but she took it, grasping his forearm. "Merry meet," she said.

"Wow," Kevin said. "Your Mark is extraordinary, but I shouldn't be surprised. Only an extraordinary priestess could've done what you did."

"Huh. You're Z's brother?"

"I am."

"You're taller than I imagined."

"So, you imagined things about me?" Other Kevin's smile was just the right amount of cute and cocky.

"Uh, did I mention Darius is Aphrodite's Oathbound Warrior and her Consort?" I added.

"You did now." He offered his hand to Darius, too. "My man, you're a lucky Warrior."

Darius grunted at him, but took his hand. Briefly. Before sitting beside Aphrodite.

"Kevin, dear, I did find some cookies left in my basket, which might truly be a miracle. Zoey and her friends remind me often of locusts." Grandma was holding a lavender-colored platter of her cookies, which she put in the center of the table before sliding in beside Kevin. "Oh, don't let me interrupt." She patted him on the cheek and flashed me a hello grin.

No one said anything. I sighed.

"Grandma, Kevin is telling me that in his world I'm dead. Are you sure you want to hear this?"

Grandma lifted her chin. "Zoey Redbird, I have battled evil beside you. I have almost been killed by the denizens of Darkness. Do not underestimate me."

"Good point, Grandma," Stark said.

"Excellent point, actually. So, go on with your story, Kevin. Z died. I take it horribly. Tell us everything," Aphrodite said with way too much glee for my taste.

"Neferet killed me. Just like she did Professors Nolan and Blake."

"Zoey's death started the human-vampyre war. Other Kevin was Marked on the same day she died. Now you're caught up," Stark explained.

"That awful, awful, creature!" Grandma said. She grabbed a cookie and bit into it like she needed to devour something.

"G-ma, if you start crying I'm going to stop talking," Kevin said.

"That, my dear, is a deal."

Kevin's gaze turned to me. "Neferet really did all of that? Killed the professors here, just like in my world?"

I met my brother's gaze. "Yes. Definitely. That and a lot more. Finish telling us about you."

"I was Marked the day the school called us about your death. It was bad, and not just because you died. At least you were Marked blue. You were normal. My Mark was red."

"Which means what in your world, dear?" Grandma asked.

"It usually means brainless soldiers, walking viruses, and killing machines. Some kids stay mostly themselves after they're Marked red, but you can always tell when someone's getting closer and closer to the Change. They turn."

"Explain turn," Darius said.

"The hunger gets them. They turn from being mostly human, to being mostly eating machines. Once a red fledgling is fully Changed, only a few—like maybe one in a hundred—can reason through their hunger. Those of us who can are made officers in Neferet's Red Army. The others are soldiers."

"And you're an officer?" Grandma asked.

"Yep. Like you, Stark." Stark stiffened, but Other Kevin just kept on talking. "Well, not exactly like you. I'm just a lieutenant. You're a general."

"But aren't you young to be Marked at all?" Aphrodite asked as she picked up one of Grandma's cookies and nibbled on it.

"He just turned sixteen in August," Grandma said.

"Yep. I was barely fifteen when I was Marked. I'm the youngest kid to ever be Marked at the Tulsa House of Night—red or blue. And I Changed faster than anyone on record—within one month."

"Why are you okay right now and no one who was with you is okay?" Stark asked.

"Other Jack's doing fine. Well, he is now," Aphrodite said.

"But the rest of the fledglings aren't," Darius said. "And of the vampyres with you, three committed suicide and the two who are downstairs are in bad shape. What's different about you?"

"I don't know. I've never known. It's not that I didn't have their hunger. I did. It was terrible. But I could reason through it. I was sure I'd lose myself like everyone else did when they Changed, but I didn't."

"What did your mentor say about it?" I asked.

"Zo, in my world red fledglings don't have mentors. They have handlers. And none of them are one-on-one. Basically, you're herded with other fledglings from one weapons class to another until you Change. Then they wait and see if you can reason through your hunger. If you can't—you're a soldier. If you can—you go into officer training. But you don't have a mentor. You have OICs."

"Huh?"

"Officers in Charge," he clarified. "And you don't talk to them about anything except fighting and killing."

"No one knew you were different?" Grandma asked before I could.

My stomach hurt for Other Kevin.

He shook his head. "I got good at hiding it. They wanted us to do things. Terrible, awful things." Other Kevin was holding his fork halfway to his mouth, just staring down at his plate.

"Kev?" I spoke softly.

"It's okay, dear." Grandma rested her hand on his arm. "We have battled Darkness. We will not judge you."

He jerked and put his fork down. He took a big gulp from his

265

glass, and then placed his hand over Grandma's and met my gaze. "Being able to think clearly most of the time is an advantage—especially when no one knows you can. I made sure I kept myself out of the worst situations. But sometimes I couldn't bear the thirst—the hunger. When that happened I made it fast for my victim. Painless." He rubbed the bridge of his nose in a gesture I remembered so well. "There were times when I was sure I was going mad—when I thought, 'Well, this is it—this is when I turn into one of them.' But then I'd have one of those Nyx dreams and I'd wake up myself again."

I sat up straighter. Grandma and Aphrodite leaned forward. "Nyx dreams?" Grandma asked.

"Yeah, what kind of Nyx dreams?" I said.

He shrugged. "I've had tons of them. After the first one, I don't remember them clearly. Just the goddess' smile and the way her hand felt resting on my head. Sometimes I'd wake up thinking that I'd been sleeping with my head on her shoulder." He glanced sheepishly at me. "Real dumb, huh?"

"Not necessarily," I said.

"Tell us about the first dream—the one you remember," Aphrodite said.

Kev grinned at her. "Anything you say, Goddess of Love."

I kicked him under the table.

"Hey!"

"Focus," I said. "On the dream."

"It's going to sound weird, but I remember every bit of it. It started at your farm, Grandma. I was trying to find you, but I was sick and dizzy and I tripped. In my dream I hit my head and when I woke up—which sounds weird because I was technically still sleeping, but in my dream, my dream-self woke up."

"Yeah, yeah, we get it," Aphrodite said. "Keep going."

"Hey, y'all aren't havin' a party without us!" Stevie Rae, holding Rephaim's hand, smacked Stark on the shoulder and he slid over to make room for them.

"We're not partying, bumpkin. Kev is telling us about the Nyx dream he had after he was Marked," Aphrodite said. "Here, have a cookie and be quiet."

I made quick introductions. "Kevin, this is Stevie Rae and her mate, Rephaim. Guys, this is my brother, Other Kevin."

"Yeah! More cookies!" Rephaim snagged one and chomped happily, nodding a hello at Kevin.

"Hi, there." Stevie Rae dimpled at him.

"Hi. You're a red vampyre." Other Kevin was staring at her like she was a science experiment gone wrong.

"She's a High Priestess," I said. "She also has an affinity for earth."

"Wow."

"Staring isn't polite," Darius grumbled at him.

Other Kevin blinked. "Sorry. It's just that I've never seen a female red vampyre before."

"What?" I gaped at him. "No girls are Marked in your world?"

"Not as red fledglings. Never."

"That's weirder than boobs on a boar," Stevie Rae said.

"Goddess, give me strength." Aphrodite rolled her eyes to the heavens.

"Let's go back to the dream," I said. "You were looking for Grandma and you tripped and fell. Then you woke up."

"Yeah, I was in a cave-thing when I woke up, only it was only my soul and not my body. My body was all crumpled back where I'd tripped, and I remember my head was bleeding, too. This woman's voice was calling for me and I floated around, following it. At first I thought it was you, G-ma, because it was singing in Cherokee, but it wasn't. Zo, real weird stuff happened. Like, I could see the color of words and sounds."

My skin felt all tingly. "Laughter is birthday-cake-frosting blue."

Other Kevin looked shocked. "How did you know?"

"Keep talking."

"Okay, um, I followed the voice and there she was—the goddess.

She was sitting by a little stream." Other Kevin's gaze went far away and the corner of his lips lifted sweetly, making him look like a little boy again. "She was the most beautiful thing I'd ever seen. She's still the most beautiful thing I've ever seen. She called me 'u-we-tsi.'"

"Son," Grandma said with a smile.

Other Kevin nodded. "I'm not as good as Zo with the Cherokee, but I do know that one. Nyx called me 'u-we-tsi' and told me I'm special. That my power is in the uniqueness of my combined blood of ancient Shamans and of the modern world. She said that I would be her eyes and ears in a world that is struggling to find the balance between good and evil. Then she said something I'll never forget. I even had it tattooed around my arm." He rolled up the sleeve of his T-shirt so that we could see the cursive script tattooed around his bicep. I knew what they would say before Grandma read them aloud.

"Darkness does not always equate to evil, just as light does not always bring good."

"Then Nyx kissed me. Right here." He pointed to the filled-in red crescent Mark on his forehead. "When I woke up I'd made the Change."

No one said a word.

Kevin's gaze went around the table. He sighed and leaned back, running his fingers through his dark, tousled hair, food forgotten. "I knew you'd think I was crazy."

"Ohmygood*ness*, Other Kevin is his world's Zoey!" Stevie Rae blurted.

Kevin stared at me and together we said, "Ah, hell."

28

Other Kevin

"The same dream. You're telling me you and I had the same dream." Kevin couldn't stop staring at his sister.

"What I'm telling you is that it wasn't a dream at all. It happened to me. Almost exactly like you described, only I actually went to Grandma's farm the day I was Marked because Mom and the step-loser refused to take me to the House of Night. Instead they thought they'd pray over me." Kevin and Z rolled their eyes together. "Wait, what happened when I was Marked in your world?"

"You picked me up from school. We freaked about your Mark, and then I went to the House of Night with you."

"I didn't go home?"

"Nope. We didn't figure there was any reason to, and we were right because when I was Marked I had already come home first. I was, um, pretty upset. You'd died, Zo."

G-ma squeezed his hand. "That must have been very difficult for you."

"It was awful. For you, too, G-ma."

269

"Did Mom take you to the House of Night?" Zo asked.

"Are you kidding? She and the step-loser wanted to start the prayer chain. I snuck out and called the red line."

"What's the red line?" Stevie Rae asked.

"It's the emergency line for the House of Night if you get Marked red. You just hit 7-3-3 from any phone and someone will come pick you up. That's what I did, and they took me to the depot with the rest of the red fledglings. And that's about it." He sat back and waited for whatever would happen next.

"You won't hear me say this very often, but Stevie Rae's right—you *are* your world's Zoey," Aphrodite said.

"I agree," said G-ma Redbird.

"Yes," said the tall Native kid called Rephaim who was with Stevie Rae.

"Yep," Stark said.

Then everyone just stared at Kevin.

"Hey, what'd we miss?"

Two guys hurried up to the table. The taller of the two had a cool blue tattoo that looked like the wings of an Egyptian god. The other was a red fledgling Kevin didn't recognize. They were holding hands. The blue vampyre was saying, "Those red fledglings are finally relaxing a little, so we were able to get away. Lenobia, Travis, and Professor P are sitting with them in the cafeteria. I really feel bad for them. They're super messed up."

On their heels was a gorgeous black girl whose blue tattoo was two phoenixes rising from flames. "Yeah, but that's nothing compared to this kid's red vamp friends. Erik's with them. They won't even leave their room. Um, could I have a cookie?" she said as everyone slid around to make room for the three of them and Zo made more introductions.

"Kevin, this is Damien—his affinity is for air. And Other Jack. He's from your world. In this world he and Damien were together, and then our Jack was killed."

"But now I have him back." The Damien vampyre looked at Jack with so much love that it seemed an intrusion to watch.

"And I have *him* back," Jack said, putting his head on Damien's shoulder.

"Yeah, and this is Shaunee. Her affinity is for—"

"Fire, I bet," Kevin said.

"Smart and handsome. I already like him," said Shaunee.

"Guys, this is my brother, Other Kevin."

"Hi," Kev said. "So, it's still bad with Marc and Dave?"

"Real bad," said the fire vampyre. "Got any words of wisdom that might help us help them?"

Kevin looked down. He was so damn torn. On one hand he was amazingly, incredibly happy that his sister was alive. On the other was the past, and the men downstairs who might never be able to get over it.

"I wish I did," he said slowly. "Time. And support. Talk to them, like Zo's been talking to me." He glanced up, smiling sadly at his sister. "Like I'm normal. Like I'm not a monster."

"You're not!" Zo exclaimed, sounding so big sister protective that it made Kevin find his smile again.

"I'm not now, but my past isn't pretty. And their past is even uglier."

"We'll help 'em get through it," said the cute blond. "A few of us have some real ugly skeletons in our closets, too."

"Your world isn't the only one with monsters," said the guy named Rephaim.

There was a long silence that had Kevin popping his knuckles nervously. Zo saved him by saying, "Um, guys, we just realized that in his world, he's their me."

And everyone stared at him again.

Kevin sighed.

Finally, the blue vampyre named Damien spoke. "Okay, I'll say it because it looks like no one else will. If Other Kevin is his world's Zoey, what is he doing here?"

"I came through the thing. You know, the bloody thing in the park. Like the rest of them did. Like Jack did," Kevin said.

"It is nice to meet you." Jack offered Kevin his hand, which he took. "How are *you* doing?"

"Fine. Good," Kevin tried not to fidget as everyone gaped at him. He looked more closely at his world's Jack. "I don't think I know you."

Jack moved his shoulders nervously. "Um, I kinda know who you are because you're an officer, but you wouldn't have known me. I, uh, avoided your kind as much as I could."

"Wait, you kept your humanity, too?" Kevin leaned forward eagerly.

"Not really. I wasn't Marked long ago. I could feel my humanity leaving me, but I've never been good at sports or fighting or boy stuff in general, so no one paid me any attention. I just kept to myself as much as possible, which was actually pretty much."

"You were alone? All the time?" Damien looked heartbroken.

Jack turned to Damien. "Yeah. It was safer alone. I hoped when I made the Change and couldn't think anymore that I would just forget everything and everyone from my real life. That's the only way I could stand it."

"It's okay now. Everything is okay now. You're home. You'll never be lonely again." Damien smoothed back his hair and kissed him gently, which gave Kevin a little start of surprise. That was the first time he'd witnessed a guy kiss a guy. He decided it was a little weird, but kinda nice, too. They seemed to love each other a lot.

Then Kevin processed what Damien had actually said. "Wait, go back to what you were saying. You asked what I was doing here, but you already knew the answer, didn't you? So, I must be misunderstanding the question."

Damien didn't answer. He looked at Zo instead. "I think you should tell him."

He watched his sister draw a long breath. He could see that she was picking at her fingers, which meant something was bothering her. So, he braced himself for bad news.

He should've braced himself for *really* bad news.

"This is going to sound stuck up," Zo began, but Damien interrupted.

"Actually, narcissistic is a better way to put it than stuck up." He paused and looked at his friends, who were all—even G-ma—frowning at him. "I didn't mean Zoey is *actually* narcissistic, just that what she's going to say will appear to be that." Damien sighed. "Never mind. Carry on, Z."

"Anyway," Zo started again. "What they want me to tell you is that I'm the reason we defeated Neferet. It's not that I did it on my own, but like Nyx said when I was Marked," then she quoted almost exactly what Nyx had said to him, too, when he'd made the Change. "My power is in the uniqueness of my combined blood of ancient Wise Women and Elders, as well as insight and understanding of the modern world. She said that I would be her eyes and ears in a world that is struggling to find the balance between good and evil. Then she said," Zo pointed at the words tattooed around his bicep, "Darkness does not always equate to evil, just as light does not always bring good."

"The same thing happened to you." A terrible sense of foreboding caused the hairs on his forearms to lift.

"Kevin, do you have an affinity for any of the elements?" Zo asked abruptly.

"I dunno."

"When you're circling for, say, a Full Moon Ritual, and the elements are called, have you ever felt anything?" Damien said.

"I have no idea."

"What do you mean, you have no idea?" Zo asked him.

"I've never taken part in a ritual. Or a circle."

Except for Jack, the entire table gaped at him.

"What in the hell are you talking about?" Aphrodite said.

"Red fledglings and red vampyres don't take part in rituals. We don't circle. We're not even allowed in Nyx's Temple," Jack explained.

"Oh, my Goddess, is that true?" Zo sounded like she might hyperventilate.

"Well, yeah. I tried to sneak into Nyx's Temple once, but I got caught." Kev paused to shake off the memory of that terrible beating. "I never tried that again. That's why I was sure my dreams of Nyx were just delusions—my brain dying or something."

"It's an abomination," Damien said.

"We need to fix that. Now." Aphrodite stood. "Let's take him to the temple. If he has what you have, Z, we'll know he really is you in his world."

"And if not?" Kevin asked.

"If not, you're just a cute red vampyre whose sister is boss of us," Stevie Rae said.

"I am not the boss of you," Zo said.

"I'll remind you that you said that next time you order me around," Aphrodite said.

"Children, stop bickering. Let us go to Nyx's Temple," said G-ma.

"Hang on, we need Shaylin," Zo said.

"She was with Nicole in the barn last time I saw her," Shaunee said. "She said she needed some barn therapy after dealing with the super-upset red fledglings. I'll get her and meet you guys in the temple."

Everyone started to file out of the dining hall, and Kevin snagged Zo's sleeve, holding her back for a second. "Hey, what if I do have what you have. What does it mean?"

Zoey's eyes were sad when they met his. "It means you're what I am—a leader, a rallying point, the person who brings people together—and when we do that, we defeat Darkness."

"Ah, hell," he said.

"Yep. I couldn't have said it better myself."

(

Other Kevin

The snow had changed from giant flakes to steady, tiny specks of white that caught the gaslights along the path to the temple and turned into starlight. Zoey's friends were talking easily together. They even waved to fledglings who called their names.

Zoey walked beside him, uncharacteristically silent.

G-ma Redbird was on his other side. She was silent too, and holding his hand.

"Do not be nervous, u-we-tsi." She spoke softly, for his ears alone. "The goddess already knows you."

"How can you be sure? Maybe they were just dreams, or delusions, or maybe some weird psychic echo across worlds of what was supposed to happen to Zoey."

"I can be sure because I know Nyx," G-ma said cryptically.

And then they were entering Nyx's Temple and Kevin forgot his nerves. He forgot his fears. He forgot everything except the wonder of Nyx.

The moment he entered the temple he was engulfed in the scent of vanilla and lavender. He heard the tinkling of running water and glanced to his right as they passed a beautiful fountain made of amethyst with candles floating in it. There were several ways they could have gone, but the group didn't hesitate. They turned to the left, walked through a thick, arched stone doorway, and entered a large room that was lit by white candles suspended everywhere. Sconces with live flames protruded from the walls. In the very center of the room was the only piece of furniture—an antique wooden table, ornately carved, that held another candelabrum, plus a luminous statue of the Goddess made of iridescent, golden onyx that was lit from within. Her arms were raised and she was cupping a crescent moon between her hands. Several thick sticks of sweetgrass incense smoked at her feet. In front of the table there was an open flame that burned from a recess in the stone floor. He thought it looked like it could burn for a century and never falter, never fade, never extinguish.

"Z, I'll get the candles," Stevie Rae called, disappearing into a side room.

"Found her!" Shaunee entered the room with a pretty, petite girl beside her. He blinked, surprised to see yet another female red vampyre. This one had an adult tattoo that looked like that famous Japanese wave, but with layers upon layers of detail. "Kevin, this is Shaylin. Her element is—"

"Water," Shaylin said. She stared at him, and as she did her eyes seemed to get bigger and bigger. "He has the exact same aura as you, Z."

"Huh?" Kevin was even more confused than he had been before he'd entered the temple. "Aura?"

"She's a Prophetess of Nyx. She sees auras," Shaunee explained.

"Really? And mine's like Zo's?" Kevin said. "What's it look like?"

Shaylin grinned. "Pretty. You both have violet auras with flecks of silver, like liquid mercury, sparkling all over."

"Do people usually have the same auras?" Zo asked.

"Nope," Shaylin said.

"What about siblings? Other Kevin's my brother."

"My answer is still nope. I've never seen anyone before with the same aura."

"Well, that's weird," Kevin and Zoey said together.

"Jinx!" Kevin yelled. "Beat ya!"

She shoved his shoulder. "Come on. You're with me." Then she gestured at the others. "Okay, circle up."

It only took a moment. Everyone knew exactly what to do. Well, everyone except Kevin, who stood next to Zoey, watching everything while he cracked his knuckles. When all were in place, Zoey turned to him. They were standing in the middle of the circle between the table and the open fire.

"Hey, stop looking so nervous. This is easy and fun. Just walk with me. Damien, Shaunee, Shaylin, Stevie Rae, and I will do everything. All you need to do is to concentrate on what you're feeling, and if you feel something—tell me. Ready?"

"Yep," he lied.

She picked up a long, wooden match and a box to strike it against. Then she walked to Damien, who was holding a yellow candle.

"From the east I summon air—the element that fills us at birth and surrounds us all the days of our lives." She touched the match to the yellow candle.

Kevin felt his hair flutter and heard the sound of wind sighing through leaves. He looked around, trying to see if he'd missed something. Was a window open?

Zoey and Damien were staring at him.

"Anything?" she asked.

"I—I felt wind in my hair and heard leaves rustling."

Damien grinned. "That's one."

"Seriously? I really have an affinity for wind?"

"Absolutely," said Zo.

"Wow. Just wow, wow, wow!" Kevin said.

"Come on. Let's see what else you have."

Everyone turned to their right while he and Zoey approached Shaunee, who was holding a red candle.

"From the south I summon fire—that element that warms us and gives us light." She didn't have to touch the match to the red candle. It spontaneously lit and Kevin jumped. He was surrounded by heat, as if he was standing a little too close to a bonfire. A light sweat broke out on his face, and he automatically wiped at his forehead.

"My guess is that's two," Shaunee said.

Zo raised her brows at him.

He nodded, unable to stop his gleeful grin. "Definitely felt that. It's awesome!"

They turned to their right and walked to Shaylin, who was holding a blue candle.

"From the west I summon water—the element that washes us and quenches us." She lit the blue candle.

The sound of waves filled Kevin's ears, and the scent of the sea filled his nose.

"I hear it! I smell it!"

"That's three," Shaylin said.

They turned to the right again and ended up in front of Stevie Rae and her green candle.

"Hey there Z and Z's bro," she said, smiling at them both.

Kevin thought he automatically liked this girl, and decided right then he wanted to get to know her better.

"From the north I summon earth—we come from you, and return to you." She lit the green candle.

Kevin could feel the softness of a grassy meadow under his feet. He smelled hay and heard birdsong.

"That's four. Right, Kev?"

"Right!" Kevin told the little blond.

"Now for the fifth." Zo led him back to the table and the fat purple candle that rested there. "Last, I summon spirit to our circle—it is our connection to each other and to our Goddess." Zo lit the purple candle.

Unbelievably, Kevin felt his own spirit leap, like there were birds fluttering around inside his chest. He gazed down at Zoey, surprised to see her eyes filled with tears.

"You feel it, don't you?"

"Yes. I feel it." Then something caught his eye and Kevin's gaze went to the circle itself. All around it was a glowing silver thread, like a ribbon of mercury. "Holy crap! Can you guys see that?"

He heard soft laughter from everyone. They were smiling at him and nodding their heads. G-ma was clapping her hands. Zoey was the only one who looked sad.

"While our circle is open I want to do something," Zo said. Her eyes traveled the circumference, meeting the gaze of each of her friends. "Help me, okay?"

All four nodded.

Zoey turned to her brother. "Bend down so that I can put my hand on your head."

Kevin did one better. He knelt before his sister, and as he did so he felt the rightness of it. She rested her hand gently on his head, and when she began to speak, her voice was completely changed—filled with otherworldly power and the strength of a goddess.

For my brother I ask a blessing from elements five
Air, fire, water, earth, spirit
No matter where he might go—what hardships he
*   might know*
Follow him. Strengthen him. If his heart is empty—fill it.
Keep him happy, safe, and alive.
I ask of our Goddess Nyx from above
To hold him close, wrapped in love ... always love.

"So she has spoken—so mote it be," intoned her friends.

Instantly, Kevin was bathed in such a sense of compassion—of endless, unconditional love—that he knew beyond any doubt Nyx was his goddess, too.

Zo smiled through her tears at him. "How about you close our circle?"

He had to wipe his eyes and clear his throat before he could answer her. "I don't know how, Zo."

"It's easy. Just go backwards—that always closes a circle, ends a ritual or spell. Start here. Release the element and blow out the candle."

"Um, spirit. Thank you for coming. And you can go now." He felt awkward, but he blew out the candle and felt the release of a little spark within him that he knew was spirit.

Grinning in spite of his nerves, he made his way around the circle in the opposite direction, releasing each of the elements. When he was finished, they all rushed to congratulate him—all talking at once. All except Zoey.

He knew what was wrong with her, but he didn't want to think about it just then. Didn't want to talk about it just then.

Aphrodite approached him. "Ya know, you're not bad for a kid."

Buoyed by the miracle that had just happened to him, Kevin put a hand over his heart and bowed to her. "Aphrodite, Goddess of Love, Prophetess, Savior, and beauty—if you would spend some alone time with me, I'd show you youth has its benefits."

Aphrodite's smile was a cat licking cream. "Ooooh, Z, I know who got all the game in your family."

"I'd like to add smart to my list of compliments," Kev quipped.

The mountain of muscle called Darius stepped forward. "Back off, boy."

Aphrodite slid her arm around the Warrior's waist. "Oh, handsome, you're adorable when you're jealous." As she and Darius walked away, she batted her impossibly long eyelashes at Kevin and blew him a kiss over her shoulder.

He fell back, pretending to catch her kiss, and almost knocked his sister over.

Zoey rolled her eyes.

"Yep, he's totally threatened by me. I can tell."

"You're gonna get your butt kicked. I can tell," Zo said.

Kevin took a Karate Kid stance, arms out like a crane. One foot lifted, he waved his hands like a giant bird and made a "*Waaaa-chaw!*" cry, jumping up and kicking out ridiculously. "That's right. Um hum. He can *try* to kick my butt."

Stark shook his head. "Pathetic. Truly pathetic. But also there's no doubt that you're Z's brother."

Zoey was staring at him. Kevin could see her struggling not to laugh and he jumped up again, yelling another "*Waaaa-chaw!*"

Zo started to giggle. She tried to stop, which made her snort, which in turn made Kevin snort. Then the whole room was laughing.

That's when it happened.

It hit Kevin hard. He knew what he had to do. He didn't want to. He wanted to do anything *but* that—except he really didn't have any choice. He realized then he'd never really had any choice.

And his laughter changed. Turned to tears. The tears turned to sobs. Kevin stumbled to the statue of Nyx and knelt at her feet, as he had at his sister's feet just a few minutes before.

Zo was there. So was G-ma. They put their arms around him. He felt the other four—air, fire, water, and earth join them in their tight circle of support and comfort, hope and love.

Then he said it. He finally said it. His voice was thick with tears, but he spoke carefully, so that it filled Nyx's Temple and, hopefully, lifted to the Goddess herself.

"I've killed so many people. I didn't want to. I didn't let them suffer. But I did it. I did kill. And I have to go back. I have to join the rebels. I have to … I have to …" his words faltered as his heart broke. He didn't want to leave. He wanted so, so badly to stay here in this wonderful world that wasn't filled with war and insanity. He wanted to stay with his sister and her family of friends.

"Atone." Zoey's voice was soft, but it carried like the scent of vanilla and lavender, permeating everything.

Kevin sighed with relief and nodded. "Yes. I have to atone. To find forgiveness—if Nyx will let me."

"Oh, Kev," Z said through her tears. "She already forgives you. Now you have to find a way to forgive yourself."

"I'll find that back there. Back in that world. I can make a difference there, just like you have here."

Zoey stepped back, wiping her eyes with G-ma. Stark produced tissues from somewhere, handing them around the circle. Even Aphrodite and Darius joined them—though Darius didn't even look close to crying.

"But how are you gonna get back?" Stevie Rae asked. "We barely know how we got you here."

Kevin blinked in surprise at her. "That's obvious. You just showed me how."

"Huh?" Zo said.

"Do what you did to get me here again, only this time, do it backwards. Like you close a circle or end a spell or ritual—with the opposite of what you did before."

"That might actually work," said Damien.

"We should practice," said Zoey.

Kevin put his hand on her shoulder. "I don't have time for you to practice. I need to get back there."

"You can wait a few days. Let us think through this. Experiment. What if we mess things up even worse than they are now?" Zo said.

Then G-ma surprised everyone. "Zoeybird, you have to let him go. Now. Don't you see? The longer he stays here, the more difficult it will be for him to leave. And u-we-tsi-a-ge-ya, how would you feel if you had been pulled from this world and sent to another, only to discover how very badly you were needed back in your old world?"

Tears were washing Zo's cheeks, but she nodded. "I—I get it. I understand. I just don't want you to go."

"Thanks, Zo. That means a lot to me. And I don't want to go, either, but I have to. You know I have to."

Zoey wiped her face and blew her nose. Then, in a loud, strong voice she said, "Okay, circle. Gather everything you had before. We're going back to Woodward Park."

29

Zoey

It took a surprisingly short time to gather the elements of the spell. My circle did it all. The only thing I did was sit with Kevin and tell him anything I could think that would help him back in that other world.

The whole time I pretended like he wasn't really going to leave. A big part of me hoped he couldn't.

"Stop it," Kev said.

"What? I didn't even say anything."

"Stop thinking about it. There's nothing we can do. I have to go. You know it. I know it. G-ma knows it. And I'll bet Nyx knows it, too. So stop thinking about it."

I blew out a long breath. "All right, where was I?"

"You just finished telling me about the weapons in the basement of the House of Night. I got it. They're worth a fortune, and a fortune is what the resistance needs. I'll figure out a way to get down there, and if there's gold and jewels in them thar hills, I'll pawn it."

"You are a goofball," I said.

"But tall. I have that going for me. And Aphrodite says I got game."

"No one listens to Aphrodite."

"Uh, Zo, she's your prophetess."

"And still. Okay, so, you're taking a copy of Neferet's journal back with you."

"Yep." He patted the inside pocket of the jacket Damien had found for him. "It's right here."

"None of that may have happened to her in your world. Or maybe just a part of it. But we found out stuff from her past is one way to get at her, especially when it's stuff no one knows."

"I'll do some digging and see if she's from Chicago. If she is I'll do a search into her past. If it's there I'll find it. I'm damn good with computers." He grinned.

"And you have to find your Nerd Herd," I said. "That's the most important thing."

"Yeah, so you say, but I'm worried about that. Stevie Rae isn't alive in our world. I remember when she rejected the Change because I was at the House of Night. And I don't know any Shaylin. Like my world's Jack says, Damien's dead, too. That leaves Shaunee. She's cool, but she's always with a girl she calls 'Twin.' And she seems like a totally different person than the Shaunee who's fire here."

"Wait, is Twin a white girl from Tulsa?"

"Blond, real hot, and kinda slutty?"

"That's her! Okay, that means you have fire *and* water."

"The slut's water? Somehow that makes sense."

"Oh! In the car Other Jack recognized Aphrodite. Only he asked where her Mark was—so she's in your world, too."

"There's no vampyre in my world with a red and blue Mark like hers."

"No, but she is in your world. Remember, Kev, who we are deep inside is the same. It's just that we've had different experiences, so our personalities might be different. Find Aphrodite. She can stand in for any of the elements, but she was air when we called you—so that's probably what I would have her personify for you, too."

"She should be fire as smokin' hot as that girl is."

"Eew. Just stop. Now all you need is earth."

Grandma joined us, sitting beside Kevin on the cushy velvet love seat in front of the fire that crackled happily in the professors' lounge. Other Kevin and I had come to the lounge to wait while my circle rushed around gathering spellwork elements. As they found each one—again—they ran in, placed it on the table in front of us, and then took off again. So far the table held the five ritual candles, matches, a crystal pyramid/tetrahedron (which Shaunee pilfered again from another trophy case) and an athame.

"I found it, Zoeybird. I knew I had a second one in my room. I just had to search for it." Grandma added a redbird feather to the growing group of things.

"So, all you need is to find one more person who can personify an element—hopefully earth." I thought for a second and then added. "Think about Stevie Rae when you look for him or her. Stevie Rae's a real Oklahoma girl—she's tied to the red earth—feels it in her soul. Remember that, 'kay?"

"'Kay, I will. Stop worrying."

"It's what I do best," I said.

"What of those poor souls who came through with Kevin?" Grandma asked.

"Kev and I already talked about that," I explained. "It'd be good for him to have an ally, but none of them are ready to go back now."

"They won't ever be, Zo. Jack's the only one who was able to save his sanity. The rest of them are broken. Promise me you won't make them go back."

"Hey, I'd never force anyone to go there," I assured him.

"Kevin, I want you to come directly to my farm as soon as you return. Tell me everything that has happened. Give me this." Grandma took from around her neck a small beaded pouch on a string of braided leather and placed it over Kevin's head so that the pouch rested in the middle of his chest, near his heart. "I would believe you anyway, but this will speed things up."

"Thank you, G-ma."

Stevie Rae jogged into the room, waving a rowan stick. "Found it! Sorry it took so long. It was in the very bottom of the spells and rituals chest." She ticked off the items on the table. "So, we just need the grooved rock."

"In the shape of a heart," I said.

"I have an idea. I'll go find Shaylin." And Stevie Rae was off.

"Okay, let me think. What else …" My mind was a cacophony of thoughts warring with an orchestra of emotions.

"Kevin, you said you do not know a Dragon or Anastasia Lankford?" Grandma asked.

He shook his head. "No. The Swordmaster at our House of Night is a really old vampyre named Artus. He's super scary."

"So, no Dragon was killed at your House of Night this past year?" I asked.

"Nope."

Grandma and I exchanged a smile.

"Find Dragon Lankford and his Consort, Anastasia. They'll help you, and I'd bet a plate of Grandma's cookies that Anastasia can either stand in for earth or can help you find someone with an earth affinity."

"Okay, got it. I'll remember."

"And Kevin, no matter what, do not underestimate Neferet. She became immortal in this world. She commanded threads of Darkness to do her nasty bidding. Hell, I even saw her turn herself into about a zillion spiders."

"That's seriously disgusting." Kevin shuddered.

"Right? So, be overly careful. Oh, and in this world she had major psychic powers, but she could never read my mind—and if other people, like Damien and Stevie Rae or the rest of the Nerd Herd, if they kept their minds busy thinking about by-rote stuff—vocab words and whatnot—that messed up her mind-reading abilities."

"Okay. Got that, too."

"We did it!" Stevie Rae and Shaylin rushed into the room. They were grinning and holding a fist-sized sandstone that had a perfect imprint of a wavy, watermarked heart on it.

"Where did you manage to find that?" I asked, running my hand over the heart, which I could swear felt wet.

"Shaylin made it."

"Because Stevie Rae helped. We got earth and water together, and we marked the rock!"

"That's perfect. It really is," I glanced up at the cool grouping of international time and date clocks on the wall. "I can hardly believe it, but we're on time."

Kevin's gaze followed mine to see the Tulsa Time Zone clock that read 11:15 pm—December 24. "Hey, Z! I just now realized—happy birthmas!"

"Oh, great Earth Mother. I totally misplaced your birthday," Grandma said.

"That's okay. There's been a lot going on today. I misplaced it myself."

"But you're eighteen, now, right?"

"Yeah, I guess I am. I thought I'd feel different, but I don't. Maybe that happens at twenty-one."

"No, u-we-tsi-a-ge-ya, that happens at sixty-one," Grandma quipped, before leaning over and kissing me. "Happy birthday, my Zoeybird."

"Dang, Z. We kinda missed your birthmas." Stevie Rae almost looked like she was going to cry.

"That's okay—I'm used to having a crappy birthmas. At least this one wasn't boring."

"You got me for your birthday. And I'm not even a Christmas-themed present," Kevin said, punching my arm.

"Gee, thanks." I rolled my eyes at him. It was either that or burst into tears, and then he might start crying. Again. And we both snot when we cry. A lot. So, just no. "Okay, guys, tell

Damien, Shaunee, Aphrodite, and Stark that we're ready. We'll meet you down at the SUV."

After they left, Grandma stepped into Kevin's arms. "I'm going to say goodbye here. I cannot go with you to the park. I wasn't there the first time. And I—I do not want to see you leave." Her voice trembled, but she blinked hard as she tried to keep her tears from falling. "I love you, Kevin. Dearly. Always. In any world. Come find your G-ma. She will be waiting for you."

Kevin smiled through his own tear-filled eyes. "With lavender chocolate chip cookies?"

"With lavender chocolate chip cookies. I promise."

They hugged for a long time. Then Kevin bent, brushed the tears from Grandma's cheeks and kissed her gently. "I love you, too, G-ma."

Grandma patted the medicine pouch she'd given him, and then slowly, sadly, she walked away.

We watched her, both sniffling. I sighed and reached into my pocket, pulled out two balled-up old tissues, and handed one to Kevin. While we wiped our eyes and blew our noses, I asked the question I'd been struggling with for hours.

"Kev, do you know Heath Luck?"

He tipped his head to the side and actually grinned at me. "You mean your grade school *and* high school sweetheart, quarterback, and all-around studly guy, Heath Luck?"

"Yes. You know that's who I mean," I said, trying to pretend my hot face was beet red from embarrassment and not from the racing of my heart and the fluttering of my stomach.

"Of course I know him." Then Kevin looked closer at me. "Wait, is he *dead* in this world?"

I nodded, not trusting my voice.

"Oh, Zo. I'm so sorry. He's totally fine in my world. Completely alive. In college playing OU football."

"Even with a war going on?"

"Vamps love them some sports—especially football. It's become like a weird hobby of theirs. So as long as you're a jock or a cheerleader, or majoring in something else vamps in general—or Neferet in particular—think is important, or at least amusing, they leave you alone. Well, pretty much. Heath's doing great."

"That's good. I'm glad. I'm really glad."

"He was at your funeral. He was real broken up."

I met Kevin's eyes. "Don't tell me anymore, 'kay?"

"'Kay. Anything for the birthmas girl." He put me in a pretend headlock and started giving me noogies. "And I have your birthmas noogies right here."

"OHMYGOD stop messing up my hair!" I was smacking him when Stark came into the room.

"Uh, we're waiting for you two."

"Good thing," I said, trying to fix my totally screwed up hair. "I was just getting ready to go all Ninja Turtle on him."

"Scared. I'm super scared."

"Yep, she's frightening when you mess with her hair," Stark said.

The two of them giggled like little boys and I looped my arm through Other Kevin's on my right, and Stark's on my left. Then, off to see the wizard–like, the three of us headed for the SUV.

(

Zoey

Woodward Park was like the rest of midtown we'd driven through—completely deserted. It was still snowing. The flakes had gone from small and sparkly to heavy and lazy.

Just like the night before.

I stared out at the winter wonderland as we trudged through the park. It was like nothing bad had happened—like the snow had covered all of our mistakes and made things new again.

The thought held as we looked down on the spot that had caused so much to go wrong—and right—the night before.

Oh, my Goddess! How could it have all happened in only twenty-four hours?

In the distance I could see snowy mounds and the reflection of streetlights off of yellow crime-scene tape, and understood that the storm had made it impossible for the wreckage that the vampyres had caused to be cleared. From this far away it looked so benign—almost like toys children had abandoned because they'd been called from their play to get ready for bedtime.

Get your head in the game, Zoey! Tonight a mistake could hurt Kevin. I shook myself mentally and checked with Stark.

"Is it time?"

"Yep." Stark went to Kevin and held out his hand. "It was really good to know you. I wish you could stay. Hey, when you see Other Stark and you want to get through to him, tell him William Chidsey would be ashamed that he's working with Neferet. He won't like it, but it will get through to him."

"Who's that?" Kev asked.

"He was my mentor, and a big part of my life. More importantly, he was a good man. A very good man. And no matter what world—I can't believe he'd be for Neferet."

"Thanks. I'll remember. It was good to know you, too. Take care of our Zo, will ya?"

"Absolutely."

Then Kevin pulled Stark in for a manly, back-slapping hug.

"I have to stay up here, like I did last night. I'm glad we met, too. Stay safe, okay?" Damien didn't hold out his hand. He went straight for the hug, which Kevin returned.

"I'm glad Jack is with you. Don't let him come back to our world. It's not good for him there," Kevin said.

"I won't. He'll stay here with me. Always," Damien assured him.

Kevin turned to me. "I'm ready."

290

"That wall is surrounding Neferet's grotto," I explained to Kevin as we made our way carefully down the snow-covered stairs.

He studied it curiously. "The grotto's inside there?"

"Yep."

"It's smaller than I pictured it."

"The Woodward Park Association told me it was a fox's den."

"Weird. It'd simplify things if I could just stuff her in there and seal her up."

"Yeah, it sure would," I said.

"Good luck with that," Shaunee told him. "She's a lot harder to stuff than you'd think."

"That's what I'm afraid of," Kevin muttered.

"Hey, you're a resourceful guy. You'll figure it out." Aphrodite sent him a flirty grin.

Kevin lit up like a Christmas tree. "Well, Goddess of Love—if you say it, then I believe it is so."

Darius snorted and mumbled something under his breath.

"See," Kevin whispered to me. "He's totally worried."

I shook my head at him and almost slipped down a step. Kevin took my hand and steadied me, and then he didn't give it back.

I didn't mind. At all.

We didn't talk much as we worked to ready the space. It was harder than it had been the first time. We were dealing with snow that in some places had drifted to our knees. We were also moving through a myriad of emotions—fear, anticipation, worry—and all the while I kept reminding my circle to focus on our intent. We took our places. I was concentrating super hard, trying to remember exactly what words I'd used in what order to invoke the elements—and feeling relieved that I hadn't made up some elaborate craziness that I'd never remember.

When we were ready, I called Other Kevin into the center of the circle with me.

"This is going to be like what we did in Nyx's Temple, only I'm going to be using different words and each of them is going to give me something. It's going to be weird, because we're working backwards. I've never called elements this way, or cast a circle like this. I'm not sure it's going to work."

Kevin's gaze was full of confidence. "I'm sure. One hundred percent. This is going to be easy. The hard part was the first time. Now, you know what you're doing."

"That's a real good way to look at it," Stevie Rae said, dimpling at him.

"Thank you."

Kevin looked super pleased with himself, and I suddenly realized that my friends liked him. *Really* liked him.

And I had to struggle not to burst into tears.

"Okay, everyone think what we were thinking then. Protection. We're casting a protection spell. Got it?"

"Got it!" the four of them echoed.

"Okay, we call spirit first." I closed my eyes, concentrated, and centered myself. *Please, Nyx, help me get this right.* I opened my eyes and knelt in the small area Kev and I had cleared of snow. "Oh, strong and powerful, all-knowing spirit, I call for you. Cast your mighty blessing upon the magick I work here. Spirit, come forth and complete my circle!"

I lit my purple candle and felt the soft, familiar brush of spirit rush through my body. Kevin's intake of breath told me that he'd felt it, too.

I thought that was an excellent sign.

Then I reached up and released the braid that held my redbird feather, just like I had the night before, saying, "I offer this feather— the spirit of my people—free and strong. It is my wish that it fills our circle and focuses our intent for our spellwork tonight."

I stood, and with Kevin by my side we went to Stevie Rae. I spoke the words to call earth, and Stevie Rae did her part, handing me the rowan twig. She smiled at Kevin and mouthed, *Bye—we'll miss you,* then she brushed away a tear.

We went to Shaylin next, and collected the rock with the watermark.

"Stay safe," she whispered to him.

Shaunee and fire were next. When she handed me the crystal tetrahedron she told Kevin, "Watch your back. We'll miss you."

Then we were standing in front of Aphrodite.

I called air and lit her yellow candle, and Aphrodite handed me the wickedly sharp athame. Then she looked up at Kevin.

"When you talk to Other Aphrodite, be exactly who you are. She'll love you, too."

Then she totally shocked me by kissing him. Softly, sweetly, right on the lips.

"Goodbye, my Goddess of Love." The kid stepped forward, cupped Aphrodite's face in his hands and kissed her—not sweetly, not softly—*sexily*. I didn't look at Darius, and was real glad he'd taken the same position he'd had last night—outside the *other side* of the circle.

I bumped Kevin with my shoulder. He let her go. Finally.

Kevin and I turned to head back to the center of the circle, and I felt the breath leave my lungs. Our circle was completely ringed in a ribbon of glowing red light.

"Is that normal?" Kevin whispered.

"No. But I think it's good."

When we were back in the center I crouched and started to recreate the last part of the spell. That's when I noticed the redbird feather was gone. I started to look around for it and a jolt of surprise lightened through my body.

It had been gone last time, too. I'd made a mistake I didn't even realize I'd made, but somehow I repeated it.

I'm doing this right!

Okay, work backwards. Cut yourself.

That's exactly what I started to do—and stopped. My head snapped up and my gaze found Aphrodite.

"Our intent! We all messed up right about now. We all thought bad stuff about your mom. We have to change that."

Aphrodite nodded. Then her eyes brightened. "I got it! We all need to think 'Frances LaFont gets a second chance.'"

"Perfect!" My eyes went around the circle. "That's what I want you to think. All of you. Now!"

I began drawing the pentacle to manifest the pentagram within our circle. And with the last stroke, I drew the razor sharp athame across my palm—directly over the still-painful scab—as I thought, *Aphrodite's mom gets a second chance.*

From there it really was easy. I added the four-sided pyramid, which represented the manifestation of fire, and then Shaylin's rock. Finally, I took Stevie Rae's rowan twig, and as I planted it, I spoke the words I had no trouble remembering, only altering them to fit the order in which my spell was cast.

"I end with earth's offering, the rowan. I return it to earth, blessed by the elements, and infused with power. May it grow strong and long—so mighty that it can withstand any negative influence." Just like I'd done the night before, I pressed end of the stick wand into the ground, planting it firmly.

There was no explosion like last time. There was only a great exhale, as if the earth herself had drawn a deep, reviving breath.

At the base of the rowan, the ground opened. It wasn't a giant hole. It wasn't really a hole at all. It was more like a shifting of the earth and the forming of the absence of something. The nonhole expanded, sucking into it the rock and the pyramid—and the athame. And as those magickally infused items disappeared, the rowan began to grow.

This time it wasn't twisted. This time it grew tall and sturdy and straight.

I stood and faced my brother. He took both of my hands in his. We held tight to one another.

"Promise me something?" he asked.

"Anything."

"Reach out to your Kevin. He doesn't know how to reach out to you. He's just a kid, you know. But he misses you, even though he'll probably never admit it. Be his big sister, 'kay?"

Tears were falling silently down my face and mixing with the snow until I couldn't tell which was soaking my shirt.

"I promise. And promise me something."

"Anything."

"You'll be careful. Really careful, and not just stupid-young-boy-hero careful." He stared to answer me, but I cut him off. "And promise me if you get into a really bad spot, you'll gather all this stuff again and get your butt to Woodward Park with four people who can help you cast a circle, and you'll come back here."

He smiled through his own tears. "That's two somethings, not one."

"Just say you promise."

"I promise."

We came together then and I hugged him like I never wanted to let him go.

And I didn't. I didn't ever want to let my little brother go.

"I love you." We spoke the words at the same time and then, as we came apart, laughing through tears, we said, "Jinx!"

"I think I beat you to it. Again," he said.

"Not a chance," I said.

"You're a sore loser. But I love you anyway. Take care of yourself, Zo. And take care of that other me, too."

Kevin stepped into the hole and disappeared.

30

Zoey

Closing the circle was anticlimactic. We did it quietly. Slowly. And then, surrounded by my friends, I went back to the House of Night. Without my little brother.

No one said much of anything. Aphrodite snuggled close to Darius, and I heard her crying softly. Darius held her gently, smoothing her hair and murmuring to her.

Stark asked Shaunee to drive again, then he pulled me onto his lap and held me like I was a little girl while I snot-cried all over his shirt.

He didn't seem to mind at all.

"I'm going to take a bath," I said when we kicked off our snow boots and trudged through the front door of the school.

My friends each took turns hugging me. They didn't say anything. They didn't have to. When Stark and I were alone, he smoothed my dark hair back from my face and kissed my damp cheek. "A bath's a good idea. I'll go by the dining hall and grab us some snacks. Do you feel like anything in particular?"

"I'm not hungry."

"How about some of that lavender tea you like?"

I nodded absently. "That sounds nice. Thanks."

It seemed like a long walk to my suite of rooms. I wanted to avoid everyone, and thought I had. But when I rubbed the tears out of my eyes and really looked around I saw that every student—fledgling or human—and every vampyre I passed stopped and silently, respectfully, placed their hands over their hearts and bowed their heads to me.

I was a snotty mess by the time I got to my room.

I meant to lounge in a hot bath for hours. Maybe even days. But once I was submerged it seemed pointless. I got out, piled my hair on top of my head, and put on my comfiest pair of old, ratty sweatpants and one of Stark's oversized T-shirts.

He was waiting in front of our fireplace, and when I came to him, he pulled me into his arms again and kissed me on top of my head.

"Would you please come with me?"

"Stark, I'm not hungry. I swear."

"We're not going to the dining hall. There's something you need to see."

"Can't it wait?" I felt exhausted. The last thing I wanted to do was to go anywhere that didn't involve my bed.

"Nope. It can't wait. Come on. Please. For me?"

I sighed. I knew Stark could feel everything I did—which meant I knew I was making him miserable. So, I gave in. I owed it to him.

"Okay, but is it going to take long?"

"That depends on you."

He held my hand and we walked slowly back through the school that I'd made my own. When we got to the back door—the one that opened to the sidewalk that led to the student dorms, I stopped.

I looked down at my pink bunny slippers. "I don't have my snow boots on. You should've told me we were going outside."

"That's okay. I wanted an excuse to carry you." He promptly picked me up, cradling me in his arms as he walked to the girls' dorm.

I couldn't help but smile when we went inside. The sights—the smells—everything brought memories rushing back. Kids were clustered around different TVs, either watching movies or playing video games. They paused when we came in. Each of them stood, put their hands over their hearts, and bowed to me.

I put my hand over my heart, too, tilted my head down, and in a voice thick with emotion said, "May you blessed be."

"Blessed be, High Priestess," they echoed.

Stark took my hand and led me upstairs, directly to a door on the second floor painted a familiar, pretty, light purple. He knocked twice.

Stevie Rae opened the door. She was in her flannel cowboy pj's that had lassos and horses all over them. A giggle escaped from somewhere within me.

"I can't believe you still have those."

"Are you kiddin', Z? These pj's are total classics. I'd as soon throw them away as my Roper jeans."

"Don't we all wish?" Aphrodite quipped from somewhere behind her.

Stevie Rae stepped to the side and I realized that not only was our old dorm room decorated almost exactly as it had been when Stevie Rae and I were fledglings together, but my friends and Grandma Redbird were all in their pj's and all crowded on the twin beds and the floor. Nala was curled up, donut style, on the end of my bed, staring with slitted green eyes at Maleficent who was grooming herself on Stevie Rae's bed. The opening frame of *Finding Nemo* was already on the screen, and my friends were passing around popcorn and more of Grandma's endless lavender chocolate chip cookies. The little sink had been filled with ice and lots of brown pop.

"Surprise!" they yelled.

I burst into blubbering tears.

"Ah, Z, don't. You'll make us all start again." Stevie Rae put her arm around me and steered me into the room. "Come open your present. It'll make you feel better, promise."

"Present?" I sniffled.

"Yes, and we promise it's *not* Christmas themed," Erik said. He and Shaunee were sharing a beanbag chair. He sent me a wink and I remembered the snowman necklace he'd given me last year and my tears started to dry.

Aphrodite and Darius scooted over to make room for me on the end of what used to be my very tiny-looking twin bed and Stark handed me a box wrapped in silver foil tied with a gold bow.

It was a very little box.

I shook it. "Is this from you?" I asked Stark.

"It's from all of us," he said as my friends nodded like bobblehead dolls.

"We all went in on it, Z," Stevie Rae said, plopping down behind me on the bed so she could peer over my shoulder. "Hurry and open it. We've been keeping it secret for ages."

"Okay, here goes." I tore off the wrapping paper and made a small, happy sound as I saw the *Moody's Fine Jewelry* sticker, which seemed a little creepily déjà vu-ish after Erik's comment. I readied myself to pretend to gush over whatever was inside, and opened the little velvet box.

My mouth flopped open—unattractively, I'm sure—as the gaslights in the room caught the diamonds and made them sparkle with white fire. The pendant was platinum, shaped in a perfect crescent moon made of diamonds.

I gaped at my friends, who were all grinning at me.

"Look at the back!" Stevie Rae said.

I turned it over to see an engraving on the back:

Happy 18ᵗʰ B-day, Z
We ♥ you!

"We had it made special for you," Stevie Rae said.

"It's why you only got one thing, because it was fucking expensive," Aphrodite said. She was holding a full glass of champagne and leaning against Darius. Except for her unusual Mark, she looked 100 percent like herself again.

"Do you like it?" Stark asked.

I had to clear my throat and swallow several times before I could answer him. "No. I *love* it! It's the most beautiful, most perfect birthday present I've ever gotten."

"Yea!" Everyone cheered and then they were all crowding me while Stark fastened my incredible, fabulous, beautiful necklace— as we oohed and ahhed about it.

In the middle of that, Aphrodite's ringtone blared Aretha Franklin's "Respect."

She frowned at the phone, handed her glass of champagne to Darius, and then answered it.

"Yes, this is Aphrodite LaFont." She paused, listening, and I watched her face drain of color. "How did it happen?" She paused again. "I see. No. That's fine. I'll take care of it. Thank you for letting me know." She tapped the END button and dropped her phone back into her designer bag. While her hand was in her bag, I watched her search around, and then she brought up a familiar medicine bottle filled to the brim with Xanax. She held out her hand for her glass of champagne, which Darius returned to her after a hesitation and a resigned sigh.

Then Aphrodite did the last thing I expected her to do. She walked over to our sink and poured out her glass of champagne over the ice. She turned and opened the door that led to our modest bathroom. I craned my head around with everyone else as we all watched her open her bottle of Xanax and pour it down the toilet, saying, "I am not her. I will never be her. I let that go." She flushed the toilet, tossed the empty pill bottle in the trash can, and then came back to her seat.

When no one spoke, she rolled her eyes. "Just ask."

"Okay," I said. "Who was on the phone and why did you pour out your favorite drink and your favorite pills? Not that we don't think it's an excellent idea, but still."

"That was the hospital on the phone. It was about my mother."

Shaunee snorted. "What, did they release her and she had not one friend who could come pick her up? No surprise."

"Tell her to call Lyft," Damien said. "You don't need to deal with her issues anymore."

"I'm not going to have to. She's dead."

"What? How?" I sputtered.

"She OD'd. Apparently, it was an accident. She mixed too many prescription drugs and too much alcohol one last time. She wasn't hooked up to monitors anymore because she was supposed to go home as soon as the snow cleared. They thought she was sleeping and she'd yelled at the nurses so many times for bothering her that they left her alone. Like she'd demanded. And she died."

I went to Aphrodite. "Are you okay?"

She looked up at me. Her eyes were clear and her expression was serene. "I am." Then she lifted a pretend glass and said, "I'd like to offer a toast." We all grabbed glasses, totally confused about what was going on, but wanting to be supportive. Aphrodite stood. "Sometimes people get exactly what they deserve. Let's hope it works like that for Z's brother, too. So, to Other Kevin! Let him get all the goodness he deserves!" "To Other Kevin! Let him get all the goodness he deserves!"

And that was something we could all drink to.

(

Zoey

I went back to Woodward Park the next night—alone. Stark hadn't wanted me to go by myself, but I'd insisted. It'd stopped snowing not long after midnight the night before, and the snowplows had worked overtime to get the streets cleared. But it was after dark, and the roads were still crappy enough that the only cars driving by the park were police cruisers and ambulances.

I made my way slowly to Neferet's grotto. The rowan tree had taken root. It stood straight and strong in the center of what was our circle, fully leafed out and looking as magickal as it truly was. As I passed it, I touched it gently, and spoke a simple prayer to Nyx.

"Please stay close to Other Kevin, Goddess. I know you love him. Please let him know it so completely that he stays strong even when Darkness tries to put out his Light."

The tree swayed and in the murmuring of its impossibly green leaves I heard the echo of Nyx's voice fill the world around me, "*Trust me, Daughter, to care for my Son.*"

I bowed my head and felt a wash of relief that lessened my sadness a little. "Thank you, Nyx."

Then I went to the wall. I knew what was compelling me. It was her journal—*Neferet's Curse*—and the lingering pity I felt for Emily Wheiler.

I rested the palm of my hand on the wall, closed my eyes, and spoke to her.

"They were wrong—that man who abused you, and the others who stood by and let it happen. The vampyres you went to were wrong, too. They should have gotten you help—should have known something was seriously wrong with you. And we were wrong. First, to let you have so much power, and now to be so quick to cast blame on you—so quick that we opened our world to monsters." I paused and added, "But goodness came of it. I found my brother. Damien found his Jack. Aphrodite found herself. And I learned something important about you. I learned that I feel more pity for you than hate, and that's a pretty big thing. So, Neferet, for the first time, I can say I honestly hope you find peace. And I wish you to blessed be."

I took my hand from the wall and turned my back to it as I pulled out my cell phone and punched the old number I'd found earlier that day. He picked up on the second ring.

"Uh, hi, Kevin. This is your sister, Zoey."

(

Zoey Redbird didn't see the thin tendril of Darkness that snaked from the almost-invisible crack in the wall where her hand had just rested. It reached for her, trembling with need. As it came within a hair's width of her body, its sightless face rippled and its maw-like mouth opened. Pointed teeth glistened with spittle. At that instant, Zoey shifted her stance, allowing the light of the newly risen moon to shine behind her. When the silver beam touched the tendril it quivered, smoked, and slowly—very slowly—it slithered back between the rocks and disappeared.

The end ... for now.

An excerpt from

HOUSE OF NIGHT
OTHER WORLD
• BOOK TWO •

LOST

Stark

"Stevie Rae! There you are! Hey, we need to talk." Stark rushed across the springy newly green grass toward the statue of Nyx standing proudly in the middle of the House of Night's main courtyard. Beside Stevie Rae were two young fledglings who had just finished lighting the myriad of votive candles that flickered cheerily around the base of the Goddess. They bowed nervously but respectfully to greet Stark. "Hi, yeah, hi. Nice job with the candles and everything. Okay, time to get to your next class!" Stark waved his hand dismissively and shooed them away.

The two fledglings practically sprinted toward the rear entrance to the school. Stevie Rae scowled at Stark. "Great. You just scared 'em. Don't you remember what it was like to be newly Marked? Those two have only been here for a week. They're still cryin' in their pillows at night for their mamas."

"They'll be fine, just like we were fine. Who's not fine is Zoey."

"What in the Sam Hell are you talkin' about?"

"Have you seen her lately?" Stark fired the question at her.

"Yeah," she shrugged. "I saw her for just a sec a little while ago. She was headin' to the depot to try to keep Kramisha and Aphrodite from killing each other over the restaurant renovations."

"That's where she said she was going. But she only stopped by for about ten minutes and then made a lame excuse to take off. She's been doing that lately. As in almost every day. Do you know what the hell is wrong with her?"

"No! I didn't know anything was wrong. Ah, oh. Is it Other Kevin?" Stevie Rae's blue-eyed gaze swept the schoolyard. "Is he back?" She squinted, half expecting him to materialize from one of the dusky shadows.

"No, he's not. But yes. I think it has something to do with her brother and that Other World. And I do not think she's okay."

"You're gonna have to give me more to go on than that. Since Rephaim and I moved back to T-Town I've been super crazy busy getting settled and figurin' out lesson plans for this dang Spells and Rituals class I was moronic enough to volunteer to teach. Jeesh, who knew teaching was so hard?"

"Every real teacher in the world knows that, but that's not the point. Stevie Rae, you need to listen to me—I do not think Z is okay."

Stevie Rae motioned for Stark to join her on an ornately carved iron bench perfectly situated near the goddess statue.

"Now, tell me what's stuck in your craw about Z."

Stark blew out a long breath as he sat beside her. "She's going to Heath's grave. Every day. And she's lying about it."

Stevie Rae hiked her shoulders. "That's not real bad. I mean, Z misses him. We all know that, and maybe she's not telling the truth because she doesn't want you to feel bad. And if she's lying how do you know where she's going?"

"I followed her. And before you give me crap about that let me say that I only did it because I'm worried. Real worried."

Stevie Rae held up her hands in surrender. "Hey, I'm not judging. And if you say there's something to be real worried about, you have my full attention."

Stark ran his fingers through his thick hair and sighed again. "So, I followed her," he repeated. "And watched her. She sits there. On his grave. And talks to him. A lot."

"She talks to his gravestone?"

Stark shook his head. "No. She leans against his gravestone, but she stares to the side of it, like he's sitting there—beside her—somewhere close. And by close I don't mean Nyx's Grove."

"Well, okay, so it's weird and sad, but maybe that's how Z deals with her grief. You know it took a long time for her to even go to his grave. Maybe this is actually a good sign. How's she been acting otherwise? And let me say sorry that I've been so dang busy moving here that I can't answer that question myself, which as her bestie is something I should be able to do."

Stark waved away her apology. "This isn't on you. It's on all of us. I think we've left her alone too much since Kevin went back to the Other World."

"But we were givin' her space. And she's been seeing a lot of her brother. The one who isn't a red vampyre. I thought that was helping her deal with Other Kevin not being here." Stevie Rae chewed her bottom lip. "I haven't asked her hardly anything about how she's been feelin'. Like Kramisha always says, it's not cool to be all up in Z's business."

"Yeah, well, space time is over. Since she's starting 'talking,'" he air quoted, "to Heath, she's stopped actually talking to me. And, obviously, you."

"Z's not talkin' to Damien or Aphrodite, either?" Stevie Rae asked.

"Oh, sure. Z talks to Damien and Aphrodite, me and you. But she never says how she's feeling. She never says anything that isn't just surface crap. Stevie Rae, she's pulling away from me. And from you, Aphrodite, and Damien. She's only really talking to dead Heath."

"You seriously don't think this is just Z dealing with her grief?"

"No, because this dead Heath talking crap didn't start until after Other Kevin came from the Other World and—"

"And told her about Heath being alive over there," Stevie Rae finished for him, eyes widening with understanding.

"Exactly," Stark nodded.

Stevie Rae sucked in a huge breath. "Ohmygoodness, Z's gonna go to the Other World!"

"Exactly!" Stark repeated.

"Ah, hell!"

(

Zoey

I pulled my bug off Seventy-First Street onto Aspen, and took the immediate left to enter through the somber gates of Floral Haven Cemetery. It wasn't long after dusk, but I'd timed it perfectly so that I could slip into the cemetery after most visitors had left, but before the gates were officially closed.

"I guess practice does make perfect," I muttered.

As if it knew the way without me steering, my little aqua-colored bug wound around the curving roadways to what had become a familiar section of the graveyard. I stopped where I always did—by the big juniper tree that marked the beginning of the path I followed almost daily.

It always felt sad when I first got here. Floral Haven wouldn't have been Heath's first choice. Not because it was a bad cemetery or anything like that. I just knew that Heath would have liked somewhere more … well … colorful. Heath had liked crazy, and Floral Haven was immaculate, structured, organized, and well regulated. The opposite of crazy.

But as I walked down the path to the Luck family plot, my sadness lifted a little—then more than a little when I caught sight of my neighborly addition to the grounds. I went to Heath's proper, modest, boring tombstone and sat right on top of his grave, which I knew he would've appreciated. I leaned against the cold gray stone that said in block letters: HEATH REGINALD LUCK—BELOVED SON, and looked to the side at the family plot closest to the Luck's. There was only one tombstone—the one I'd purchased immediately after I'd purchased the family plot. It was as unboring as the very proper rules of the cemetery had allowed. I'd commissioned a stone made from smooth blue marble, the exact color of a perfect fishing hole. The artist, who had been more than mildly confused by my unorthodox idea, had carved a scene of Heath sitting on a small wooden dock casting his rod out into the water. I'd had him make it so that Heath was looking right at me, grinning like he always did when he went fishing.

"Hey there. How ya doin'?" I asked the carving of Heath. "Yep, it was one of those awesome Oklahoma spring days today. Not too hot, not too much ragweed and pollen, and not too ticky. Yet. You'd say it was good fishing weather, but then again you thought every day was good fishing weather."

Okay, let me be clear. I haven't lost my mind—at least not totally. I am not under any delusion that Heath is actually here, listening to me. I know where he is—or at least one version of him. Heath Luck is hanging out where I last saw him, with Nyx. He was probably fishing right now up there somewhere.

But I like pretending to talk to him.

I need to pretend to talk to him.

Especially now.

"Zoey? It is you! I thought I saw your bug turn in here."

I jumped at the voice and spun around on my butt.

"Kev! Sheesh, you scared the bejezzus outta me. Make some sound next time."

"How about you tell me when you're gonna visit Heath's grave next time and I'll meet you here?" Kevin said, settling in beside me. "You don't ever find this creepy?"

"What? Sitting on his grave? Heath would love it," I smiled.

"Well, that and *that*." He pointed to the carving of fisherman Heath.

"Heath would love that, too," I said. "Do you not remember he had a sense of humor?"

"Sure. Do you not remember he's dead?"

I jerked back as if Kevin had slapped me. "Of course I remember. I was there. Losing him almost killed me. Why the hell would you ask me that?"

"Because of what Other Kevin told you."

I didn't say anything. I couldn't say anything. Since Other Kevin had slipped from his world into ours, and told me that Heath—the kid I'd been in love with since third grade—was alive back in that other world, I'd had one thought obsessively circling around and around my mind.

Go see Heath … go see Heath … Go. See. Heath.

"Zoey, I'll go with you. All you have to do is ask." Kevin spoke into the silence swirling between us.

My gaze snapped to his. "You can't! I'm not alive in that world, so I could get away with sneaking over there, but you are—and you're a rogue red vampyre who has probably been leading the resistance for the past several months. It's not safe for you over there."

"Z, it's not safe for anyone over there."

I looked away from Kevin and my gaze found Heath's smiling image again.

"I understand that," I muttered.

"Do you really?" Kevin cracked his knuckles and flexed his fingers—a sure sign he was stressed.

I answered my brother's question with one of my own. "You know I'm going, don't you?"

"Yep, I do. And, Z, if I know it, so do your friends."

Foreboding surged through my veins like ice water. "No! I haven't said one word to any of them."

"You haven't said one word to me, either. I figured it out."

"Which means they will, too," I said.

"Uh, yeah. For sure."

This is going to break Stark's heart, I thought, swallowing against the lump building in my throat. "Ah, hell …"

ACKNOWLEDGMENTS

First, we want to thank our superfan and friend, Thiago Marques, who is part of the Brazilian Nighters. Thiago, your research help was invaluable. *Nós te amamos.*

Thank you to our agent and friend, Meredith Bernstein, who said those three magick words so long ago, "vampire finishing school." The House of Night would not exist without her.

We have vast appreciation for our longtime editor and friend, Christine Zika. Your brainstorming is always awesome! Thank you for helping us make this the best book it could be. You are truly our Goddess Editor.

We want to send a big WE HEART YOU to our new publisher, Blackstone. You are a dream team. Thank you for letting us join your family. Team Cast and Team Blackstone make a perfect pair!

XXXOOO

DISCUSSION QUESTIONS
for
LOꝹED

1. A main reoccurring theme in the House of Night series regards acceptance and tolerance. Often this theme is demonstrated externally, as in Zoey's quest to open the House of Night to human students. But sometimes this theme is an internal struggle, as in Aphrodite's relationship problems with her mother. Discuss the difference between internal and external acceptance and tolerance, and how both affect character development.

2. Early in the book, Zoey believes Kalona visits her in a dream, though later she discovers that it was not Kalona because he has sworn never to return to any location where he caused Zoey or her friends pain. Do you agree with Kalona's decision, or do you think he's simply avoiding responsibility for past mistakes?

3. In *Loved*, Aphrodite comes to the realization that she cannot make her mother love or value her. Discuss Aphrodite's path to this realization and whether you believe it will or will not affect her personality and her future decisions. What are some healthy ways teens can cope with abusive parenting?

4. There are several political scenes in *Loved*. How do they mirror current events? How do real-world situations inspire and/or influence fiction?

5. In *Loved*, we see D; struggle with depression. What signs and symptoms did you notice that illustrated the depth of Damien's illness? Discuss the steps Damien began to take toward healing. In real life, what resources are available to aid teens who are struggling with mental illness?

6. In *Loved*, you meet two characters who are from a completely different world than the characters they mirror in our House of Night world. These characters are different, yet similar enough that they have many of the same likes, dislikes, loves, and even idiosyncrasies as the characters they mirror. What does this say about nature over nurture? Do you agree or disagree?

7. Damien's actions in the Other World wound Other Jack deeply. Do you think Other Jack's reaction to Damien is credible? Do you agree with Other Jack's eventual acceptance of the new Damien?

8. Weather always plays a big role in HoN books. Discuss the symbolic nature of the snowstorm in *Loved*.

9. In her essay entitled "Reimagining 'Magic City'" for the Smart Pop anthology *Nyx in the House of Night*, Amy H. Sturgis writes, "The novels can be read together as one extended and creative love letter to my hometown (Tulsa)." Discuss how Ms. Sturgis' statement can be supported providing examples from *Loved*.

10. We discover the White Bull is orchestrating chaotic events at the House of Night and Tulsa in general. Is chaos always evil? Support your opinion.

FAN Q&A

You have questions? P. C. & Kristin have answers for you!

What inspired you two beautiful ladies to bring HoN back? The fans of your beloved series? Just because it's the tenth anniversary? Or another reason entirely different?
—RHIANNON "RHINNY" RICKETS

P. C.: I'd always planned on writing another HoN book, but I thought I should wait about five years or so and then write a book set in the distant future—at least fifty years after the events of *Redeemed*. Then Kristin and I realized the tenth anniversary was upon us and we wanted to do something special for our fans. Though neither of us read reviews, we do interact with fans a lot, and we listened to what our readers were saying—what they missed most about the HoN, what they most wanted to see if/ when I wrote a new book. Then we brainstormed a few different possibilities, like a new novella or perhaps an anthology of short stories, because I didn't think I'd have time in my schedule to write an entire book. But Kristin and I kept circling around to a new idea we had that would open up a whole other dimension to the

HoN world. We decided I should go for it and see if I could get the book done in the time I had—and I did! It was such a pleasure returning to the HoN world that we outlined a second book as well, and I'm currently working on it!

P. C. and Kristin Cast, not only mother and daughter, but a wonderful writing duo. As coauthors, how exactly do you work together so successfully and what role do each of you play when writing the HoN series?

—LUC WEST

P. C.: For the HoN series, I do all of the writing and Kristin serves as my frontline editor. Early in the series she made sure Zoey and the gang didn't sound like fortysomething disgruntled schoolteachers. As the books progressed, the characters' voices became set, so Kristin shifted to being much more involved with plotting and brainstorming with me. I rely on her editorial advice completely.

Kristin and I do actually coauthor books. Together we wrote *The Scent of Salt and Sand* (a novella in Kristin's new-adult series, the Escaped), and we're coauthoring a new YA paranormal series scheduled to debut in 2018 titled *The Dysasters*. When we co-write we choose our own characters and decide whose turn it is to write which chapter according to whose character has the main point of view in that particular chapter. Careful outlining is very important when we co-write.

People often ask what happens when Kristin and I disagree and how we resolve fights between us, and that question makes us laugh. We don't fight! We work together with mutual respect and very little ego. As to final plot and character decisions—if we're actually co-writing, we tend to leave that up to whomever is writing that part of the novel. If it's a HoN issue, I have the final decision as I'm doing the writing, but I pay close attention to Kristin's advice—she's usually right!

When writing the outline for the story of House of Night, was Nyx the only Greek goddess considered, or were there other options that may have been chosen but for certain reasons, they didn't make the cut?
—ELLA MAY FLEMING-CHRISTIE

P. C.: I had help finding Nyx! As I was creating the HoN I asked a student of mine if he would like to research goddesses for my new series. He was excited to help, and all I told him was that I needed a vampire goddess and I would prefer she be based on one of the lesser-known mythological deities. He brought me this poem of Hesiod's, and I knew immediately that Nyx was my goddess and the House of Night was what the school would be called. In return my student helper was the inspiration for Damien!

There also stands the gloomy house of Night;
ghastly clouds shroud it in darkness.
Before it Atlas stands erect and on his head
and unwearying arms firmly supports the broad sky,
where Night and Day cross a bronze threshold
and then come close and great each other.
(Hesiod, *Theogony*, 744 ff.)

What was your inspiration to write the series? A lot of writers don't keep a series going for as long as HoN. What kept you going with it?

—EVEE HILTON

P. C.: In 2005 my agent, Meredith Bernstein, and I were having dinner at a writers' conference and she said she would like me to write a series set at a "vampire finishing school." She wanted me to write something really hot (for adults), but I was teaching high school and I immediately envisioned it as a YA series. I proposed it to her as young adult and she fell in love with the House of Night!

I had a story arc outlined for the House of Night, and because of my deadlines and my word count restrictions, it simply took twelve books to get to the conclusion.

At what point in the series did you decide to make the dynamic between Aphrodite and Zoey change to where they become best friends? When did you decide to make her one of the "good guys"?

—FELICIA CAREY

P. C.: From the very beginning! I knew I wanted to stay away from clichés, whether they were vampire or teenage in origin. I believed it was important to show the multilayered personalities of girls who, like Aphrodite, get labeled bitches or bad guys. I also wanted to allow all of the main characters the opportunity to develop, mature, and grow.

I would like to ask a two-part question. From all of the phenomenal characters in HoN, who was the first one? How did you decide if they were going to be good or evil? Thanks :)
—NANCY WENTE

P. C.: Zoey was the first character I created. Sometimes I planned the character development very early and intended them to be good or evil all along, as in Aphrodite and Neferet. Sometimes characters stepped up and demanded I pay attention to them, like Rephaim, Nicole, and Aurox.

Who is your and Kristin's favorite character from the series?
—JAZZ ALEXANDRIA SCHAGANE

P. C.: My favorite to write is Aphrodite, but Zoey will always hold a special place in my heart.

K. C.: Heath is my absolute favorite character! He's super loosely based on a guy I went to college with, who is very, well, Heath-like.

I have a question. Are there transgender vampyres and would Nyx gift them with the body they truly want?
—EMILY FRIESEN

P. C.: There absolutely are transgender vampyres! In the HoN society, ALL are accepted by Nyx and her followers. I'm not going to say Nyx would never gift one of her people with the body that truly reflects who she or he is, but the Goddess doesn't like to manipulate human events. Instead, she blesses her people with strength, wisdom, kindness, tenacity, etc., and allows them to find their own paths.

Sister Mary Angela … Maya Angelou. Intentional or just a happy coincidence?

—RACHEL FORRESTER

P. C.: Intentional! And I'm thrilled that an ex-student of mine caught that! XXXOOO

Zoey's love life is so complicated and stressful it always made me relate it to myself and my real life. Why did you choose to continue the strenuous love complications for so long for Zoey instead of cutting it short and simple like most writers would have to avoid the conflict of fan opinions?

—CHRISTINE CARECHILD

P. C.: I'm glad you asked this! From the beginning of the House of Night, Kristin and I felt strongly about making a clear point about treating Zoey's love life realistically. The truth is teenagers are confused about who they should date, and that's great! Thinking that a young person who isn't even old enough to vote is old enough, mature enough, to choose a life partner is ridiculous. You have to know yourself well before you can choose with whom you'd like to spend your life. Teenagers are just beginning to discover who they are. They need to move through that journey of discovery without being shackled to a life partner before they've barely begun to experience life!

It is also a sad truth that young girls are consistently slut shamed if they dare to date more than one young man, but the young men? They're hailed as studs and heroes for being popular with the girls. I created a matriarchal society for our vampyres in the HoN, and one of the beauties of a society run by women is that women aren't judged for choosing their own way—and that often means they date more than one guy at a time, especially if they're barely eighteen years old.

K. C.: I do have to stand up for all of my fellow authors out there who chose to equip their characters with a more simplified relationship status. They most likely did not do it to avoid the conflict of fan opinions. As authors, we love you. We appreciate you. We need you. That being said, a lot of authors write the book they want to write whether or not readers will have conflicting opinions. Actually, as an author, I hope readers have different opinions. It means you heard me. It's a fabulous feeling to have one of my books be the catalyst that gets people talking to and learning from each other.

Which character did you find the most enjoyable to write, and which did you find the most challenging and why?
—TED RYAN

P. C.: I enjoy writing Aphrodite most. She and I share a sense of humor and a few other personality traits (it's probably best I don't elaborate on that!). Neferet is the most challenging character to write. Her descent into Darkness was a tough journey to follow.

Why did you kill Loren Blake?

—MARYON PEFFERLE CONCHA

P. C.: I'm glad you asked! Loren Blake was a predator. He manipulated and used Zoey. Adults who abuse their positions of power (teachers, the clergy, politicians, public servants) instead of serving and protecting those in their care should be held responsible. Loren is *not* a romantic character—no matter how handsome and charming he appears. He's an abuser and a predator.

As the authors, if you could bring one of your characters off the page and into our world to have dinner, which character would it be and why?

—CATHRINE JAMESON

P. C.: That's a hard question! I would really like to have dinner with the entire Nerd Herd! But if I have to choose one character I would probably pick Lenobia. She and I share the same horses!

K. C.: I would love to have dinner with Aphrodite! Can you imagine all of the HoN gossip? It would be fabulous!

Here's a question for ya, I don't know if it was ever touched on in the books if the adult vamps could have kids? Little Zoey/Starks running around would be adorable. But I'm guessing they probably can't reproduce?

—MEGAN MCGURN

P. C.: It is impossible for vampyres to reproduce in the HoN world. The Change increases a fledgling's metabolism and body temperature so that by the time they are adult vampyres women no longer have periods, which means they no longer ovulate, and men no longer produce viable sperm.

K. C.: This will never change. No HoN vampyre will ever have a child. Never ever. No way. Not happening.

Was there any inspiration from a fan or any fans on certain characters or any inspiration from fans on the settings, plots, and themes of any of ya'll's books? And I love ya'll's books so very much!

—JEREMY GRACE

P. C.: Yes! Some of the characters were inspired by real people. Example: Zoey was inspired by Kristin at sixteen years old. But Zoey and sixteen-year-old Kristin are also very different. Once I put a character in his or her fictional world that character begins to take on a life of his or her own. Because the world is different than our own, the characters develop as unique people and often end up having little in common with the "real" person who inspired them.

As to setting, plots, themes … For *Loved*, Kristin and I did take into consideration the things fans have been asking us about for the past three years, and we wove answers into the story!

What was your favorite part about writing this book? Is it hard to pick back up after being done with these characters for the last three years?

—LEAH GEORGE

P. C.: My favorite part of writing this book was the whole thing! It surprised me how nervous I was to write another HoN book. I felt a lot of stress about it, and it took me several months to begin writing, but as soon as I dove back into the HoN world the book took off! It was like I'd traveled a long, difficult distance to visit a group of very close friends, but once I got to their "house" I was completely at home again and had a fantastic time! I'm already working on the second book and loving it! No more stress—no more nerves. All is well at the HoN (for me, that is—for the characters, not so much).

Did you plan out how the whole story would progress, major plot points and such, or did you just make it up as you went?

—THERESE EWA KLINGBERG

P. C.: For the HoN, Kristin and I brainstorm major plot concepts and write a very loose outline. I usually begin with a clear opening scene and know where I want to be at the conclusion. What happens in the middle is much less clear and often changes and surprises me!

THIS is a question for you both—If you could change one thing in the entire series, what would it be and why?

—ANITA JOUBERT

P. C.: I'd definitely change the length of the books! I love writing long books, and I would have vastly preferred writing six big books instead of twelve regular-sized books.

K. C.: I would have encouraged P. C. to write a novella about the origin of our vampyres. It's a really interesting story that no one else knows, and I think readers would enjoy it so, so much!

What is the hardest part of dealing with publishing? Are there any secrets to dealing with publishers as an upstart author? Do you ever get so tired of editing your drafts that you begin to think your novel sucks? How do you keep inspiration flowing when you hit a really bad writer's block or just lose interest?

—ALYXANDREA JADE LOFFER

P. C.: The hardest part of publishing is that the outcome and success of your career is such a fluid, subjective thing. As an author, I write the best books I can, and that's the last bit of control I have over them. Then they go out into the world and I basically have to just wait and see what happens with them! Example: *Chosen*, the third book in the HoN series, was my first book to hit any bestseller list. *Chosen* was my eighteenth published novel.

Secrets to dealing with publishers? YES! The best advice I can give to aspiring authors is to research the job of being a professional author as you would any other profession. You wouldn't walk into a dentist's office and announce, "Hey! Someone hand me a drill and I'll get to work!" without years of training. It's the same with the business of being a professional author. Know the steps that have to happen to take a manuscript all the way to becoming a book on the shelf of a bookstore. Know an editor's job. Know an agent's job. Decide whether being an author is your career choice or a hobby. Then read and read and read, and write and write and write.

If you get tired of editing your drafts, you need to choose a different career. Writing is rewriting.

How do I keep inspiration flowing? Writing is my job. I'm under contract to produce books. I don't look at publishing through rose colored glasses or treat it like a hobby. I write whether I feel like it or not, just like I used to teach whether I felt like it or not because it was my job and I had a responsibility to do it well. Professional authors don't have time to indulge in writer's block.

K. C.: For me, the hardest part about the publishing industry and the secret to dealing with publishers go hand in hand—develop thick skin. Major publishing houses are not in the business of candy coating. If they think you suck, they'll tell you, but in a more eloquent way. There's an enormous chance you'll be rejected more times than you thought you were able to deal with, but if this is your *career* and not a *hobby*, you will persevere.

If you're hitting a wall with your writing, whether it's "writer's block" or losing interest, you're not writing the right thing. Go back a scene. Skip to a new chapter. Take a walk. Don't just sit there trying to force the sentence, scene, chapter, whatever. It's clearly not working, so it's time to try something new.

My mind is fried after noticing that this question might be published in my favorite series. I'm simply over the moon and floating amongst the stars with the prospect of another HoN book. But I do wonder … How are you able to not only juggle writing this book, but your new series, the Tales of a New World?

—DANIELLE BITSCHE

P. C.: I've been writing for a long time and I know how to move from world to world and book to book without having my characters and plots blend together. I also schedule my deadlines so that they don't usually run over the top of each other. As I'm answering this question, I'm working on copy edits for *Loved*, the draft of the next HoN book, the first book in Kristin and my new YA series, *The Dysasters*, and *Wind Rider*, the third book in my Tales of a New World series. It's about focus and dedication and hard work.

Of all the stories you (and Kristin) have written, which is your (and her) favorite?

—CAITLIN EVANS

P. C.: That's a really difficult question to answer. Books are a lot like children or fur babies—it's hard to have a favorite. I'll always love my first published book, *Divine by Mistake*. Currently, I'm really enjoying my new fantasy series, Tales of a New World, particularly *Sun Warrior* (October 2017 release). I think my favorite book in the HoN series is *Burned*, but *Loved* is a close second.

K. C.: *Scarlet Rain*, book two of my Escaped series. I've always wanted to write a book about a super gross pandemic/disease creature/bug thing, and I did (but with a heavy dose of magic and Greek mythology)!

Is there going to be a HoN movie?

—SARAH NORMAN

P. C.: In November 2011, Samuel Hadida at Davis Films purchased the film rights to HoN. Kristin and I met with Hadida in Paris and had a lovely time discussing what was supposed to be the first of five major motion pictures. Hadida hired a fantastic screenwriter, Marc Haimes (*Kubo and the Two Strings*). Marc wrote a wonderful screenplay that has my full support. Hadida has done nothing with it. There isn't anything more Kristin and I can do until the rights revert to us in 2020. Yes, we find the situation very frustrating. If you want to make your voice heard and tell Samuel Hadida you would like the HoN to come to film (or TV!). Here is his contact information. He's not listening to the authors. Maybe he'll listen to the fans!

Twitter: @Metropolitan_Fr
Facebook: https://www.facebook.com/DavisFilms.us/
Email: info@metropolitan-films.com
Mailing address:
Davis Films
29 Rue Galilée, 75116
Paris, France

Would HoN be better as movie or TV series?
                                        —JACKIE RAE HANSEN

P. C.: I'd like to see it as a cool cable series!

K. C.: Me too!

Are you guys planning on coming out with anymore "products" based off the series? Like the candles and the wisdom cards?
                                        —MEGAN CHAPMAN

P. C.: Yes! Stay tuned to our websites, www.PCCastAuthor.com and www.KCastAuthor.com for new merchandise!

What's next for you two?
                                        —DEREK CHARLES

P. C.: Thank you for asking! In October 2017 *Sun Warrior*, the next book in my YA fantasy series Tales of a New World releases, and HoN Other World book two releases in 2018.

K. C.: P. C. and I are also working on a new YA series, the Dysasters, which releases in 2018 as well. As for my solo project, I'm busy writing something that is absolutely amazing and that you will totally love!

And always remember
You are powerful! Your choices matter. Thank you for choosing us.
Sending you light and love ... always love.